The 25th of October

Christopher C. Curtis

Copyright © 2018 Christopher C. Curtis
All rights reserved.

'The only people for me are the mad ones, the ones who are mad to live, mad to talk, mad to be saved, desirous of everything at the same time, the ones who never yawn or say a commonplace thing, but burn, burn, burn.'
– Jack Kerouac, *On the Road*

Prologue

Saturday, 13 October 1979
Oxford, England

The minute hand finally struck quarter past with precision and purpose. The time was six-fifteen. The laboured, mechanical sound continued, concise and authoritarian in its delivery. I took a deep breath. It had been a long five minutes since the museum attendant had last walked down the aisle. I checked the cabinet door again, just to make sure. Not only did it open, but still no alarm was activated.

Then I caught sight of her from the corner of my eye. She was an attractive lady, well presented, middle-aged, thick dark hair with matching eyeliner. We made eye contact again as she walked past, and – for the second time – a brief smile was exchanged.

The heart started to pound, synchronizing to the beat of the handsome Regency timepiece, which now said six-sixteen. It provided a fitting background for the conflicting morals and emotions that were taking precedence. The mind soon followed, confused in its motives. I knew I had a choice, but impulses can be powerful, capable of overriding the most rational thought.

It was too late. The clapperboard had been slammed, the director had shouted 'Action!' I opened the glass cabinet, carefully selecting the chosen print.

After dismounting from the board, it was held delicately between finger and thumb. I opened the programme I'd bought at the match earlier, and after placing it into the centrefold, I gently closed the door.

Signor Leonardo da Vinci himself would have been impressed with the dexterity – as well as the respect and dignity – one of his famous works was being shown, as both were duly dispatched neatly inside my overcoat pocket.

For peace of mind, I waited to see if the missing sketch was noticed. It was going to be a long four minutes. There was a manuscript, *Of the Woman's Birth* by Isabella Andreini, on display in the same cabinet. The sound of the clock amplified, becoming louder, as I began to read the Venetian fable.

'The suffering women are content to live in that subject, in which they are born into a modest and modest life. They content themselves with the short border of the house for a sweet prison.'

I couldn't make sense of it. I couldn't make sense of anything really, except for the rhythm of the clock. It was six-twenty-five.

I heard the attendant. She was close. I didn't look, I couldn't. The gap was obvious, and very noticeable. I felt overwhelmed and nauseous. The emotive had become physical. She walked past. I looked at the clock for the last time. The manufacturers were Thwaites & Reed of Clerkenwell, probably a piece from the mid-nineteenth century or thereabouts. It was now six-twenty-six.

I made my way back down the stairs to the ground level as calmly, and as in control, as possible. I played it cool, not even using the handrail, opting instead to sweep down the centre of the stairs and into the foyer area. Next to the entrance was a gift shop. I selected three Da Vinci postcards. *The Drawing Of A Woman's Head*, *The Female Head* and *The Vitruvian Man*.

'They're all on display upstairs,' said the salesgirl.

'Just saw them. Incredible,' I replied.

'I know, we're very fortunate to have such a connected curator.'

'What's a curator?' I asked.

'The curator is a custodian of a museum or gallery,' she informed me, as I was handed a brown envelope she had kindly wrapped the postcards in.

'Oh, I see,' I replied. 'Anyway, thank you,' I added, as I walked towards the exit, then out onto the concourse.

I crossed the road to the Randolph Hotel. The rain was becoming heavier, so I took refuge under the canopy of this five-star antiquated fare. Richard Burton and Elizabeth Taylor had resided here in 1966. Sixty-six, the year The Beatles had 'Eleanor Rigby', Michelangelo Antonioni had *Blow-up*, and Joe Orton had *Loot*, playing at The Criterion in London's swanky West End. I looked at the three steps, imagining them both walking up, Richard holding the door for Elizabeth. It may even have been raining, who knows.

From the short distance, I looked for the first time. I expected some drama, and some chaos, both accompanied by police sirens, but apart from a few tourists gathering around the main entrance, nothing was happening.

The prestigious Ashmolean Museum looked as inspiring as ever, providing a picturesque silhouette against the damp Oxford sky. The anxiety had waned, so after a few minutes I decided to make a break for it. With the rain now in torrential mode, I didn't get very far, this time having to take shelter in the nearby Oxford Playhouse. The evening's play was a cutting-edge piece called *Class Enemy*.

Gloucester Green coach station was less than five minutes away. After looking at the rain pounding the pavement for a few minutes – and checking to make sure both programme and print were dry – I decided to make a move, to throw caution to the wind. The nonchalant – though hasty – walk to the coach stop that followed was surreal to say the least.

It was the same driver from that morning. He was in front of the coach adjusting the rear-view mirror, oblivious to the rain.

'Good timing, Son, just about to leave. Enjoy Oxford?' he asked, as he ran back onto the coach.

'Lovely city. Been here once before, four years ago. Today was very eventful, though,' I replied, as I passed him the ticket which was promptly checked and returned.

'A smaller London, Son, always something going on. So, what was so eventful if you don't mind me asking?'

'Oh, we lost,' I stuttered.

'Not again, who against this time?'

'Millwall.'

'Typical,' he sighed, as he started the engine and began to reverse.

'Yes,' I agreed, before taking the same seat as that morning. After sitting down, I looked out the window. The rain was still relentless. Combined with the darkness, it meant I couldn't see a thing. I couldn't read my programme, and I couldn't compare the authentic sketch to the postcard I'd just bought. Oh well, *The Vitruvian Man* had to wait.

I nestled into the seat. Football and art, what a combination. Both have the capacity to produce some wonderful – and impulsive – emotions, sometimes for the better, but sometimes for the worst.

I thought of the usher. The salesgirl. The people in the cafes – both in Victoria – and in the covered market. I even thought of the driver. I started to feel uncomfortable and guilty. *The day wasn't supposed to end like this*, I thought, as the coach headed down the wet and bleak-looking A40 towards London.

Chapter One

The reception was everything you'd expect from a radio station being transmitted from a ship somewhere in the North Sea. Rain was imminent, Radio Caroline had said earlier in the morning. *No, not today*, I thought, as I was preparing to go to Victoria to catch a coach to Oxford. I stayed to listen to 'Sweet Talkin' Guy' by The Chiffons, before switching off the transistor and making my way downstairs.

After closing the front door, I looked up at the mid-October sky. Heavy purple-laden clouds were hanging ominously above, as if ready to burst. It was only a question of when the downpour would materialise.

I made my way through the desolate streets to the nearby Arsenal underground station. Walking down the tunnel towards the Piccadilly southbound platform, the wind began to whip up, discarded newspapers scattering in its wake. It was seven-thirty, and apart from the ticket inspector, I hadn't seen one person.

The walk from Victoria underground along the Buckingham Palace road to the coach station had a little more activity and life, although, to be honest, I was paying more attention to the elements – continually scanning the skyline, hoping the inevitable would hold out a little longer. I'd waited a long time for today – four years, in fact – to return to Oxford, so any notion of the game being postponed due to weather conditions just wasn't an option.

Victoria coach station looked tired. It always does. Maybe it was still a little hungover from Friday evening's activities. Let's face it, this place does have more than its fair share of hustlers and the like. The cafe inside bore testament to this. Men and women scattered at different tables, seemingly up to no good. Some did the talking, some did the listening, all did the observing. One trait they shared was that they noted my appearance as I opened the condensed glass door. An uncomfortable silence followed, before I discreetly closed the door and went to the ticket hall.

National Express had the monopoly, and were running the show. There were three routes from the capital to Oxford. The 190 – via Heathrow – taking two and a half hours; the 290 – via Henley-on-Thames – one hour and thirty minutes; and the 390 – non-stop – just under an hour. A 390 was parked up, the doors were open, and looked ready to go. The driver was adjusting the rear-view mirror. 'How long?' I asked.

'Leaving in five minutes, Son,' came the abrupt answer.

As I waited for the comforting sound of the engine being started, I noticed a poster advertising a new movie. *The Great Riviera Bank Robbery*. It was about a bank robbery in Nice. Isn't that the place where Albert Spaggiari had robbed the Société Généraleas bank three years earlier, in seventy-six?

His gang had taken nearly thirty million francs from that one. They left a message on the walls, '*Sans armes, ni haine, ni violence.*' 'Without weapons, nor hatred, nor violence,' was the translation. My friend Douglas has the same ethos. Was in it for the buzz. Never to hurt anyone.

I went to take a closer look for more depth and detail. As I noted the directors, producers and the cinematographer, I heard the roar of an engine in the background. I hastened to the door, climbed on, and handed him my ticket. 'Do you know where Nice is?'

'A long way, Son. South of France.'

'Have you been there?'

'Too far for me, Son.' He gave me back the ticket, looked into the rear mirror, then shifted into first gear. 'Why?'

'Heard it's an interesting place,' I replied, before walking down the aisle and settling into a seat in the middle.

Nice sounded cool, glamorous and sophisticated. I visualised it being full of amiable Raffles-type criminals. Art, crime, bank robbers, sea, cash and – according to the poster – sun. *What more could one wish for?* I thought, as I checked for any signs of rain again.

The interiors of the 390 were a good representation of the late seventies, basic and threadbare. What a year it had been so far. On the third of May, a greengrocer's daughter from Lincolnshire had been victorious in the general election. The 'Iron Lady' had been introduced onto the international stage. In literature, *Kane and Abel* was published. Jeffrey Archer had arrived. Such was the political landscape.

Liverpool were the new English First Division champions. Terry Venables had somehow miraculously brought south London's Crystal Palace into the top flight, and Nottingham Forest were the kings of Europe. Incredible stuff.

Compensating for the lack of comfort, the scenic journey through the capital was some consolation. I looked out the window as the coach proceeded to Marble Arch via Hyde Park. The rain had started. I sat back. It didn't matter, I felt happy and content. 'Oxford here I come!' I exclaimed.

The cool, white stucco environs of the ultra-chic Notting Hill and Holland Park followed, but quickly dissolved into Shepherds Bush. The White City estate was visible, providing the last slice of urban before the suburbia of Park Royal, Uxbridge and Hillingdon took over.

With the exception of the art deco Hoover Building on Western Avenue, the A40 isn't that imaginative. The grey motorway soon passed, and a *'Welcome To The City Of Oxford'* sign greeted me, and the sparse group of passengers I had shared the journey with.

Just past the Headington roundabout I stood up. The Manor would soon be in sight. The floodlights towered above the nearby Bury Knowle Park. I grasped the headrest in front of me even tighter, as I felt the surge of goose-bumps.

Passing the ground, I remembered the specifics in detail. The exact spot where David had bought the matchday programmes four years previous was still there. I recalled him taking me to my first game, the walk, the talk, and the arrival. Buying the matchday programmes was poignant. Hopefully the same vendor would be there a little later. As with the Hoover building, though, the ground passed quickly, not even giving me the luxury and time to enjoy the memory.

I still have that programme. Still in pristine condition. Little did I know that in a few hours' time – sandwiched between the pages of an Oxford United v. Millwall matchday programme – would be an original, priceless Leonardo da Vinci sketch, courtesy of an impulsive decision made inside the prestigious Ashmolean Museum.

We quickly approached The Plain, a dainty ring road of sorts. There was a water fountain with a roof in the middle. On the top was a clock. It was ten-thirty.

On the left – just past Magdalen Bridge – was Rose Lane. That's where David lived when I visited him four years ago. The actual flat was around the corner, but the Botanical Gardens opposite was still visible. Queens Lane was next, where some passengers had to disembark. I looked across the road. The coach stop he had walked me to after the game was still there. I remembered waving as the coach was leaving. *Wish he could come to the game*, I thought, but – as you learn – life just isn't like that. Life is full of twists and turns, and people come and go. The only certainly was that you never know what's going to happen next.

'You okay, Son?'

I looked up. It was the driver. 'I'm good,' I replied.

'Seemed miles away. Time to get off.'

Gloucester Green had finally arrived. 'Thanks,' I said.

'How old are you, Son?'

'Seventeen,' I replied, as I descended onto the pavement.

'Well, stay safe, Son,' he said, as he disappeared into the cafe.

It was approaching midday, and the rain had stopped. There was an hour or so to spare before embarking on the trek to The Manor. Having just had a head full of twisted bicycle frames and rows of punts – courtesy of the High Street and Magdalen Bridge – I needed to empty the mind a little.

There were some good cafes in the centre of Oxford; one was in St Giles. This intimate, old red-leathered seating affair was full. The covered market – an old medieval market, dating from 1774 – was close by.

As I walked down George Street I noticed Annabelinda down a side road. Howard Marks – an ex-Oxford graduate – co-owned it. The rumour was that this bespoke dress boutique was a front for hash smuggling. Further along was The New Theatre. The Cure had played there last month, and The Buzzocks – supported by Joy Division – were coming in two weeks' time. Nice and quaint, but small in comparison to London's music illerati.

The next five minutes were a fusion of architectural delights, as I weaved through the back streets. Tom Tower, the High Street, the Radcliffe Camera, were all nicely glued together with the swarms of tourists and masses of bicycles.

Annabel's was in the market. This was the place to be. As I ascended the stairs, the chattering vibe became louder. It felt good. There I was, not only in a cultured different city, but mixing with the future elite.

Students can – and will – create a scene. Sometimes arty and cultured, other times intellectual and academic. It appeared Oxford had both. I sat back, observing the so called 'beautiful people'. I must admit, it did look alluring. The girls with their good genetics and fine bone structures. Heads were slightly tilted, fingers constantly running through the luxuriant, thick hair. The boys were similar – both bore no indication of marriage, not for now at least.

I didn't buy the happiness vibe, though. Behind the scenes these people go through a lot, probably more than most. Drug overdoses, car crashes, accidents, you name it, they are part of it. The coffee was strong and good. After paying, I navigated my way back to the top of the stairs.

Along the wall on the way down were an array of prints, posters and flyers. All in juxtaposition, they were temporary pinned – and glued – onto the wall. One caught my eye. The image was one I'd seen many times before, though at present where escaped me. The illustration was a fine line sketch of a naked man. He had long hair, and his were limbs rotating. It was a beautiful piece, but I just couldn't remember the source.

Art from the Italian Renaissance at the Ashmolean Museum was the exhibition. It was open until seven, and wasn't that far from Gloucester Green. The match finished at four-forty, then a forty-minute walk into town – *plenty of time*, I thought. Another flyer advertised a production of a new play. It was called *Class Enemy*, and was at The Oxford Playhouse.

On the way to The Manor I passed Headington Hill Hall, a stately home. The Morrell Family – founders and owners of the local brewery – had resided here. Oscar Wilde had even attended their infamous lavish, aristocratic May Day balls.

After they sold up, the owner of local publishers Pergamon Press rented it. His name was Robert Maxwell, and he was taking more than a little interest in Oxford United. No one took him seriously, though. I mean, what money could possibly be made from football?

As I passed under the private bridge linking the house with South Park, I suddenly remembered where I'd seen the image on the flyer. It was in the opening credits of *World In Action*, a contemporary television programme that was accompanied by a haunting opening soundtrack. It had been designed to synchronise with the bleak, desolate isolation of the period. The subject matter was always frightening. Political and social affairs were the topics, depicting the grim life of the early-to-mid-seventies.

Sadly, the vendor wasn't there. 'Haven't seen him for a long time,' said the man as I gave twenty-five pence for a programme.

The Millwall fans had predictably arrived early. Separated by a wire-mesh fence, they added to the atmosphere. We lost 2–1. *Damn*, I thought, as I made my way out onto the High Street. The rain started again, becoming very heavy, very quickly. There was a London-bound coach stop outside the ground. I declined – the fix of some Italian art took precedence.

Further down the road, a small crowd had gathered outside Radio Rentals for the final scores. Tottenham had won. 'Good,' I quietly uttered. I placed the programme inside my coat, then began to walk to the Ashmolean in the cold October rain.

The sky had become dark, as I cut through the Radcliffe Camera into Broad Street. The Sheldonian Theatre – a marvellous Sir Christopher Wren piece – looked daunting against the dark amber-blue sky. It provided a fitting backdrop for the fourteen carved stone heads that Wren had somehow deemed suitable to surround the building.

It was the first week of the exhibition, so the opening hours were extended. I entered the six-pillared entrance of the world's first university museum with excitement. The ground-floor lobby area was a large white space, cool and airy, with a high ceiling. I was met with noisy tourists, who – though about to leave – were still mingling. A concoction of French, Italian and Spanish filled the air. Polished Greek statues – made of marble – were neatly placed in each corner. The wide concrete staircase – itself looking like an exhibition piece – was on the right. I used it as I ascended to the first floor.

The room had row upon row of polished wooden and glass cabinets symmetrically laid out. Five were dedicated to the fourteenth- to seventeenth-century Italian Renaissance movement. One had given priority to Leonardo da Vinci, and rightly so. Except for the sound of a clock, it was quiet as I stood in front of the *Drawing Of A Woman's Torso*. *Remarkable dexterity*, I thought, as an attendant walked past. We smiled, as she continued on down the aisle.

You couldn't help but marvel at the composition of *The Female Head*. A master craftsman for sure. I observed the two pieces for a while before moving on. Then, bang, right in front of my eyes appeared *The Vitruvian Man*. There it was. *Wow*, I thought, as I took a few steps back. *Why is art so beautiful, so captivating?* I wondered, feeling a stimulation akin to a football match.

I looked at the clock. It said six-fifteen. They say it's a long way from the heart to the mind. The decision that followed would have consequences some twenty years later.

The coach had been pelted with heavy rain for the previous hour as it flew over the Westway and passed the Kensington Hilton. There was now a sense of urban security. I felt safe as the city lights became focused. I could actually see buildings and people again. Because of the rain, I hadn't noticed a car that had been following us.

Instead of Victoria, I disembarked at Notting Hill. 'Thank you, Driver,' I said, as I waited for the door to open.

'Hope one day you get to see Nice, Son,' he replied.

With the sketch in possession, I felt qualified. 'You never know,' I replied.

I stood there in the rain, and watched as the doors closed. The red indicator lit up, blending nicely as the coach merged with the other traffic. As with David, the vendor, the attendant, and the salesgirl, I felt some sadness. I'd probably never see him again.

Just before the underground, I checked the print again: it was still dry. I then hastened the short distance to the underground. As I reached the top of the stairs, I was quickly apprehended by three detectives. Two were from the Thames Valley Police Force, the other from the Met – all three were from the Art and Antiques squad. After being placed in an unmarked police car, I was driven back up the A40, where I was taken to St Aldates police station, ironically a ten-minute walk from Carfax.

Chapter Two

'You are now in London, that great sea, whose ebb and flow at once is deaf and loud, and on the shore vomits its wrecks, and still howls on for more. Yet in its depth what treasures!'
– Percy Bysshe Shelley

20 August 1999
Piccadilly, Central London

The West End Central Police Station is located on the junction of Boyle Street and Savile Row, right in the heart of London's West End. Opened in 1940, it somehow seems at odds amongst the splendid eighteenth-century Palladian architecture of Old Burlington Street and Savile Row.

Savile Row is famous for its bespoke tailors. Hardy Amies, Henry Poole & Co., Gieves and Hawkes: they all reside there. Past clientele include Admiral Lord Nelson, Sir Winston Churchill, Charlie Chaplin and Ian Fleming. Some possess the coveted royal warrants, some don't. Gieves and Hawkes have three: HM the Queen of the United Kingdom, HRH the Duke of Edinburgh, and HRH the Prince of Wales. Of latter years, though, Moschino, Evisu and Ozwald Boateng – and a few others – have entered the scene. The new boys have arrived, shaking things up a little.

I startled as the hatch crashed down. 'Quick. They're hot.'

I recognised the voice. 'Alexios?'

'Morning. Quick. This is the one with one sugar.'

I got up and looked through the hatch. 'Morning,' I said, as I took the cup etched with a single line down the side. 'What's the time?'

He looked at his watch. 'Eleven exactly. Oh, never guess who I just saw in Starbucks?'

'No idea.'

'Terence Stamp.'

'Really?'

'Was sitting there.' He shook his head in disbelief.

'Think he lives around here.'

'Piccadilly?'

'Probably one of those mansion blocks down by St James Church.'

'Heard he also lived in India, some Ashram, studying under the Bhagwan Shree Rajneesh.'

'Tom would know,' I said. *Pune and Piccadilly, cool or what?* I thought, as I stirred the coffee. 'Heard he speaks Italian as well,' I added.

'Would have been there the same time as The Beatles, sixty-eight.'

'What a time to be around.' I thought of our friend Tom. He's obsessed with that period. 'Anyway, wasn't as glamorous as what we think,' I added.

There was a pause before the subject matter changed. The tone suddenly became monosyllabic and more serious. 'So, what happened?' he asked.

'I was dragged out of bed at six in the morning by the Metropolitan Police's elite serious Art and Antiques squad,' I said, taking a sip of the medium americano. 'They were going on about a painting or something.'

'Let me go and find out when the first interview will be,' he said.

An hour later, I was taken for the first formal interview. An officer collected me and took me to an interview room. It was as one might expect. Furnishings were sparse, and kept to a minimum. There was little in the way of imagination, and the feeling was one of emptiness.

An imitation wooden table was in the centre of the room, with two plastic chairs placed on each side. Detective Chief Inspector Smith – and his colleague, DCI Jones – were sat opposite old friend – and my lawyer – Alexios Kanaris.

From Greek Cypriot stock, Alexios grew up in Upper Holloway, north London. Being a childhood friend of myself, Tom and Rich, and growing up in the late seventies and early eighties, he encompassed the scene. Smoking weed and going to the Arsenal was the thing. From the local secondary, he left us, progressing onto the North London University, choosing law. King's College for a Masters was next.

His training at Middle Temple was tough, but he survived. Though an outsider, he held his own. Mixing with the judicial elite became a joy and the norm. Progressing from article clerk, he eventually went solo. His practice now had a reputation of representing the big boys in the European Court of Human Rights. Allegations of money laundering and tax evasion are his speciality. Strings the case along, using loopholes. The acquittal rate is high. The government hate him, a thorn in the side. An expensive one at that.

Having reached the dizzying heights of knowing – and representing – international drug dealers, politicians and celebrities, he still kept an eye on his own, not forgetting where he came from.

'I do have an alibi,' I replied.

'Which is?' asked Jones, a dark-haired man, in a soft southern Welsh accent.

'I told you. Visited a friend.'

'That was from one-thirty until two-fifteen. The theft took place at four,' replied Smith, a blond-haired man with a deep north-east lilt.

'Would have been home by then.'

There was silence. 'The three witness statements all add up,' said Jones, holding up his supporting documentation.

'Detailed description. All say the same thing,' added Smith.

Jones reclined into the chair, his hands joined over his stomach. 'And—' there was a pause '—you've done it before.'

'A da Vinci. From the Ashmolean Museum in Oxford,' said Smith.

'Nice choice. Prestigious venue. Impressed,' Jones added.

'Come on, that was twenty years ago,' interrupted Alexios. 'My client was seventeen years old. Acted on impulse, not unusual for a teenager.'

Smith looked at Alexios. 'In my experience, the art world is – and can be – very seductive.'

Jones looked at me. 'Say it's a buzz. Difficult to let go.'

'It wasn't vindictive, or malicious,' I said. 'Simply an opportunist act. No more than that, and – more importantly – I paid the price,' I added, looking at them both.

'Where is the painting?' asked Jones.

'No idea.'

'Needs to be returned to its rightful owner,' said Smith.

'Don't know what painting you are talking about.'

'We'll resume a little later,' stated Jones, as he gathered up the paperwork.

'Give you a little time to have a think,' added Smith.

'This lot are serious. They only investigate the fraud, theft – and money laundering – of valuable listed art,' Alexios explained, as I was escorted back to the cell by a uniformed officer.

'I don't know what they are talking about,' I said.

'Also ceramics and artefacts,' he continued, as the officer unlocked the door. 'High-level stuff,' he added.

'I'm telling you, I don't know what painting they're talking about,' I said, as the door closed behind me.

'See you tomorrow,' he said, as the officer slammed the hatch closed.

I took a deep breath, sighed, then headed towards the mattress, trying to make some sort of sense from the day's events.

'We have enough evidence to charge you anyway,' said Jones, abruptly, two days later, and nearing the end of the fifth interview.

The four of us had finally realised that no progress was being made. It wasn't going anywhere, the format had become the same. They wanted to know where I was, I told them I was at home. They wanted to know where the painting was, I told them I didn't know.

'Your clothes match the description from the witness statements,' added Smith.

'That's enough,' concluded Jones, as he gathered the array of paperwork from the table.

In the early evening of Sunday, 29 August 1999, I was charged as follows. That on Thursday, 26 August 1999, at approximately 15:00 hours, Mr Stephen Vincent stole a listed artefact from The Fifth Street Art Gallery, 26 Cork Street, London W1.

Bail was refused due to likelihood of absconding. I was summoned to appear at Bow Street Magistrates' Court the following day. After accepting – and signing – the charge sheet, I was escorted back to the cells by a uniformed officer.

As the door slammed shut behind me I looked to the ceiling. '*Sick and tired of being sick and tired?*' was the slogan above. A Crime Stoppers number was next to it.

'What's the time?' I asked, as Alexios stopped by a few minutes later.

'Just gone seven,' was the reply. Not that it mattered. Time was irrelevant at the moment. There was no concept of it. It made no sense. Could have been any time, or even anywhere. He passed me a book.

'Thanks,' I said.

'That da Vinci from the Ashmolean in Oxford. Was that really twenty years ago?'

'Nineteen seventy-nine,' I confirmed.

'What was the name of Douglas's friend, the one who had got into Oxford?'

'David?'

'David, that's it. Whatever happened to him?'

'Went to Amsterdam. Not heard of since.'

'He was my inspiration. A boy from an inner-city council estate getting into a university at Oxford.'

'Shows it can be done,' I said, vividly remembering the man who had also made such an early impression on me. It was during a visit to see him in seventy-five that I was introduced to the world of literature, music and football.

David was a friend of Douglas. They were the same age. Seven years older than myself, Rich and Tom, we looked up to them. For some reason, I started to hum the riff of 'Get Back'.

Further down is number three Savile Row. This was once the former HQ of Apple Records. Apple was set up in 1967 after the death of Brian Epstein. John, Ringo, George and Paul played their last ever gig on the roof there. It began with 'Get Back', and ended with 'Dig a Pony'. This historical event took place no more than a five-minute walk from where I was currently residing exactly thirty years later, accused – would you believe it – of taking a valued piece of art from a gallery. This time it was an ancient Taoist painting from the Shang dynasty. This time I was innocent.

'See you tomorrow,' he said, tapping the hatch with his knuckles.

'Alexios?'

His face appeared again. 'Yes?'

'What does the painting look like?'

'Don't know. Think it's worth a lot, though.'

'The witnesses, who are they?'

'A Chinese lady, and a couple. He's English, she's Italian,' he replied.

I looked at the book he had given me. *On The Road*, Jack Kerouac, I took a deep breath, and started to read it, yet again.

Someone was being shown to the cell opposite. Another West End hustler, caught feeding his habit, had been taken off the streets. It was going to be one long night as I paused, again thinking of David.

He had been accepted into Balliol College, Oxford. It was big news at the time, something completely at odds with what you'd expect someone from an east London housing estate to do.

Balliol was a noted academic establishment, preserved for the likes of British prime ministers – Edward Heath, H. H. Asquith and Harold MacMillan had attended – and international alumni. Shyamji Krishna Varma and Mirza Nasir Ahmad also had the privilege of being educated there.

David was from different stock. Though bright and capable, he hailed from the London Borough of Hackney, somewhere not noted for its academia, especially in the 1970s.

Would love to see that man again. Twenty five years ago? Wow, I thought, as I fell asleep on the blue mattress, holding the bible of music and travel.

Monday, 23 August

Great Marlborough Street Magistrates' Court had closed the previous year. With its imported Italian marble tiles, oak floorboards and Robert Adam's period interiors, this stunning piece of architecture from the 1800s would have provided an apt backdrop for the case of a missing painting, said – on the current market – to be worth at least a cool one million.

The past list of attendees there read like musical, artistic and literati alumni. Rock stars galore appeared there. Jagger in the sixties. Richards, Rotten and Lennon in the seventies. The first three were on a drugs rap; Lennon was the exception, showing explicit art in a New

Bond Street gallery was the charge he had to answer to in 1970.

Speaking of art, Francis Bacon had also appeared in the same year. He was found in possession of cannabis. Representing literature, the writer Oscar Wilde took the Marquis of Queensberry to court on a libel charge, 104 years ago.

The court had also seen politics. Christine Keeler had been summoned in sixty-three. Apart from nearly bringing down the British Government, she was captured by photographer Lewis Morley for that iconic naked pose on a chair. Turned out the chair wasn't really an Arne Jacobsen original, after all. It was a copy.

The same chair had been used by Islington's bad boy, the playwright Joe Orton. Unlike his working-class counterpart Keeler, Joe wasn't afforded the luxury of the West End to answer the charge of damaging Islington Council library books in sixty-two. An appearance at the poverty-stricken Old Street Magistrates' Court was the venue. Seems like counterfeits, court appearances, art, drugs, music and political intrigue have been around a long time.

With the London Palladium on the right, Sony Music Entertainment to the left, and Liberty's department store across the road, it was prime location. Overlooking Carnaby Street was the cherry on the top. Rumour was, it was going to be a hotel. I wasn't surprised, such changes were becoming the norm. As this decade retired, our capital city – its global landmarks and cultural icons – were fast succumbing to places of service and leisure. Character was being lost to accommodation and food, designed to serve the transitional people, the ones who came and went.

The door was unlocked. 'Let's go,' said the officer, as I was led to the reception area.

'Which court?' I asked.

'Bow Street,' he replied.

The man who had been in the opposite cell was sitting there. 'Stephen,' I said, as I introduced myself.

'Howard,' he answered. He was looking rough, the junk was obviously beginning to leave his body.

'Hoisting?' I asked.

'Jeans, Armani, five pairs. Selfridges, Oxford Street. £350. You?'

'A painting. Fifth Gallery, Cork Street. £1 million.'

'Big difference,' he said, as we were cuffed and led to the waiting van.

It was raining as we headed down Regent Street towards Piccadilly. Hamleys was on the left, Austin Reed on the right. In between was Heddon Street. This was the location for the cover of Bowie's *Ziggy Stardust* album. I knew this because Tom had had the insight to have his picture taken when the iconic red telephone box was still there. For some reason, Westminster Council had it removed. What other city would do such a thing? They'd encourage it, market it for tourism.

Even at eight on a Monday morning, Piccadilly Circus still looked enticing. I love it here, especially at night, and when it was raining. The neon aglow, reflecting the garish, bright corporate colours above onto its wet pavements.

At the top of Wellington Street – opposite The Opera House – was Bow Street Magistrates' Court. After passing through a wooden gate we were taken from the van to the building. The ride was short. Back to back, not even fifteen minutes.

The weekend's hustlers were being dealt with first. They were given fines, adding to the existing ones, which – more than likely – hadn't been paid. They were continuing the history of Hogarth's London, still creating the Dickensian underbelly of the West End. Not much had evolved in this genre. Prostitution, touting and pickpocketing were the name of the game, the only consequence being a twenty-pound fine on a Monday morning. No more than a mere occupational hazard.

These folk couldn't hack another town or city. They were free here. Nobody would bother them. Less attention was paid to them. Only here would they find the acceptance to continue to indulge in pastimes that had been around for centuries.

At eleven-thirty, I was summoned. The time had come for the higher echelons of crime to stand up and be counted. The adrenaline started to flow as I stood up. I straightened the back, rolled the shoulders – forwards and backwards – and took three deep breaths. *Cometh the age, cometh the man*, I thought, as I was escorted up the stairs to the courtroom.

Every London magistrates' has its notorious judge. Here, it's Evans. He loathes petty crimes, and is more prone – and willing – to hand out custodial sentences for anything he perceives as trivial, unjust and antisocial. So far no one had been jailed. Maybe he was enjoying a much-need day off.

I quickly ran my fingers through my hair, tried to straightened my now crumpled shirt, and took another deep breath. 'Do you know who it is?' I asked the gaoler, as we stood at the top of the stairs.

'Mr Evans has just started,' came the reply, before opening the door.

The clerk was a slightly overweight young man with thick, dark, gelled-back hair. He glanced up briefly as I entered the narrow dock. Alexios was to his right, leaning back in his chair, a slight nodding of the head being the only acknowledgement. To his left was the prosecutor, a bespectacled, timid-looking man in a navy blue pinstripe suit. He was seated, reading some papers.

This was Court Number Two, and had hosted such luminaries as Giacomo Casanova, the Kray twins, and more recently General Pinochet. I was in esteemed company, I thought, as I took a seat. You could smell the history, the surrounding polished wooden panels looked fine, and gave a rich aroma. *These four walls have certainly soaked up some drama over the years, if only they could talk*, I thought, as I enjoyed the silence.

The clerk stood and made an announcement. 'Please stand.' The room dutifully followed – myself included – and after a few seconds Evans entered, taking the seat opposite me.

The next instruction followed. 'Please be seated.' I was then asked to stand to confirm my name, date of birth and current address. After the charge was read, the prosecutor took up the mantle. How looks can deceive. He was convincing. Even I would be hard-pressed to not to think I was the guilty party. There was a particular emphasis on the value.

'How much?' asked Evans.

'Market value? One million pounds, Sir.'

'Has the painting been retrieved?'

'Not as we speak, unfortunately, Sir,' he replied, as he sat down.

Alexios, as good as he is – and he is – didn't stand a chance. There was no way he could make a case. There was a plea for bail – which, to be fair, was strong – but the look as Evans left the room to deliberate said it all.

Less than five minutes later, I was directly informed that the application for bail was refused on the following grounds: 1) The seriousness of the offence; 2) That I may interfere with witnesses; and 3) The risk of not appearing for the next court date. The case was to be adjourned for three weeks until Monday, 13 September, during which time I was to be remanded in custody.

I was back in the same small, green, ceramic-tiled room I'd left barely ten minutes earlier. On the way I asked the gaoler which jail served the West End.

'Brixton,' he replied.

It was lunchtime. A vegetarian hotpot was the choice. *Not bad, had worse*, I thought.

Alexios came down with some paperwork a little later. They consisted of the witness statements, charge sheet and the transcribed police interviews.

'Returning to jail after twenty years, interesting,' he said, as he handed them over.

'Very,' I agreed, as a feeling of anticipation – as well as excitement – came over me.

We shook hands. 'I'll come and visit in the next few days.' He looked at his watch – a Rolex Oyster. 'Have to go, another appointment,' he said, as he picked up his bag and made his way to the desk.

A benevolent act is all well and good. Sometimes, though, a charitable deed, such as befriending someone, can have a consequence further along the line, as I was about to find out. 'Wants to join you,' stated the gaoler, as he opened the door. Before I could see who he was referring too, or answer, Howard was in. The door slammed quickly behind.

'Been up?' I asked.

He sat on the floor, head propped on his knees. 'Three months. Result,' he replied. 'That's it, no more, have to get clean,' he added.

He told me he'd been out five weeks this time, and had three kids. The problem was that he just couldn't give up the dope. I read my book until the gaoler opened the door. 'Let's go,' he said.

Howard struggled to get to his feet, and we were both taken to the waiting van.

The Royal Opera House was looking superb. Its glass and metal exterior was pure splendour, both grand and modern. We took a left into Wellington Street and drove south towards The Strand. Penhaligon's was on the right. Douglas was a fan, loved the stuff. He always proudly displayed it wherever he went. On the other side, Christopher's was looking smart and swanky, as did most of the new bars, restaurants and clubs, sprouting up like weeds in – and around – the London landscape in the run-up to the Millennium.

After collecting someone from the law courts, there was a total of five on board: three prisoners, one gaoler, and one driver. We then headed down Fleet Street towards our destination: HMP Brixton.

Blackfriars Bridge was opened in 1869. Designed by a Tottenham boy, Joseph Cubitt, it became notorious when, on 17 June 1982, the self-proclaimed 'God's Banker', Roberto Calvi, was discovered underneath. His fate was suspicious, and shrouded in conspiracy theories.

As the van moved slowly in the rush-hour traffic, I scanned every one of the five wrought-iron arches, trying to visualise the exact spot where he may have met his demise. Outside Blackfriars station was an *Evening*

Standard billboard: '*West End Smash And Grab Gang Captured*' ran the headline of the West End Extra edition.

The Elephant – and its Walworth Road – was busy, Kennington not so. Within twenty minutes we were passing Brixton Hill and the turning into Jebb Avenue.

Like all the London prisons – except Belmarsh – this was a Victorian jail. Famous dignitaries included Lee Harvey Oswald, Robert Blake and, of course, the Kray twins. The irony that I had been here visiting my friend James just four days previously wasn't lost on me, as I was taken into the reception area.

Chapter Three

HMP Brixton, South London

It may have been twenty years, but it could have been twenty months, twenty weeks, or even twenty days. It didn't really matter. Such is the ambience of a jail.

We showered, got fed, had our photo taken and were given a number. A visit to the doctor was the final stop before being taken to a wing. This was important for Howard and the others. They needed the medication. Of the eleven intakes, only myself – and one other – were not dependent on class-A narcotics.

'A' wing was noisy. It was association time, pool was being played and television watched. We waited to be allocated a cell. As nice as Howard was, I wasn't really up for sharing a cell with a heroin addict in withdrawal. It wasn't exactly what I needed right now. We walked up the wrought-iron staircase to the first floor, aka the 'ones'. Three were allocated there – excluding Howard and myself. Then it was on to the 'twos', where four were dispatched. Howard stayed with us. On the 'threes', Howard took leave. We shook hands, safe in the knowledge that we'd see each other in the morning. 'Take care,' I said, as he walked behind an officer to his cell.

Myself and two others continued to the 'fours'. A man leaning over the railings on the opposite side was looking somewhat inquisitively as I was shown to cell number twenty-five.

The occupant wasn't there, but it was neat and tidy. A large pile of brown folders was in one corner, a chess set in the other. I went to the window and looked out. It looked down onto the exercise yard; it was still raining. The bottom bunk was vacant. I put the paperwork on a table, made my bed, then lay down. After ten minutes, the door opened. The man leaning over the railings entered.

I got up. 'Stephen,' I said, introducing myself.

'Dimitri,' he replied.

He was on trial for fraud. He didn't say what for at first, and I didn't ask. An unwritten rule is that you never ask what someone is in for; this takes time. I understood his earlier concern on the landing. One of the worst things about prison life is not knowing who you're going to share a cell with.

'Been here long?' I asked, as he put the kettle on.

'Six months,' he said.

'You play?' I asked, alluding to the chessboard.

'Of course. I'm Russian,' he replied. 'We play tomorrow,' he added.

'Definitely,' I answered.

He had a cleaning job, and just as important, a routine. After lunch – when the jail wound down – he tuned to Classic FM, before settling down for some reading. I liked Dimitri.

As promised, Alexios visited a couple of days later. It was brief. 'Pay particular attention to the statements,' he said. 'There are two men, and one woman. They all describe exactly what you were wearing.'

'How can they know?' I asked, a little perplexed. 'I came here to visit Tom that day, I didn't see anyone else, went straight home.'

'Oh, the painting has been found and returned,' he said, ignoring my question.

'What does it look like?'

'Here,' he said, as he passed me a brown envelope. 'Look at it later.' He said that he was working on another case, and needed to see someone else. A spate of smash-and-grabs during the summer had plagued the capital. The ringleader – who was from Islington – was in the prison, and he was representing him. 'I'll come next Monday,' he said.

'From Islington. What's his name?'

'Ted. See you next week.'

'Fraud. Cashpoint. Credit cards, millions. Trial next week,' said Dimitri, summarising his incarceration, as we settled down to a game of chess the following day after lunch.

'Old Bailey?'

'Blackfriars. What about you?'

I got up to find the envelope Alexios had given me. 'This,' I said, holding up a copy of the painting I was supposed to have stolen.

He squinted his eyes. 'Wow, nice picture. Here, put it up,' he said, handing me some Sellotape.

It went up next to the window, where we could both see it. He was right, it was nice, very nice in fact.

It was a rural setting with trees in foliage, and colourful flowers in bloom. There were some birds, and a river gently flowing. A Buddha was sitting in the middle. Behind him were five figures – four men and one woman. Three seemed to be collecting wood, one was fishing and the woman was carrying something. The colours were hues of red, gold and green. Along the bottom were three beautifully calligraphed Chinese characters.

I slowly acclimatised during the week. Every now and then I regaled Dimitri with fables of past prison life, and how it had changed in twenty years. 'No toilet then,' I said. 'Only a small plastic container for everything, placed under bed until unlocked for meal times, then you went to empty it.'

I didn't think he could comprehend it, and – to be honest – neither could I.

'And you stayed in your cell for twenty-three hours a day.'

'You are kidding me, right?'

'And no breakfast pack,' I added, holding the polythene bag up with the contents of cereal, teabags and bread you are now given every day. 'Only porridge, and a mug of stewed tea.'

I was enjoying the company. Drinking tea, playing chess and listening to classical music suited me. I was happy, I felt at peace. I didn't see Howard for a few days. When I did, he looked a different person. The eyes were bright and alive, the conversation was more meaningful.

Monday, 6 September 1999

The door unlocked early. 'You're moving to "C" wing. Quick, I'll be back in ten minutes,' said the officer. I was settled, and didn't want to move, but I had no choice. I gathered my belongings, and when he returned walked down the landing. I saw Dimitri on the other side mopping the floor.

'"C" wing,' I said, as he looked over.

'That's a good one. TV there,' he smiled.

'I hate television. Prefer the radio, chess and drinking tea,' I said. The thought of being in a cell with someone watching daytime television filled me with absolute dread. The officer beckoned. 'Bye, Dimitri,' I uttered, trying not to sound too emotional.

'Bye, my good friend. All the best. Good luck.'

He came around. We hugged. It felt comfortable. 'Thanks, you too, brother.' I hate saying goodbye, especially to someone I've come to like. It doesn't get any easier, that's for sure. I then navigated the four flights of stairs down to the ground level, where two others were waiting. I didn't get time to say goodbye to Howard.

It was cell five on the second landing in 'C' wing. 'Hi, Stephen,' I said to the occupant, this time lying on the bottom bunk.

'Duggan.'

'Pleased to meet you, Duggan.' There was a TV, but it was off. A radio was playing Magic FM. I felt relieved, Dimitri was quickly forgotten. Such is prison life.

A Turkish Cypriot from Green Lanes, Stoke Newington, Duggan was on a 'intent to supply class A' rap. It was a few kilos of heroin. Like myself, he was on remand. I thought of Howard. Hoping he was coping, and seeing it through. After some small chat, Duggan fell asleep. The routine was a little different, there was to be no more post-lunch chess.

I put the picture up, climbed into the top bunk, placed my hands behind my head and lay back. I felt comfortable, and reflected on the week. Prison can sometimes be like that. Can be a little monastic and solitary. A sanctuary-type place where – if so desired – you can relax and reflect. Such pastimes can be a little difficult in modern-day life with all its distractions.

Not long after, there was a rap on the door. With Duggan in a deep slumber, I went to see who it was.

'Steve?'

I recognised the voice. 'James, how did you know I was here?'

'Teddy told me. Have to go to work. Ground floor, number five.'

'What about exercise?'

'Can't, working in the kitchens.' He stood back to show the all-white uniform. 'Come on association.' He quickly vanished, and I returned to the bunk.

James was who I had visited on the day the painting went missing. We went back a long way. From the twenty years I'd known him, he'd been inside for at least ten.

Duggan stayed in the cell as we were called for exercise. It started to rain, as we began to walk around the paved circle, so we were called back inside. As I was going in, a young man – no more than, say, twenty – approached me.

'Steve?'

'Yes?'

'Teddy. John's nephew.'

'Good to meet you,' I said.

He was your typical Islington boy. From the Caledonian Road, and it showed. The pink Ralph 'Ralphie' Lauren polo was a given. Offset with grey tracksuit bottoms, and finished off with the mandatory white Reebok Classics.

Brixton Jail is predominantly the domain and preserve of south London. You do get the occasional east, north or west Londoner, the ones who have been apprehended in the West End. They are few, though. The look is the difference. They prefer the hair a little longer north of the river, as opposed to the contemporary Bermondsey crop.

Islington has – depending on who you're talking to – various connotations. For some it's a trendy and posh, the birthplace of New Labour, and current home of its leader,

Tony Blair. Behind the scenes, though, it can be a different story. There lurks a darker side. One of council deprivation. The estates, back streets and alleyways could be unpleasant. Sometimes, it could be a dangerous place. It had a history. Granted, it had its fair share of political elite and high-flyers of media and business. Ted only spoke to me for two reasons. I knew a member of his family, and we shared the same lawyer.

The fathers were responsible for the spate of armed robberies in the capital during the sixties and seventies. They knew where the money was. After accessing the cash, it was quickly invested. This ethos was handed down, and the sons continued the culture, only instead of vans, banks and post offices, the swanky designer boutiques of the West End and Knightsbridge were targeted. Instead of Jaguars, it was scooters; hammers had replaced the coshes. The only similarity was the deed itself. Still being carried out with acute aplomb and accuracy.

Ted was a little irked about a rumour. A De Beers diamond exhibition was to be held at the Millennium Dome next year, and a number of jewels were to be on display. Apart from some priceless blue diamonds, the 'Millennium Star' was featuring. This was said to be worth a cool £20 million. Word was out that his south London rivals were planning an audacious heist to prise the gem away. 'See you on Association,' he said, as we parted on the second landing.

Duggan was on a visit when I returned. The cell was all mine for a while. Hoping he wouldn't mind, I switched the radio on, tuning to Virgin. Chris Evans had just acquired the station. A new audio show covering football had been devised. Terry Venables was in on it.

Two new songs played: 'Just Looking' by The Stereophonics, and 'The Bad Touch' by The Bloodhound Gang.

Duggan decided to stay as I made my way downstairs to cell five on the ground floor. Every prisoner has a cell card that displays identity, name, number. religion and length of sentence. James's had said five years. *Strange, I thought he'd been given ten*. The door was slightly ajar. 'James?'

'Come in,' a voice said.

The room was dark, a piece of cloth was over the window giving it a comfortable feel, similar, I guess, to an opium den. 'One of the perks of being in the kitchen?' I asked, making reference to the plush single cell.

'Anything for some peace and quiet. Tea?'

'Please.'

I sat down. There was a large picture board on the wall.. He still had this occupation with African American culture. Subway art from New York, politics from Martin Luther King, Malcolm X, Louis Farrakhan or Angela Davis, he loved it all. Motown, Funk, Jazz, Herbie Hancock, Quincy Jones. It was all his, and still visible.

There were posters and pictures on another wall. The focal point was Pam Grier, standing, hands on hips. 'Amazing features,' he said, referring to her nose and eyes.

The picture was surrounded by an array of African American females in various promo black and white prints from the record companies. The Chiffons, Martha Reeves and the Vandellas, Brenda Holloway, they all stood out. Brenda looked luxuriant in a portrait piece. They served the space and did it justice. It made sense, adding beauty and warmth. Then again, James did have at least ten years' experience when it came to the decor of a prison cell.

His look hadn't evolved much over the years, and – despite being in his late thirties – he still looked boyish and youthful. I guess not having to take care of household bills really does lessen the stress of everyday life.

Even the blond, foppish hair – complete with the same short back and sides, and centre parting – was still there. A legacy from his borstal days.

That was where we first met, October 1979, twenty years ago. Says it was the best time of his life. I knew what he meant. 'So what happened?' he asked.

'Some painting was taken up west. Got arrested for it. Remanded for three weeks,' I replied, concisely.

'You're kidding, right? Where?'

'The Fifth Street Gallery, some independent place in Cork Street.'

'How much?'

'Been told a million.'

He whistled while pouring the water. 'What?'

'Exactly,' I said.

'How's Tom?' he asked.

'Thanks man,' I said, as he handed me a cup of tea. 'Still crazy, but good,' I added, regarding Tom.

'Rich?'

'Haven't seen him for a while.'

'Heard he's into Buddhism.'

'Me too, can't be a bad thing though,' I said, remembering Rich's heyday with Tottenham's main firm.

'Doug?'

'He's good, shame you couldn't see him the other week. Said he wasn't feeling well when we arrived at Brixton station, thought that was a strange one,' I replied.

'I understand, probably needed to score.'

'Maybe,' I said, though I didn't think that was the case. Why arrange to visit a friend when you need to find a fix?

'So, who would have a million-pound painting in a gallery open to the public anyway? The Victoria and Albert maybe – or the National – but a small gallery in Mayfair?'

'Yeah, I know, doesn't sound right,' I sighed.

We shot the breeze for a while. Mostly nostalgia, mostly remembering Portland Borstal. Oddly enough, it was all happy memories. Recalling bad times – though we tried – proved difficult, there didn't seem to be many.

It was getting late. 'Better get going, thanks for the tea James,' I said as I stood up, stretched and went to the door.

'What is it with you and art, Steve?'

I turned around. 'What do you mean?'

'It's similar to when we met. The charges, both involve art. Then it was a priceless da Vinci piece, now it's a million-pound item.'

'The first one I was guilty, and admitted to it,' I replied.

'Twenty years ago, long time,' he said, with what seemed a little sadness.

We hugged. 'Later,' I said, as I slipped through the door.

On the first landing I stopped and looked down. A man went into James's cell. He looked around before closing the door. I saw Ted on the second landing, he was playing some pool.

Duggan still hadn't left his cell. 'What for?' he said, as he listened to Magic FM whilst drinking some tea. He pointed to the wall. 'Nice picture,' he added.

'Yes, yes it is,' I agreed, as I climbed to the top bunk. I faced the picture, thinking about what James had said about it being similar to when we met. He was right, it was about art, and yes, twenty years is a long time.

Chapter Four

'The two great turning-points of my life were when my father sent me to Oxford, and when society sent me to prison.'
– Oscar Wilde

Monday, 4 September 1979

I pleaded guilty to the theft of the Leonardo da Vinci sketch at Oxford Magistrates' Court, and had to appear at Oxford Crown Court in a month's time. There was no bail. I was taken to Oxford Prison until the date at Oxford Crown Court.

HMP Oxford

Oxford Prison opened in 1073. Once a castle, it sits discreetly in the city centre. An evergreen mound is placed to its side. The reception orderly, Reg – an ageing lifer – informed me that every daffodil that grows on that mound represents someone who was hanged there. That – and being handed a small dose of disinfectant shampoo – was my introduction to the joys of life on the inside. Because of my age, I was classified as a YP (Young Prisoner) and taken to the wing for the under-twenty-ones.

    I shared a cell with Aadesh, whom I became friends with. He was nineteen, and a vegetarian Hindu. He had been there for one month on a fraud charge. After lengthy debates and discussions, I made a request for the vegetarian diet. It was granted. Under the influence of George Bernard Shaw and Aadesh, I adhered to the concept – and principles – of vegetarianism. One of the best decisions I've made. I also managed to read *Down and Out in Paris and London* by George Orwell.

I also learnt that Oxford wasn't so dreamy behind the scenes. Sure, the city centre is quaint and picturesque. Its green university quadrants, etched masonry and rows upon rows of cute bicycles were pleasing to the eye. But there was also a sinister side behind this facade of academia. The surrounding housing estates – Barton to the east, Rosehill to the west – and the most notorious of them all – Blackbird Leys to the south – were a social experiment that could go wrong if the car industry were to falter.

Built to accommodate the influx of workers that fed the car factories, they became hotbeds of working-class family life and culture. Men had walked and cycled from the towns, cities and valleys of south Wales to seek work in the 1950s. Rovers, Minis, Morrises, MGs and Rolls Royces – this was where they were manufactured.

During the late sixties and early seventies the housing estates were slowly becoming a hotbed of delinquency. Petty crime was constant, hidden from the world of degrees, PhDs, and Masters. In the early nineties raving scene, joyriding was in. Cars were stolen, driven and displayed in front of large, baiting, joyous crowds who had gathered to witness the frustrated police looking on helpless. Blackbird Leys had become a trendsetter, and the media took note. The film *Shopping* was influenced by this unique environment.

1979 was one of those transitional years that normally succeeds a changing of government. Musically, it was the year of ailing punk. The genre had nowhere to go, was tiring a little. The Pistols were gone. The Clash were beginning to fade. The Cure, along with The Skids and The Ruts, became the popular alternative.

On the celluloid front, Coppola gave us the masterpiece *Apocalypse Now* with its haunting soundtrack. Roddam had created *Quadrophenia*. Islington boy Phil Daniels was the star of the show; different music, but just as potent. Fulham boy John Bindon also played a part in the film. He once had a fling with Christine Keeler. Both had somehow managed to move into the murky waters of the higher echelons of British society.

As well as the funky, soulful disco beats that were coming to the fore, two-tone was in. This interracial mix of reggae and ska was making headway into popular culture. It had been manufactured in Coventry. The Specials were leading the way. 'Ghost Town' was an eerie piece, filling the airwaves with its take on what had happened some five months earlier.

Tuesday, 25 September 1979

There was a tunnel that ran underground from the prison to the courthouse. 'Only one in the country,' Reg proudly stated, as I sat in reception. He also kindly informed me that Donald Neilson – known as The Black Panther – had made the same short journey four years earlier.

'How do you know?' I asked.

'I was here,' he replied, quite proudly, whilst rolling a cigarette.

Borstal training was the sentence. Nine months to two years, depending on behaviour. I was quickly allocated, and dispatched to a borstal the following Tuesday.

Tuesday, 2 October 1979

Saying goodbye to Aadesh was difficult. We became close in the four weeks, and got on well. We talked for hours, and hours, and hours about everything you could imagine. We talked on association and walked together during exercise. We did promise to meet up. I haven't seen – or heard – from him since.

'The last public hanging on the mound was of a seventeen-year-old boy,' Reg said, as I waited in reception.

'What did he do?' I inquired.

'Theft, stole something,' came the inevitable answer. 'Found he was innocent not too long after,' he sighed, shaking his head. 'How old are you, boy?' he asked, as he was folding some clothes.

'Seventeen,' I replied.

'What you in for, boy?'

'Theft,' I said, quietly.

'All the best, boy,' he uttered, as I was lead to the waiting coach to join two others.

'Bye Reg,' I said. Never again will I forget those tales, and that awful smell of the disinfectant shampoo.

The early October Dorset sunshine greeted us as we arrived on the south coast in the late afternoon. Passing through Weymouth, I was struck by how much it looked like Nice on the poster at Victoria station. The buildings looked the same, only the sea was a different shade. On the way we had to stop off and collect someone at Reading, and two at Dorchester Prison. At Reading, I looked at the gate as we entered. *Oscar Wilde once passed this exact spot. Incredible*, I thought.

Chapter Five

'Borstal Boy, don't you cry, just do your bird, and time will fly.'

Portland Borstal, Dorset, England

Built by French convicts – ironically, to imprison them – Portland Borstal is an imposing venture. Opened as a prison in 1848, it became a borstal seventy-three years later in 1921. The island is connected to the mainland by one road. This road is a mile long, with a Royal Navy base at the beginning, next to Weymouth. Prisoners are checked every five minutes, so the chances of a successful escape are remote. As of yet, no one has made it – and many have tried. Some have even perished in the English Channel by trying.

Famed for its stone, the exported granite was used by many for various structures. John Nash was a big fan, using it for many of his Regency edifices. Oxford Circus and Regent's Park, not to forget Piccadilly Circus, are fine examples of the aesthetics – and longevity – of this stone.

Cells were inspected every day, and had to be in pristine condition. Bed packs made with precision. No dust. The tiled floor had to be so clean you could see yourself in it. The smell of the polish is still with me. Sunday was when we wore our 'best clothes'. Pale green nylon shirt, jacket and tie with black trousers. The house senior officer would enter. The rules were simple: fail the inspection, no association.

The decor had to come from publications such as *Smash Hits* or *The Melody Maker*. *Sounds* – for some unknown reason – was prohibited. James had Chic, The Supremes and Anita Ward; I decided on Depeche Mode and Tubeway Army, such was the allure of the then popular culture.

Two LPs were allowed. *The Specials* by the Specials and *Off the Wall* by Michael Jackson were my choices, *Funkadelic* by Funkadelic and *The Dude* by Quincy Jones were for James.

After five months, James accepted a transfer to Guy's Marsh, an open borstal. It was still in Dorset, just a little more inland. The evening before he left we gathered in the record room with the prized vinyl under our arms. Particular attention was paid to the handling of the stylus, as well as the vinyl.

Many abscond from Guy's Marsh, only to be returned to the familiar discipline of Portland. Say they miss the routine. It must have suited James, he stayed the remaining four months.

I made friends with Yusef, a Somali boy from Tiger Bay, Cardiff, and Marc, a Clash fan from the Isle Of Wight. Marc had the first two Clash albums, *The Clash* and *Give 'Em Enough Rope*. Great as they both were, I did miss *The Dude*.

The nine months passed quickly. I managed to read five books: Brian Friel's *Lost in Translation*, Arthur Miller's *Death Of A Salesman*, George Orwell's *Down and Out in Paris and London*, and Jonathan Swift's *Gulliver's Travels*. The other I read near the end. It was a new publication by Carey Schofield. *Mesrine: The Life and Death of a Supercrook* had a profound impact on me then, it still does.

Jacques Mesrine was a notorious French bank robber. Forever in the company of beautiful women, this charismatic figure started out robbing jewellers, fashion stores and banks. He had evaded the authorities many times with daring escapes. The so called 'Man of a Thousand Faces' met his fate in November 1979.

Pink Floyd's 'Another Brick in the Wall' was the pivotal song of the time. The youth from Islington Green school singing the backing vocals still haunts me today.

10 June, 1980 was a pleasant, sunny Dorset day. I said farewell to Yusef and Marc. Again, agreeing to meet up; again, never materialising. There was sadness, but it passed, I'm learning. People come and people go, that's just the way it is. The closing of the carriage doors was vivid as the train departed from Weymouth. The billboard for the *Dorset Evening News* said that English clubs had now won the European Cup for four consecutive years, after Nottingham Forest had just defeated Hamburger SV. I sat in a seat facing the direction the train was heading. There I was, eighteen years old, in possession of a discharge pack – consisting of soap, toothpaste, toothbrush – and a borstal haircut, en route to Paddington.

Chapter Six

**Sunday, 12 September 1999
HMP Brixton**

'Good luck tomorrow,' said Ted, after failing to pot the yellow ball.

'Thanks,' I replied, as James stepped up to neatly pot three, before placing the black ball into the top right-hand corner with the concise precision that comes only with consistent practice.

After playing pool a while, we retired to James's cell for some tea. The man who I saw from the landing three weeks ago joined us. 'Paul.'

'Steve,' I said.

Paul was coming to the end of a five-year sentence. 'Fraud,' he said. There was a slight accent I couldn't quite fathom. Maybe Italian, I thought.

There were three new pictures on the board. I knew Tammi Terrell. She was Marvin's soul mate. Stunning, I thought. 'Who are the other two?' I asked.

'Diahann Carroll, and original Supreme, Florence Ballard.'

'Beautiful,' I remarked.

'Died at thirty-two. Depression and drink.'

'Young,' I said.

'Life,' added Paul.

Paul liked to talk about his prison life as if there was some sort of kudos attached to it. He especially like to regale us with his time in Ford. We spoke of many things, except my case tomorrow, as if it was a foregone conclusion and I was returning. As Ted and I were leaving, James handed me a book. 'Came out three years ago, a good read,' he said.

'Thanks dude.' We hugged. 'Nice to meet you Paul,' I said.

'*Piacere. Ci vediamo domani*,' he replied.

'*Certo*,' I said. Like the rest of them, I'd somehow managed to convince myself that I'd be returning tomorrow.

Ted and I continued to the first landing. His case was coming up, and it was big. A series of smash and grabs were still happening, though. The Gucci, Prada, Louis Vuitton stores in the West End and Knightsbridge were being hit, big time. Bond Street, Sloane Street and Piccadilly being the principal targets.

There was pressure from the top for this activity to stop. A scooter gang from Islington had been taken out. Five – including Ted – were arrested, and dispersed to different London jails: Belmarsh, Pentonville, Wandsworth, Wormwood Scrubs, and here. It was still continuing, though. Someone, somewhere, was still organising the operations. We shook hands. Tomorrow wasn't mentioned.

Duggan was awake. Heart FM was now the station of choice. 'Spacer' by Sheila B. Devotion was playing. It came out in 1979, and suited my present mood. Buddha was still there, sitting peacefully, still in harmony, not only with nature but more importantly with himself.

'Looks like that other picture, you know, the woman's face,' said Duggan. I looked puzzled, not really understanding. 'The one where she's always looking at you, no matter where you are,' he added.

'The Mona Lisa?'

'That's the one. Probably worth a lot more than that, though. How much this one. The price?'

'A million.'

'A million,' he laughed, as he put the kettle on. 'Tea?'

'Please.'

'One million,' he said, as he continued laughing. After a few seconds I joined in, couldn't help it. So there we were, two complete strangers, one accused of supplying kilos of heroin and the other accused of taking a painting worth a million, laughing at some photocopy in a prison cell in south London. *You couldn't make it up*, I thought. I climbed onto the top bunk, tea in hand, and looked at the book James had given me. *Mr Nice* by Howard Marks.

Sleep was difficult. I was nervous. Lying there, I wondered about James, Howard and the others. The ones who find the world a frightening place. *Maybe they have a point*, I thought, as I finally fell asleep in the early hours, listening to the rain.

Chapter Seven

Monday, 13 September 1999

'See you later,' I said, as the officer unlocked the door.

Duggan turned over. 'See you, good luck,' he replied, before going back to sleep.

The case had been switched from Bow Street to the City of London Magistrates' Court. As we progressed towards the city, the rain became heavier.

'Looking good,' I said, observing the subtle tan.

'A week in Kefalonia,' Alexios replied, as he came to see me.

'Isn't this place mainly for motoring and white-collar offences?' I asked.

'Even though it's in the city, the court serves Westminster,' he explained. 'Also, another change. There's a circuit judge, Donald Hayden-Bowen. He's fair,' he added.

'You know him?'

'Not personally.'

'Still Oxbridge, though.'

'Of course,' he replied, with a shrug.

Though historic – and steeped in history – this place was missing something. It didn't have the sleek, rich interiors of Bow Street or Great Marlborough Street. I took to my place in the dock at eleven. The prosecutor – a handsome, blond, Robert Redford type – was on the right. He appeared relaxed, confident, looking the part. Alexios was on the left, looking a little nervous. The game, it seemed, had been taken to another level.

Though the personnel were different, the format was the same. Just a little more hectic. The clerks appeared more busy. Folders being moved from one desk to another in haste. The ushers likewise, running a lot more. It was all very administrative. *Cheap law degrees being handed out cheaply*, I thought. The suburban mock-Tudor townhouses with tarmac drives had somehow replaced the authentic urban Clerkenwell.

The judge had the countenance of a distinguished person. The long, bespectacled face, with thick silver hair, was to be respected. He made the time – and effort – to smile, acknowledging all. Within minutes of him taking a seat, the case proceeded.

'Mister Stephen Vincent. On Thursday the fifth of August, 1999, you are accused of a theft from the Fifth Street Art Gallery, Cork Street W1. How do you plead, Mr Vincent; guilty or not guilty?'

'Not guilty, Sir,' I answered, looking straight ahead.

'Thank you, Mr Vincent. Please be seated.'

The clerk continued. 'Your Honour, this case has been referred to the Crown Court. We now have an application of bail.'

He leaned forward, looking to the prosecution. 'Thank you, proceed.'

The prosecutor stood up before pausing. He looked pensively at his paperwork for a few seconds. 'Not guilty. The defendant's words, not mine. A bold and courageous thing to say, would one not agree? Let's not forget why we're here. Your Honour, let's be clear. This is a very serious offence. A serious criminal act, acted out with intent. Your Honour, one million pounds is a lot of money. You have to question the mind of a man willing to act upon this intent.'

This was going to be a tough one, I thought. I looked towards Alexios, who stood up, becoming more animated. 'Objection, Your Honour.'

The judge motioned towards the prosecution. 'Please continue.'

'Three people have clearly identified the accused as the perpetrator. May I draw your attention to this.' He held up a copy of *The Vitruvian Man. Long time*, I thought. It was like seeing a former girlfriend. *Still as beautiful as ever.* He looked at me. 'Familiar, Mr Vincent?'

'Objection, Your Honour,' repeated Alexios.

'Continue,' said Hayden-Bowen.

'This defendant must not be granted bail on three accounts. One: the seriousness of the offence. Two: he has a history, running the risk of reoffending. Three: the financial implications. One million pounds, a lot of money,' he said, emphasising the amount. 'The risk of the defendant also not attending the date of the trial is high,' he added.

I looked at Alexios. He seemed fixated on his counterpart, sitting motionless, with a look almost of awe.

'Finished?' the judge asked politely.

'Yes, Your Honour,' he answered, before taking a seat.

'Has the painting been retrieved?'

'That, I'm not too sure of, Your Honour,' he said, again rising to his feet.

'Thank you,' concluded the judge.

All eyes were now upon Alexios. He edged a file forty-five degrees to the top left-hand corner of the table. This movement gave emphasis not only to well-manicured nails, but also the Tag Heuer watch nicely displayed underneath the bespoke Italian suit.

'Thank you, Your Honour. First of all, I'm pleased to say that the painting has been retrieved, and returned to its rightful owner.'

'Good,' said Hayden-Bowen.

'As of yet, no one is disputing the witness accounts. However, I've asked for CCTV from the Metropolitan Police.' He paused. 'Who have stated that as yet, there is none available.'

I like it, I thought. The confidence was there. 'Your Honour, this case has not been put before a jury, therefore we cannot assume guilt. The man you see in front of you – the man I'm defending – has not committed this crime.'

Already, I sensed Alexios gaining ground. Watching these guys battle was clever, as if it was a game of chess. They were seasoned pros, all was said with clarity and concision. To my surprise, Alexios was in the ascendancy. Seven days of good food, a little rest – and a tan – was proving crucial.

'Regarding the alluded-to previous offence, my client was seventeen years old, he acted on impulse, pleaded guilty, and more importantly – justice has been done. I'll therefore be proposing for an application of conditional bail. My defendant must be granted bail on three accounts. One: no persons were harmed before, during – and after – the alleged offence. Two: his history was a single offence committed twenty years ago. Three: he has not been placed before an independent jury. And last – but not least – the painting has been returned.'

'Objection,' came the cry from the prosecutor.

The judge motioned. 'Thank you. That's all. Court adjourned.'

'Please rise,' said the clerk, as the court stood in unison.

The prosecutor looked both calm and collected as he sat down. I looked over to Alexios, who seemed – for some reason – little nervous. It looked personal. The two gaolers at my side sat unperturbed. It was a long ten minutes.

The judge entered. 'Please stand,' said the clerk.

'Mr Vincent, please stand. This is a very serious offence. But as of yet – as has been brought to my attention – you have not been in front of a jury and convicted. I have looked very closely at the application for bail, both for and against. I have come to a decision that conditional bail is suitable at this present time. I see no evidence you will contact – or seek to contact – any of the witnesses, and the painting has been returned.

'The date set for the trial will be Monday, 25 October at The Old Bailey. The conditions will be as such: that you reside at your current address; you do not go within five hundred yards of The Fifth Street Gallery; and you do not contact – or try to make contact – with any of the witnesses. That's all, thank you.' He gathered some papers and left. I quickly followed suit, as I was ushered back down the stairs.

Alexios came down straight away, fist clenched. 'Yes!' he exclaimed, as if victorious in battle.

'The prosecutor. What's his name?' I asked.

'Peter Smith-Cresswell,' he said, fist still clenched.

'You know him?'

'Seen him mostly on the Crown circuit. Surprised to see him at a Magistrates. Anyway, have to go to Brixton now. Come and see me on Thursday. Say hello to Doug, Rich and Tom. Well done.'

59

'Thanks, and say hello to Ted.'

'Will do.'

'Where is Smith-Cresswell's practice?' I quickly asked.

'Clerkenwell. Listen, look through the statements, and please, remember the bail conditions,' he stated, as he ran up the stairs.

I collected my property, and signed a few forms. Twenty minutes later I was standing in the midday drizzle. There was a City of London emblem above my head: *'Domine dirige nos'* it said. 'Lord, direct us' was the translation. I took a deep breath and descended the three steps to the pavement.

Bank underground station was nearby. I began to up the pace. The walk soon became a run, then a jog. After three weeks, the breathing soon synchronised to the familiar heartbeat of London life. It was lunchtime, and it felt good to be amongst cars, people and activity.

'Think I'll spend eternity in the city, let the carbon monoxide choke my thoughts away,' I sang, courtesy of 'She's Gone' by Hall and Oates, as I reached the top of the steps at Bank. I had a choice: Northern or District line. I chose the former. The oldest line on the system was tired and worn, but also felt comfortable and reassuring.

At King's Cross it was either the dark blue Piccadilly line – my favourite – or the lighter blue Victoria. The latter was noisier, but faster. The train had Walthamstow Central emblazoned on the front, it was still nice to see a familiar destination. I walked to the end of the platform, before settling into a carriage the back on the train where there weren't as many people.

Please, never change this convenient and intimate arrangement, I thought, as I sat on one of the two long seats that face each other. I rested my head against the glass, and closed my eyes. I thought back to Brixton. It would now be post-lunch. Duggan would be sleeping, Dimitri reading. As the driver announced that we were approaching Finsbury Park, I opened my eyes. On the platform there was an big ad promoting an upcoming event: The Millennium.

The year was almost finished. In less than five months, we would welcome a new century. The Millennium was waiting. It sounded promising, the Blair government had even constructed a monument to commemorate the occasion. £1,789,000 was the cost of the Millennium Dome. It was taking a lot of criticism. I quite liked it, though. I'm all for art.

The polished marketing of the 'Cool Britannia' concept was truly kicking in. A neatly packaged set of ideals, designed to attract the beautiful people from afar to the capital. Contemporary culture was awash with creativity, supplying everything we needed. Ramsey and Oliver took care of the food, Evans the airwaves, Blur and Oasis the music. Not forgetting the arts, courtesy of Emin and Hirst. Literature had *Loaded*. Fashion had McQueen. All the genres were there – at a price, of course.

No more of the windswept, barren – sometimes shabby – city that some of us had come to know and love. *London is changing*, I thought, as I made the short walk from the station home.

Both the front door and living room seemed larger than before, such was the illusion. I guess three weeks away can do that to you. I threw down the three plastic bags containing my belongings, and – before hitting the shower – turned on the radio. Sadly, Melody 105.4 finished last year. Some jazz, funk and uplifting soul became the choice, courtesy of 102.2 Jazz FM. The court date was the 25th of October. I had five weeks to find out who had set me up for this – and why.

Chapter Eight

'When you want something, all the universe conspires in helping you to achieve it.'
– Paulo Coelho

Tuesday, 14 September 1999
Islington, North London, England

The following morning was – understandably – a little disorientating. It was six when I woke up. I reached for a pen to quickly write down the name Peter Smith-Cresswell, before I forgot.

After some meditation, I became more focused. I'll go to the Central Library, then visit my good friend Tom. I hadn't seen him for a while – no one had, he had just disappeared for a while. Feeling refreshed after a cool shower, I decided on a pale blue Margaret Howell shirt, navy blue jumper, and dark jeans. The rain during the night had left the morning feeling fresh and vigorous. The late September sun was trying to break through as I stepped out for the less-than-ten-minute walk to Finsbury Park station.

I saw the 19 bus leaving the station from a distance. Previous experience taught me that it got caught in the traffic lights on the junction with Seven Sisters Road, and a short sprint was just enough to catch the life-saving chrome pole as it began to drive off. *I hope the Routemasters never disappear*, I thought, as I climbed the stairs to the upper deck. How would we function without these iconic buses?

It quickly passed along the Blackstock Road. This short thoroughfare – once home to the Irish, West Indian and Greek/Turkish Cypriot immigrants – had more recently become a hub of North African/Algerian activity, with coffee shops, barbers and patisseries aplenty. A little further on, Highbury Stadium was visible through the terraced houses on the right, as we ascended Highbury Hill.

As always, the Victorian clocktower was looking magnificent at the Highbury Barn. The old North London Polytechnic opposite appeared a little shabby in comparison. I got off at the next stop and cut through the fields to Fieldway Crescent, where the Central Library is located.

I needed the reference section, which was on the third floor. The lift wasn't working, so I took to the stairs. The silence of the reference and studying area was intense. So many books, thick and bound, were neatly shelved in rows along the walls.

I didn't know where to start, so I approached the desk for some assistance. 'Do you have the *Who's Who*?' I asked an attractive librarian with long, jet-black curly hair, and matching eyes.

'Follow me,' she said, as she lifted the counter.

I tried to keep up with her as she weaved through some tables and chairs to one of the corners. 'There,' she said, as she pointed to the most handsome-looking navy blue leather-bound books on the third shelf. 'Anything else?'

'No, no thank you,' I replied, as I carefully removed the S–Z edition, before sitting down at a vacant table.

There were three Smith-Cresswells. One was a retired accountant, eighty-six, and residing in Bermuda. The second was twenty-five, living and working in Scotland. The third was thirty-nine, and living in Amersham,

Buckinghamshire, and working as a Queen's Counsel. Listed hobbies included gardening, travel and art. It said he also resided in Nice, the South of France. He was a member of The Sloane Club – a gentleman's club located in Lower Sloane Street, SW1. *That's my man*, I thought, as I closed the book and returned it to the shelf.

'Where can I make a photocopy?' I asked, as I went back to the desk.

Again I followed, this time to another corner where a photocopying machine was.

'Do you know how to use it?'

'No,' I answered truthfully, as I passed her the copy of the painting. 'Just the one,' I added.

'What's your name?' I asked, as we walked back to the desk after.

'Laila.'

'Stephen. Thank you for your help, Laila. What's the book?' I asked, seeing a paperback on the table.

'*The Fall*.'

'Who by?'

'Albert Camus.'

'Any good?'

'Just started it.'

'Novel?'

'Yes, with a philosophical twist.'

'Sounds interesting,' I said, as I heard the rain lashing the windows around the room. 'Summer's leaving us,' I added.

'I love autumn,' she replied.

'Winter?'

'In the depth of winter, I finally learned that within me there lay an invincible summer,' she quoted.

'Who said that?' I asked.

She held up the book and smiled. 'Albert Camus,' she replied, as she attended to the next customer.

Outside the library, an old red telephone box had *ER* emblazoned across the top. The door was difficult to open, becoming stuck halfway. After squeezing through, I made a call. 'Who is it?' a voice said.

'Tom, it's Steve.'

'Hey, long time.'

'Where you been? Still at the same place?'

'Yeah man.'

'You busy at the moment?'

'No man.'

'Give me twenty minutes, I'm coming over,' I said, as I looked through the broken glass of the phone box. There was a crack of thunder as I pushed the door as hard as I could.

Tom lived in Stoke Newington. The easiest way was to catch a bus going towards Dalston, which meant going to Highbury Corner.

St Mary Magdalene's Church was opposite. In the grounds were the public conveniences where producer Joe Meek was arrested. A man before his time, some say. Meek's studio was a little further down the Holloway Road. It was there that he had masterminded his distinct, novel sound of the sixties. In 1967 three Islington residents – Meek, Orton and Halliwell– died within six months of each other.

Further up – towards Highbury Corner – is the infamous 'Black House'. 95–101 Holloway Road is a reminder of the black civil rights activist – and racketeer – Michael X. This self-appointed leader of the 2a black power commune had resided here before being executed in Trinidad for murder in 1975.

John Lennon and Yoko had visited in 1970, bringing their newly shorn hair to raise money for renovation. I was trying to picture the scene. John Lennon – one of the Beatles – entering that building, literally yards in front of where I'm standing. *I just stood there. To think that he had opened that very door, incredible*, I thought.

The adjacent shops had only just disappeared. Demolished, no more Highbury Jeans – relocated to Chapel Market – a garish-looking Tesco was its replacement. Highbury Magistrates' Court was still there, and – by the looks of it – was getting busier. The old Overton taxi building was now a pile of rubble; blatant vandalism, sanctioned by Islington Council.

I disembarked from the 30 bus four stops later on Balls Pond Road. From there, I walked through Newington Green onto Albion Road.

Tom's place was next to the old Hackney Town Hall. It was one of those handsome GLC red-brick blocks, discreetly nestled between Clissold Park and Stoke Newington High Street.

'Yes, brother,' he said, greeting me with a handshake and shoulder hug. 'Remember,' he stated, pointing at my shoes.

He looked well. 'Long time,' I said, as he made a quick U-turn and ran back inside.

I complied with the instructions. First the shoes, then – without touching anything – to the bathroom to wash my hands. I knew from experience that he couldn't relax until this ritual had been completed. I had to respect the trauma chronic OCD must cause.

Along the hallway was a long row of trainers, all neatly lined up. 'Coffee?'

'Please,' I said.

I followed him to the kitchen, where – like the trainers – a selection of coffees was neatly aligned along a shelf. We decided on some Ethiopian. While the coffee was brewing we went to the living room. 'Wow, what's that?' I asked.

'That, my friend, is an Apple Mac, just on the market,' he stated proudly.

It looked neat in the corner, matching the colour of the brilliant white walls. I took a closer look as he went to bring the coffee. There was a dating site on the screen. A profile of a Chinese lady was on display, a half written message was underneath.

The living room was airy, cool, minimal, and had a good energy. 'Something's different,' I said, as I sat down.

'Had it feng shui'ed. Rich did it,' he said, shouting from the kitchen.

'Heard he's studying at a temple.'

As I waited I looked around. The fresh paintwork highlighted the original sash windows, which were neatly glossed. The slightly worn, dark brown Dutch leather sofa where I was sitting was placed strategically on polished floorboards. A mahogany bookshelf – with a golden Buddha statue in the middle – was against one wall. It was the same Buddha as in the painting. On the top shelf was a row of football hooligan books – all predictably lined up in alphabetical order. Opposite was a big mural of the Arsenal badge – a cannon – 'Pride of London'. It had been tastefully done in eighties New York hip-hop graffiti style. The letters *E.I.E.* – Arsenal's firm – were circled above.

The room soon filled with the aroma of freshly brewed

coffee. 'Where you been? No one has seen or heard from you for a few months,' I said, as he placed the cups on a table.

'Just getting on with a few things, mainly work,' he answered, as he returned to the computer. 'Don't know whether to do a cut-and-paste job, or maybe take the time to say something a little more personal, you know, something different, with feeling,' he said, coffee in one hand, mouse in the other, and cursor waiting in the message box.

'What's cut and paste?'

'Oh man, what a technique,' he said, excitedly. 'You only have to write something once. You simply place the mouse over the intended piece you need to use. Click copy, go to the new document, click paste, and job done,' he added, by demonstrating. '*Hi. You look nice. I live and work in central London. Looking forward to your reply, Tom*,' was the message he sent. 'It's the latest fad, Steve.'

'What is?'

'Internet dating.'

'Sounds a bit calculating and impersonal.'

He wiped the top of the Mac with his sleeve, turned the monitor so it was facing us, then joined me on the sofa. 'Don't be so cynical Steve, the days of chatting for hours in a pub or a club have gone,' he said.

'How is work?'

'It's— sorry, one minute,' he said, as he quickly got up and raced back to the computer. 'Got a reply,' he added. Nothing else seemed to matter, as he looking attentively at the screen. I went to the bookshelf, as he proceeded to type, choosing *Bloody Casuals: Diary of a Football Hooligan* by Jay Allen.

'Any good?' I asked.

69

He looked over his shoulder. 'One of the first on the subject, written ten years ago.'

'Surprised more haven't been done.'

'Don't worry, give it a few years. Damn. No pic, no reply, why do they always say that?'

'Want to see who they're talking to. Send a picture.'

'Don't know where they can end up. Imagine a photo of you floating around cyberspace. The scammers can use it for anything.'

'It's only fair.'

'Then, when you do send one, and they don't reply, your self-esteem takes a knock,' he admitted.

Tom does the emotions stuff well. Having been to rehab, he's clued-up on such things, well versed in it. He sounds eloquent when it comes to the self-esteem, feelings, stuff. It seemed as though his obsessive traits had transferred to the dating sites.

'Still in therapy, Tom?'

'Of course.'

'That'll do,' he said, finding what he thought was a suitable picture.

'Who is she, anyway?' I asked.

'Chinese, living in Earls Court, works as a researcher in a museum. Same interests as me. Photography and history, different to the theatre and walking that you normally get.'

'I was away for nearly a month, you know,' I said.

He came and sat down again. 'Yeah, I heard. What happened?'

I explained the situation briefly. 'Can you believe it?' I concluded.

'Sounds crazy, dude. Someone wanted to give you bail, someone didn't. Guess you've now got a chance to delve into it. This Smith-Cresswell character certainly needs a second look, that's for sure.' A notification came through. 'Sorry Steve, SW5, that is Earls Court isn't it?'

'We've been there enough doing the tickets at the Exhibition Centre, check an A–Z.'

'A–Z? Watch.' He typed in 'SW5'. The relevant information came up: it was the postcode for Earls Court. 'No more A–Zs, Steve,' he added.

I put the book down and joined him. 'Speaking of Earls Court, any work around?'

'Ascot. Sunday. Speak to Rich. Yes!' he exclaimed. 'Wants to meet tomorrow.' The Mac was then switched off; the high was to be enjoyed, before it wore off.

We shot the breeze a while. Arsenal had sold Nicolas Anelka to Real Madrid in the summer and had signed a player from Monaco called Thierry Henry. 'Any good?' I asked.

'Have to wait and see. Only scored three goals at Juventus, though.'

'You've got Fiorentina in the Champions League next month. You must have been to their stadium when you were working in Italy.'

There was silence. His countenance had changed. 'How are Oxford getting on?'

'Lost away to Wrexham on Saturday, Luton at home next,' I replied. 'Tell Rich I need to speak with him about some work,' I added, as I got ready to leave.

He got up, switched the Mac back on, and went into the bedroom. 'Take this, it's a Nokia 7190, it's new on the market,' he said, on his return.

'Nice one,' I said, as he went back to find the box with the charger.

'It's even got games on it,' he shouted, from the bedroom.

I placed the book back into its allocated slot on the shelf. 'You have a new message,' I said, as I walked to the door.

After a quick hug, he ran back to the living room. 'Be careful,' he shouted, as I closed the door behind me.

It was still raining, but not as heavy. I wandered down to Dalston. It was still raw and edgy. Passing the Four Aces nightclub next to the station confirmed this. There were more artists per square mile here than anywhere else in Europe, they said. I can see the attraction; even on a wet Tuesday morning, there was a vibe. The 277 took me to Highbury Corner, where I took the train home.

Chapter Nine

Wednesday, 15 September 1999

'Steve?'

'Speaking.'

'It's Rich.'

'Hey.'

'Tom gave me your number, about some work.'

'He mentioned Ascot on Sunday.'

'There's that, but I need some help at the office today, if you're interested.'

'Have an appointment at ten. Can come at eleven?'

'No problem,' he said.

I looked out of the window. It was a little overcast, but the rain had stopped. I decided on a faded, dark blue hoodie, jeans, and white Moschino trainers. *Perfect attire for a day in the office*, I thought, as I walked to station to take the number 19.

'I'd like five more copies please, Laila.'

'You remembered my name.'

'Of course,' I replied, handing over two pieces of paper.

She lifted up the counter, and I followed her to the photocopier. 'Black and white or colour?'

'This one black and white, one copy,' I said, handing over the details of Smith-Cresswell. 'And this one, four colour please,' I added, referring to the picture of the painting.

'Makes a change from all the school and college work we normally get,' she said, as we waited for them to print. As she collected them from the tray, she looked a little intrigued. 'What's the connection between the

Maitreya Buddha and the man's details?'

'You know the name?' I asked, a little surprised.

'I'm studying philosophy. I'm writing a paper on people's different spiritual beliefs.'

'This is far from spiritual,' I sighed.

'Known as the happy Buddha,' she said, as we walked back to the desk. 'They say he's the last of the lineage,' she added.

'Really?' I replied, not really knowing what she meant.

'Is everything okay? I mean, you're not in any danger are you?'

'It'll take a little time to explain,' I said. 'Would you like to meet sometime? Maybe for lunch, or a coffee?'

'Wait.' She got up and went to a drawer, returning with a large envelope. 'In case they get wet,' she said, as the five copies were placed inside.

I thanked her, and made my way downstairs. On the way to the station I passed the old Highbury lavatories. Orton used to hang out there – now, ironically, it's a victim support agency. I thought of Joe, and how it must have been around here then. Highbury, Islington, London. The people, how did they communicate, and when they did, what about? Was it better? I had this notion it was, like it was more interesting, more exciting.

The phone rang, it was Tom. 'Sounds strange I know, but do you need a car? I mean, with all the running around you'll be doing before the court date, a set of wheels may suit you.'

'Would be nice,' I admitted. 'Why?'

'An old friend, Charlie – known him a while, he deals in cars – might be able to help you out.'

'Who?'

'You won't know him, lives in the sticks, but still dabbles in the city. He's down tomorrow for some business. Can arrange a meet-up if you want?'

'What time?'

'I'll speak to him, then call you.'

'Cool,' I said.

'*Ci vediamo dopo, ciao.*'

He'd already hung up, before I had the chance to ask him what he said. Definitely Italian though, I thought.

The office was in Leicester Square, so I went to Upper Street to catch the 19 again. On the way the sun suddenly broke through. The bus stop was in front of the Union Chapel, a discreet yet beautiful church nestled amongst some beautiful Victorian houses. Though slightly set back, it was still visible to the eye, courtesy of a stunning, protruding clock face. It was made by Thwaites and Reeds in 1888. The time was exactly ten-thirty a.m.

Who Dares Wins was filmed there in eighty-two. Tom was obsessed with film locations: where they were made, if they still existed, or still looked the same. Maybe this was a little late for him, he liked the sixties. He liked going to the locations, captured them with a Polaroid camera, then had them documented and catalogued. Though he was often in Italy for business, he'd never fulfilled his dream: to go to the location of *The Italian Job*.

I was observing – and taking note – from the top deck of the fast-changing skyline. It was happening a little too fast for me. I wondered whether the Italians or the French would destroy their heritage with such mindless vulgarity and vigour.

I got off at Shaftesbury Avenue by Cambridge Circus. I walked past where Sportspages was. The habitual ritual of spending many an hour sifting and browsing independent publications about football was over. Four-two-four and ninety minutes had muscled in, giving the novel football fanzines a more professional – and commercial – edge. I always doubted their interest in football anyway.

Sportspages had probably one of the finest books ever created. The bible for football fans: Simon Inglis's *Football Grounds of England and Wales*. How the grounds were built, the architects, the funding, was endless and fascinating reading. Each ground having something idiosyncratic. I've been to a few and so had Tom, who'd nearly joined the 'ninety club', an honour bestowed on someone who had been to all the ninety football grounds in England and Wales.

It was a short amble to the office. The sun had now disappeared behind some dark blue clouds, which allowed the inevitable follow-up drizzle. The shop window was still the same, displaying its juxtaposition of theatre posters – old and new – with various garish half price cards.

I didn't recognise the man working, but he was expecting me. 'Steve?' he said, lifting the desk to let me through. 'Phil,' he added, as I made my way downstairs to the office.

'Good to see you Steve, tea, coffee?'

'Coffee please, need a little boost,' I said, as we shook hands.

He went to the bottom of the stairs. 'Phil, two coffees, one with one sugar, one without, the cafe on the corner opposite the Empire is the best,' he hollered.

'Heard you're going to a temple,' I said, as I sat down.

He took a deep breath. 'Need something more than this,' he said, pointing to the piles of tickets and envelopes for the concerts, sports events and theatre he was selling. Rich was Tom's business partner. Tom looked after the football, Rich everything else; especially the corporate side. 'I have the money, but need something else. There's more, I know there is,' he said.

'Where is it?'

'Walthamstow. It's called I Kuan Tao, which means 'one way'. It's a philosophy, and though it respects the five main religions, it's not a religion in itself. All the prophets, saints and sages who were enlightened all come from the same source,' he said.

'Even the Maitreya Buddha?'

He looked at me and was about to say something when the phone rang. 'John. Yes, I'm here, no problem, see you in a minute.' He turned to me. 'Yes, he was, I need to find that source,' he added.

Rich was always a little different. I knew him as the young white kid with the dreadlocks. He was always searching for something. We used to meet at Doug's flat, and he'd take us all the way to west London for the blues and shebeen parties. Being a little older than us, Doug was always up-to-date on the latest music and fashion. His flat was always complete with the latest – mainly reggae – vinyl releases. Hours were spent listening to Linton Kwesi Johnson, Burning Spear and Black Uhuru, on his latest state-of-the-art gadget: the Akai Hi-fi system. Life was so cool in the mid-seventies.

The coffee arrived in two white polystyrene cups. John entered not long after. A tall well-dressed man – quite elderly – he looked the part in a beige camel hair overcoat. A brown envelope was promptly given to Rich.

The gesture was reciprocated, with John receiving a white envelope Rich took from the drawer. 'Have a good day, gentleman,' he uttered, in a soft Scottish accent, as he made his way back up the stairs.

The next two or three hours were spent checking invoices, answering phones and allocating tickets to various clients. There was a big fight coming up, as well as some Champions League games. We put the tickets in the allotted envelopes, ready be sent to the respective companies, all in time for the final post.

'Let's go,' Rich finally said, after the task was completed. He paid Phil and locked up. Before taking the tube, we went to the Oxygen bar opposite to relax a while. A DJ was playing some cool electro-house as we ordered two colas with ice and lemon. 'Tell me more about the temple,' I said, liking what I'd heard so far.

'I was invited by a member there about a year ago. It felt right immediately. I've just kept going back, basically.'

'So what is the philosophy?'

'Buddhism, Taoism and Confucianism mainly, and some teachings from the religions.'

'Tom said you did the feng shui in his house.'

'I'm learning under a master at the temple.'

'Do you know the Maitreya Buddha, then?'

He repeated what Laila had said, that he was the last Buddha in the lineage. 'Why?'

'Just heard the name,' I replied.

'Everybody knows him, the one with the belly, the one who's always smiling,' he said, as we found somewhere to sit and chill.

After an hour or so, we walked to Leicester Square station to take the Piccadilly line.

'Still in Finsbury Park?'

'Of course. Still in Tottenham?'

'Southgate now.'

As we sat on the train, he took a book from his bag. 'What you reading?' I asked.

'The *I-Ching*, or the book of change, from the Chinese Zhou dynasty.'

'Never heard of it,' I said, as I sat back. Eight stops later, we arrived at Finsbury Park. Before the doors opened I gave him a copy of the painting.

He handed it back. Something had been written on the back, and as I went to give him another copy the were doors closing. 'See you Sunday,' I said.

'A good traveller has no fixed plans, and is not intent on arriving,' he said.

'Who said that?'

'Lao Tzu,' he said, as I stepped onto the platform. After the train disappeared down the tunnel, I looked to see what was on the back of the copy. It was an email address. *Laila*. I smiled.

On the way home, I tried to figure out how a renowned football hooligan was now reading the book of change and quoting Confucius.

A text came through: '*Call tomorrow*'. It was from Tom, he'd sorted something out regarding a car.

Chapter Ten

Saturday, 18 September 1999

It was six when the phone rang. 'Tom?'

'Morning, hope it's not too early. Spoke with Charlie, mentioned your predicament, let's just say that he has access to a few cars, and he's willing to loan you one until you go to court.'

'How much?' I said, a bit surprised.

'Nothing. He owes me. Interested?'

'Where do you know him from?'

'We were in Ford together. He was in there for insurance fraud, you know what these rich boys are like. Get bored, wanna buzz, so they commit a crime, serve some time, get some cred.'

'Has been known,' I said. 'When can we meet?'

'Today at two, Baker Street?'

I had to see Alexios at eleven. 'I'll be at yours for one,' I said, as I rolled back over.

There was a spring to my step when I got off at Holborn. Though it was a Saturday, Alexios's practice was open. The air smelled sweet and refreshed as I walked the short distance to his office in Lincoln's Inn Fields.

'Nothing. I've looked a few times,' he grimaced, alluding to the witness statements in front of him. 'All three say the same thing. I mean, how did they know what you were wearing?'

He had a valid point. The Arts and Antiques squad had taken the clothes, they did match the description.

'What's today?' He paused to look at his watch – this time an Rolex Oyster. 'The twenty-fifth… we have three weeks, it'll be fine, don't worry,' he stated, as he walked to the window.

'What's wrong?' I asked, sensing some uneasiness.

He walked back behind the desk and sat down. 'Just heard the leasehold is being sold. May not be here much longer.'

'How long have you got left, did they say?'

'Weeks, days, don't know,' he sighed, as he opened the statements again. 'Highlight anything you're concerned about in the statements,' he said, 'and I'll see you next week.'

I had to meet Tom, so after making an agreement to see each other every Thursday, I got up to leave. 'How well do you know Smith-Cresswell?' I asked, as I opened the door.

'Told you, just seen him around.'

'Thought the law circle was a close-knit affair?'

He went back to the window. 'It can be. See you next Thursday. Any problems, call me.'

I closed the door, and walked down one flight of stairs. It had started to rain again. I hastily made my way to Chancery Lane to take the 341 straight to Tom's. On the way, I wondered why Alexios had avoided my question regarding knowing Smith-Cresswell.

'Yes, brother.' Tom opened the door, topless, hair wet whilst brushing his teeth. He ran back to the bathroom. Tom – like me – did like an appointment. The preparation was the best part. Taking the shower, choosing the clothes, deciding on the cologne.

'*Faccio del al caffe*,' he shouted, as he passed from bathroom to bedroom.

'Huh?'

'Make some coffee. The water's boiled. Just needs to be poured into the moka pot.'

After a few minutes I took the thick espressos to the bedroom, placing them on the side. As he was choosing a jumper I noticed three black and white photos of him in different locations. 'Like the pose,' I said, referring to the sideways glance adopted in all three.

'You like them? Taken yesterday. That one's in Notting Hill, same location where Marvin Gaye walks in front of a Rolls Royce,' he announced proudly. 'That one was in Montague Place where Jimi Hendrix stood,' he said proudly.

In the third one he was standing in front of some wrought-iron railings. 'Where Joe Orton stood?'

'Cheyne Walk, Chelsea,' he confirmed.

I looked at all three one by one, wondering if they knew their fate.

'Can you help me set up an email address?' I asked, as we went to the living room to finish the espressos.

'Of course,' he said, and after less than ten minutes at the Mac, I was the proud owner of my first email address. I sent Laila a message, thanking her for her help.

'How did it go with the lady from Earls Court?' I asked.

'Met yesterday, went well. We need to go to Baker Street,' he said, as we walked towards Balls Pond Road to catch the 30 bus.

'Thought Charlie lived out in Hertfordshire?'

'He does, but he has to see someone in Baker Street, it's more convenient for him. How is James, by the way?'

'Good. Had his sentence reduced.'

'I heard. If anyone needs a break, it's him. I mean, not a lot to show for someone in their late thirties,' he said, as the bus came.

He had a point. It wasn't only James who didn't have a lot to represent such an age, none of us did really. Rich, Tom and myself, we were all the same age.

As I looked out the window, King's Cross was having one of its bad days; it looked bleak. 'Don't you find it sad, Tom, that there's no marriages, kids or careers?'

'We grew up in the late sixties and early seventies, Steve. We got distracted by the music, fashion, clothes, the television programmes they offered. We bought into it. The middle class aren't sold it. They get educated, make sure they get married, get a career and have kids. I've spoken with my therapist about this a few times, she doesn't understand the working-class environment.' He looked at me. 'We were influenced by the media, Steve.'

I looked out the window again, this time we passed through Euston. I thought of the potency of the *World in Action* programme, how it was edited, produced, all designed to alarm and cause fear. The Euston Road was looking grim.

'Interesting concept, Tom, but – like the therapist – disagreeable. I mean, there were others from the same communities who progressed. What about Alexios and David? They lived in the same community, they went to the same schools as we did.'

'They are the exception, but very few,' he said.

The truth is that while others were serving apprenticeships, and going onto further education, we were doing the borstal gig. In hindsight not much use, but the experience was worth it.

We were continuing this candid, honest and thoughtful conversation until we disembarked at the next stop after Baker Street station. After walking a block or two, we arrived at a handsome 1930s mansion block.

'Hello?'

'It's Tom, come to see Roberto,' he answered, after ringing the intercom.

'Number twenty-five, third floor,' came the concise instruction.

We entered the building, and walked down the marbled-tiled floor that had a plush red runner neatly placed on top. 'Who's Roberto? Thought we were coming to see Charlie,' I said, as we approached an iron-gated lift.

'We are.'

'Then who's Roberto?'

The wrought-iron gate crashed as it closed behind us. 'He was in Ford with Charlie. It's Roberto's house, and Charlie's coming here to meet us, don't worry,' he replied, pressing the third-floor button. The red lighting that illuminated the buttons against the polished wood looked cool as the lift slowly – but surely – made its way to the third floor.

'Prison? What for?' I asked, as the lift shuddered to a halt.

'Forgery. Six years,' he said quietly, pressing his forefinger against his lips.

'So you know him?' I whispered, as we came out of the lift.

'No, he arrived when I left.'

'But you know Charlie?'

'Yes.' He then walked quickly ahead down another marbled hallway, until we reached a large wooden door.

Tom rang the bell, and a few minutes later the door opened.

'*Bonjourno*,' a man said.

'*Bonjourno*,' replied Tom, as we entered. The interior belied the exterior. The hallway was long and expansive. We proceeded to follow what looked – from behind, anyway – a tall, thin man, who then abruptly stopped.

He held up a hand. '*Aspecto*,' he said, as he went to close a door on the left-hand side. As we waited, I noticed a large map in a gilded, brushed-gold frame on the wall. It detailed a certain region in Italy called 'Regione Piemonte', which was written in beautiful calligraphy along the top. There was a gesture for us to continue, and we entered a spacious lounge area.

'Roberto,' he said, holding out a hand.

'Stephen,' I answered.

His hand felt sincere, genuine and warm. The almost classical biblical features were framed with long silver hair and matching beard, which was trimmed to almost perfection. It was all not too dissimilar to his namesake, the respected Italian psychiatrist and psychologist, Roberto Assagioli.

He turned to Tom. '*Tu come stai?*'

'*Bene, bene, grazie, a tu?*'

'*Bene.*'

'Please,' he said, ushering both Tom and myself into the room, which was in a baroque style, only with a slightly independent edge to it. Two life-sized porcelain leopards placed facing each other either side of the window caught my eye. Soft, classical music came from a radio on a cabinet. 'Haven't seen one like that before,' I said.

'New concept in audio. Called DAB.' He demonstrated its usage by pressing the tuning and volume buttons. The tone was clear, more crisp. *Different*, I thought, remembering the AM/FM transistor in Portland, the difficulty of trying to tune in to Radio Luxembourg in the evening, the interference.

'Are you okay?' Roberto asked.

'Yes, I'm fine,' I said, much to Tom's merriment. After resetting back to Classic FM, he looked around. 'Li Xing?' he shouted.

A few seconds later a slight – though attractive – Chinese girl appeared. 'Sorry,' she said, sounding apologetic.

'Li Xing, Tom and Stephen.'

'Pleased to meet you,' she said, before offering tea and coffee.

Tom's Ethiopian coffee was still kicking in. 'Tea please,' I said.

'And me,' Tom added,

Roberto shrugged. 'Guess I'll have the same.' He smiled as he sat on an expensive-looking, luxuriant cream sofa. Tom and I joined him as Li Xing was making the tea. Not much was said, so I marvelled at the spacious apartment.

Li Xing placed a tray on a table in front of us. The sound of the boiling water being poured broke the silence. *Some rituals are both universal and reassuring*, I thought, as it provided a cue for Roberto.

'Tom informed me of your plight,' he said, looking at me with blue-grey eyes. 'I feel for you,' he added, as he sipped from his cup. He looked at Tom. 'Tom is a friend, he's helped me in times of need, so, I'm just returning a favour.' He placed the cup on the table. 'The rites and rituals of public transportation are not what you need at the moment. The car is a gesture. Nothing more,' he added.

The classical music gave the words a certain ambience, as though the gesture was genuine, done in good faith, all with good intentions, and shouldn't be questioned.

'Thank you,' I said, as Tom's phone rang.

'No worries. We're here. Take your time. See you soon, bye.'

'Charles?' asked Roberto.

'Twenty minutes, half an hour. Stuck in traffic.'

'We have a little time. Anyone play chess?' he asked, as he looked at me.

'A little,' I replied, still in the zone after my board-game work out with Dimitri a couple of weeks ago.

He turned to Li Xing. 'It's in the bedroom,' he said, and she dutifully got up to collect the chess set. She returned, producing a beautifully crafted red wooden box. 'Part of my daily routine, at least one game a day. Keeps the mind and spirit both active and alert,' he added, as Li Xing started to set the game up.

I couldn't disguise my bewilderment as the ivory figures were placed onto the board, and it didn't take long for my confusion to be acknowledged.

'Chinese chess, you play?' she asked.

'Never,' I answered, truthfully.

Roberto went to the large granite fireplace and rearranged an ornament on the mantelpiece. It was a Chinese lady wearing a kimono and holding a lotus flower.

'A Gianninelli,' he said, proudly, as he sat down opposite Li Xing.

I watched with intrigue as the red and black pieces – so alien to me – were being arranged on a board. 'Soldier, canon,' informed Roberto, holding up the relevant two pieces.

'This a river,' said Li Xing, pointing to the middle of the board.

'The object is to take the General, similar to the King,' added Roberto. Before he could say any more, or even make a move, there was a chiming of the doorbell. Roberto glanced at Li Xing, who, again, obediently responded.

There was a distant conversation for a few minutes before a tall, slightly tanned, slender man entered the room. *Very Jermyn Street*, I thought, as he uttered 'Hello' to the four of us in a nervous, neurotic manner

'Tea, coffee?' offered Li Xing.

'Tea please,' he answered, as he sat down next to me. 'Apologies for being late, damn traffic. Also forgot the damn portfolio with the selection of cars in.'

'Not to worry,' assured Roberto, as he moved his Warrior towards the river.

'Can come back tomorrow. It's no problem,' he said, looking at the three of us.

Tom looked at me, we were going to Ascot tomorrow for the races. 'What about Monday, same time?' he said.

Charlie glanced at Roberto, who nodded. 'Brilliant. Monday it is, same time?'

I looked at Roberto who nodded again. *Take it now*, I thought, *while it's there*. The court case was in four weeks, and every week, day, hour, minute and second was crucial. 'That's fine,' I said, as Li Xing moved her Warrior towards the water.

I was intrigued by the chess and enjoying the tea. Charlie explained a little about the selection of cars he could offer, while Roberto was briefly explaining the rules of the chess. The cars were mainly of British and Italian extraction. Aston Martin, Ferrari, Triumph, Maserati to name a few. The exception was a Japanese Lexus. I was getting excited as he spoke passionately of the dynamics, how they ran, the timing between the shift of the gear changes. I could smell the oil as he spoke about the best rural roads he went for. The only part omitted was how he acquired them. As the chess was being played, the thought of driving one of these sleek machines for a few weeks was awesome.

Tom mentioned the rush hour. 'Don't want to get caught in that,' he said.

'You can play chess with Li Xing on Monday,' Roberto said. He turned to Tom. '*Ci sentiamo dopo.*'

'*Va bene*,' was Tom's replied.

'Nice to meet you Roberto, and I'll see you Monday, Charlie,' I said, as Li Xing kindly escorted us to the door. As we entered the hallway, she quickly made sure that the door Roberto had closed earlier was locked.

On the way to Baker Street station, I asked Tom what Roberto did for a living. 'A lecturer, teaches at the St Martins School of Art,' he said.

'Li Xing?'

'She's a student there.'

'Why is Charlie lending me a car?' I asked.

'Roberto told you, he owes me a favour.'

Though you meet so many different people in prison, I couldn't quite place Roberto in a jail. Charlie, yes, but not Roberto.

Though not technically the five–seven p.m. rush hour, it may well have been. The term 'rush hour' is antiquated anyway, it's always busy now, no matter what the time – such is the contemporary appeal of the capital. 'You in?' I asked, as we both squeezed into an eastbound District Line carriage.

We changed at King's Cross. I paused just before the escalator leading down to the Victoria line. 'Wasn't James in Ford as well?' I asked.

'I think so. Come on, it's getting late,' he said, running ahead down the escalator.

'So James, Charlie and Roberto were all there together?' I said, following suit.

The question was avoided. He was in a hurry, and seemed a little anxious. I knew why, the dating bug was getting to him, he had to get home to check.

It seemed the thrill of cocaine had been exchanged for the Internet. We parted at Highbury and Islington. 'See you tomorrow,' he said, as he hurried up the stairs, as if to score.

On the way home, I pondered the notion of having a car. *I'm a subterranean*, I thought. *I pride myself on my astute knowledge of the underground, knowing where all the stations are, and on what line.* Which the best carriage was that stopped outside an exit was a speciality. The deeply held principles – and ethics – of pollution, congestion and the environment would also have to cease for a while if Charlie's promise came to fruition.

Fifty pence for half an hour, one pound for one hour, was the tariff at the local Internet cafe. I opted for the former. My inbox was empty, so I had twenty minutes left to play around with.

I typed in 'Peter Smith-Cresswell', and some information came up. He was a director of a museum in Nice, the Musée des Beaux-Arts de Nice, South of France. *Cool*, I thought, as I clicked on a link to the website. It said that there were some events coming up in the next few weeks. Time was running out, so I asked for a printout. With a few minutes left, I went on to the Oxford United website and printed the fixture list.

When I got home, a silvery blue light coming from a lamppost filtered through a gap in the drapes. It illuminated the pile of witness statements on the table, as if to highlight their importance. *Tomorrow*, I thought. The two printouts took precedence.

Chapter Eleven

Sunday, 19 September 1999
Ascot, Berkshire, England

The fluorescent lighting of the previous evening had been replaced by the more natural glow of a sun rising from the east. It filtered through the same gap, only with a different energy. It was six o'clock in the morning, and I could smell the freshness as I lifted the window.

I passed on Marvin Gaye – 'Jam On Revenge' by Newcleus was more appropriate, as I took a shower. Clothing had to be discreet. So after choosing a Hugo Boss shirt, jeans and a grey sweater, I headed to Waterloo with that Sunday feeling. The arrangement was to meet under the clock at Waterloo for ten. I was feeling a little nervous. The four of us were to be together again, the first time in as long as I remember.

Doug was waiting, and looking sharp. A juxtaposition of Joe Orton meeting Noel Coward – with some Quentin Crisp thrown in – was the choice of attire.

'Can't believe what happened,' he said.

'I'll find out what's going on,' I replied, as I thought of the meeting with Charlie tomorrow, and Rich joined us.

I heard a voice. 'Do you understand the significance of this?' It was Tom, he was pointing to the beautifully crafted timepiece above us.

'Where Terry met Julie, "Waterloo Sunset", The Kinks, know it well,' said Doug.

Rich took some pictures with the Polaroid Tom had brought.

'Nice,' Tom said, as they were beginning to dry.

An announcement said our train was about to leave from platform five. 'Quick!' yelled Tom, as the four of us made a dash for the gates. On the way we laughed. *If you could contain that feeling of happiness, life would be awesome*, I thought, as we somehow managed to board the Bristol-bound train.

I felt safe and secure as we sat facing each other. The four of us were together again, and it felt good. As we passed Virginia Water, Tom looked for the house where John Lennon filmed 'Imagine'. 'It's around here somewhere. My favourite Beatle,' he said, as we all scanned the passing Berkshire countryside in vain.

'Preferred George Harrison,' Doug said.

'Ringo for me,' Rich added.

I was left with my fellow vegetarian. '"Band on the Run", seventy-five. Remember you playing it at your flat in Tufnell Park.' I said to Doug, who was opposite me.

The journey to Ascot was a little over half an hour. Before getting off the train we separated. I linked up with Rich as Tom and Doug walked ahead. Selling a few tickets had become something of a liability and a risk. For some reason, politicians and the media had taken this moral high ground. Endless debates in Parliament, new legislations, committees being set up, you name it, all in the name of buying and selling a few tickets. I mean, in the context of what's going on in the world, surely there are more important issues. If someone wants to buy a ticket at any price to see a show or a match, then so be it, it's their choice, a one-off event, an experience money can't buy. Many a time these guys have been a saviour, what's the problem?

As expected, they went fast. The last two went to a Russian. '*Спасибо,*' he said, sincerely thanking us, with a handshake.

'*Пожалуйста,*' I replied.

Rich looked puzzled. 'You speak Russian?'

I thought of Dimitri. '*Маленький,*' I smiled, as I called Tom to say we were all done. They still had a few left. 'He'll call me when they've finished,' I said.

'The days of the ticket game are numbered anyway,' lamented Rich, as we walked to a cafe.

'You think so?'

'There will be something on a PC or phone soon where you could buy and sell items.'

'So what are you going to do?'

'Been thinking about this anyway. This doesn't sit right with me anymore,' he said, holding up a wad of cash. 'It's at odds with the principles I'm learning at the temple. I study hard under Master Qianyao, Steve. Sitting in a classroom for five hours can be tough, trust me. Many people come to the temple thinking we meditate all day. Far from it. To learn is always difficult and the purpose of learning is to cultivate, so you are rewarded later.'

It sounded like a dilemma, I thought, as we went to a cafe and ordered some tea. I acknowledged the glow he had, the one that comes from inner peace and happiness. 'Stick with the temple,' I said. There had to be something more to life, he said, and whatever it was, I wanted some of it,

'What is the Tao, anyway?' I asked, as we sat down.

'The Tao is the essence of everything. It's the spiritual truth behind all religions, philosophies and schools of thought.' He took a sip of tea. 'The heavenly Tao has being transmitted for 4,800 years. It is the source of everything, the driving mechanism of evolution, the life force of the universe. Basically, it's the driving force behind everything.'

I became mesmerised, and before he could continue the phone rang. It was Tom.

'At the cafe by the station,' I said, but the allure of free hospitality was too much. They had decided to stay. After finishing our tea, we headed to the station.

'Come to the temple. Master Qianyao will be pleased to see you.'

'I'll come before the court date,' I promised.

'He has been blessed with the heavenly mandate, to transmit the three treasures. The heavenly Tao has being transmitted for 4,800 years Steve, in ancient times you had to study – and wait – maybe forty years for this transmission.' He looked at me solemnly. 'The Bagua is now full. The Maitreya Buddha is the last Buddha.'

'As in this picture?' I asked, as I passed him a copy of the painting I'd meant to give him on the train the other evening.

'Can I keep this?'

'Sure,' I said, as the train lumbered into Waterloo at quarter past seven. As we walked from British Rail to the underground, I thought about loving the city life. The feeling of walking in the opposite direction of everyone else, the surreal feeling of loneliness, not being part of it, but at the same time being part of it. I thought of Laila, as a tune entered my head, it came out a few years ago. '5:19' by Rialto.

I got home and counted the cash – just over a grand. *Not bad*, I thought, as I took advantage of an early night.

The short melody of '5:19' was still there. I also wondered when Laila would call.

Monday, 20 September 1999

'Can't make today,' said Tom. 'Have a date. Call Charlie,' he added, as he gave me his phone number.

He was still in Ascot, and didn't too sound great. I took the number and rang Charlie.

'Charlie. It's Stephen, Tom's friend, about the car.'

'Good morning. Apologies, can only offer you a choice of two cars, insurance stuff. A Triumph or a Maserati?'

'What Triumph. Stag?'

'A Vitesse Mark II.'

A Maserati or a Triumph? I was excited. 'How many seats in the Vitesse?'

'Four.'

'I'll go for that. You still coming to Roberto's?'

'Midday. I'll drop it off.'

'Thanks Charlie. See you then.'

'Pleasure.'

I looked out the window. Rain was on its way, that's for sure, the clouds bore testament to this. *Time for some jazz*, I thought, as I selected Miles Davis. 'Nefertiti' sounded good, and – as always – never failed.

I arrived at the block bang on eleven forty-five. 'Hello?' said the same voice as yesterday.

'It's Stephen.'

The door opened, and this time I opted for the stairs rather than the lift. On arrival I gave number twenty-five a resounding knock.

The door opened slowly. 'Hi, Li Xing,' I said, as her face appeared.

'How are you?' came the unenthusiastic response, before I followed her to the lounge area. Again, a point was made of checking the door. 'Tea?'

'Please.'

'I make Chinese tea.'

'Is there a difference?' I asked, as I sat on the sofa.

'Big difference,' she replied, as she walked to the kitchen area. 'We don't use milk or tea bag,' she said, shaking her head, as if appalled by such a thing.

'We haven't always used tea bags,' I said, as I remembered visiting David at Oxford. How fastidious he was with the regular tea ceremony. The preparation, the seriousness of the ritual. Even the consumption, it was all there. Armed with these fond memories I went to the kitchen, feeling that our long – and historical – tea-drinking culture deserved perhaps a little more respect and credit. 'We used to use real leaves.'

It suddenly came back, I was there, in alignment with David, 1975, Rose Lane. A little hot water into the pot, swirling it around. The careful choice – and placement – of the leaves. The use of a strainer, as it poured into the cup made of the finest bone china. The precision, the art. *Twenty-five years ago, long time*, I thought, as a significant piece of my life came flooding back.

Chapter Twelve

'Oxford is a little aristocracy in itself, numerous and dignified enough to rank with other estates in the realm.'
– Ralph Waldo Emerson

Saturday, 18 January 1975

The city of Oxford is no more than fifty-five miles from London. My friend Douglas had invited me to visit David, an associate of ours at this picturesque university city. Doug had been arrested the previous evening in the West End, so he couldn't make it. The coach tickets had already been purchased, I had no option other than to go it alone.

Like many, David had decided to stay on when studies at Balliol had ended. The lure and attraction of the 'City of Dreaming Spires' and its culture had held sway. He continued to reside there, staying on at his student digs in Rose Lane, after graduation.

It was one of those bright January mornings, and the sunshine was impossible to escape, as it bore through the coach windows. I arrived earlier than expected, so I had some time to spare. I naturally gravitated to the city centre from the coach station. I sat down on a bench in Carfax – a crossroads of sorts in the heart of Oxford – to read the directions Doug had written for Rose Lane. On my right was Carfax Tower, a fourteenth-century church. Its Quarter Boys kept me amused for a while. These two cast-iron figurines – adorned in medieval regalia – were situated each side of the clock face. On the hour they moved to strike the two visible bells.

I was fortunate enough to witness the one o'clock ritual. As I got up to leave, I heard some shouting followed by three synchronised claps. 'Villa!' came the roar again, with the clapping following again in unison. 'Villa!' it echoed, for the third time, louder and closer. Two minutes later – like the curtain raising at a theatre – between fifty and a hundred young men entered the vista. Surely actors, I thought, as they were dressed resplendent in the contemporary fashion of the day. Tank tops, with high-waist jeans that were turned up at the bottom. The iconic Doctor Marten boots were favoured. They were in vogue, and a must. The cherry-red shine glistened in the light of the January afternoon, as they aped their contemporary musical heroes. South London's finest, Bowie, had pin-ups. East London boy Bolan was fading. The west Midlands was on it. Slade currently ruled the roost.

The colours were the same as the Quarter boys: claret and blue. We were going in the same direction. I followed for a while, obsessed, intrigued and fascinated, until I turned right into Rose Lane.

'Oxford United are playing,' explained David, as I relayed the experience.

'Against who?'

'Aston Villa,' he replied, as 'Philadelphia Freedom' by Elton John was playing on the stereo. He was drying some leaves of a cannabis plant he'd just hoisted from the medicinal section of the botanical gardens, which was placed conveniently across from his flat.

Being a Tottenham fan, he admitted missing White Hart Lane, home of the illustrious Tottenham Hotspur FC. Spurs were currently bathing in three post-glory years. They had won the Football League Cup in seventy-one and seventy-three, and the UEFA cup in seventy-two. He also sometimes missed the desolate, barren streets of Hackney.

'Maybe one day it will change, become desirable,' I said, optimistically, to which he laughed.

He had the newly released albums. *Tubular Bells*, Mike Oldfield; *Selling England by the Pound*, Genesis; and *Captain Fantastic and the Brown Dirt Cowboy* by Elton John. *Tubular Bells* was the most consistent, being played over and over again. The homegrown had also dried enough to be sampled. The digs were cool, a studio flat. One room, painted white, with a cheese plant in one corner and a record player in the other. I was impressed. *What a cool life*, I thought.

I was intrigued with the way he made the tea, such art and perfection.

'How's Rich?' he asked, as we were waiting for the tea to settle.

'Good,' I said.

'Tom?'

'He's good,' I answered, in reference to my two close childhood friends.

I only stayed a couple of hours. I was fourteen, and had made an effort. The gesture was reciprocated. 'If you want to see Oxford United sometime, I'll come with you,' he said, as we walked to the nearby coach stop on Queens Lane.

'When's the next one?'

'Two weeks. Manchester United,' he replied.

The format of football was simple back then. One home game was followed by an away one. Then home again, then away, and so on, and always on a Saturday, except cup games. They were played in the evenings during the week, and under the floodlights.

'The name of the ground?' I asked, as I boarded the London-bound National Express.

'The Manor. Here,' he said, as he gave me a book to read on the journey.

We waved as the coach made its way towards the M40. The Manor. *What a cool name*, I thought, as I sat back and started to read *The Absolute Beginners* by Colin MacInnes.

I kept to my word, and so did he. I returned a fortnight later, again without Douglas.

Saturday, 1 February 1975

Nothing prepared me for my first ever football match. Saturday, 8 February 1975 was the date, Oxford United v. Manchester United were the teams, and the Manor ground, Oxford, was the venue. David met me at the same stop on Queens Lane. After some more homegrown, an unconventional guided tour followed. My favourite being a visit to the top of Tom Tower. *Some vista*, I thought, as I scanned the skyline.

'A mini London,' David said, as he toked on another spliff. He was right. The red Routemasters and black taxis – both visible from above – were familiar.

A Derek Clarke header sealed the two points. There was no three points then. It was simple. Two for a win, one for a draw, and nothing if you lost. It was a second-division match. Who could envisage the conquerors of the mighty Benfica in the 1967 European Cup Final plying their trade in the second tier of English League football? The majority left The Manor happy with the one–nil result. The cost was also affordable. Entrance fee, programmes and beverages were kept to a minimum.

There was no middle-class media ready to turn this epitome of the working classes into a hyped-up, over-sensationalised, rigged, money-making racket for the television. It wasn't ready to sell its soul to the highest corporate bidder.

We walked down Headington Hill to the flat, where we drank tea and talked. He told me of his plans to visit Amsterdam. I could listen for hours, such was the stimulating conversation. *Wish You Were Here* by Pink Floyd and the obvious *Tubular Bells* were the soundtrack.

As he walked me to Queens Lane, he spoke of his plan to go to a local Caribbean club later for an evening of rum, weed and reggae; you could tell that he was a friend of Doug's. 'Here, I bought two,' he said, handing me a match-day programme.

'Thank you,' I replied, placing it neatly in my jacket.

As the coach came, I asked whether he missed Hackney. 'Sometimes,' he replied. When the coach came I said goodbye, hoping to see him again soon.

There would be no more David. True to his word, he did go to Holland, and hadn't been heard of since. Why do the Davids of the world – the interesting ones, with character and meaning – never seem to hang around.

I started to read the team line-up and the player profiles as the coach connected with the A40, but it quickly became dark, so the programme was placed neatly inside my pocket.

As I disembarked at Victoria, I knew I'd go back one day. I'd seen what football meant, a return to The Manor was imminent.

Monday, 20 September 1999
Marylebone, London

'What's wrong?'

'Nothing, why?'

'You looked lost. Sugar, milk?'

'Neither,' I answered, acknowledging the subtle sarcasm. I made my way back to the sofa. 'Where's Roberto?'

'Lecture,' came the terse reply. She placed a tray with biscuits on the table. The cups were smaller, with some painted, detailed Chinese imagery.

Mine had a river and some trees. From what I could see, Li Xing's piece was more sombre, with a moon and a silhouetted mountain. 'Friday you said you'd play chess?' she asked, taking the chess set from a shelf. On closer examination, it was a very beautifully crafted with porcelain and ivory trimmings.

'We call this Xiangqi,' she informed me, as she began to assemble the figures. After taking a biscuit from the tray, I sat back and observed my new opponent. She was attractive, and she knew I knew. Thick jet black hair, cut straight into a sharp bob at the back, fringe cut just above the eyebrow at the front. The black eyeliner and the subtle metallic blue eyeshadow matched her eyes. The clothes were simple: a loose, soft cashmere top over black skinny jeans, turned up at the bottom with bare feet on show, completing the look.

'Nice top. Designer?'

'Designer Chinese. You won't know,' was the abrupt answer, as the last piece was moved to its respective place.

The setup was now complete, the game was about to start. I took another biscuit. 'Nice,' I said.

'Almond,' she replied.

The tea was different and strong, and I couldn't disguise it. 'Sip, then contemplate the move,' was the advice.

'From?'

'The Wuyi Mountains in the Fujian province. It's called "Da Hong Pao",' she stated.

Before she moved, she put on a CD. *Ultra* by Depeche Mode was the choice, I was impressed.

'This Warrior, you say Pawn. This Emperor, you say Queen,' was the brief explanation of the rules. After this brief information, battle commenced. I was quickly getting into it. My Warriors were slowly but surely making headway towards the focal point – the Emperor – to the tune of 'Barrel of a Gun'.

A pattern to her play was emerging: after she moved, she asked a question. It started with the obvious. 'How you know Roberto?'

'From Charlie.'

'How you know Charlie?'

The only problem was that it wasn't working. After I moved, she got the reply. 'From Tom. How do you know Roberto?'

'He was my lecturer,' she answered, as she moved a Chariot. 'You can call me Li,' she added.

104

'Lecturer?' I asked, as I moved a Horse, to counter the threat.

'For my Masters.'

'Cool, for fashion? Your move.'

'Art.'

After each sip of the rich, golden tea, I was not so much contemplating the next move, but more contemplating an answer to her question. I was enjoying it. The conversation – like the game – started to flow.

'Beijing?'

'Many cities in China, not only Beijing. I come from Shanghai. You?'

'Here.'

'And what do you do?'

'Just applied for university.'

'To study?'

'English history, your move.'

We both seemed a little relieved when the doorbell chimed, the disruption was welcomed – without letting the other know, of course. I could hear voices in the background before Charlie entered, a soft, black leather portfolio under his arm. 'Apologies, my God, the traffic, couldn't move on that damn M20.'

'Where did you come from?'

'High Wycombe.' Li looked at him. 'Well, near High Wycombe. Not disturbing anything, am I?' he asked, looking at the chess.

'Not at all, have a seat,' I replied.

'Not bad for a novice,' he remarked, placing the portfolio on the table. He handed me some glossy photos, and what looked like an official document.

The photos showed a quality racing green Triumph. *Unbelievable*, I thought. 'The car?'

'Nice isn't she?' he said, as he proceeded to fill me in on the specifics, history and dynamics.

'Has Tom explained everything?' I asked, still a little unsure of the gesture.

He looked around. Li had got up to go to the kitchen. 'Don't worry, Tom's explained everything to me, I understand. The insurance, tax, it's all taken care of,' he said quietly. 'And a beautiful machine at that,' he added, as Li returned.

'Totally,' I concurred, handing back the photos.

Roberto arrived soon after, looking the part with a cashmere overcoat over the shoulders. An amazing sun-burnt orange pashmina – the largest I'd ever seen – was wrapped around his neck. As Li took his coat, a black Merino sweater was revealed. 'Good afternoon,' he said.

'Afternoon,' we replied, in unison.

'Getting nippy now,' he said, with a slight shake of the shoulders.

He came over to observe the game. 'Good isn't she, beats me all the time.'

Li returned, and seemed nervous. A sense of a tutor/student relationship was in the air. She – like Charlie – had changed.

I could only think about the car. I needed to see it, to make sure it was real. I said I had to leave. 'An appointment,' I explained. Roberto was insistent I stay. I noticed a slight Germanic tone to his voice.

'Interesting. I'm Italian, from the north, not too far from Germany,' he explained.

'Is there a difference?' I asked.

'Between the north and the south of Italy?'

I nodded my head.

'A big difference. Let's say we are more industrial, more business-minded, and—' he paused '—a little more conservative.'

We spoke a little about how Italians have been coming to London for a long time, settling mainly in the Clerkenwell and Farringdon areas.

'We love London, always have, and always will. Londinium. AD 43,' he said, with a smile.

I understood. London does have an energy that cannot be matched, or explained. An energy no other European city – no matter how historical or architecturally beautiful – has.

'Well, it's creative, dynamic, alluring. Who would want to be anywhere else?' I said, as I got up to leave. 'Coming Charlie?' I added.

I thanked Roberto for his hospitality, and Li for her kindness and patience. 'I'll collect those on the way back,' I said, referring to the documents on the table. 'May I?' I asked, as I held my camera up to take a photo of the chess set, after which Charlie and I proceeded to follow Li to the front door. Again, the door of the room in the hallway was checked.

I made a promise that we would continue the game of chess very soon.

'The designer is Vivienne Tam,' she whispered, referring to her top, as she closed the door.

Trying to keep up with Charlie was a tough task. He had a nervous disposition about him. He waltzed down the two flights of stairs and out of the block with ease. 'Parking is sparse around here, had to park nearby,' he said. The anticipation made me keep up with him, as he raced down the street.

He finally stopped on the corner of Marylebone and Praed Street. I began to follow his gaze as he scanned the cars. 'There it is,' I said, unable to contain my excitement. I pointed towards the vehicle. It looked sleek and elegant, a jewel in the crown, amongst the other cars.

He then ran to check the windscreen. 'Thank God for that,' he said, relieved he'd been spared an infamous Westminster parking ticket. 'When's the court date?'

I went to the driver's side. 'Twenty-fifth of next month,' I replied. 'I'll return the car the day before, if that's okay?'

He threw the keys over the roof. 'No rush. Here, all yours.'

'Thanks,' I said, catching them. Unlocking the door felt good, and as I got into the driver's seat I could smell the leather and wood.

Charlie came to the driver's side and knelt on the pavement. 'No more buses, tubes, trains and people sticking their elbows, and God knows what, into you.'

'Can't say I've experienced that,' I answered, vowing to stick to my public transportation roots, no matter what. 'Charlie, what can I say? Much appreciated.'

'I know it's for a good cause.'

'Need a lift anywhere?'

'It's okay, Marylebone station is only around the corner, I'll walk. Any problems, give me a call,' he said, as we shook hands.

'Will do,' I said. I sat there for a few seconds, watching him walk towards the station. I inserted the key and started the engine. The vast array of clocks on the wooden dashboard suddenly came alive. The phone rang. It was Tom. 'Good timing,' I said.

'Finished?'

'As we speak,' I replied, pressing on the accelerator.
'You sound happy.'

'I'll be twenty minutes,' I said, as I slowly pulled away from the kerb. As I passed Charlie, I beeped the horn. He turned, smiled and waved.

The engine sounded retuned and sharp, the changing of the gears emphasised this. There was a rawness that synchronised to highlight the acceleration. I then pulled over for a few minutes, before reversing, to pass Roberto's. I slowed down as I saw Charlie entering Roberto's block. I was tempted to sound the horn again. *Next time*, I thought, as I reversed again and purposefully sped off.

The drive from Baker Street to Hackney was a joy. Each traffic light was a kaleidoscope of colours, each worthy of the wry smile I mustered as dusk was approaching. I avoided Upper Street, for obvious reasons – what would Joe Orton make of the transformation his old stomping ground had undergone? The thoroughfare that joined Highbury and Islington to the Angel was once a working-class area, it had meaning and character, before the transformation to the middle-class enclave of bars, clubs and restaurants it's become. Thinking of Joe reminded me to contact Douglas.

Tom was leaning over the balcony, again with no top on. The LCC crest was underneath. I gave the accelerator one final push as he pointed to a vacant parking space. I took out the keys and sat back. For a few seconds I didn't want to get out. The sound of the door slamming was authentic, as I finally made the effort. After admiring the perfect parking, I looked up and smiled.

He looked disappointed. 'No Maserati?' he shouted, arms aloft.

'Difficult choice,' I said, as I took the flight of stairs. When I reached the balcony he'd gone inside. After removing my shoes, I entered the living room. 'Difficult choice,' I repeated.

He got up from the Mac and gave me a hug. 'Man, that was hard work. She's from India. Doing a Masters, looking for marriage.'

'Another one? I need a coffee,' I said.

'Worth it, though, meeting her tomorrow. Good old Arsenal, we're proud to say that name…' he sang, as he went to the kitchen.

'Didn't know you could speak Italian, Tom?'

'One second,' he said, as I sat down with *Awaydays* by Kevin Sampson.

He came back with two espressos. 'Sorry?'

'On Friday, you were speaking Italian with Roberto.'

'Oh, just a little, you know, the basics. How were Charlie and Roberto?'

'Good,' I said, as I tried to visualise them both in a jail. The English aristocrats always have done a bit of time, they have a history of imprisonment, but an Italian art lecturer from the illustrious St Martins School of Art? This was a little more difficult.

'Was Li Xing there?'

'I can call her Li now,' I joked. 'Can't work her out,' I added.

'These Chinese students do like the ageing academic type, trust me. As for Roberto, you know what these lecturers are like, always have a young lady in tow.'

'Wish there were more books like this. There must be a market,' I said, referring to the few books currently dedicated to football firms. I thought about contemporary media, and what was currently being promoted. The

'Mockney' genre was in. *Lock Stock and Two Smoking Barrels* was leading the way with its take on London's underworld.

I checked my emails. Yes, Laila had replied. I understood Tom's feelings now. She left her number. *Later*, I thought, *first I need to contact Doug*. 'Any idea where Doug's living now, Tom?'

'He mentioned something about Whitechapel on Sunday.' He wrote something down. 'This is his number,' he said.

'I'll give him a call. Thanks for sorting a car, Tom, I have a feeling it's going to get interesting.'

'*Ci vediamo un altro giorno mi amico,*' he said, as we walked to the door.

'I don't understand.'

'Means we'll see each other another day.'

It was raining as he opened the door. I stuck my head out over the balcony. It wasn't that heavy, just the average drizzle. Looking down, it made my new acquisition look glittery and shiny. The rain was rolling down the exterior.

The walk down the stairwell felt good. Maybe it was the car. Maybe it was Laila. Maybe it was both. Who knows. Who cares. Seize the moment, enjoy it. Tom was on the balcony, still no shirt. 'It's raining!' I hollered.

'Good!' he exclaimed, arms stretched out. He looked up to the sky and took a deep breath, smiling.

I unlocked the door. '*Ci vediamo un altro giorno mi amico,*' I said, as I switched the engine on. The CD player and the radio looked a little antiquated. I tuned in to Unknown FM. I felt good, and took advantage.

'Laila?'

'Who's this?'

'Stephen. From the library.'

'Hi. How are you?'

'Sorry it's late. I'm good. Yourself?'

'Tired. Just finished reading.'

'Camus?'

'Good memory.'

'It serves me well.'

'So tell me. The picture I photocopied. What does it mean?'

'Are you free tomorrow. During the day?'

'I'm not working tomorrow or Wednesday.'

'Do you know Clissold Park?'

'Of course. I live in Hackney.'

'I'm just driving through Dalston Junction.'

'You drive?'

'Not really. I was offered a car that I collected today.'

There was a pause. 'You bought one?'

I was starting to get confused. 'Laila, I'll explain tomorrow. Do you know where the cafe is?'

'Love it there. My favourite, that and Springfield Park.'

'Midday?'

'Perfect.'

'Great. See you tomorrow.'

After saying goodnight, and the car having warmed up, I felt even better than before. I returned to Unknown FM, increasing the volume. A Swedish, Peruvian girl with a sexy voice was laying down some serious Latin techno beats for a Monday evening. I revved the accelerator, then did a semi U-turn. Tom was still on the balcony. I waved before entering the now becoming twilight zone that can only be Dalston.

The different colours of dials, gauges and switches were illuminated in front of me. With my left hand on the wheel – the other parallel to the side window – I surveyed my surroundings. Instead of turning left towards Highbury, I drove straight along Kingsland Road. The hip and wonderful were out in force. The atmosphere was creative and exciting.

A French movie was showing at the Rio cinema on my left. *Cool, I like French films*. The avant-garde. The new wave. Brilliant. As I manoeuvred through the gears my thoughts shifted to Leila. She knew a little, but not a lot. I had to tell her. I took a deep breath, and increased the volume even more. The rain became heavy as I hit Stamford Hill. It didn't let up all the way home.

I made a successful dash for the door. Morrissey was the choice as I tried to unwind. The picture of Buddha was upright on the table. I stared between that and the pile of statements next to it. 'Vauxhall and I' did sound the part. *Tomorrow*, I thought, on the decision to read them, and with that I went to bed.

Tuesday, 21 September 1999

I went straight to the window. I slept well, but had to make sure the previous day wasn't an illusion. Had to be sure that arranging to meet a beautiful librarian – and acquiring a sublime car – was in fact reality, not a pleasant dream. The sun was shining, and the car was there. I checked the phone, I had spoken with Laila yesterday. On top of that, Charlie, Roberto and Li Xing did actually exist. I remembered the documents I'd left behind, and needed to collect.

The noise of poles and planks being dragged and the thud of metal brackets being thrown served as testament to the power of meditation. Though distracted by the scaffolders, I got through it. *This is life*, I thought. *It's never-ending, always ongoing*. Buddha was consistent as always. On the table, smiling. Rich knew about him. I could see some similarities. Both had a peaceful demeanour. Feeling a little calmer and focused, I attended to the statements. I reached for the highlighter Alexios had given me.

There were three witnesses: a couple and a woman. The woman was from China, the couple were an Italian woman and an Englishman, all three were tourists, and described as 'avid art lovers'. The lady said she was at the desk regarding the purchase of a displayed piece, when she noticed a man unmount a painting from the wall. After placing it inside a brown leather bag, he then calmly walked to the door, opened it, and left the gallery.

The couple were about to enter the gallery as a man holding a brown leather bag was leaving The man opened the door for him. The description was the same from all three: blond hair, five eleven to six foot. Black silk jacket – Versace embroidered on the back – blue jeans and white training shoes. That was exactly what I was wearing on that day, I remembered James commenting on the jacket. The police had taken it, along with the other clothes, for evidence.

I didn't know what to highlight, or what to go on. There was no CCTV footage, strange for an establishment with such valuable assets. There was also no statement from any person working there. I placed the pen down, tied up the folder, and sat back. I had to see

Alexios on Thursday. I'd continue tomorrow, I had to meet Laila in an hour.

I needed some music to help me through the shower, the statements had made me nervous. It was a choice between Pink Floyd's *Dark Side of the Moon* or Marvin Gaye's *What's Going On?* I opted for the latter, as I knew from experience that it never failed, no matter what.

Though twenty-eight years old, the lyrics were still contemporary and relevant. Ecology issues, relationships with fathers – it's all timeless stuff, it's still here. *Probably more so*, I thought, as the goose bumps highlighted the haunting melodies.

The weekend rain had left the Tuesday morning air feeling fresh and vigorous, so I thought I'd go for it by choosing a red and blue checked tartan Vivienne Westwood shirt.

The Triumph looked even better on closer inspection. I still couldn't believe it as I sat behind the rosewood dashboard, lowered the roof, and drove down Fonthill Road towards Seven Sisters Road. People were communicating, talking, laughing, as if the sun had nudged them out of hibernation.

The majestic Rainbow Theatre overlooked the junction. Only recently converted to a church, it had seen it all. The Beatles, The Stones, Bob Marley, The Who, The Clash, David Bowie, you name it, they had all graced its stage. The stage door was visible on the right. Tom had a picture of him next to it, mimicking the Bowie image of seventy-two during the Ziggy Stardust tour.

Akin to a wise old man overseeing his disciple, The Sir George Robey was in its shadow. Once the Clarence Hotel, it was a fine looking building. A lesser venue, maybe, but it had still played to the likes of Steve

Marriott, John Cooper Clarke and assorted pub rock. Rumour was that Ringo had frequented it after a soundcheck at the Rainbow.

As I sat there, waiting for the lights to change, I imagined Bowie, Starr, Hendrix and all the others entering and leaving the door right there in front of me. The sounding of a horn behind reminded me to take a left into Seven Sisters Road, eastbound, towards Manor House.

The park was on my left. My second home. The amount of time I'd spent in there. On the right were the endless row of B&Bs. Once the preserve of the northern and Irish tradesman coming to the smoke to ply their particular trade, they now stood either boarded up or turned into cheap hotels. The Hornsey Wood Tavern looked excellent with its curved glass frontage – slightly set back from the road, looking grand. As with The Sir George Robey – and the bed and breakfasts – I couldn't imagine developers demolishing it and wanting to turning it into housing.

The sun was bright and glaring as I turned and drove down Green Lanes. I pulled over and called Laila.'

'About to pass Old Shoreditch Town Hall,' she said.

'I'm here. Keep walking, look for a green car,' I said.

I saw her on Stoke Newington Church Street, and gestured for her to stay where she was. After a U-turn, I drove slowly whilst opening the door, all in one fluent motion.

'Morning.'

'Morning,' she replied, as she got in.

'Enjoying your day off?'

'Of course, the seats are so low.'

'I know. Takes some getting used to,' I said, wanting to take advantage of the weather and drive some more. 'Change of plan,' I announced. 'Kenwood House, have you been there?'

'Never,' she smiled, as I headed back towards Manor House.

As we waited at traffic lights at Turnpike Lane, she turned to me. 'Are you okay?'

'What makes you say that?'

'Seems as though something is bothering you,' she sighed.

I took a left at Wood Green station. Five minutes later we were in alignment with the magnificent Alexandra Palace. Ally Pally looked glorious bathed in the autumn sunshine. *One of the seven wonders of the world*, I thought. The visible London skyline was clear to the left. 'One of my favourite landmarks used to be the old PO Tower,' I said, pointing out the BT Tower. To the left was the emerging Canary Wharf skyline, it looked separate. *Hope it stays that way.* I tried to see if the Millennium Dome was now part of it.

Muswell Hill and Highgate were traffic free, so we arrived at Kenwood not long after. I parked in a quaint looking gravel courtyard next to the house. Before switching off the engine, I asked what she thought.

'Never been here before, very nice.'

'A hidden treasure,' I said. 'Do you like art?'

'It's the reason I asked about that painting you had copied.'

'Then you are in for a treat,' I said, switching off the engine.

'Let's take advantage of the nice day, find a seat outside,' I said, as I ordered a peppermint tea for Laila, and an americano for myself.

She had chosen a table next to a trellis. Red and white roses were still in flower. I placed the tray on the table, and sat down. 'Why the interest in the picture?' I asked.

'It's striking, has a scene of tranquillity, though there's something more to it.' She took a sip of the peppermint tea.

'It's only a picture,' I said, liking the idea of being drawn into a swirl of psychological debate.

'Just a feeling, that's all. This tea is nice.'

'Earlier you asked if I'm okay.'

She looked at me. 'I don't know, I just sense some trouble, that maybe… I don't know, it's difficult to explain.' Her voice trailed off, as though she wanted to say something, but couldn't.

'Laila, I need to be honest with you about why I came to the library, and why I had the painting.'

It took no more than ten minutes, and was no big deal. In fact, it was quite liberating. I presented it in a neat and compact manner. The conclusion was that not only was she understanding, but intrigued, very intrigued.

'Do you know why anyone would want to do such a thing?'

'At the moment, no idea. That is what I intend to find out in the next three weeks.'

'You sound confident.'

'Quietly so,' I admitted. 'So, you said you like art. Do you realise you are sitting yards away from some of England's most celebrated and talented artists? Gainsborough, Rembrandt, Reynolds, their original works are exhibited right over there,' I said, indicating the house.

We quickly finished our beverages with a surge of anticipation, then headed next door. We spent a while admiring the old masterpieces and portraits. Laila liked *Mary Countess of Howe* by Gainsborough. My favourite was *The Hon'ble Mrs Tollemache as Miranda* by Joshua Reynolds. We both agreed that Rembrandt's *Self-Portrait with Two Circles* was magnificent.

Before leaving, we went to see Robert Adam's neoclassical library. 'Amazing,' Laila said.

'Very,' I agreed, seeing the similarities with the interiors of Marlborough Street Magistrates' Court.

'They all look so sad in the paintings, don't you think?' Laila asked, as we made our way to the lake.

'Art wouldn't be so powerful or enticing if it wasn't melancholic, emotional, and drawn from sadness. Art not only affects the artist, but the people who see it,' I replied.

The water was still, shimmering and sparkling under the afternoon sun. As we sat there I could see the attraction for the artists, the poets, and other creative people. 'How did they know what you were wearing? It doesn't sound right,' Laila asked after a few minutes of silence.

'Good question,' I replied.

She had a point. Only Doug and James knew what I was wearing that day. How did these witnesses know? 'The prosecutor wasn't happy I got bail,' I said, recalling Smith-Cresswell's facial expression. 'Not only had his ego been shattered, but there was something else, like a concern that the last thing he wanted was someone delving into his affairs.'

'As if there is something to hide?'

'Maybe, that's what I'm going to find out,' I said, as we walked back to the car. I thought of Keats, and what Hampstead would have been like then. '"White barred clouds bloom the soft dying day." Keats, he lived here,' I said.

'You think he wrote that here?'

I looked to the sky. There were clouds, though not barred, not today anyway. 'Not sure, poets have always come to Hampstead for inspiration.'

'Kenwood House is so beautiful.' She paused. 'Wish my dad could see it, he'd love it.'

We stopped by the car. I didn't know what to say. 'That's the beauty of London,' I uttered. The sun that filtered through the trees surrounding the car park suddenly began to disappear, replaced by darkness, I looked up to the sky, then at Laila. 'Quick,' I said, as I opened the door.

I started the engine and shifted into reverse. The sound of the tyres pressing against the gravel made a wonderful, gritty noise. '"Thou watchest the last oozings hours by hours",' I said, as we waited at the gate on Hampstead Lane.

'Keats?'

'From "Autumn",' I replied, as the first drops of rain hit the windscreen. It didn't really matter though, we did what we had to do. A foundation had been laid. 'Let me drop you home,' I insisted, against her polite reluctance.

Highgate Village was still classy. 'Rod Stewart's house,' I said, pointing out 507 Archway Road. 'Should be Arsenal and England, not Celtic, Man United or Scotland,' I added, my football tribalism coming to the forefront. 'Credit to him, though. One of the few people in the media who actually is a football supporter.'

Rod has always been into it. 'Celtic, United, you'll never be divided,' he sang, whilst playing with a football on *Top of the Pops* way before Albarn and his 'Cool Britannia' mob turned up, pretending to like the beautiful game in order to sell records.

'Isn't our prime minister a Newcastle United fan? And Alastair Campbell an Arsenal fan?' I looked over, hoping she wasn't serious. The smile said she wasn't.

'I like a good sense of humour,' I said, as I headed down the Holloway Road.

As we approached Dalston, I asked where in Hackney to go.

'Do you know the Lea Bridge Road?'

'Very well,' I replied, remembering The Swan, back in the day. I was aware of her mentioning her father at Kenwood, thought maybe I should say something.

'Where do your parents come from, Laila?

'Father's Algerian. Mother's French, came from France in the mid-seventies.'

'Straight to Hackney?'

'Kensington for a few years, then Hackney.'

'Seventy-nine?'

She looked over at me. 'How did you know?'

I thought about David, Oxford, Aadesh, Portland, James. 'Hackney must have been a little different then,' I said.

'I love it here, despite the criticism, it has a sense of community, character, wouldn't live anywhere else.'

'Heard they're building an overground line soon. Going to Whitechapel, even heard Croydon mentioned.'

'I've heard that. Will be good.'

'Always a bit isolated. Having no underground doesn't help. Investment in infrastructure will make it appealing for the middle classes,' I said. I noticed she relaxed more as I came to Hackney Central.

'I'm the same. Love where I live.'

'The treasure is in front of you. Not somewhere else.'

'You have read *The Alchemist*?'

'One of my favourite books.'

'Mine too. Where in France did you live?'

'When my parents left Algeria, they went to Marseilles, then to Paris.'

'You lived in Paris, cool.'

'Not as glamorous as it sounds, I'm afraid,' she said, as we drove down the Lower Clapton Road. 'You can drop me here,' she added.

'Sure? I can drop you at home, it's no problem.'

I found a space and pulled over. 'Thank you,' she said. As she opened the door, she turned to me. 'Do you know the name of the artist who painted the picture?'

'I don't. All I know is that it's about an ancient Chinese dynasty, it's very old, and is a collector's item.'

'I'll try and find out, do you mind?'

'Not at all,' I said, not knowing whether to mention her father. 'One last thing, Laila,' I said, as I took Smith-Cresswell's details from my pocket. 'Smith-Cresswell, he's a member of the Sloane Club. Can you call them and find out when he's next in town?'

After a few minutes speaking to the receptionist, she handed the phone back. 'He's checking in tomorrow at eight,' she said.

'Thank you Laila,' I said.

She walked a while down the Lea Bridge Road before turning into a street. The sun briefly appeared between the clouds, after which followed a crack of lightning. I leant over the wheel, looking up to see the advent of a heavy downpour. It didn't bother me, in fact I enjoyed it. I turned on the radio and cranked up Unknown FM, before making my way home through the back streets of Stokey.

Rich called later, on his way home from the temple. 'There's a cricket game at Lord's tomorrow I need to attend, can you cover the office in the afternoon? I'll be back by six.'

'No problem. I need to check out the Sloane Club after. Fancy it?'

'Of course, see you then.'

Chapter Thirteen

Wednesday, 22 September 1999

After Kenwood, I was in the mood for some more art. It was raining again as I stepped out onto the busy pavements of Holborn. Nearby was the John Soane's Museum. *This house never fails to amaze me*, I thought, as I approached the entrance.

Inside was a labyrinth of artefacts, sourced from around the globe. Two pieces caught my eye. One was a bronze statuette of the figure of Guanyin, the Goddess of Mercy. It was from the Chinese Ching dynasty, who ruled from the seventeenth to eighteenth century.

The other figure was from the Doccia porcelain factory in Italy. It was a Pietro Tacca piece of a chained captive. He was also responsible for the monument to honour Ferdinand de' Medici in Livorno, Italy. Another representation of slaves, Tacca is controversial to say the least. It didn't go unnoticed that both pieces were from China and Italy.

All this global history recorded in art, right here on my doorstep, amazing, I thought. Laila was correct: the treasure is where you are, not where you may think it is.

Maybe the car would be more apt for the visit to the Sloane Club, any excuse to drive, I thought, as I quickly went home to collect the now familiar machine. Fifteen minutes later I was in Soho. *More treasure*, I thought, as I parked in the NCP in Lexington Street. Rich had to dash. 'Back at six,' he said, heading out the door.

The next couple of hours were spent answering the phone. Hotel concierges were requesting good seats for clients, and tourists were inquiring as to prices and availability. In between, I learnt something new. I was introduced to 'surfing'. I was fast becoming fascinated by this new world.

Intrigued after hearing about the Ching dynasty at the Sir John Soane's, I scrolled down the lineage of the dynasties. I was entering a sphere I never knew existed. I startled when my phone rang.

'Ready for some information?' asked Laila.

'Ready,' I said.

'The artist was a Chinese philosopher called Mei. He was alive during the Chinese Shang dynasty. The Shangs ruled from 2070 to 1600 BC.'

'Anything from that time has to be valuable, especially to an overseas buyer,' I said. 'Will the Orton books be worth something after a few hundred years?' I added.

'Very funny. He stole our books. Defaced them, people still come to the library asking about him.'

The office phone rang. 'Laila. Got to go, speak later.'

It was Rich. 'Brother, have to stay here a while, entertain some guests, going to be a late one. Can you lock up, and drop the keys over at the Oxygen. Give Douglas a call, the Sloane Club is right up his street.'

'No problem, I'll call Doug now,' I said. After spending a few minutes looking at the golden lineage of the Tao, I rang Doug. 'Need some help tonight,' I said.

'Is six okay?'

I looked at the clock, it was four. 'Perfect,' I replied, as it gave me a couple of hours to surf.

I researched Mei. He had been commissioned for a set of five paintings for the Shang dynasty, to represent the five paths of Buddhism.

1. The path of accumulation.

2. The path of joining.
3. The path of seeing.
4. The path of meditation.
5. The path of no-more-learning.

For some unknown reason, Mei painted several copies of the first two, and the fourth. They were commonplace, not much value. I was accused of taking the third one, of which only one was recorded. Only a few copies of the fifth had been recorded. The third and fifth were the rare ones, making them extremely valuable and sought after.

They were all lost during the Opium Wars. The third and fifth ones had never been recovered. Unlike the third, there was also no recorded image of the fifth; basically, no one knew what it looked like. 'The path of seeing' had never been recovered? Was the judge not told by Alexios in court that the painting had been retrieved, and returned to its rightful owner? This played a big part in my getting bail. Was Alexios telling the truth? I picked up the phone.

'Alexios, the painting. You said it had been found and returned to the gallery.'

'So the Art and Antiques squad told me. Why?'

'Was wondering, that's all. See you tomorrow.'

'Don't forget the statements.'

'I won't.' I printed the four images, not the best of quality, but they'd do. I needed some fresh air, so after placing the '*Back in five minutes*' sign on the door, I strolled to nearby Trafalgar Square. The rain – thankfully – had abated.

I sat overlooking the square. It was originally designed by the Prince Regent's favourite son, John Nash, the figurehead of the Regency period, though it was later revamped by Sir Charles Berry.

The pigeons matched the sky. Grey and dull. They were sparse, the legacy of our current mayor, who was intent on phasing them out. Like them or not, they were a part of London life. Next, the Routemaster buses would be culled. The four lions were still there, though, looking to each corner as if desperately trying to preserve the heart and soul of the city. It felt as though it was about to rain again, but somehow just holding back.

I paused at the National Gallery on the way back. Another sixties exhibition by another sixties photographer was being shown. Jean Shrimpton, Mick Jagger and David Bailey being the usual suspects. Three Japanese girls bumped into me. I turned, and after a slight bow they ran inside giggling. The sixties culture still holds sway. *How we take this stuff for granted*, I thought, as the rain started.

Once inside, I turned the sign back to '*Open*' and looked out. The rain returned with a vengeance. During the day there was only one complaint. A ticket had been bought from Phil yesterday. He sold a restricted view, which is fine, as long as you inform the customer. Problem was, he hadn't. 'Screamers,' we call them. The only way to deal with them – without causing too much hassle – is to apologise, refund the money – cash only – and hope it doesn't go any further. The anger is understandable. Nobody likes being ripped off.

'A *pleuville*! That's what I am!' exclaimed Douglas, who – after hanging up his overcoat and dispatching an umbrella – gave me a well-deserved hug.

'What's that?' I asked, glad to see he was on form.

'Someone who likes the rain.'

Rich, Tom and myself grew up with Douglas. Being a little older, we looked up to him, thought he was an amazing guy, he taught us a lot. A juxtaposition of Joe Orton, Kenneth Williams and Quentin Crisp, he kept the Regency vibe alive in the twentieth century, a real dandy.

He introduced me to alternative music, to the hip literature and movies of the day – as well as the hashish and weed. Problem was that he didn't stop there. It evolved, choosing the lifestyle of harder drugs. Going to his flat in Tufnell Park was always edgy – and cool – especially for young teenagers. We saw, and heard, it all. We grew up fast.

Another talent was crime, a pastime we aspired to at the time. He did it with style, panache and swagger, and was rarely caught. When he was, the consequence was a couple of months' loss of liberty here and there. 'Occupational hazard,' he would say. We admired the way he never hurt people. It was white-collar fraud, nothing physical. He prided himself on this 'moral criminal' vibe.

Mine and Tom's goal was to go to every football ground in England and Wales with our respective teams. Doug's was to serve time in every jail in England and Wales. Because of Oxford's inconsistency – getting relegated and promoted on a regular basis – along with Arsenal's solid foundation in the first division, I was in the lead.

I looked at the clock. Five forty-five, nearly time to close. I needed to eat. 'Gaby's?'

'Of course, where else?'

After locking up, I took the keys across the road to the Oxygen bar. It was still raining, so we ran to Gaby's on the Charing Cross Road. We ordered a falafel and soda, before taking a seat at the counter by the window.

'We can take the tube from Leicester Square to Victoria, then the District line to Sloane Square, or walk down to the Embankment to take the District line,' he suggested.

'I have a car,' I said, much to his disbelief.

'What?'

'It's in the NCP, Lexington Street.'

'Where did you get that from?'

'A friend of Tom's. Hasn't he told you?'

'Haven't seen or heard from him since Ascot. Since that Chinese girl he's gone quiet.'

'Must be the dating sites, Internet addiction,' I said.

'Goes from one thing to another, always has done.'

I watched as the rain hit the window. I followed the drops and noticed how they merged with several others on the way down until it reached the bottom. Some drops didn't connect, simply falling to the bottom on their own. These reached the bottom a lot faster. I thought about life and how we connect with some, and not others.

Maybe there is a purpose to why some of us go it alone and do life solo, who knows. The rain on the window was just another one of life's many analogies, I thought, as I felt some sadness.

'You okay?'

'Yeah.'

'Coffee?'

'Sure,' I answered. We were on the cusp of Leicester Square and Covent Garden, spoilt for choice really, as we went to pay.

'Bar Italia?' Doug suggested.

I looked at the time, six forty-five. 'Too busy. Anywhere else nearby?'

'There's a new Italian place in Monmouth Street.'

'Perfect, let's go,' I said.

'*Andiamo!*' Doug exclaimed, as we headed in the direction of the Seven Dials.

We passed Bunjies, an old folk, beatnik coffee house joint on Litchfield Street that had closed earlier in the year. 'Making way for a restaurant,' Doug lamented.

'Not a Ramsey or Pierre White thing?'

'Hope not. To think Art Garfunkel, Paul Simon and Bob Dylan played there.'

'As did Sandie Shaw, Cat Stephens and Rod Stewart.'

'Not forgetting Phil Collins and David Bowie,' he added.

The New Covent Garden Hotel looked refreshed after a makeover. Doug liked hotels. He enjoyed the ambience. 'A world within a world,' he used to say. 'Love the brickwork,' he said.

We diverted to pay respect to the founder of Neals Yard, Nicholas Saunders, who died the previous year. He put it on the map. A true visionary and collective, he was always on a continuous journey of self-development.

He had paid something like £7,000 to purchase this old warehouse back in seventy-six when Covent Garden was rundown, shabby and in a state of disrepair. He created a sense of community by opening a wholefood warehouse. This former squatters' haunt had – thus far – eluded the 'Cool Britannia' folk. They had nothing on it, even if they tried.

'Need to see the water clock,' I said. This contraption was the same concept as the Quarter Boys in Oxford. The difference being that, on the hour, built-up water passed down tubes, filling up buckets, which in turn created the sound of bells being chimed, as opposed to the bells being struck.

'Heard anything from David?' I asked, in vain, as well as hope.

'Nothing,' came the inevitable answer.

'Wonder what he's doing,' I said, picturing what would now be a handsome forty-something in the Dutch capital.

The coffeehouse did look good – he was the man, knowing every crook and cranny of the capital. As he ordered, I looked at the neatly placed bags of pasta, and rows of bottled olive oil displayed all around. '*Produto da Brescia*,' said the labels. There was a large map of Italy on the wall, indicating which region products were manufactured in. The region Roberto was from wasn't far from Brescia.

'You okay? Look miles away.'

'Just wondering where Tom goes when he's out there,' I said, as we sat outside. I explained about Roberto. 'The map made me think of him. Do you know him?'

'Heard of him.' He looked at my cup. 'Finished?'

'Nearly,' I said, as I drank the last of the coffee. Without saying anything else, he took the cups to the counter. '*Grazie*,' said the barista.

'*Grazie*,' Doug replied.

'*Chi vediamo un altro journal*,' I added, as we made our way to the door.

Doug was pointing out lots of things on the short walk through Soho to Lexington Street. Mostly were of a bygone era that included drugs and crime. It didn't take long for contemporary culture to get a mention, though. 'That Oasis, Blur, Chris Evans, and the rest, all coming to the capital, regurgitating some old format to make money, makes me sick,' he said.

'Let's see if they continue to live here when the party's over,' I replied.

'Creating this "Cool Britannia" nonsense,' he continued. 'In the meantime, it's us that have to live through it,' he added.

'How do they all make so much money? Where does it come from?'

'The media,' I answered, as we got in the car.

'Result,' Doug observed, looking around the interior.

The slight ramp led us out from the claustrophobic car park and into the bright lights of Soho, glowing as dusk was upon us. We entered the realm of Knightsbridge within a few minutes. The designer stores were on each side. Gucci, Prada, Louis Vuitton, they were all colourful, shiny and enticing as I thought of Ted.

There were two sides to the industry. On one side were the designers, the buyers and sellers, the advertising, the models and their agencies, and the shows. On the other side were the Londoners, who wanted some of it. The postcode gangs. The fence, the planning, the scooters, the hammers, and finally, the buzz. They both needed each other. I mean, what a compliment, your product was being sought, targeted, money cannot buy that advertising.

I was looking for the Gucci handbag store. 'Look on the right, I'll look on the left,' I uttered, as I slowed down, leaning over the steering wheel. Typically, Doug spotted it. 'There,' he said, pointing on my side. It looked out of sync with the rest, more like a bank, or a hotel. It was a new building – maybe late sixties or early seventies. The black and gold lacquered exterior glittered in a tacky way. This was probably the intended look, though. On first impressions, not somewhere you would buy extravagant accessories.

I imagined the scooters descending. Organised, planned, well researched, riding to carry out the job, nothing would stop them at that stage. Then the precision of the blows, the onlookers – who were both shocked and amused – the aftermath. There was a sound of a horn. 'The light's green,' Doug said, pointing above. I took a left at Sloane Square, then another into Lower Sloane Street.

'Number fifty-two,' I said.

'Over there,' Doug said, again showing the way.

There was no space to park. I continued driving, speeding up a little as we turned into Pimlico Road. As we went around Sloane Square for the second time, Doug pointed out the Royal Court Theatre. 'Orton had a play there, *Entertaining Mr Sloane*, 1975.'

I glanced up briefly as we passed the handsome venue, trying to figure out whether he would have crossed the square, taken the 19, or walked around it.

'Just another working-class boy. Out of his depth, devoured by the middle classes ,that's all,' I said, finding a space alongside Sloane Gardens.

It had a good view of the club, which was a little further on the right, and looking exactly like the picture on the website. As we listened to Heart FM, the rain started to pelt the roof, totally out of sync with the disco and club classics.

'You think Orton was starting to move in circles a little alien to him?' I asked, keeping an eye on the royal blue canopied entrance.

'Definitely,' he replied.

'Same as Christine Keeler?'

'The middle classes really don't like us, you know. They adopt some of our ways, then adjust them to suit themselves, and suddenly it becomes their culture. We connect more with the upper classes.' He mentioned The Barrow Boy and the Banker pub by London Bridge. 'A good example of the connection between the upper and working classes,' he added.

'Speaking of the upper classes, do you know Charlie?'

'Heard a rumour, may not be true though.'

'About?' I asked, still keeping an eye on the entrance.

'Him, James, and another man in Ford.'

'What other man?'

'Paul, I think.'

A porter quickly dashed from the club as a taxi pulled up outside the entrance. After collecting two suitcases, he ran back inside, reappearing a few seconds later with an umbrella.

'Doug?'

'Yes?'

'Let me introduce Mr Peter Smith-Cresswell,' I said, as a blond man climbed out of the cab, paid the driver, then sheltered under the umbrella as he walked to the door.

'He's in London for a reason,' Doug said.

I pondered a few seconds before starting the engine. 'What's the time?'

'Seven-thirty.'

'I'll take you home.'

'Too early, meeting the boys for a game of snooker at eleven.'

'Bagel and a cup of tea then?' I suggested, which was agreed. I did a U-turn and headed back towards Knightsbridge. I accelerated as we approached the

Piccadilly underpass. The cold tunnel felt good as we headed east towards Whitechapel.

Two cream cheese bagels and a cup of tea later, we felt better. Doug said he was tired. 'Need to go home,' he said. Really, he needed a fix. I understood. 'I'll drop you at Aldgate Station,' I said.

I watched as he walked away. His behaviour was different than a few hours ago. This was what the junk did, it dictated your whole being. Like a silhouette, he faded into the background, such was the anonymity of Aldgate. My thoughts switched to Smith-Cresswell. Why would he be in London? Maybe a court case? Maybe something else? We'd see. I tuned to Unknown FM and hit the road, wondering what Doug had meant about James, Charlie, and someone else.

'Hi Laila,' I said, briefly stopping on Shoreditch High Street to make a call. I suggested a walk along the River Lea on Saturday, if she wasn't busy. She wasn't, so we agreed on one at Tottenham Hale station. I felt a warm glow. Needless to say, the rest of the drive was pleasant.

I listened to *Animals* by Pink Floyd and burnt some sandalwood incense, but still found it difficult to relax. I sat down, ran my fingers through my hair, took a deep breath and thought about the characters in this emerging drama.

Tom. Childhood friend. Suffers from OCD. Ex-addict. Ex-criminal.
Ritchie. Childhood friend. Buddhist. Ex-criminal.
Douglas. Childhood friend. Addict. Criminal.
Alexios. Childhood friend. Lawyer.
James. Childhood friend. Criminal.
Leila. Librarian. Studying philosophy.
Charlie. English aristocrat. Fraudster. Ex-criminal.

Roberto. Italian aristocrat. Senior art lecturer at the prestigious St Martins School of Art. Ex-criminal.

Li Xing. Roberto's student. Artist.

Saturday, 25 September 1999

The Saturday vibe never changes. People come and go, music and fashion will change. For some reason though, the feeling of a Saturday never does. Today was no different. *Sounds of the Sixties* with Brian Matthews on BBC Radio 2 always started the day nicely. The mix of psychedelic, blues and pop from the decade provided a perfect two-hour soundtrack.

The sun was shining, and a denim shirt was a good choice. Fonthill Road was a joy to behold. I looked at the Triumph. Though tempting, I stuck to the plan of taking the train. The rag trade of the seventies and eighties was dissolving, as a fusion of African, Caribbean, Arabic and Turkish beats came from speakers the shopkeepers had meticulously placed above the doors and on the window ledges above. Why go elsewhere? What can be more beautiful than this? *The treasure is certainly here*, I thought.

I hadn't seen Laila for a few days, but it seemed like a lot longer. 'Nice to see you,' I said, as we proceeded to take the overground train to Enfield Lock.

Five minutes from the station was a section of the River Lea. A beautiful row of terraced cottages sat on the other side of the river. Some weeping willows were gently swaying in front of the houses, as if dancing in appreciation of some extra September sun.

The river itself was motionless. Not as much as a ripple could be seen, such was the stillness.

The conversation was similar. Not a lot was said, neither of us wanted to disturb the peace. When we reached the cafe at Stonebridge Lock, we sat down and had a coffee. 'Did some more research on Mei,' she said. 'He was commissioned by Emperor Lao Shi for five paintings about nature. They were completed in a five-year period.'

'Must be these,' I said, as I passed her three of the photocopies I'd done at the office.

'This must be the path of accumulation,' noted Laila, as three men were in the background gathering wood.

'Then this would be the second one, the path of joining,' I said, as it depicted them crossing a river with two other men.

'The path of no-more-learning? That has never been recorded. No one has seen it. This must be the second.'

'Then it must be the fourth, the path of meditation.'

On the third one, the five men had gone, replaced by what looked like a girl standing by a river. Three ducks were in the background.

'Would be interesting to see the fifth.'

'Probably in the hands of a wealthy New Yorker or Japanese.'

'Or even the Chinese themselves.'

'What was one doing in London anyway?' She got up and went to the edge of the lock. Three swans had arrived. As she stood there, I held up the third painting. It looked exactly the same.

We walked back along the path to Tottenham Hale. 'Never been this far,' she said.

'Each part is different. I like the Hackney section, more derelict and industrial. Lesneys matchbox factory is great,' I said.

Nostalgia was kicking in as you could smell the aroma of burning wood from the houseboats. The sight of the grey smoke rising upwards against the amber, orange sky was a sure sign that autumn was well and truly here.

'I enjoyed the walk,' said Laila, as we waited at a bus stop. Her bus came soon after, and after watching it head towards Seven Sisters, I disappeared into the underground.

Chapter Fourteen

Monday, 27 September 1999

'Good morning. The Sloane Club. Martin speaking, how can I help?'

'May I speak to Mr Peter Smith-Cresswell, please. It's regarding a taxi he booked for midday tomorrow.'

'Mr Smith-Cresswell isn't around at the moment, won't be back until later this evening. May I take a message?'

'What time is he returning?'

'He normally returns about ten.'

'I'll call back then. Thank you.'

'Thank you, Sir.'

'Doug. I need a favour, just found out Smith-Cresswell's out until this evening. Need someone to go to the Sloane Club, check him out.'

'Come at four. Call me when you get to the station,' he said.

Aldgate was fresh in my memory. I liked the energy there, I couldn't wait.

'When you leave the station take a left, then the first right. Walk down a little, you'll see me on the left,' were the instructions as I left the station. After walking alongside some rundown warehouses in a side street, I came to a dead end. As I turned around to walk back up, the phone rang. 'You've gone too far, walk back and look up on your right.'

Above what looked like an abandoned clothes shop, I saw him beckoning from a third-floor window. 'Door on the left, third floor,' he shouted, as he opened the window and threw down some keys.

Outside, a faded sign denoting a clothing and sewing business was still visible above. Inside was a different story, though. The interior was in stark contrast. It was spacious and clean, from the fifties I thought, noticing the polished green ceramic tiles that ran all along the lower half of the wall.

Each floor had two doors. They were those safe, solid wooden doors – not too dissimilar to Roberto's Marylebone pad – that made you feel secure. On the third floor, one was slightly ajar. 'Doug?' I said quietly.

'Yes, come in,' came the reply.

It was a large studio space, all one room, except for the bathroom and toilet. Original brickwork was visible. A brown leather sofa – similar to Tom's – was facing a renovated brick wall. On a shelf was an old Panasonic Hi-fi system, that included a built-in cassette player. 'From Drayton Park?'

'Of course. Serves me well,' he replied.

In between the wall and the sofa was a white table with some books on it.

'What you reading?'

'*Junky*, Burroughs.'

'Again?'

'Still a good read, man. The style is so neat and well-written. Though forty years old, still cuts it.'

'Ready?' I asked, looking at the time.

'One minute,' he said, as he disappeared into the bathroom. Douglas was a long-time heroin addict, must be over thirty years now. He was still in the game, though. Others came and went, but he somehow survived. You wouldn't think he was in his late forties.

I looked around. The days of listening to new music and being introduced to weed were still very vivid in my memory. It was fun then, but he progressed to harder drugs. Speed, LSD was temporary, until finally arriving onto the infamous Junk. He accepts his situation, an addict, no partners, just the brown. That's just the way it is.

'People have been doing this for hundreds of years,' he used to say, quoting various ancient tribes and cultures from around the world that used opiates. 'Keeps you looking young,' was the mantra. His life was a montage of jails and rundown areas of London.

As I waited by the door, I saw a neat array of colognes, aftershaves and eaux de toilette displayed on a shelf. I took a burst of the Davidoff cologne. The memories continued when I saw a black and white poster from the seventies nicely framed on the other wall. It was a classic image depicting a Rastafarian smoking weed. The smoke was thick and bellowing, I could taste it. I was fascinated with this poster in Drayton Park, staring for hours. 'Drayton Park?' I asked, when he returned.

'Of course. Fancy some snooker later?'

'Why not.'

He took a shot of the Penhaligons. '*Andiamo!*'

'The flat has a nice vibe,' I said, as we walked towards the station.

'Rich feng-shui'ed it for me.'

'It's amazing what we are capable of,' I said, as we entered Aldgate underground en route to Sloane Square.

'Did you applied for that course you were interested in?'

'Should hear from them soon,' I said.

'I'll wait on the square,' I said, as we came out of Sloane Square station. I went and sat down, having to put my collar up to combat the wind that was whipping up. The remaining leaves fell from the branches to the ground under the sudden gusts. Some were swept into the water under the fountains, others just plummeted straight onto the concrete. Similar to the rain on the window at Gaby's. I wondered which were the more fortunate.

Doug returned twenty-five or so minutes later. 'Wasn't a lot there,' he said, as he came and sat beside me. 'A small attaché case was on the bed, but was locked.'

'Probably here a day or two for a court case, travelling light,' I said, as we crossed the square to the station.

He showed me a flyer. 'These were on the table.'

It was an invite. '*RSVP. You are cordially invited to a preview opening of The Victoria and Albert Museum's Chinese porcelain and artefacts event on Wednesday, 6 October. Venue: The London Guildhall, EC1.*'

'What's today?' I asked.

'The fifth.'

'Tomorrow, so that's why he's here.'

'The Guildhall, nice place for it.'

'Yeah, saw a nice Chinese artefact at Roberto's. I'll go and check it out tomorrow. What about the snooker you mentioned.'

'Too early, the boys will be there about eleven.'

There was a couple of hours to spare, so it was agreed to go back to his to chill a while, then a tea and bagel, followed by something to eat before moving on to the snooker hall.

It was a joy to browse through some vinyl. I chose *Sticky Fingers* by the Stones. It was like the old days as

142

we spoke about books, art and music. Though the conversation flowed, I sensed some regret, as if being chained to the shackles of addiction was becoming too much. Before leaving I changed the mood, playing some classic jazz funk cassettes on the hi-fi. It was fun and carefree, all shared against a backdrop of Patrice Rushen, The SOS Band and the Brothers Johnson.

The touts acknowledged Doug as we walked to the top end of Brick Lane for a bagel. The energy for hustling was reserved for others, a nod of the head sufficed. He pointed to a pastel green restaurant. 'I know the owner, Zahir, he owns a few around here, we'll eat there later.'

Sitting outside the bagel shop, I noticed the young crowd moving in. These were the cool, artistic crew though, not the Camden Britpop lot. These were different, more cultured, edgy, and less materialistic. They were prepared to take risks, and bringing a vibe that only art could provide.

'Good that James got his sentence reduced, though,' I said.

'Let's hope he can now build a good life.'

'You mean a new life?'

There was a few seconds' silence. 'Let's go,' he said, as if I'd touched on something.

Zahir was pleased to see Doug, and the sentiment was reciprocated. The potato and spinach curry hit the spot. After we all shook hands, we headed in the Whitechapel Road direction. 'Love it here,' he said, as we ambled towards the snooker hall. On the way, I thought of the boy in *The Alchemist* and his quest for the treasure.

'Have you read *The Alchemist*, Doug?'

'Never,' he replied.

Maybe he doesn't need to, I thought.

The snooker club was some rundown building on the Whitechapel Road. 'Going to bulldoze it soon. Can you imagine?' lamented Doug, as we approached the entrance.

To be truthful, it had seen better days. The moss outlining the once grand – still intact – sash windows paid testament to this. The sign above the frontage was broken, and barely working. '*Snooker. Pool. Billiards played here,*' it stated, in flickering, fragmented red neon.

Similar to his abode, the facade deceived the interior. Inside was resplendent. Deep red and heavily hung crushed velvet drapes created a warm, secure space. The main hall still had the original fixtures and fittings, untouched by greed. Hopefully the exterior would keep the 'Cool Britannia' crowd away for a while.

'Steve, this is Mo, Shah, Ali and T.'

'Nice to meet you,' I said, as I shook five warm and engaging hands in the above order.

'Nice one mate,' was the unanimous reply, as more attention was paid to the action on the table, rather than a visiting outsider. It felt better and more comfortable that way.

It wasn't long before a thick layer of smoke was wavering across the green baize. The aroma of damp, heavy skunk followed. 'Don't worry, the police never enter,' assured Doug.

Nice little setup, I thought. I could see the appeal. Safe and secure from any interruptions. *That's why Doug likes it, he's at home here. Always was with other cultures. From the Rastafarians of the seventies to the Bengalis of the nineties, he digs it.*

Gucci scarves purchased on a day trip to the Bicester designer warehouse in Oxfordshire became the topic of the day, before they decided to go up west. Sadly, I declined the invitation.

Ali insisted on giving me a lift, so after a few goodbyes, I was safely dispatched in a shiny blue-grey, metallic BMW. The cream leather seats were comfortable. Doug joined us for the ride, sitting next to me in the back. Doug said he needed to collect something from his home, so we stopped there first, before Ali took the longer – and more interesting – route through the Bank, and Aldgate, to Liverpool Street. The ride was like a sci-fi movie. I was lost in a fantasy, where the world was all chrome and concrete, offset by the neons and traffic lights the city provided. Very quickly, it all became desolate and lonely.

How it must be growing up here, I thought. *The shadow of the City – and its corporate culture – always looming overhead. It must be beneficial in some ways though, some of the money must – like a well-kept secret – somehow trickle through.* The irony was that there seemed to be a freedom here like no other. Everything was so transitory that nothing really existed, and what did exist was left alone. Ali stopped outside Liverpool Street station. We shook hands again. 'Nice to meet you guys,' I said, before closing the door.

As I walked towards the station, Doug called me back. 'For you,' he said, handing me a box.

The wind was really beginning to take hold. I put my collar back up, braced against the cold air, said thank you, and ran into the station, hoping that I didn't miss the last train.

Tuesday, 28 September 1999

'Drinks reception at six. Starters at seven. Main course seven-thirty. Desserts, coffee, and a small dance after,' I said, reading from the back of the flyer.

'No problem. Where shall we meet?' asked Rich.

'Stamford Hill train station. Five-thirty?'

'Cool. See you then.'

I sat back and looked at the camera Doug had given me last night. It was a Nikon DF DSLR, and it made a nice, concise clicking sound as I zoomed in on a few things on the table.

Outside Steve's newsagents on Stroud Green Road was a billboard. The poster was for the *Islington Gazette*: '*Islington smash and grab scooter gang jailed*,' ran the headline. I parked up, and bought a copy for twenty pence. There were five facial shots on the cover. Teddy was in the middle, the focal point, the ringleader. He got seven years, the others five. On the back page was a review of Arsenal's upcoming Champions League game at Wembley against Italian side Fiorentina.

'Tom's and Doug's flats have a nice ambience,' I said to Rich, driving through Stamford Hill.

'It's about the five elements being linked to the five senses,' Rich replied, when I asked about the feng-shui. 'At the moment, don't block the north-east corner with any furniture. This is where the money flow is at the moment.'

'And the happiness?'

'You have to meet Master Qianyao. Been studying the Tao for three years now. The knowledge is awesome, there's some amazing stuff. You know, insights into why things happen, and for what reason.' He looked at me. 'Don't worry about anything Steve, it's all happened before, everything will be okay.'

'The Victoria and Albert Museum presents The Secret Treasures of Ancient China.' Chinese characters were in gold against the large red banner hanging across the magnificent Guildhall. We parked opposite. *A Kind of Blue* by Miles Davis was the cassette I'd brought along, as we sat back and waited.

'What does Smith-Cresswell look like?'

'That's him,' I said, turning the music down. He was walking with a Chinese lady. Near the entrance they linked arms, before showing their invites and entering. I took a series of shots with the camera Doug had lent me.

'Can you take one of the Chinese characters?' Rich said, pointing up to the banner.

'Job done,' I announced, as I put the cap on the lens. 'Let me drop you home.'

'Southgate station is fine. Stop by tomorrow, we can take a look at the photos.'

'Sounds good,' I said, playing the Miles Davis tape again, as we drove through the Barbican. And as with all masterpieces, it sounded a little different than before.

Wednesday, 29 September 1999

The tree in front of the flat was now almost bereft of its foliage. Yesterday's wind and the gusts throughout the night had seen to that. Autumn was coming to an end, I thought.

Rich's place was a small apartment block just off the main road, less than a ten-minute walk from Southgate station. 'Mac?' I asked, noticing the now familiar piece of technology in front of a window. Tom's was white, Doug's was silver, Rich's was apple green.

Except for the Mac, a table, desk, table lamp and sofa, furnishings were kept to a minimum. Like Tom, there was no television, and everything was white. On the table was a book, *The Twelve Buddha Concepts*. A Chinese map was positioned in the centre of a wall. 'The *bagua*, used for feng-shui,' Rich said.

'Not much space,' I said, noticing most of the squares were filled, bar one.

'The last space, that's the white period, then it's full up, won't be another one for thousands of years. The Maitreya Buddha is our saviour.'

'The one from the painting?'

'You need to come to the temple, Steve.'

It was beginning to sound tempting. 'I promise I'll come,' I said, continuing to look at the *bagua*.

'It's used for chess and Chinese astrology as well.'

I showed him the photo I took at Roberto's after the chess game with Li.

'Can I keep this?'

'Of course,' I said. 'What do you do for entertainment, Rich?'

'Listen to ambient music online and read.' He went to the Mac. 'I downloaded this.'

'SHOUTcast,' I said, reading the name of the website.

'You can listen to stations from everywhere. The US, Germany, Sweden, you name it. Listen.' After a couple of clicks some cool music came from the white speakers placed each side of the Mac.

'Can't listen to words or lyrics anymore,' he said.

There was a balcony overlooking a shady wooded area, a white mansion was visible in the distance.

'That's the Priory, once a golf course, now a rehab clinic. Tom went there,' said Rich as he joined me.

The soft breeze felt good after the harsh wind of yesterday. We stayed for a while, before going back inside to eat.

Rich was now vegan. 'Eat five colours every day,' he said, as he placed some salad on a table. 'Green, red, yellow, orange and white, very important.'

Veganism is something I aspire to. Though the thought of no cheese and eggs was a little difficult.

We discussed Charlie loaning me a car until the court date. 'Do you know him?'

'Never met him, just heard some stuff.'

'Heard what?' I said aloud.

'You didn't know, him and James?'

'James?'

'Was getting friendly with some lord dude, who was a good friend of Charlie's.'

'And?'

'Well, something happened. James threatened to go to the press, Charlie wasn't too happy.'

'What happened?'

'Now, that I don't know.'

'What was the lord's name?'

'Can't remember, well connected in the political sphere, though.'

'Presumably why he didn't need unwarranted attention,' I added, not giving it much thought.

'Precisely, makes you wonder what happened to keep James quiet.' He changed the station, PSYCHEDELIK.COM was more up-tempo, the trance beats became deeper, and more hypnotic. Nothing more was said about James and this mystery companion.

I opened the camera and handed over the SD card so he could downloaded the images onto the Mac.

'Definitely him,' I said, looking at the piece of paper with his details on.

He printed out a copy of the banner at the Guildhall, and put it with the photo I gave him of the chess game to one side. 'What's the name of the museum in Nice?'

'The Metropolitan Museum of Nice.'

'They'll definitely have a website, I'll go and check it. Charlie's surname. Is it Hackett?'

'How did you know?'

'He's also a patron at the Metropolitan Museum of Nice.'

'You serious?' I asked, as he continued typing.

'Not only that, both are benefactors of the Arts Council as well.'

'So, Charlie must know Smith-Cresswell,' I said, as I went back to the sofa.

Charlie knows Smith-Cresswell, James was mixing with some politician, the bagua *was nearly complete, and this techno is so damn cool, what a night*, I thought, reclining into the sofa

As the evening evolved, I felt a connection with Rich that had been missing before. As we walked to the station we became close, there was a shift.

'Thanks for tonight,' I said.

'No worries man. It's starting to get interesting.'

'Very,' I replied. *Time to return to Marylebone to collect the insurance documents*, I thought, as I entered the station.

As I ascended the escalators to the platform, the art-deco lamps were passing by one by one. This suited the mood, a little sombre, but with a flicker of life. It was then that I drew up a plan of action, as it began to dawn on me that maybe I was about to embark on one hell of a three-week period.

Thursday, 30 September 1999

There was a gentle knock on the door. I got up, and looked instinctively from the side of the curtains. It was Laila. I ran quickly to the bathroom to put on a clean T-shirt, used some body spray, before opening the door.

'Sorry it's early.'

'It's okay,' I smiled. 'Not working?'

'Home today, college tonight, have to revise. One's almond, one's chocolate, the other plain,' she said, handing me a brown paper bag.

'I'll make some coffee.'

She was dressed fine. Black corduroy trousers and white shirt. Being shoeless added to the elegance. As we drank the coffee – and shared the croissants – I explained the Guildhall, and that Charlie and Smith-Cresswell were on the same board at the Metropolitan Museum of Nice.

'He must know Roberto, then.'

'Smith-Cresswell?'

'Yes.'

'I'm seeing Alexios today in Holborn, from there I'll go to the St Martins School of Art, see what he teaches.'

'Be careful what you say to Alexios.'

'True. If I say anything, he'll report me, he has no choice, which means I go back to jail, and he could get his licence revoked. It's in neither's interest.'

'My father was a lawyer. He helped people from his heart, but…'

'But what?'

'Unfortunately there aren't too many practising with the same humanity. It can be lucrative, and this affects morals and judgements, money becomes the be all end all.'

'You mean they make a lot of money whilst not really having people's interests at heart, like politicians?'

'I'm not saying Alexios is like that, but just be careful, it'll be whatever best suits his interests, that's how life is. Remember, if you breach, you won't have the chance to clear your name. The judge gave you a chance, don't ruin it.'

I looked at her. 'You know, I never looked at it like that,' I said. 'I'd forgotten his name, I'll ask Alexios today. Laila?'

'Yes?'

I looked her in the eye. 'Do you think that I'm innocent?'

'I do.'

'How do you know? I mean, what makes you think that?'

'A feeling.'

'Speaking of politicians, James was caught up in something with an MP, or a lord. Both Rich and Doug have alluded to it.'

'Do you know what it was?'

'They won't say, only that it involves a friend of Charlie's. Anyway, enough of that, tell me about your father, he sounds a good man.'

'He believed in justice, in equality, and helping the less fortunate. Because of this he was hounded by the government in Algiers. We had to leave, so with my mother – and older two brothers – we fled to Marseilles.'

'Who did he help, anyone in particular?'

'People persecuted by the government. Intellectuals, writers, journalists, anyone who opposed and questioned the regime.'

'When was this?'

'The war ended in sixty-two. France was still continuing to back the government after that, though. Would have been the late sixties when we left.'

'The media here didn't cover that one,' I said.

'He loved London, called it home. What about your mother and father?' she asked.

'Father lives in America. Mother is sadly no longer with us.'

'I'm sorry.'

'It's okay.' The early morning sunlight was beginning to filter through the windows, as we finished the coffee and ate the remaining croissant.

'Have to go now, revision time,' she said.

As I opened the door, I asked whether she'd been to Nice.

'Several times, why?'

'What's it like?'

'Very nice.'

'I've always wanted to go,' I said, remembering the poster at Victoria coach station.

'Don't you dare,' she said, as she started to walk down the steps.

I looked up. The rising sun was beginning to take refuge behind the clouds. I couldn't stop my thoughts as they turned to Nice.

'No update Stevie, except I can now devote more time to your case, things will start moving now, trust me,' Alexios said.

'I saw in the *Gazette*. Is he pleased with the result?'

'Out of seven, he'll do three, plus he's been on remand for nine months, which gets deducted. All in all, he has just over two to do, so I'd say he is,' he explained, sounding a little relieved.

Ted doesn't have to commit crime. The families have money. The dads robbed the banks, the cash was then invested in pubs, clubs and restaurants. Two decades later, these investments have become assets which in turn have bought profit. But it's the culture, a reputation has to be kept. The banks and building societies are no longer viable, so they now go and hit the designer shops. If apprehended, Alexios will help them out. He has no choice, he wouldn't want to fall foul of the Islington families.

Heeding Laila's words about being careful, and as tempting as it was, I didn't say too much.

'I'm away for a few days, don't do anything stupid. I'll see you when I return,' was the quick conclusion.

'Anywhere nice?'

'Marrakesh.'

He did looked tired. Maybe the pressure of having to get a result for Ted, or the building being sold, was taking its toll. 'Cool. Heard any more about the move?'

'Seems inevitable now,' he sighed.

'Well, enjoy the break, see you next Thursday,' I said, as I closed the door and headed towards Charing Cross Road.

'Foundation, Degree or a Masters?'

'Foundation,' I replied.

'This brochure has all the information regarding courses for the upcoming '99/2000 term. Applications to be submitted before November.'

'Is there a website?'

'It's on the back.'

'And the lecturers?'

'Profiles will be on the website.'

'Thank you for your help,' I said, as I looked about the rabbit warren of a place called the St Martins School of Art. The Pistols played here in seventy-six, probably hadn't changed much since then, but that was the attraction. Helped and aided creativity, I guessed. Alexander McQueen amongst others had graced this illustrious abode.

'Tom, how are you?'

'Not too bad.'

'How do you say that in Italian?'

'Say what?'

'Not too bad?'

'*Non che male.*'

'*Non che male,*' I repeated, before being corrected.

'*Che* is pronounced "chair".'

'Tom, a quick one. Thought I was going to get pulled the other night, Hampstead of all places. It didn't happen, but what happens if they do stop me, I mean regarding insurance? I left the papers at Roberto's, need to go and collect them.'

'I'll call you back,' he said.

As I reached Euston, the phone rang. 'Can you collect Monday?'

'What time?'

'Morning.'

'No problem, you coming?'
'Finishing my book.'
'Which one?'
'*Ultras Torino Granata Orgoglio*,' he said, fluently.
'Any good?'
'Blinding, all about the Torino Ultras. They're just about to play Napoli at home, arranging a meeting just outside Turin.'
'Is Roberto from Turin?'
'Not exactly Turin, from the surrounding district. Is that the time, five-thirty? Have to go, see you later.'
'How do you say that in Italian?'
'What?'
'See you later?'
'I told you the other day.'
'Forgot.'
'*Ci vediamo.*'
'*Ci vediamo.*'
'*Correcto*,' he said.
'Thanks Tom. Have a good one. Catch up soon. '*Ci vediamo.*'
'*Pronto, perfecto. Ciao.*'
'*Ciao.*'

Friday, 1 October 1999

'Roberto Di Giovanna is the senior lecturer's name,' said Laila. 'And guess what else he's involved with?'
'Not on the Metropolitan Museum of Nice board?'
'I looked into the committee, a certain Mr Roberto Di Giovanna is listed as a non-executive director.'

'Busy man,' I said. The thought of going to the South of France to check out this gallery – especially this time of year – suddenly became very appealing.

I needed a walk, needed to clear the head a little. After hearing about Roberto I needed something. The Parkland Walk – an old railway line from Finsbury Park to Highgate, with its green, open space – was appealing. The alternative was to retrace Joe Orton's Islington. I opted for the latter, distraction took precedent.

My trusted Asics trainers were as comfortable as ever as I stepped out into the grey, overcast day. Twenty minutes later I was outside Holloway Road station, about to begin the fabled odyssey mentioned in his diaries.

He used the tube, so he would've come out of the exit. I stood in the entrance, trying to visualise him walking across the road. The public lavatories were opposite, though now concealed, you can still make out the detail of where the entrance was. The diaries mentioned that he went around the corner. I tried to figure out which corner, probably Hornsey Road.

The new London Metropolitan University building looked dull and crude amongst the old railway arches and used car dealer showrooms. There was a rumour that Arsenal were to build a state-of-the-art stadium on the nearby Ashburton Road rubbish dump. Zaha Hadid had also been commissioned for a project here. *It needs them both*, I thought, as I began to walk towards Noel Road.

Islington Town Hall looked stunning in the autumn sun. A wedding was taking place. The bride and groom were on the steps, being showered with multicoloured paper. A bright red Routemaster was waiting to take the happy couple and their family and friends on a jaunt around the capital. As in Regent's Park, I stopped to observe. Everyone was smiling and happy. Doug, Tom, Rich and myself didn't belong in this genre. Marriage? That was an alien concept to us, not part of our tapestry. There weren't that many weddings in our world.

The South Library on Essex Road was where most of the books were taken from. After Joe and Ken altered and rearranged them, they were ingeniously returned to the shelves for their amusement.

The foyer was magnificent, almost baroque in its detail. Inside the main room, I tried to picture where Joe and Ken would have sat as they observed the reactions of the public who had the misfortune to stumble across the books.

The final scenes of *Prick Up Your Ears* – with Gary Oldman playing Joe –-was filmed in St Peters Street. Around the corner was 25 Noel Road. I stood opposite the house, looking up to the third floor. Not a lot had changed, in fact very little. The two windows were still there, as were the wrought-iron railings. Joe liked the railings, they featured in many photoshoots of him. This house was a big part of who Joe Orton and Kenneth Halliwell were. Twenty-two years ago both were never to see it again. 1967 was also the year Spurs beat Chelsea two–one in the all-London FA Cup Final at Wembley.

I took the 43 bus back to Holloway Road. I needed to walk a little more, I was in the zone. I decided to walk home via Hornsey Road. This was Don McCullin territory, the renowned photographer who took many black and white photos around the area in the late fifties. An infamous image was *The Guvnors*. As a Finsbury Park boy, he had access to the local hoodlums, and photographed this local gang in a disused building along Fonthill Road, the seven of them, all posturing in suits. A policeman was murdered nearby by the same gang not long after. I always tried to locate that damned building, never could. Not much in the background to go on. One day, maybe Tom could assist me.

My favourite was a black and white image from sixty-three, of an American car on Fonthill Road that belonged to a local boxer. Again, I was still unable to locate it, as the only clue was two trees. McCullin lived in Somerset now. I guessed that after being in global war zones, he deserved it. Sometimes one had to been thankful for the sanctuary only a home could offer, no matter where it was. This was one of those times, as I crashed on the sofa.

Monday, 4 October 1999

'What happened?' asked Li.

'Maybe from the run this morning, it's okay, I'm fine,' I answered, as I limped along the hallway.

Before she took my bag, she closed the door on the left again. 'This bag is heavy.'

'It's my camera, going to Regent's Park after, take some photos of the refurbed Victorian gardens, especially the roses.'

The board was set up, very neat, concise and inviting. Tea was served, and Mozart – upon request – was playing. I thought of Dimitri as I sat there. Although the circumstances were different, it was the same, in a bizarre way. So, with a sip of the tea, battle commenced, for the third – and hopefully final – time.

I was more experienced this time. I was expecting the questions, and she knew I was expecting them. And so they came, some subtle, some not. She wore a black

Public Image Limited T-shirt. 'John Lydon's from Finsbury Park,' I said, after I made a move.

It didn't really matter that I was playing naive in a smart way, or smart in a naive way. The fact was my Soldiers were making headway across the river, heading towards the General.

Twenty minutes of intensity accompanied the moves. The questions being answered was a skill, a little like seduction, and she was falling for it, or, on the other hand, maybe she wasn't, maybe she was letting me think she was falling for it, to let me assume that I was in control.

'Checkmate,' she announced, soon after.

I took a deep breath, then rolled back on the sofa. There was silence, the questions had ceased, the answers had grinded to a halt, the game was over. No more pretence. No more niceties. We were exhausted.

'Who's John Lydon?' she asked.

'Need to make a phone call,' I said. I searched my pockets. 'Damn, my phone,' I added, checking every pocket. 'Must have left it in the car.' I stood and tried to walk, getting as far as the edge of the sofa. 'Do you have Tom's number?' I asked, rubbing my ankle.

'No, I don't.'

'Need to call him, it's urgent, do you mind going to get it?' I asked, as I walked gingerly to the window. 'It's the green one,' I said, handing her the keys.

I waited at the window until I saw her. I waved, pointing to the car, before quickly running to my bag, taking out the camera, and running to the door in the hallway.

Inside the room were three easels. A large canvas was on one, two smaller ones on the others. Oils, brushes, paints and other materials were scattered around. The two smaller canvases appeared completed, the larger one nearly finished, all three looked spectacular. I ran back to the window. Lei looked up, holding up the phone, and I waved as she disappeared. I went back to the room, taking shots with the SLR. The shutter speed sounded clinical, as I snapped some close-ups and some distant from different angles. I checked the quality of the images, they looked good, not bad at all, I thought, as I closed the door. Before returning the camera to the bag, I went and took a few shots of the chessboard.

'Where was it?'

'Down side seat,' she replied, not too pleased.

'Where's Roberto?'

'He teach today,' she replied.

I asked about her work.

'Nature. Flowers, plants, trees, anything natural.'

'Rivers? Mountains?'

'Where I live in China, many mountains.'

'Thought you were from Shanghai?'

'I studied in Shanghai. I'm from a province called Shanxi.'

'Maybe one day I can see your work,' I said. I called Tom. 'At Roberto's, got the documents.' I turned to Li. 'Have to go, thanks for the tea, we'll arrange another game sometime soon.' As I went to collect my bag, I remembered my disability. 'Feels better now,' I added.

As we walked down the hallway, I noticed I hadn't closed the door properly. She closed it with a concerned look.

As I left the building I was aware of being observed. The reflection in the car window confirmed Li was at the window. I put on a CD Rich had given me. *Moon Safari* was by a new French band called Air. 'La femme d'argent' proceeded to fill the car with electronic ambience. A small adjustment of the rear-view mirror confirmed she was still there. A wave was tempting, but as the intro of 'Sexy Boy' kicked in, it was time to accelerate. The saying 'you may have won the battle, but not the war' struck a tone, as I headed towards King's Cross.

The drive home was clean, fast and precise. I sent a text to Laila: *Been a good, productive day. Call you tomorrow.* The reply was almost instant. *Same. Speak tomorrow.* The rest of the day was spent between the looking at the statements and admiring Li's artwork.

Tuesday, 5 October 1999

I arrived early. There was a little time to spare, so I took advantage of the colourful – but noisy – aviary. The sound of the birds was in contrast to the grey morning. They looked exotic, out of place with the grey London morning. *Clissold Park never fails*, I thought, as I passed a few deer in the next enclosure.

'One chocolate, one almond, one plain, and two medium americanos, one with soya please,' I requested. 'No work again?' I asked, turning to Laila.

'Holiday,' she answered, as we went to sit outside. After sitting down she took out what looked like a small computer from her bag.

'What's that?'

'A laptop. Same as a PC, except portable.' She switched it on, and waited a few seconds. 'This is what I found out yesterday about Roberto. His name is Roberto Di Giovanna, a sixty-five-year-old member of the Savoy family, an Italian aristocratic family who are a notable presence in the Piedmont region of Turin, northern Italy.' She took a sip of her coffee before looking at me.

'Heard of them,' was all I could muster after the initial shock.

'Stephen, these people are massive. They are like royalty. This man is a member of one of the most powerful and influential families in Italy, if not Europe.'

The Roberto who I met the other day now took on a different meaning. The charismatic art lecturer had been replaced with something different. 'This is going to be difficult,' I said.

She searched some more – there were many links to the Savoy family – before clicking a link to a Di Giovanna's family tree. Roberto was the second son of Enrico Di Giovanna. His brother – Gianfranco – had a business producing and exporting fine wines around the world. Gianfranco also had two sons. Roberto had no children. Enrico had detached himself from the Savoy politics early on. 'Smart move, he did himself – and his sons – a favour,' I said.

Other links suggested that Roberto was seen as an outsider, a maverick, someone who, though privileged and well connected, never quite played the game. He had defied his father by not choosing business, and instead opting to pursue his love and passion of art. He gained a first in fine art from the Institute of Turin. A PhD in Menton, France, followed. He stayed in the South of France for a while, earning a living by teaching. 'Took up the post of senior lecturer at the Central School of St Martins College of Art three years ago,' Laila said.

'Sounds legit. Nothing incriminating. Where is Menton?'

'A small town next to Nice.' She then clicked on another link. 'In 1989, Roberto Di Giovanna was sent to prison.'

'What for?'

'Doesn't say. It's a scanned article from the *Journee Di Torino*.'

'Probably has a contact in the paper, that's why they won't say. My guess is tax evasion. Isn't the Internet amazing?' I said, finishing my coffee.

'While we're here.' Laila passed over the laptop, and I typed 'Charles Hackett'. Charlie lived at The Manor farmhouse, Sawbridgeworth, Hertfordshire, and was schooled at Eton, before going to Oxford.

'I feel sorry for some of our aristocrats,' I said. 'I mean, they have property, but no cash. The estates are the only asset, and most of them are falling apart.'

'They'll be fine. People have always been fascinated by royalty and aristocracy.'

I liked Charlie though, a little insecure maybe, but harmless. 'I don't think we should worry about Charlie too much. Roberto Di Giovanna and Peter Smith-Cresswell seem more worthy of our attention,' I said, as I handed back the laptop.

'What about Li?'

'A little temperamental, but pleasant enough,' I said.

After finishing our coffee, we walked up Stoke Newington Church Street together, before parting at the high street.

As I sat on the 106, I thought about Roberto, who had studied and taught art in three different countries, whilst running the wrath of his father. *Interesting*, I thought.

Thursday, 7 October 1999

Alexios had returned from Morocco, and the tan was topped up. A post-summer radiant orange glow greeted me. 'Nice watch,' I said, as I sat down.

'De Tag,' he replied, shaking his wrist in admiration. 'Did you bring the statements?'

I placed them on the desk. 'Dry and highlighted,' I announced, in reference not only to shielding them from the morning rain, but also last night's research.

He opened a drawer, taking out a silver Dictaphone. 'Brilliant invention,' he said. 'One, two, three,' was repeated a few times as he tested it out. 'Received the prosecution papers today, had a quick look. The main case for conviction is the witnesses, that and being convicted of a similar offence, which shouldn't be used against you, but it is. I've been thinking and I believe you didn't do it.'

'I didn't,' I stated.

'The witness accounts are the fly in the ointment. We now have two weeks until the trial. If we could get to the bottom of who these people are – and why they're saying this – the case will be thrown out, that's for sure.' Whether it was Morocco or the fact that Ted's case was done, it didn't matter – he sounded assertive and confident. He looked at me. 'Leave it to me now, please,' he said, as the Dictaphone was switched off, and returned to the drawer.

I knew what he meant, and he knew I knew what he meant. I nodded in agreement. 'I will,' I said.

'Promise?'

'Promise.'

'Then see you next Thursday.'

I stood and went to the door. He stayed seated, continuing to marvel at his watch. I noticed that some photos had been removed and placed into boxes, as I closed the door behind me. I headed towards Embankment to contemplate, with the rain as company.

Friday, 8 October 1999

'Here we go,' I said, as an image appeared on the screen.

Rich zoomed to a small white card placed in front of the canvas. 'Zheng Chunhua.'

'Thought her name was Li Xing?'

He scrolled on her profile. 'Zheng Chunhua, from Shanxi province. Studied at the Traditional School of Chinese Art of the Beijing Education Academy. Now completing a BA at London's St Martins School of Art.'

We looked closely at the paintings. The themes were consistent. Each had birds, flowers and trees against a backdrop of either mountains, waterfalls or fields. The hues of the pastels were telling, but sublime. The subtle shades of greens and greys against the splashes of dark, almost calligraphic brush strokes, seemed almost at odds with Li Xing the person.

I was trying to link the personality of Li Xing with the artwork of Zheng Chunhua. 'Not much competition, insecurity or nervousness shown in the paintings,' I said.

He was paying particular attention to the unfinished one. 'Good composition. The style is elegant, flowing, traditional. Nice brush strokes. Something that's missing from contemporary Chinese culture.'

'Might be making a comeback. Maybe there's a market for it, who knows?'

'You mean a new demand?'

'Who knows who wants what in the art market, it's a very secretive game.'

'Seductive, and can be a buzz,' I added, remembering what DCI Smith had said in the interview.

'She must have an exhibition, or a showcase coming up.'

'Or a graduation show.'

'Doubt it, this is more professional.' Without saying anything, I think that we both knew what could be going on. It was one of those defining moments when the previous confusion is placed into some sort of context. I began to feel a little surge of adrenaline.

We chilled for a while, drinking tea on the balcony and reminiscing about the old days. We spoke about the good times at Benjy's in Hackney, Cork's in Bond Street, and the SW1 Club in Victoria. The music appeared in my head, like a soundtrack. 'Keep Your Body Working', Kleeer, 'Movin', by Brass Construction, it all became very vivid for a while.

Nostalgia is powerful stuff, it's a trigger for emotions. Many feelings come through the associations it brings, more often than not linked to some sort of tragedy. 'We've lost a few,' I sighed.

'We have indeed,' came the reply, as we went into the living room to listen to PSYCHEDELIK.COM.

'Man. Woman. Heaven. Earth. Sun and Moon. Hard. Soft. It's all change, all yin and yang,' Rich said, referring the *bagua* on the wall. He showed me where the yin starts and the yang ends, and vice versa. 'This is life, it's all synchronised, be yourself, make honest decisions and go with the flow,' he added.

After a few more anecdotes, I left feeling good. I made a promise to visit the temple on the Sunday before the court case. Outside, the beech trees had been refreshed by the earlier downpour, you could almost taste the sweet aroma.

Life was about decisions. It didn't really matter if they were right or wrong. No decision, no change. No change, no evolution. No evolution, well, there was… nothing. Everything and everybody is in the process of change. Nothing stops, nothing waits, the yin and the yang, as Rich so eloquently put it.

Change would inevitably happen because someone, somewhere, had made a decision. Another decision would then be made because of that decision, and so on – it was a cycle. Everything was evolving. Fonthill Road was changing. Islington was changing. London was changing. England was changing. The United Kingdom was changing. Europe was changing. Even the world was changing. The clever ones would – and did – accept the concept of evolution, and, more importantly, embrace it.

As I approached home, I noticed how the car was parked under a lamppost. The luminous glare of light from it made the Triumph the star of the show. It seemed to bask under the spotlight. I closed the door, and looked at the picture of the Maitreya Buddha. He was still smiling. 'Turin here we come!' I shouted.

Chapter Fifteen

Saturday, 9 October 1999

'Didn't know you worked on Saturdays.'

'It's half a day, it means I can take a day off during the week. How many copies?'

'Three, one of each. Oh, I've made a decision.'

Laila looked slightly puzzled standing next to the photocopying machine. 'Which is?'

'I'm going to Italy.'

'When did you make it?'

'When I left Alexios on Monday, I went to Embankment to weigh a few things up. After speaking with him I felt helpless, got the feeling he did as well, but won't admit it. I haven't got an alibi, the witness accounts are consistent, and I can't deny a few seconds of opportunist irrationality when I was younger. I need to do some research, check out Roberto and Smith-Cresswell. I need to get to the museum in Nice, see what's happening, then onto Turin.' She handed me the photocopies. 'Would you like to come?'

'When?'

'Thursday. Maybe you can take a few days' holiday, take a break.'

'I'll let you know.'

Not long after, when I was walking past Highbury, I received a text. *'Can meet you in Nice. I'll then travel to visit family in Marseilles while you go to Italy. Looking forward to it.'* Laila.

Now some planning, I thought, as I hurried home. *I'll need some company, and some help.* Rich, Doug and Tom came straight to mind. Tom loved travelling to Italy, and there would be some cool jazz spots as well as new movie locations to explore. Rich could be persuaded – I'd ask him later. Doug, though, was different. He'd never left the UK.

'How long you going for?' asked Rich.

'Leaving Thursday, returning Monday.'

'How we getting there and back?'

'Driving the Triumph. I want you, Doug and Tom to come.'

'Doug? Maybe that's not a good idea, considering his addiction and the problems it could cause.'

'Logistics?'

'Drive to Dover, catch the ferry, drive through France to Marseilles, stay the night, then to Nice. We'll check out the museum Roberto and Smith-Cresswell are involved with there, then drive to Turin, check out Roberto, then drive back. Four, five days max.'

'You make it sound so good Steve, there must be some temples to see.' After a brief pause he made a decision. 'Count me in.'

He could do that, had mastered the art of making his life simple. Create a life without expectation and obligations, then you can plan without worrying. *Amazing*, I thought. 'Sounds a good place to be,' I replied, in acknowledgement. Though I felt far from that level, I could feel what he was saying. I had an inkling that this place did exist, and – when attained – must be awesome.

'Are you still coming to the temple tomorrow?'

'Looking forward to it,' I replied.

I sat back and looked up. Even though it wasn't until next week, and I'd yet to ask Doug and Tom, I was excited. The Maitreya Buddha was still smiling.

Sunday, 10 October 1999

'We'll only be a couple of hours,' Rich said, sensing my nervousness.

There were some CDs in the hallway. I grabbed a few. *Time for some Beatles*, I thought, as we left his flat and continued to the car. *Revolver* was the choice.

The riff of 'Taxman' exploded as we tore down the Grange. 'Eleanor Rigby' become poignant as we crossed the reservoir into Walthamstow; 'All the lonely people, where do they all come from?' sounded about right.

'Remember that?' I said, pointing out the Royal Standard pub as we approached Blackhorse Road station. 'Good for some live Saturday rock, saw The Tygers of Pan Tang there in eighty-nine.'

Rich ignored what I had just said, he had a serious look on his face. 'The *bagua* is full Steve, time is running out. Centuries ago, only disciples who studied under a master received the transmission of the three treasures. Some had to cultivate for forty years or more, can you believe that? Now it's available to us all. We are very fortunate.'

'Doesn't that mean it's been a little demeaned?'

'Not everyone will have the privilege of being introduced, you have to be the right person at the right time. It has to be auspicious, which is a shame because what we do here, and how we behave, will determine where we go after, and unfortunately not everyone will understand that.'

I like it here, I thought, *I don't want to die, or go anywhere else after. I love life, I love living.* The thought of not going home, or to the park, or to the shops on

Stroud Green Road, not being able to catch a bus, the underground, or listen to The Beatles was unthinkable, as well as unimaginable.

'Got to Get You into My Life' became more amplified as he continued. 'There are three periods. Green, red and white. We have lived through two. The first was green, when the planet was destroyed by floods. The second was red, when fire wiped us out. Now it's the white period, this is the final one. Then the cycle will be completed. The *bagun* is now full. There won't be any more blessings for 129,000 years.'

'What will destroy us now?'

'The white period will not be tangible. It will have no substance. It will come as the wind. The wind will blow around viruses. Also, it will manifest itself in the form of the Internet.'

I was intrigued. The past week had so far been positive on the Internet. Downloading photos, researching Mei, Smith-Cresswell, sending emails to Laila. 'How?' I asked.

'Social groups will be created. Harmless at first, but – like everything – they will be abused. Big corporations will move in, they will start to feed us opinions. The next level will be to create images that will pollute the mind, becoming more and more graphic. It'll be a slow process. Our minds and beings will quickly become obsessed with politics, creating identities that divide humankind, then creating war, all while selling us advertising.'

The Beatles slowly wound down with 'Tomorrow Never Knows' as we got caught up in traffic.

The I-Kuan Tao Temple was located at The Old Town Hall, Walthamstow, a magnificent building at the top of

Orford Road. After parking at nearby St Mary's Church, we took the short five-minute walk to the temple.

After being greeted at the door, I followed the example of Rich, who – after taking a respectful bow – wiped his hands on a cloth provided by the cadres.

'Have to say hello to Buddha first,' he said, as I followed him up the stairs. A beautiful wrought-iron handrail was aligned on each side. It was nice to know the original features were respected and intact.

We reached a double door at the top. 'This is the prayer room,' he said, after we entered.

I felt as though I was in the company of something magical. The sun was filtering through the large bay windows, giving the room an added golden hue. The strong sandalwood incense added to the sensation. The small Buddha statues surrounding the room were aglow. 'Three hundred and sixty altogether,' Rich informed me.

'Incredible,' was the only word I could muster.

Again, Rich led the way as I followed him to the middle of the room, where he stood behind a row of beige cushions. I awkwardly bowed and knelt, as he uttered some words.

We were facing the most magnificent statue, cut from probably the finest marble going. I had to look closely. As well as amazing, it looked familiar. After a few seconds, I smiled. The Maitreya Buddha – as always – smiled back.

We bowed, left the room, and headed back down the stairs. 'Let me introduce you to Master,' he said, as he knocked on a door.

'Stephen, this is Master Qianyao. Master, my good friend, Stephen.'

The room had a cool feeling. It was airy and smelt of crafted, polished wood. There were cabinets that had various items inside. On the tables and shelves were marble carvings of ancient Chinese warriors, some on horses, some not.

I held out my hand. 'Pleased to meet you,' I said.

He put a manuscript he was reading to one side. 'Pleased to meet you. Please, sit. English, no good.'

'Your English is fine,' I replied. I couldn't help but notice the warm handshake and the radiant smile that accompanied it.

We sat down on a sofa that faced another sofa. There was a table in the middle, a chess set was arranged and ready to go. Before I could say anything, Rich said we had to go to the office.

'Thank you, Master,' I said as we left the room.

'Thank you,' he replied, as he continued to read a manuscript.

'Master plays chess?' I asked.

'That's for the feng-shui,' Rich said as we came to another room.

There were two others waiting to be blessed, Ash and Maddie. After completing the necessary paperwork, Rich took the three of us up to the prayer room. The sun was continuing to hold up, filtering through the windows, keeping the Buddha statues bathed in the golden glow. The aroma of the freshly imported Malaysian sandalwood incense was uplifting, complementing the visual aesthetics of the fresh flowers that were placed neatly around the Maitreya Buddha. Maddie stood on the other side of the room with the other women, a sign of discipline and respect.

'Yin and yang,' Rich quietly uttered to me.

He left the room, and returned – accompanied by four others – dressed in white robes about fifteen minutes later. I observed the offerings as they systematically placed fruit and chocolates on the altar.

Master Qianyao then entered. He had three rolled manuscripts in his hand. Made from rice paper, they had been written in classic Chinese calligraphy, and individually tied with a red ribbon. A cadre lit a large bunch of sandalwood incense, which he placed in a bowl in front of the Buddha.

Master Qianyao untied one of the manuscripts. 'Stephen Vincent?' he asked

A cadre looked at me. 'Are you Stephen Vincent?'

'Yes,' I confirmed.

I was then blessed, and transmitted the three treasures. A short lecture followed. As Rich promised, I wouldn't face any disasters or calamities. All there was to do was come back to the temple regularly to learn and cultivate. The history – albeit brief – was awesome. The golden lineage of the Buddhas, saints and sages sounded cool. It was emphasised a few times not disclose this information to anyone. Bring them to the temple to be blessed instead, was the message. The right person at the right time was the ethos.

'This food is amazing,' said Ash, as we sat together in the dining room after the lecture. It was vegetarian: rice, vegetables, noodles and fruit.

After the meal we relaxed and drank tea. 'What's in the bag?' I asked, as we were getting ready to leave.

'Some paperwork. I'll be a few minutes,' Rich said, as I waited by the door. He then went into the master's room before they both emerged a few minutes later.

Master was smiling. 'This man, good man,' he said, with his thumb in the air. 'When he come here to temple, sunshine. Yesterday rain, today sun.' He was right, the sun was noticeable by its rare appearance. 'Keep coming back to the temple, we'll go deeper into the explanation of the Tao.' He made a circle with his forefinger, as circular – and concise – as when he drew the Ying Yang circle earlier in the lecture.

'I will,' I promised, and after a thumbs up – and a smile – we left.

The sun was still present as we stepped out onto Orford Road, and I felt as good as gold.

I'd never really liked the Walthamstow, Blackhorse Road, or the Tottenham Hale areas. No particular reason, just didn't. All warehouses, empty, sparse and derelict. Walthamstow village, though, was special. It had a Hampstead feel to it. You could see the potential. Rows of old shops faced each other, these – with the period houses that were neatly placed in between – were crying out for gentrification.

'Do you think this area will ever become trendy, Rich? I mean like Fulham, or some parts of Islington?'

'It's inevitable,' he replied, as we walked back to the car. 'The middle classes are growing. They're finishing university, and now want to move to London for a career. They need places to live, eat and shop, and the local authorities – with the planners – are providing.'

This was a bleak outlook. London only used to appeal to the creative or the single people from the north, the ones who needed a challenge. It was a big thing to uproot and move, you had to be dedicated. It wasn't pretty in the sixties or seventies. It really was a 'dirty old town'.

I felt safe and secure in the knowledge that Finsbury Park – so far – was exempt. I mean, who would want to live – let alone invest – in a rundown inner city district riddled with criminals, drug addicts and drunks?

As we sat in the car, Rich opened his bag. 'Here.' He passed me *The Magical Mystery Tour*. 'Can't wait for France,' he added.

'Me too,' I said, as I reversed, then pressed on the accelerator. As I turned right from Orford Road into Hoe Street, the tune of 'The Magical Mystery Tour' sounded poignant.

'Came out in sixty-seven,' Rich said.

'Same year as Orton died.'

'And Tommy Simpson.'

'Who was he?'

'A cyclist. A working-class boy from Nottingham. Went to France to race. Was on the Tour de France when he died. Twenty-nine years old.' We swept over the reservoir on Forest Road. 'Fool on the Hill' sounded eerie. 'Drop me at Turnpike Lane. I'll walk up to Wood Green, maybe take the tube from there.'

It was a pleasant evening. A stroll up Green Lanes would be a fine tonic, especially with the shops all lit up. A good walk after any meaningful occasion was always clever. Time to reflect. After Forest Road, it was up to Seven Sisters, across West Green Road, then Turnpike Lane. I pointed out the Body Music record shop. 'Think it'll ever close down?'

'Body Music? No way, inconceivable,' he said, as he got out.

'Don't forget this,' I said, noticing the bag with the paperwork on the seat.

'Thanks dude. Would be nice if Tom and Doug could come to France.'

'I'll ask when I get home,' I said.

I also need a breather, I thought, as I continued to Alexandra Palace. After parking the car I walked to the blue railings that looked over the metropolis. Staring into the illuminated city I felt emotional, a mixture of sadness and regret came over me. I pondered. We were ageing, our icons were ageing, life was passing us by. I was hoping Doug and Tom could make it, but we were growing apart, taking different directions. It wasn't the same anymore. I got back in the car, and played 'Magical Mystery Tour' again.

'*A pretty nurse is selling poppies from a tray.*
And though she feels as though she's in a play.
She is anyway.'

As I drove home it started to rain.

Monday, 11 October 1999

'Just back from the therapist, man.'

'Good session?'

'Always a good session. You come out feeling great or not so great. But it doesn't matter,' answered Tom. 'Which,' he paused, 'happens a lot. It's a good sign, you know, means you're getting in touch with some deep feelings. You only make progress by getting in touch with your feelings and exploring them.'

'Sounds like therapy ain't for the faint-hearted,' I said.

'That's for sure,' he added, as he put some coffee on.

Tom had been in therapy since he left rehab and continued with the process. I went to the kitchen. 'Wow, never seen these before,' I said, commenting on three black and white framed prints on the wall.

'Good, eh?'

'I looked closely. The first was taken outside a Victorian house. 'Where's that?'

'Marc Bolan's house. Newington Green. Where he was born, amazing eh?'

'And this one?'

'Bob Marley lived there. Russell Square.'

I recognised the third one. 'The Pegasus, Green Lanes, where the Pistols played?'

'Yeah man, just down the road.'

'Good composition, who took them?'

'Some photographer I know. Interested in British fashion, music, film, etc. You know the sort.'

'I do. So, you coming?' I asked, after disclosing plans for the jaunt.

He gave me a hug. 'You bet, man.' Seems the buzz of travelling – grabbing the Head bag from the carousel, throwing it over your shoulder, then jumping on a train heading for whatever La Citta –was a powerful lure. Seemed a little healthier than sitting and waiting for replies from dating sites, that was for sure.

For some reason he loved Turin and Milan, especially the San Siro, preferring Inter to AC.

'It's not quite what you'd expect, and definitely not glamorous,' he said of the latter. 'Very industrial,' he added. He then briefly mentioned a friend from Turin.

'Coffee?'

'Please.'

As he went to the kitchen, I noticed *The Torino Ultras* on the shelf. The author was Gianni Agnelli. I sat down to have a look.

'I'm reading that,' he said. 'Up to the bit where they're planning a meetup just outside Turin with Roma.'

'What are the firms like?'

'Different. They look up to us, but different.'

Tom should know. He's made a successful business from organising packages to European football matches, mainly Italy.

I walked towards the door. 'Looking forward to it?'

'Can't wait, man.'

'How do you say "another day" in Italian?'

'*Un altro giorno.*'

'Tom, *che vediamo un altro giorno.*'

'Bravo. Not bad, more accent on the *giorno* though.'

'Have to polish up my French as well,' I joked. I made my way down the red-brick stairwell, holding on to the cold iron railing. 'Tom?' I shouted, as I walked to the car.

'Yes?'

'*Che vediamo un altro giorno.*'

'*Giovedi,*' came the reply.

I inserted an old cassette. *Jam On It* by Nucleus, which, when driving down Kingsland Road, sounded scary. I headed towards Aldgate. For some reason I was on a roll.

'Do you have a passport?'

'Of course, why?'

'Thursday, you're coming to Italy.'

'Italy, Thursday?'

'Italy, Thursday,' I repeated. 'Rich and Tom are coming.'

There was a delay in the reply. I knew it depended on whether he could get the gear through customs, which wasn't a certainty. There was a choice: buy it here and take with you, with a risk of getting busted, or try your luck over there. The dilemma was a tough one. 'Let's speak tomorrow,' I said. 'Oh, was James in Ford a couple of years ago?'

'Think he was. Why?'

'Did you hear anything about a friendship with another prisoner there?' I worded the question very carefully.

'Not as far as I know.'

'Heard he had a little disagreement with someone there.'

'Who said that?'

'No one, just heard. How's Mo and the boys?' The change in the subject was a little crass, but it worked.

'Seeing them tonight. Coming? Shoot some pool?'

For a brief second I smelt the vibe, the subtle red lighting, accompanied by the smell of fresh weed. 'Tempting,' I sighed, 'but I have to plan the trip.' I got up to leave. 'Let me know by tomorrow.'

'Steve?'

'Yes?'

'Count me in, man.' We hugged. I felt that there was something more than his first trip abroad.

'We're gonna enjoy it,' I said, as the idea of myself and my three best friends hitting the Continent suddenly became a reality.

Tuesday, 12 October 1999

'Need a few days off anyway, been studying hard. Will also be a good time to go and visit my relatives,' said Laila. We were sitting in a cafe at Manor House, drinking mint tea. She said that talking about her father a few days previous made her think of her family in Marseilles and

Paris. 'Don't really see them much, which is sad. There's something about family,' she said.

'On your mother's or father's side?'

'Father's. Where are your family? Do you have any brothers or sisters?'

'Two brothers,' I replied. 'How was work today?'

'Same as usual. Look,' she turned on her laptop. 'Did some research, checked out Charlie, this came up.' She turned it around. There was a piece from the *Hertfordshire Gazette*. It was an article about his trial. Similar to Roberto's, it was small.

'Three years for fraud,' I said. 'Go on *Who's Who*, see what clubs he's a member of.'

'The Wellington Club, Knightsbridge.'

'Anything else?' I said, hoping to hear the Sloane Club.

'A country retreat in Buckinghamshire.'

'Buckinghamshire?'

'The Cliveden.'

I sat back. 'That's where Christine Keeler was.'

'Who?'

'I'll tell you later. It's a stately home. The Astors lived there. They were the epitome of the English aristocracy,' I said.

I thought about Christine Keeler. I visualised the pool where she met Lord Astor. She went from Maidenhead to London's West End. From Murray's nightclub to mixing with the elite at Cliveden.

It was a similar story to Orton's. I made another decision. A visit to Cliveden would follow France and Italy.

'Says it's exclusive. These people move in high circles,' Laila said. She switched off the laptop and looked at me. 'Be careful,' she added.

'I will,' I replied.

'So, when are you taking me to my first football match? You promised me, remember?'

'Soon,' I said. We walked to the bus stop. As she boarded the 253 I asked if we could met in Paris on the way back.

'I have an uncle and aunt there – from my mother's side. I'll show you around.' She waved as the bus departed. It was dusk, and the sky was a blend of grey and orange. Nice, Turin, and now Paris. *How cool is that?* I thought, as I walked home through the park.

So, there you have it. The personnel for the excursion to find any evidence against Roberto and Smith-Cresswell included four childhood friends. One was a quintessential Englishman in his late forties, who, having travelled all over the country to various jails – and a few day-trips to Margate – had never left the Smoke. The other two were in their mid-thirties. One now meditated every day, soon to become a master of feng-shui. The other, a chronic obsessive compulsive disorder, now enjoying the trappings of success by indulging in designer clothing – Lacoste, Stone Island, Gucci – and dating sites, as well as speaking Italian. We were honoured to be joined by a stunning, intelligent French-Algerian librarian who studied philosophy and fluently spoke French, Spanish, Italian and Arabic. Then – of course – there was myself. The journey would be courtesy of a Triumph TR6.

Wednesday, 13 October 1999

The only break from planning the logistics and browsing the statements was a trip to the new Costa opposite the station. Once the preserve of central London, they were slowly branching outwards. Some were better than others. This was one of the better ones, a good mixture of Ethiopians, Somalis and Algerians were catered for. I ordered the obligatory americano. A little milk, one sugar, in a takeaway cup.

There was a table near the window looking onto the Seven Sisters Road, which I was grateful for.

'What's the book?' I asked.

The man at the next table showed me the cover. *The Prophet* by Kahlil Gibran.

'What's it about?'

'It is about everything.' He smiled.

'Everything?'

'Everything,' he repeated. 'You should read it.' I asked him to spell it as I quickly wrote it down.

He had a suitcase next to him. On top was a bag. It looked like as instrument.

'It's a Qanun,' he answered when I asked. He'd come to play some concerts and was going home. He had a nice face. Approachable, and friendly features, warm, blue-green eyes with light brown tousled hair.

'Where do you come from?'

'Damascus. I am Syrian.'

'How did you find London?'

'Different. Busy. Anyway, have to go. Nice to meet you,' he said, before politely placing his cup in the refuse. 'Always rain in London,' he added, as he opened the door.

I watched as he quickly crossed the road to the station. He had the suitcase in one hand, the Qanun was over his shoulder. I wanted to run out, ask him to stay a little longer, to prolong our conversation, talk about literature, music, art, Syria, anything, but he had gone, vanished into the underground. I could still catch him, he'd be walking down the steps to the train, now he'd be on the southbound Piccadilly line platform waiting for the Heathrow train. *I'll still be able to catch him if I run*, I thought, as an all too familiar feeling began to overwhelmed me. Like the coach driver, the salesgirl, the vendor, and particularly David, I'd never see this person again.

You meet some good people on the journey of life; the problem is, they always leave. I also felt the bombing of neighbouring Iraq last year. Our current prime minister – and his entourage – cooperated in the criminal act called Operation Desert Storm. I finished my coffee, and as I walked home Rich called, saying he wanted to see me.

There was a frown. 'What's wrong?' I asked.

The look of confusion was still there. 'Nothing.'

'C'mon man. You thinking what I'm thinking?'

Rich was looking studious in gold-rimmed tortoiseshell glasses. 'Well, it does look a little familiar, I must admit.'

'A little like Zhang's artwork?'

'Same style of brush stroke, that's for sure.'

We both sat down looking in more detail at a copy of the painting I was supposed to have stolen and one of Zhang's pieces.

'Alexios says it's worth a few million,' I said.

'Must be big business, especially in China. The new money there seems to be buying them back.'

'A little ironic, don't you think? Buying back your own history and culture.'

'Probably as an asset. The content doesn't really mean anything. It could be anything. Wine, books, property, it's all the same, just an asset, a commodity.'

'And status, means you have the wealth to invest.'

'Look at punk. The whole genre has become lucrative. The Jamie Reid posters. The Vivienne Westwood clothing. The vinyl, all collectable.'

This was true. The second-hand record shops had been scoured and pillaged, now finding a new home in Japan.

'She's from a city called Jinan in Shandong province.'

'Rich, you said that you're studying the *Twelve Analects* by Confucius.'

'Also known as Lao Shi. Lao Shi means teacher.'

'Which province was Lao Shi from?' I asked.

'One second. Man, I love the web,' Rich said, as he was typing. 'Right, here we go. Confucius was from Qufu, which is in—'

'Shandong? Who were the rulers?'

'When Confucius was around, it was the—'

'Zhou dynasty?'

'Clever boy, Steve. Impressed. How did you know?'

'There's a connection, Rich. They're up to something. If we can find something in Nice or Turin, something tangible that can outweigh the witness statements, I have a chance.'

'I'd say Zhang is painting copies for Roberto, so he can place them on the black market.'

'And Smith-Cresswell?'

'He's a director and patron of the museums, probably adds some credibility to push them through. Who's going to Italy?'

'You, Tom, Doug and myself. Laila will meet me in Nice for a few hours. She will then go to Marseilles to visit family. Then we'll meet in Paris on the way back.'

'Where we gonna stay?'

'Pensions. There are lots around the station areas. It's only for four, five days max.'

'We'll be okay in Turin. Tom knows people there, he's linked-up with a firm, the Torino Ultras. Knows the leader. Heard him mention the name Gianni a few times when he's on the phone. Stays with him when he works out there.'

'I'm excited, Rich. I gave him a hug. Can't wait. See you Friday,' I said, as I made my way to the door.

'Steve?'

I turned around. 'Yes?'

'It does not matter how slowly you go so long as you don't stop.'

'Lao Shi?'

'Clever boy, Steve.'

In the car, I realised how fortunate I was to reconnect with Rich. We'd grown apart in the last few years. I was closer with Tom. We all go our own ways, but we need people. Apart from looking after your health, life is about relationships, about connecting with people. The choices we make about who we connect with determines our happiness and wellbeing. I put on 'Magical Mystery Tour'. 'Roll up for the mystery tour,' sounded touching. I felt better.

Thursday, 14 October 1999

'Tower Hill.'

'It's nice around there,' I said, in response to Alexios's office relocation.

'Heard it's coming up,' he replied, as he walked to the window.

'Tower of London, Trinity College, Fenchurch Street. Nice area. Anyway, time for a change. New start, new chapter. Embrace.'

He returned to the desk and sat down. 'You're right, London's changing. We have to change and adapt with it.'

'Not only London,' I said. 'Everywhere.'

'It's brand new, open-plan. Main feature is a glass spiral staircase in the middle.'

'Sounds exciting.' I looked around the office. The interiors were a rich, dark, polished mahogany. Old-school. One wall was like a gallery, photographs of Alexios with various ageing London gangsters and sporting celebrities – footballers, snooker stars, boxers – all signed with '*Best wishes*'. If only walls could talk. There were also photographs of clients. These were the money launderers, property tycoons and business associates, all smiling, grateful for their liberty.

'When you moving?'

'Waiting for the date. It'll be soon.'

'Any update on the case?'

'Still sifting through. Don't worry, it will be prepared before the court date.'

'I'll be away for a few days, from tomorrow,' I said.

'Anywhere nice?'

'Just up the road for a few days. Oxford. Going to chill, clear the head. Might see David. Oh, before you go, the painting. It's now worth five million sterling.'

'Serious?'

'That's about seven million dollars, 148.57642 Japanese yen, and 8.6977 Chinese yuan.'

'Since it went missing the value has gone up.'

'What am I looking at if convicted?'

He suddenly came alive, as if relishing these types of conversations. 'As it stands, seven minimum, ten max.'

'That's more than Ted's gang.' As he got up to go to the window, something fell from his pocket. It was a card from the Wellington Club. 'Here, you dropped this. Have you been there?'

'Went last night.'

'Any good?'

'Just opened up. One of these new superclubs. Trying to the attract celebs and footballers. You know the sort.'

'Politicians?'

'Probably. Listen, enjoy the break. If anything comes up, I'll be in touch.' He continued to look out, as if to savour the view of Lincoln's Inn fields for the short time he had left there.

I left feeling a little liberated. France was tomorrow. It was up to me now. The great Alexios, mastermind of the criminal elite, was – it seemed – failing. He couldn't get out of this one, and he knew that I knew it. He couldn't break the statements. They were watertight. There was no way for him to question them. He knew Smith-Cresswell had the upper hand. He was going to lose, and his pride couldn't handle it.

Later, I threw the statements down. If I could produce any evidence to show that Peter Smith-Cresswell,

Roberto Di Giovanna or Charles Hackett were part of a global fraud scam, my chances of liberty were plentiful. I took a relaxing bath, listened to 'Walking Wounded' by Everything but the Girl, and began to pack.

> 'Live travel, adventure, bless, and don't be sorry.'
> – Jack Kerouac

Friday, 15 October 1999

We assembled in Aldgate. It was six in the morning and the air had a bite to it. Tom and myself were both wearing tracksuits, and – dare I say it – looking similar. Tom's was a burgundy Burberry, mine a navy blue Puma. Rich looked relaxed in loose cotton trousers and shirt. Doug – as ever – looked the part. Corduroys, merino sweater, complete with a cravat. This was the style. Space was limited, it was one bag per person, dispatched neatly into the small boot.

'How do you say "Torino here we come" in Italian, Tom?'

He was beside me at the front. '*Italia, siamo, andare*. Remember Turin is at the bottom of the Alps. It's going to be damn freezing,' he said.

I placed the key in the ignition and turned it. The engine sounded good. Before changing into first gear, I took a quick glance at Doug through the rear-view mirror. He looked okay at the moment. The journey was about six hours, hopefully the junk would hold him. '*Italia, siamo, andare*,' I shouted, as we headed towards the Dover Road, which meant passing over nearby Tower Bridge. Tom pointed towards Tower Hill just before the bridge. 'That's where the opening scenes to *Alfie* were shot,' he exclaimed, as I thought of where Alexios's new office would be. 'Can we take a picture where Alfie and Nat were hustling?' he asked, Polaroid in hand.

'On the way back,' Doug said, bearing more than a striking resemblance to the actor Murray Melvin.

Just before ascending the bridge I lowered the roof, and placed a cassette in the player. It was early morning, and not many cars were on the road. A mid-October sun was in place, as *Messages* by Orchestral Manoeuvres in the Dark set the tone. The Thames continued to ebb and flow – as it always has, and always will – below us. 'Incredible,' Rich said, as we passed over the bridge.

Tommy noticed a sign by the Old Kent Road that gave directions to Millwall's new ground. It was called the New Den. 'Remember Highbury in the Cup, 1987? Over five thousand,' he informed us.

'And the rest,' I added.

'North v. South.'

I remembered going to Millwall v. Leeds at the Old Den, Cold Blow Lane. Eighty-six. 'Never forget that one,' I said. All the pubs, bars and cafes along the Old Kent Road were lined with Millwall's finest. The northern visitors were given the honour of a police escort, waiting to be unleashed to the baying Lions. Hardly a local derby, but a massive game.

'Eighty-six. The Blow Monkeys, "Digging your Scene",' said Tom.

'Swing Out Sister, "Breakout",' Rich added.

'Erasure, "Sometimes",' was Doug's choice.

'David Bowie, "Absolute Beginners",' I concluded.

We entered the Garden of England, quickly settling into the surroundings. The sun continued to cast a golden hue over the surrounding fields. 'Soon be in Marseilles,' I said.

'Is it true what they say about Marseilles?' Doug asked.

Tom looked over his shoulder. 'About what?'

'That it's dangerous? A hotbed of crime.'

'It has problems like anywhere else. Don't believe the media.'

'Were you at the World Cup last year, Tom?' I asked.

'Missed it.'

'He was living in Italy then, weren't you Tom?' said Doug.

I was surprised. 'You've lived in Italy? I didn't know.'

'Only for the football, weekends and stuff,' he answered, a little sheepishly, as he was looking through some CDs I'd brought along. 'Any good?'

'Good choice. There're a new French band called Air. *Moon Safari* provided a cool ambience until we were within reach of Dover.

So far so good, I thought. Rich had his head tilted back, enjoying the breeze, and Doug was still present. Tom seemed a little nervous, always looking at his phone. He was probably missing the dating sites on the PC. I was sure that one day they would find a way to apply such technology to the phone.

'You okay, Tom?' I asked.

'Trying to remember if I switched off the…' He couldn't finish, unable to convey and express his obsessive fears.

Turning off the gas and the taps was a constant worry for him. Rich stepped in. 'Water and fire are basic human fears. It's a subconscious fear, quite common. Fire and water are fundamental needs. We need them both to live.

Phobias about property catching fire or flooding is irrational, and not true.' Cool personified, I thought. He added that fire and water were two of the five elements. 'Something I'm studying,' he added.

It was Friday, so there were the expected delays to the ferry to Calais. We had two hours to spare. Rich suggested a walk on the white cliffs of Dover, to which we all agreed. There were some wooden steps remarkably close to the port which led to the cliffs. At the top were ruins of an old castle that had once served as a prison. Tom and Rich were in Dover Borstal together. 'There it is,' said Tom, pointing down below. There was silence, as if in mourning. I understood the feeling. Douglas was in Rochester.

We didn't venture too far. There was a National Trust cafe conveniently placed for a coffee before heading back. The skies were beginning to clear, and the sun was evident every now and then. The view was awesome. 'England can be so beautiful,' said Rich. A falcon soared above, and looked like it was following us as we made our way back to the car.

'The National Trust do a good job,' I said.

'Nice to see decent, honourable people not only interested in the money,' said Doug.

'They have morals,' added Tom.

'Who?'

'The upper classes.'

'So do the working class,' Doug said. 'It's the middle classes who are the problem. They have no culture, no history, no set of values. No consideration for others, just care about themselves,' he added.

'Remember the board of visitors in borstal? They used to come and see we were treated in a humane way?'

'I do.'

'Upper class.'

The middle-class Britpop culture only had consumerism. All they wanted was convenience and careers.

Rich was leading the way as we headed back. 'Rich?' I yelled, as I paced to catch up with him. Tom and Doug continued the conversation about the class system.

'How do you know this place?'

'Been here a few times for coastal walks. I go all around.' He divulged his itinerary. Leaving London early in the morning. Catching the train. Arrive at ten. Have a nice walk, something to eat. Take a coffee, then catch the train back at around six. 'Just a day return. The next day you wake up refreshed, as if you've been on a holiday.'

How cool, I thought. 'Favourite place?'

'To visit? Eastbourne. To walk? Dorset.'

Doug and Tom caught up as we approached the top of the steps.

'Favourite station you leave from?'

'Fenchurch Street.'

'Liverpool Street,' interrupted Doug.

'Definitely Waterloo,' said Tom.

'Marylebone or Paddington,' I concluded.

Halfway down, Rich pointed out an old sixteenth-century church. 'Shame we don't have the time to visit,' he said.

'Another time,' I said.

It wasn't long before we proceeded to drive onto the ferry.

I walked to the rear. The white cliffs of Dover were becoming distant, dissolving, fading into the background.

Calais, on the other hand, was looking clearer, focused, and sharper.

After showing our passports, we were soon driving on French soil. Rich was in charge of the logistics. With an atlas on his lap he directed us to Marseilles. I put a cassette of Malcolm Mclaren on. The Stoke Newington boy sounded good. This time singing about the bohemian Parisian nightlife. I thought of Laila, then of Nice. Couldn't believe that I was going there. I remembered asking the coach driver where it was, I didn't know. Now I did, and I'd see for myself tomorrow.

'Where are we?' Doug asked.

'This is the Roman Theatre of Orange,' I replied.

'Where The Cure played in eighty-six?' Tom said, jumping out of the car. We all quickly followed, eagerly anticipating.

It didn't disappoint. Though small, I could feel 'Shake Dog Shake' being played. On the way out we climbed onto the walls, and mimicked the band. On the video 'Sweet Talking Guy' played over the credits as they played around after the gig. I thought of James, that was his favourite song. *What he's missing*, I thought, as we got back into the car laughing, before heading south.

As we approached Marseilles, my heart started beating. The feeling of hitting a new town – or city – was engulfing me. What a feeling, to be entering the unknown. Checking in at the accommodation, having the key, looking for the room, switching the TV on, putting on the kettle. Checking out the bathroom, having a shower. Selecting the clothes from the case, then hitting the local nightspot. There are some habits you just cannot shake, no matter what.

We headed to the Gare de Marseilles train station area to check for a cheap pension. Doug was looking a little agitated, as well as excited, as we moved further into the urban environs.

'Not enough rooms,' I said, as I got back into the car.

'Looks like a dive anyway,' said Doug.

'There'll be somewhere. What's the time?'

'Eight.'

'It's still early. There's loads around here,' I said.

We eventually found somewhere. Two rooms, each with two single beds. I shared with Rich. After a shower I made my way to the floor below, where Doug and Tom were.

'Where's Doug?'

'Where do you think?'

'Probably thinks he's on a *French Connection* film set,' I said, visualising him looking to score in the back streets around the station.

'Was it filmed here?' asked Tom excitedly,

'No idea,' I replied. I didn't want to lose another one on the first day.

Tom decided to stay as Rich and myself went for a walk. When we returned, he'd gone. Seemed the obsession with movies, photographs and publicity photos had gone European.

As we settled into our basic – but comfortable – room I asked if he had found out the name of the politician.

'I'll tell you later. Chill dude,' came the response.

I understood. Travelling can drain you. I sat on the bed. I heard the sound of a clock. There was a cheap plastic one above the door. 'You'll meet Laila tomorrow.'

'Does she have family in Marseilles?'

'They moved here from Algiers. Had to flee civil unrest there. Stayed here awhile, then Paris and London. Her aunt and uncle are here.'

'She's showing an interest.'

'From what I can make out, she doesn't like inequality. Her father was the same. He was a human rights lawyer. Championed people's causes, much to the dislike of the government. This is why they fled.'

'Persecuted.'

'Exactly, and given Smith-Cresswell's and Di Giovanna's somewhat privileged background, she may feel they think they're above the law.'

'She has a point. Must really believe in you.'

'It's amazing who you meet,' I said.

He took out the copy of the second painting and placed it on a shelf next to a window. Like the first, the Buddha was the focal point, but the scenery behind was different. A man and a woman were rubbing two sticks together. They were surrounded by healthy trees and flowers were underneath. There was a bird that looked like a falcon flying, similar to the one on the cliffs at Dover.

He then placed one of Zhang's next to it. 'Uncanny,' I remarked. 'Speaking of which, what exhibitions are on at the museum?'

After finding the Continental plug, he plugged the laptop in. 'Currently there is an exhibition about the Italian Renaissance in the main room, and – in the smaller room – an exhibition by… His voice trailed off. 'You're not going to believe this. Chinese art in the twenty-first century, by guess who?'

'Zhang?'

'She must have finished the third painting. And in Turin?'

'It moves to Turin next week, then London. Christie's. There's also ceramics in Turin and London.'

'The Italian Renaissance is what Roberto specialises in.'

'There's just been a spate of thefts in Italy, especially around the Turin area,' he said, reading the news from the Internet.

I sat up. 'Recently?'

'Last one was a few days ago. Press are calling them "The School of Turin". Been at it a while now.'

'What are they targeting?'

'Art, diamonds and ceramics.'

'And ceramics are being exhibited at auction houses in Turin and London?' We looked at each other across the room. 'This is crazy,' I said.

'That's some cool name, man,' Rich laughed. 'And they haven't been caught.'

'Brilliant name,' I agreed.

I looked at the clock. It was ten, still no sign of Doug and Tom.

Chapter Sixteen

Saturday, 16 October 1999
Marseilles, South of France

It was eight when we headed towards the sea. We agreed that breakfast down in the port would be a befitting send-off. The sun was beginning to take its place in true Mediterranean fashion, as we sat down at a cafe.

Already the tension was fading, and though it had only been a few hours it felt as though a holiday mode was kicking in. 'Look at that sea,' I said, as we ordered breakfast.

'Yesterday Hackney, today the Med,' said Tom, as he tilted his face towards the sun.

Doug was more relaxed. The edginess of last night had gone, replaced with a calmness. 'Went for a coffee by the station. Man, have you been there? Amazing. Those steps, hundreds of them. Railings on each side.' He was animated. Hands and arms – driven by the dope – making reference to the layout of the station. 'Some cool bars and cafes here,' he said, spoken with a eloquence that was – as we all knew – temporary.

I looked at him. This beautiful man was numb, not feeling anything, not present in reality. Feelings and emotions were void. Only a physical shell was present. Somewhere inside was a lovely warm spirit, a buried soul, that would shine if given a chance. The process of scoring, finding a dealer – as any addict will tell you – is the fun part. Then the transaction, then the hit. The latter was totally omitted in Doug's glamorous account of the previous evening.

I'm free, I thought. *So is Rich, and Tom. Free from the shackles of the hell that is heroin addiction. How lucky am I.* The croissants – followed by coffee – went down a treat. 'Let's go,' I said.

On the way back to the pension, Tom explained how some of *The French Connection* was filmed here. 'Was told by someone last night that it was shot in Marseilles.'

'Did you find out where exactly?' Doug asked.

'Nope. I'll watch it again to see where, and come back.'

For some unknown reason, Doug and Tom then began conversing about tower blocks in Hackney.

'The Trowbridge Estate in Hackney Wick. The one Hackney Council tried to demolish, but only half came down.'

'Didn't Sid Vicious live there?'

'He lived in a block in Queensbridge Road. Graham Norton lived in the same block.'

'When was the Trowbridge demolition?'

'Eighty-six,' replied Tom.

'One of my favourite years. Pet Shop Boys, "West End Girls",' I said.

'The Blow Monkeys, "Digging your Scene",' Tom replied.

'Swing Out Sister, "Breakout",' said Rich.

'David Bowie , "Absolute Beginners",' Doug concluded.

'"West end girls" was filmed in Aldgate.'

'Wentworth Street, Petticoat Lane market,' added Doug.

This was news to Tom, who – as expected – became excited.

At the pension we collected our bags and passports. 'Damn,' exclaimed Tom, as we settled into the car.

'What's wrong?' I asked, as I looked over my shoulder and reversed.

'Nice are away tomorrow evening. Never been to the Stade du Ray,' he said.

'Monaco are at home, though,' added Rich.

'That's where Arsene Wenger came from.'

'Was that really three years ago?' I asked, as I stopped the car to ponder.

'Time flies, man,' Doug said.

'Who's that player he brought with him?'

'Thierry Henry.'

'That's him.'

'And Emmanuel Petit.'

'Won the double last year,' Tom added, with a look of satisfaction.

'Are we riding inland or along the sea?' Doug asked.

Rich had prepared the route the previous evening, and briefly explained the journey.

'Both,' I answered.

'Next stop, St Tropez,' announced Rich.

'After we visit the Stade Velodrome,' Tom stated.

We parked outside the home of Olympique de Marseille football club. 'Doesn't feel the same when there's no match,' said Tom.

'Chris Waddle used to play here,' added Rich.

It did look nice, though, after the development for France's ninety-eight World Cup tournament.

After a few minutes I started the engine, and as the roof lowered, Doug looked behind. '*Au revoir*,' he said, as he waved goodbye to the centre of Marseilles.

We weaved our way towards the outskirts of Marseilles, getting admiring glances from the locals. Before taking the D559 we stopped at a Casino, where we loaded up with some bread, fresh tomatoes, cheese and water.

The main road felt liberating. I inserted a tape, *Selim* by Johnny Lytle. The joy of the music turned to utopia as I dared to take a few hairpin bends. We soon caught a glimpse of the dazzling azure-emerald sea. Though in the distance, its aesthetic seemed closer. I mixed up the sights, sometimes turning inland, sometimes aligning with the sea. Driving became a pleasure. Roaring through the lemon and lime groves, the vineyards and the lavender fields was a joy to the senses. The wooded areas were more than welcome as the sun filtered through the trees, creating a kaleidoscope of colours and sensations.

Doug had taken the occupancy beside me. The sunglasses camouflaged his eyes. Tommy and Rich were in the back. Both somehow mirroring each other with one arm hanging over the door.

'Anyone fancy Toulon?' I asked.

'It's a rugby town,' Rich informed us.

'Hate rugby,' said Doug.

'Me too,' added Tom. So, with such enthusiasm, I drove past.

'St Tropez!' Tom shouted.

I looked up. It was true. A sign had those magical words. 'Need some sun badly,' I said.

The feeling was mutual. I pressed on the accelerator so we had some time to enjoy the bronzed, Bardot-inspired mecca.

Tom took out a pile of papers. 'Need to find the spot where Bridget Bardot and Roger Vadim filmed *And God*

Created Woman,' he said, as we were closing in on the resort.

The port was surprisingly small. We parked in front of some grotesque looking yachts. 'I'll stay and look after the car,' Doug said, still oblivious to the world.

Tom quickly headed to the beach to find the exact spot where Vadim and Bardot were filmed. Rich and myself went and sat on a small wall under a tree facing the sea. 'You can see this was someplace back in the day,' he said.

'Indeed,' I replied. I closed my eyes for a few minutes. I used the three treasures that had been transmitted on Sunday. Immediately, I felt a certain peace and calmness. With this, we both went and sat on another wall to catch some rays.

'Can't seem to find it,' yelled Tom, on his return. Using his hand to shield the sun from his face, he continued in vain to pan the small beach.

After ten minutes he came and joined us. 'Any luck?' I asked.

He sat down and looked towards the sea. The silence said it all.

Though the sun felt pleasing against the skin, it soon approached midday. 'Let's go,' I said.

So it wasn't a complete failure, we walked to where Vadim and Bardot were photographed in the harbour.

'Interesting,' said Tom, holding up a photograph. 'Vadim's car was white, when he had black hair, and Bardot's car was black, and she had blond hair.' A frown confirmed his perplexity.

I looked at the photograph. 'Shame you can't really see much of the background.'

Rich took a closer look. 'Stylish though. What year?'

'Fifty-six.'

'French movies are very stylish, always have been,' quipped Rich.

'Especially the new wave period, well chic,' I said, remembering the posters outside the Rio.

Tom took another photo from his book. 'This one is better, more background. Look, you can see where it is. The cafe is still there.' He took a deep breath. 'Taken the year Vadim cast Bardot in *And God Created Woman*, 1956. Amazing.'

I looked around as we walked to the car. 'What do you think it was like here then?'

'Brilliant. Can you imagine? The cars, the cafes, the music?'

'And a lot cheaper. It's expensive here,' I said, comparing the food prices to Marseilles.

'Marseilles isn't exactly a tourist spot, so it's bound to be cheaper,' Tom said, as we got in the car.

Doug was in the same position as we left him. 'I prefer Marseilles,' he said, joining in the conversation. 'This place is sterile, it has no character. Marseilles has culture, meaning, life.'

'And a football team,' added Tom.

I agreed. With Doug, though, it was worth noting that he would probably find it a little more difficult to score smack here, which came into the equation.

Crowds were assembling in front of us to marvel at – and take photographs of – the obscene, monolithic seafarers facing us. 'Horrible place,' Doug uttered, as we ate the food we'd bought in Marseilles.

After eating I reversed, making a sharp U-turn. As the dust that shrouded us began to settle, I put my foot down. Off we went, oblivious to the rubberneckers, and drawing subtle looks from the local folk, who continued playing boules.

To say St Tropez disappointed was an understatement. Doug summed it up: 'Probably an inspiring place if you want to look at rich folk getting on and off big yachts all day, but that's about as good as it gets.'

Nice: 14 km, said the sign. This was the cue I needed to insert The Stranglers' *Dreamtime*. It was refreshing to get back onto the road, which occasionally ran parallel to the mass of sparkling water. Despite being October, the sea still matched the open blue skies. Equally enjoyable was the weaving in and out of small hamlets and villages to 'Always the Sun'. We began to laugh again. There we were, the four of us. Not one marriage, not one child, or a career between us. But you couldn't buy that feeling of excitement, freedom, liberation and collective bonding that we were feeling at that particular moment.

St Maxine – like Toulon – didn't really appeal. 'David Ginola is from here,' said Tom, referencing the charismatic Tottenham winger, which was about all the enthusiasm we could muster.

'Anyone heard anything from David?' I asked.

'The one who went to Oxford?'

'Doug's friend,' I said.

'Nothing,' came the reply.

It wasn't long before we caught sight of Nice. There was something that stuck with me straight away, and even though it was still way off in the distance – and the fact I'd never been there before – I felt something. It wasn't tangible, and I couldn't explain it, but it was there. The poster in Victoria station, the journey along the promenade at Weymouth to reach Portland, both in seventy-nine, suddenly became reality. *If only I could tell that driver, if only I could see Reg*, I thought, as 'So Nice in Nice' by The Stranglers was playing.

'Been here, Tom?' I asked.

'You know what, no, I haven't. It's a real sore point amongst some Italians.'

'Why?' I asked.

'Nice was once a part of Italy. Was known as Nicca then. Came under the rule of the Savoys.'

'The Savoys of Turin?' I asked.

'Until they signed it over to France under the Treaty of Turin, in 1862.'

'Amazing,' said Rich, looking at me, as if to say, don't say any more.

'The football badge of Nice FC is a clue. An eagle, sign of Napoleonic times.'

'Impressive, Tom. When were they founded?'

'1904.'

'Not as old as Oxford United,' I said, with a wry smile. We were now in the centre. 'Look at that sea,' I said, pointing to the right. 'What's the name of this road, Rich?'

'The Promenade des Anglaises.'

'Means "Walkway of the English",' Tom said.

'The "Promenade of the English"? Brilliant. Looks Victorian, little Weymouth.'

'Only with palm trees,' said Doug, who again became more energised, thanks to the urban environs.

'There are palm trees in Weymouth,' I said.

'Don't remember any when I was in HMP Verne.'

We gravitated towards the station vicinity, and found somewhere not too dissimilar to the previous evening in Marseilles. *One o'clock, not bad*, I thought, as we carried our bags from the car to our rooms.

After unpacking, we slowly walked down to the Promenade des Anglaises.

'Do I need this,' said Rich, walking with his face towards the sun. Tom and I agreed. Doug opted to walk on the other side of the road in the shade.

We sat down for coffee and lunch. Seems we each had a plan of sorts. 'Have to meet Laila at five,' I said.

'Going to Nice FC's stadium. Then hopefully try to locate the police gaol where The Stranglers were taken after being arrested in 1980,' said Tom. He proceeded to show us a photo of the band outside the station. Jet Black was holding his arms aloft.

'Going to Menton. Aubrey Beardsley, artist – and friend – of Oscar Wilde. He's buried there. Came to recover after catching tuberculosis in the UK. Thought some sun would do the trick. Sadly didn't make it.'

'Only a short train ride away,' said Tom, pointing to the east.

'How old was he?'

'Twenty-five.'

'Young.'

'Four years older than Sid Vicious,' Tom remarked.

'What era was he and Wilde around?'

'Victorian.'

That made sense. The Victorians would have needed a debauched playground. A hideaway, away from the prying eyes of London. Somewhere warm, pleasing to the eye. They did like their coastal jaunts.

Rich said that he'd be going back to the hotel after taking in some sun.

We walked together along the promenade, marvelling at the magnificent array of architectural splendour. After a good strong espresso at a Moroccan cafe on a street running parallel behind the promenade, we went our separate ways. I went north, back to the hotel to change. Doug ventured east to Menton. Tom headed west for the Stade du Ray. Rich simply crossed the road to hit the beach.

Laila called from the train a few hours later. 'Have you arrived?'

'We're in a hotel by the station.'

'I'll be arriving at five past five,' she said.

I looked at my watch, it was four-thirty. 'Okay, see you then,' I said. I quickly showered and put on a neat, newly pressed Margaret Howell shirt.

'Looking good,' commented Rich, as he walked through the door.

I remarked on his newly acquired golden glow. 'That, in two hours?'

'Half an hour on the front, half-hour back, half-hour each side, job done.'

'And it's a nice sun, a post-autumn, soft heat.' I glanced at my watch. 'Gotta dash,' I said, quickly running to the bathroom for some cologne. As I was leaving I noticed he'd placed a copy of the third painting next to his bed. 'A little different,' I said. 'Buddha's the same, but the rest is different. That's a new Mandarin character in the middle. What does it mean?' The phone rang. It was Laila. 'On my way,' I said.

Rich was at the table, switching his laptop on. 'We'll speak later. Have a good one.'

'See you later,' I said, as I closed the door and hastened to the station. There's something about meeting someone new. A certain adrenaline. The anticipation, the nervousness, the elixir that filled the air. I didn't really care if it was a distraction. I liked it.

208

The Gare de Ville was something else. Opened in 1867 to much publicity and pomp, the Louis-XIII-style structure was stunning to say the least. The gabled iron roof was intricate. I noticed the clock; it was the focal point, handsome in its being. The interiors were also pleasing. I went to the arrival board, the train from Paris was on time.

After Nice it continued to Genoa, Italy – via Menton – its final destination. I thought of Doug, wondered how he was getting on. He'd be in Menton. Well, I hoped he was, hope he was making a day of it, and hadn't decided to return to frequent the vicinity around the station in Nice.

I had five minutes, so I went outside to look at the clock. It was in a Baroque style, and obviously had an Italian influence. Though different in style, I remembered the clock at the Ashmolean Museum. Two different clocks, two different circumstances, but a similar theme. Art.

The excitement returned as I went to the barrier, though as the train rolled in to the platform, a part of me wanted to run away. I caught sight of Laila, she was one of the last. *Typical*, I thought.

'Hi,' she said, placing her cheek next to mine.
'*Bonjour*,' I replied.
'*Bonjour. Comment allez-vous?*'
'*Bien merci. Et tu?*'
'*Je vais bien merci.* Impressed,' she said.
'Thank you. Are you familiar with Nice?'
'Not really, why?'
'Something to eat.'
'I've heard there's a student quarter nearby. Let's go there.' I took her suitcase as we exited the station.

After passing a flower market, we entered into a labyrinth of sorts. Bars, cafes and various eateries were punctured with graffiti-clad walls and artistic flair, in this warren-like environment.

We settled on a dimly lit bistro bar on a corner. It had faded ageing posters on the windows and walls. It looked comforting.

'Vegetarian?'

'Yes,' I replied.

'Thought so, I've noticed you avoid meat.'

'Want to be vegan, though. I've always aspired to veganism. You?'

'Soon. Can you seriously live without cheese or eggs, though?'

'Difficult. At the moment no, but I'm determined to give it a go.'

'For what reason?'

'To be honest, health. Also seems like a natural evolution from vegetarian.'

We ordered some food, and finished off with a hot chocolate. 'Tommy keeps reminding us that the best hot chocolate is in Turin,' I said, as we went to sit at the bar.

'He's probably right. Have you known him long?'

'Most of my life. He's a good guy, just a bit excessive. Goes from one thing to another. He's in therapy at the moment. He has about fifty pairs of trainers.'

'Wow, that is excessive.'

'All neatly lined up in the hallway. Forty-five of them have never been worn. He's currently looking for a location where a punk band were arrested nineteen years ago.'

'Wasn't he going direct to Turin?'

'Initially, but said he wanted to be with us,' I answered, not giving it a second thought.

'Went through some archives at work, found this.' She handed me a printed page of the West Hertfordshire news from 1996. A local businessman from Hitchin had been found guilty of living off immoral earnings. 'What's new?' I said.

'Read on,' she said. It said that two other people were involved: another local businessman – named as Mr Charles Hackett – and the local MP, who could not be named for legal reasons. There was also a charge of possession and intent to supply at a party, which had been dismissed by the court. 'I found the local MP thing interesting, after what you said about James.'

'You think it's the same person? Can I keep this?'

'Of course, I have another copy.'

I folded it before placing it firmly into the top pocket of my shirt. 'This is a nice song,' I said, referring to a haunting tune playing in the background.

'"Poem de Michelle" by Teri Moise,' she answered. 'Anyway, I have to go, my train's at five past eight.'

The amble through the back streets to the station was better than before, more relaxed. Passing the flower market was different as well. Even though it was closed, the aroma gave a spring to the step.

'Did you know the Savoys were once in charge of this place?'

'Must still have connections and hold influence.'

'You mean Roberto?' I asked, as we entered the station.

'I'll see you Tuesday. Be careful here.'

'Say hello to your family,' I shouted, as she passed through the barrier and walked to the train.

'Will do,' she replied, with a wave. I stayed and watched the train depart for Nice, before beginning the walk back to the hotel. Outside, I paused briefly to acknowledge the clock, as well as the building. *Very similar in design to the train station in Slough*, I thought.

'Where's Doug and Tom?' I asked, as I took off my shoes and sat on the bed.

'No idea,' was the reply, with a shrug.

He passed me the copy of the latest painting. Behind the Buddha were four young men, just sitting there, next to a river. The landscape was bright and colourful, the trees green, the flowers orange and yellow. They had no expression except for one of concentration. The bird had gone.

'The fourth painting was stolen during the Opium Wars. Never to be seen again until Mao came to power in the forties,' Rich said.

'Probably stored away for being too bourgeois, not fitting into the Communist ideals. At least it wasn't destroyed.'

'So there's one more. The fifth one. Wonder where?'

He held his arms aloft. 'No one knows. No record, hasn't been seen for centuries.'

'I know the first one suddenly reappeared in 1970 when it was sold to an anonymous buyer. Then it was resold to another anonymous buyer here in France, twenty-five years later. Maybe the fifth one will suddenly make an appearance.'

'If the price is right.'

'We're talking millions, Steve. Value going up every day.'

'How do you know all this?' I asked.

'Been surfing the Internet, man.'

'I like that term.'

'Which one?'

'Surfing the Internet. Sounds cool.'

The three copies I printed the other day at the office were in my bag. I put my shoes back on and took them out onto the balcony. One by one, I neatly placed all four of them on a ledge in front of the Mediterranean. Dusk was approaching, and the sun was beginning to set. This made them look even more magical. The subject matter behind Buddha varied slightly in each. In the first, mountains were the theme. Second was a waterfall. The third, a forest. In the latter, there looked like a fire in the forest. Two figures – a man and woman – were comforting each other in this turmoil.

In the second, there was what looked like two parallel paths. The figures from the first were walking down one path, three other people on the other. I was beginning to get lost in the themes, trying to connect them, when I was interrupted.

'This is one cool place,' Doug announced, on his return.

'You like it?'

'On a par with Marseilles,' he answered, placing some croissants on the table.

Rich came and joined us. 'How was Menton?' he asked.

'Dude, amazing. Can you imagine riding some old wooden train that ran parallel to the sea, can you imagine?' He took a bite of the croissant. 'Awesome,' he added.

'See what you've been missing,' quipped Tom, who also suddenly appeared. He was making reference to Doug's first jaunt abroad.

'This beautiful lady sat opposite me, had long dark brown hair.'

'I'll put some coffee on,' said Tom.

'We just sat there in silence. I could feel something. When I got to Menton, she stayed on, I said goodbye and…' There was a pause. 'Do you ever wonder about people?'

'In what way?' Rich asked.

'I don't know, that you'll never see them again. I mean this stunning woman – who I shared a journey with on a mid-October afternoon in the South of France, who I connected with spiritually – I'll never see again.'

I knew where he was coming from, knew what he meant. You do connect with some people on a deeper level, even though you've never met them before. They always seem to be the ones who go. 'Life is like that,' I said. 'Enjoy the moment,' I added.

'Sometimes the feelings of a memory are more interesting,' Rich said.

Tom arrived with the freshly brewed coffee. 'So why didn't you get her number then?' he asked.

'It's not about getting numbers. I'd like to think there's more to it than that. Something you can't quite put into words.'

'Don't see the point if you don't get a number at the end of it,' continued Tom.

'What if you ask and don't get it?'

'You have to be able to deal with the rejection, now that's a feeling, I can tell you,' Tom answered, clearly displaying his therapy work.

'Then you move on,' Rich concluded in a diplomatic way.

'Can you imagine what the real ones are like?' I said, as I knelt to marvel at the four images. 'Maitreya Buddha is exactly the same in all four,' I added, as Doug, Rich and Tom came and knelt behind me. We were serious and silent as we contemplated the artwork. Rich plugged his laptop in, and hooked up some speakers. The radio sounded cool, providing a fitting backdrop to the scenario.

'This is an eerie song,' Tom said.

'"Poem De Michelle" by Teri Moise.'

'I'll check the museums out, see the setup,' Rich said, as we sat around the table drinking coffee. A Barnsbury boy, he was always good at logistics. Pulled a few decent jobs in his time, including a string of fine Knightsbridge heists in the eighties. He was a young boy then, but only got caught for one. At the tender age of eighteen, he received a ten year sentence, serving four.

'This is the place,' he said, turning the laptop around so we could all see.

'Cool,' remarked Doug, marvelling at the interactive graphics.

Tom read the description. 'The Modern and Contemporary Art Museum. Located in Nice, a modern, tower-like building, it contains – and exhibits – collections of avant-garde art, particularly from North America and France.'

'Avant-garde art from American and Europe? Guess that's where the money is,' said Tom. 'Oh, by the way, who is the Maitreya Buddha?' He looked at me, but I let Rich answer.

'The Maitreya Buddha is the last Buddha before the calendar is full.'

Doug and Tom looked at each other, their faces puzzled, as well as confused.

'He is the reincarnation of the Shakyamuni Buddha.'

'Where was the Shakyamuni Buddha from?' I asked.

'India.'

'Buddhism came from India?'

'Thought it originated in China.'

'China had Taoism before.'

Doug sighed. 'I'll make more coffee,' he said.

'So today, this is popular?' Tom asked.

'Today the avant-garde is in vogue, but remember, art is an investment. It's an asset, so tomorrow maybe it'll change, then the buyers will invest in something different. The sellers are always one step ahead.'

'So the next investment could be Chinese art?'

'Exactly. They're preparing for something big to happened. Something new to hit the market.'

'Hence Zhang's artwork being prepared.'

'They must be beginning to put the counterfeits on the market,' said Doug.

'The work she's doing isn't the same, is it?'

'Could be doing her own work for a cover to get exhibitions booked. No attention.'

'Then they exhibit the fakes? Do you think they've been doing it a while?'

'I'd say so. The art world is secretive.'

'Maybe the buyers know they're fake, but don't care. I mean, as long as it's shown they've been legally bought at an auction house, who cares?'

'Probably can't tell the difference anyway,' I said, referring to the dexterity of Zhang's work.

Doug returned with some more coffee. 'Well, tomorrow we can have a look.'

'How we gonna play it?' inquired Tom.

'Two go in, you and Rich. Doug and myself will wait in this park opposite,' I said, referring to a green space opposite the museum we could see on the laptop.

'The coffee is good, man,' commented Tom, as he held up the silver moka pot.

'Italian?'

'Common misconception. Contrary to what most people think, Italy does not actually grow coffee. It makes the coffee. Big difference. They've devised the best machines to roast the beans. This gives the flavour, but it doesn't actually grow the beans, they're imported.'

'You know a lot about Italian culture, Tom,' I said.

'He's very fluent with the language. Impresses a lot of people.'

'Time to get ready,' was Tom's response, as he finished his coffee and left the room.

We were leaving for Turin tomorrow evening after checking out the museum in the afternoon, so we agreed to hit the town tonight. Rich found a club. I reminded him that student areas were a little more cutting edge. So, the preparation began against a backdrop of Depeche Mode. All in all, it took an hour and a half.

I dressed head to toe in Alexander McQueen. Tommy was in Armani. Rich was wonderfully attired in a loose black shirt, flared black trousers and brilliant white trainers. All for comfort, of course. Doug wore, well, a juxtaposition of anything dandyish and Piccadilly, really. The navy blue cravat and matching cufflinks did look good. The choice of cologne was Penhaligon's, Trumper, Hugo Boss and Sandalwood. Not much discretion was assured.

The walk to the student quarter was relaxing, not a lot was said. We passed the bar Laila and I were in few hours earlier. The table and chair were still there, except occupied by another couple. Being with her in that moment was enough, though. Life certainly doesn't stand still, not for me, not for you, and not for anyone. As Rich said, it just keeps flowing.

Doug was walking in front. I remembered him taking me several times to the Hare Krishna centre in Soho in the late seventies. In the window was a model called the cycle of life. I used to be fascinated, following the newborn baby from the cot through to the old man on his deathbed. It used to frighten me. *I don't want to die*, I remembered thinking. I didn't then, and I certainly didn't now. I was frightened of death. The notion of not seeing, thinking, doing, reading, listening to music, walking, not watching football, everything really, didn't appeal to me.

'I understood the beginning – and the end – but what is the middle?' I asked.

'This,' replied Rich, looking all around, hands with the palms facing upwards extended.

'And it doesn't last long,' said Doug.

'So make the most of it,' added Tom.

'Two things in life are a given. We're born, and we die. Everything else is, well… this.'

We arrived at the club. Well, more of a bar really. After paying the twenty francs entrance fee, we ventured inside. The main room had no decor and was all black. A DJ was in the corner behind some silver decks. 'The French are so cool,' Doug commented, as we stood at the doorway. 'I mean, only they can take an empty room and fill it with a cool ambience.'

There were other smaller rooms where you could talk and relax. 'Chill out rooms,' Tom informed us. We ordered some soft drinks, and settled on a sofa. The clientele seemed happy, paying no attention to the visitors from another capital. This didn't last long, however. The club was getting lively, and after twenty minutes or so a girl approached our table. '*D'où êtes vous les gars?*'

'*Où pensez-vous?*' I said, with a smile.
'*Tu parles français?*'
'*Oui. Tu parles anglais?*'
'England?'
'Correct,' said Doug, standing up to adjust his cravat in a mirror behind the sofa.
'Nadine.'
'Stephen, nice to meet you Nadine. This is Doug, Rich and Tom,' I said, in consecutive order, after which Nadine beckoned her three friends to join us.
'French girls are beautiful, man,' Tom whispered, as they walked over.
'Better than Italian?'
'Different,' replied Tom.
'Claudette, Maxine and Terri,' said Nadine.
'Thought you English people drink lots of beer,' said Maxine.
'Some do,' replied Tom.
'Some don't,' added Doug.
'So, what brings you to Nice?' asked Terri.
'Holiday, travelling around for a few days,' I answered.
'You like Nice?'
'Love it,' Doug said.

So, we began to engage. Tom with Claudette. Rich with Maxine. Myself with Nadine. Doug wasn't really present, he just sat there, joining in the varied and different conversations. I couldn't understand it, why sedate your emotions? Here we were, in a nice city, good company, cool music, being alive, being free.

'What's wrong?' asked Claudette, suddenly.

'What do you mean?' Doug asked.

'I don't believe you're on holiday.'

'Why not?'

'*Quelque chose douteux à propos de ce lot,*' Terri uttered to Claudette, as they both got up to go to the toilet. Nadine joined them, after which they decided upon three German men who looked a little more fun and entertaining.

After some dancing and laughter, we left the venue in the early hours of the morning. The fresh air felt good as we navigated ourselves back to the hotel. 'Man, Claudette was a stunner,' said Tom, exhibiting her phone number in the streets of Nice like a worthwhile trophy.

'She certainly was,' I agreed.

'When did you get that?' Doug asked.

Tom didn't reply, the smile said it all. We diverted and walked to the sea. As we sat down, I was amazed that I was here. It wasn't filled with bank robbers and cash, far from it, but I liked Nice, felt comfortable here, it had a nice energy. There was a shop selling football and music memorabilia.

'Remember to come here tomorrow,' said Tom. 'Didn't know you could speak French.'

'I'm learning,' I replied.

Sunday, 17 October 1999

After a swift hit of espresso we packed our bags, leaving them at reception after checking out. The Musée des Beaux-Arts de Nice was on Avenue des Baumettes, This handsome ochre orange-coloured mansion was built in 1878, and was barely a ten-minute walk from the hotel. Tom and Rich proceeded to the building as Doug and myself found a bench in the surrounding gardens.

It wasn't long before contemporary politics came into the equation. 'This Blair thing is something else, totally not Labour,' he said.

'I don't remember Wilson, Callaghan, Hattersley or Foot.'

'Blair, Campbell, Mandelson. It's all a setup. A Hackney and Islington firm. Mandelson worked for LWT. Savvy in the media, knows how to influence people, how to work it.'

'Knows how to sell an image, you mean?'

'Exactly. Create a product, market it, add a theme song, job done. The public will fall for it.'

'"Things can only get better." Used to like that song,' I said.

'Seeing Blair's PA team outside Millbank singing along and waving flags was the worst. Some went on to become lobbyists for the multinationals. Not very Labour.'

'What about Noel Gallagher, going to number ten?' I said.

'Another working-class person being used.'

'Helped sell more records, though.'

'Which was the whole point of it. They helped each other. Meanwhile, innocent Iraqis are dying.'

'Music, politics, the media, all complicit.'

'That guy from Blur started it all, saying why support American music like Nirvana, and other early nineties grunge.'

'Another middle-class. What do you expect.'

'Some of that was good stuff. Who is he to tell people what – and what not – to listen to?'

'It was all a setup. He wanted to stop people buying it, so they'd buy his so he could make lots of money. Typical middle-class.'

'Brit this, Brit that, we'll see the consequence in about twenty years, trust me. This movement is killing art. Be it music, film or literature. They're destroying creativity, only interested in themselves. Soon it'll be all manufactured, coming from television shows.'

I brought along the fourth copy of the painting, and began to look in more detail. The colours looked even more vivid. 'Wonder what the fifth one looks like,' I said.

'Here,' he said, handing me a neatly folded piece of paper.

'What's this?'

'The fifth one.'

'What! Where did you get it from?'

'Rich's case.'

'How. When?'

He smiled. 'When I went to make the coffee.'

I unfolded it. The landscape was bright and colourful, the trees green, the flowers orange and yellow. There were clear blue skies again. This time there were six people at the river, four boys and two girls, all smiling and happy 'The five birds have gone,' I said.

'Except that one,' Tom replied. I had to look closer. There was this most amazing looking eagle against the sky, soaring, majestic, magnificent.

'Are you sure this is the fifth one?'

'Positive.'

'How do you know?'

'Here they come,' Tom announced. I quickly folded it and placed it into my top right-hand pocket.

'Anything?' I asked.

'The main Italian Renaissance exhibition was quite good. Zhang's work was in the small room. None of the five paintings were there,' Rich said. He showed me some pictures on his phone.

'Good quality,' I said.

'Nokia 3210e, just came out.'

'There was this.' Doug handed me a flyer. 'Picked it up on the way out.' It was for a Chinese porcelain auction in Turin.

'But this is for tomorrow?'

'And it wasn't advertised on the website,' said Rich.

'And look where else.' He handed me another flyer.

'Christie's?'

'Next Sunday,' said Rich.

'The day before the Old Bailey. Hope it doesn't interfere with my case.'

'It won't,' Rich said.

'How do you know?' asked Doug.

Tom and I looked at each other, waiting for the answer. 'Just won't,' came the measured reply.

We ambled back towards the Promenade des Anglaises. Doug was mesmerised. 'Looks like Brighton as well,' he said.

'Aubrey Beardsley was born in Brighton,' added Tom. 'How was yesterday anyway?'

'Not a lot there really. Menton is small, a few shops, small beach, that's about it.'

'What was Beardsley's grave like?'

'Couldn't find it,' he lamented.

'At least you have memories of the lady on the train,' Rich said.

The streets behind the promenade were a fusion of Regency prime and modern squalor. Doug wanted to stay and mingle in the Algerian cafes. Tom wanted to go back to the Nice FC football shop we saw last night. It was eleven o'clock. 'Remember, we leave at midday,' I announced, as Rich and myself walked back to the hotel. I stopped to buy a pair of titanium black-rimmed orange driving glasses.

'So?' I asked, as we continued with a slow stroll back to the hotel.

'What you expected, really. Grand, baroque and traditional. A collection of statues, and a ceramic collection by Picasso greeted you in the foyer.'

'Must have been a lot of security. I've noticed that the banks here are very security focused.'

'They have a history of high-level crime.'

I felt the same feeling as when I saw the poster in Victoria. I felt alive. Life had meaning.

'The Renaissance wasn't all that, though. Blatant cover for the expensive stuff.. The Chinese art was more interesting. Zhang's work did look good. You couldn't tell it was painted only last week, blended in well to the unsuspecting eye.'

'Did you take some pictures?'

'Of course,' he replied, holding up his phone.

After collecting our bags we sat in the foyer area waiting for Doug and Tom. I watched various people checking in. It was a pleasant hotel, well kept, and within budget. After the pension in Marseilles, we had decided to treat ourselves. 'I'll put the bags in the car,' I said, as he downloaded the pictures onto his laptop.

As I placed them in the boot I put the piece of paper Doug had given me back into Rich's case. I had forgotten what it felt like as I got in the car. The smell reminded me of London, Alexios, Charlie and Li. That seem a long time ago. *It's amazing what you can forget in two days*, I thought, as I played *Dark Side of the Moon*.

I called Laila to see how she was getting on, and to give an update. 'How are your family?'

'Very good, pleased to see me. So glad I came. How are you?'

'I'm good, love Nice by the way. I have some more photos for you. We're leaving for Turin soon, I'll email them when we reach there.'

'Okay. Be careful,' she repeated.

'Will do, say hello to your family,' I said, as Rich came and joined me.

'The School of Turin are at it again,' he said. 'This time last night in Verona.' The Castelvecchio Museum was hit. Three paintings and a ceramic were taken. 'Look.' He showed me what looked like a vase. It had a distinctive blue serpent on the side.

'How are they going to get rid of that, looks too obvious,' I said.

'There's no such thing as bad publicity, Steve. I'm wondering why they're going for this and not the Picassos or Rembrandts anymore? Surely they're worth a lot more.'

'Not as conspicuous, or well documented. Ceramics and porcelain can be very lucrative as well. Especially in the eastern markets such as China, Japan and Malaysia,' I added, as 'Money' played in the background.

'What happened to New York, Paris and London? Surely they'll be in the game?'

He turned down the music. 'Money moves around, Steve. In the 1800s the money – and industry – was in Europe. In the 1900s it was in the United States of America. The next millennium, the one we're about to enter – it'll move to China. The transition is beginning as we speak.'

'You think Roberto knows this?'

'That's why the Renaissance stuff isn't being taken anymore, and why it is cheap compared to what it used to be.'

'It'll pick up again in a hundred years or so, but that's no good to people now, unless you want to invest for the future generation.'

'I get it. Create something that will be in demand in the future. Hold on to it for a couple of years, so the value will rise. And if you get caught stealing, the penalty won't be as severe because the value isn't high at that particular moment.'

'Think about it. If you're a judge and there were two separate incidents. One involved a Rembrandt, the other an ancient Chinese painting. Who would you give a harsher sentence to? Even though the latter is worth more money.'

'The Rembrandt. How does that work?' I said.

'So the ancient Chinese paintings will soon be at an all-time high. Get the word out, tell them demand will be so high that they're already being targeted now.'

'From galleries in London?'

'You got it. They need to make as much money as possible before they devalue.'

Roberto seemed to know the next market and was preparing for it. He'd got Zhang to do the artwork. Smith-Cresswell was a director and patron at some galleries, which meant he could showcase and exhibit the work. As a noted lawyer, he was a good cover. No one would suspect, or ask questions. Roberto was as well, but because of his history he was more liable.

'What happens if two collectors meet, and have the same painting?'

'The Chinese are more discreet. They won't display them. No one will say what they have. Each will think they have an original.'

'So you can sell a lot more,' I sighed, as 'Us and Them' was playing.

'Love this album,' Rich said.

'Me too. Brings back memories from Drayton Park. Speaking of which, here they come.'

'Nice glasses,' commented Tom.

'Thanks. How was the shop?'

'Bought this.' He showed me a pin badge. Whenever he went to a ground or stadium he bought one. 'For the collection,' he added.

Doug looked relaxed again, though his eyes were hidden behind a pair of sunglasses. It was obvious how his jaunt around the station had ended.

'Should be in Turin by four or five, all being well,' I said, as we drove along the Promenade des Anglaises for the final time. As the city faded behind us, Doug turned around. 'Bye Nice,' he said, with a hint of sadness, a sentiment that was shared by us all.

'We have a choice,' Rich announced. 'Either carry on inland, or take the coastal roads towards Genoa then up to Turin.'

'Which is quicker?'

'Inland three hours, coastal just over three,' he replied. I looked to the others. We decided to continue along the coast, even though it was a little longer.

Pink Floyd was done. The time was right for *Milestones* by Miles Davis. The roof was down, the weather cooler, and we caught the breeze. The fading sun was now shaded by large, strong, healthy, Mediterranean foliage as we drove inland. The senses were treated as we passed the lemon and lime groves. 'This is where they make all the top colognes,' I said, as Miles blew the horn. It sounded a treat as we headed up towards Italy.

Rich pointed out Menton. Doug mentioned the lady on the train again, making reference to the long brown hair. The French/ Italian border arrived soon after. One by one we each handed over our passports to the customs officers. We waited as one of them took Tom's to a room for what looked like a more detailed inspection. After deliberation, he came back and asked him to come with them to an office. I parked a bit further on to wait.

'What was that about?' I asked, as he got back in the car a few minutes later.

'Nothing,' he replied, unable to make eye contact. 'You know what they're like, bored. Had to single someone out.'

The road signs changed to Italian. Tommy Boy seemed subdued, not himself. The earlier incident seemed to change him. The SS20 went straight to the north. For the first time, Rich put down the atlas. There was no need for it. The roof went up as the chilled air of northern Italy was beginning to take hold. Doug chose *Tubular Bells* by Mike Oldfield. David entered my thoughts.

'We staying at a pension or a hotel?' asked Doug.

'That's a point,' said Tom. He borrowed Rich's Sony Ericsson Nokia. '*Ciao Gianni. Sono Tom da Londra. Si, si, bene, bene. Gianni, siamo per strada. Si, si, ci vediamo subito. Non lo so, forse im un quarto d'ora. Si, si, ci parliamo quando sono al centro. Ciao, ciao.* Done,' he announced, giving the phone back to Rich.

'Who's that?' I asked.

'A friend from football,' he replied.

Tom went on to explain that Gianni was the head of the Torino Ultras, a notorious firm from Turin. They carried a lot of weight in the wild, murky world that was Italian football. Seemed he was more than delighted to play host for his Arsenal associate and three trusted English colleagues.

'When I travel to Italy for the games we link up. Known him a while.'

We stopped just outside a small town called Cuneo for some fuel. Doug and Rich took the opportunity to stretch their legs. I had to check the oil. Tom stayed in the car. 'Need to tell you something,' he said, as I went to get out.

'One minute, let me get this out of the way,' I replied. 'Oil is fine, what's wrong?' I asked.

'Early last year, I went to Milan for a football match. Inter were playing Torino. Charlie asked me to meet a friend of his, said he had something for him.' He paused before continuing. 'Well, I met him, said he wanted me to bring some antiques to the UK. No problem, Charlie was good to me in Ford, so I was given a package to bring to London. Anyway, I was stopped at customs in Milan. Turns out it was a valuable artefact that under Italian law wasn't supposed to leave the country. I was arrested, charge and convicted. Got six months in jail, served four.'

'Who was this man?'

'Roberto.'

'So that's why they stopped you back there, it's still on record?'

'Always will be.'

'What happened to Roberto?'

'I didn't say where they came from. They knew, though. He was on the same flight, took five plates with him.'

'Expensive?'

'Priceless. Told me they were artefacts from something called the Chinese Zhou dynasty, worth a fortune. He didn't even get stopped, let alone questioned.'

I remembered what Laila had said about him and Smith-Cresswell being above the law.

'So basically, he set you up, used you, so he could go through.'

He looked at me. 'That's one of the reasons I'm here Steve, I want revenge. That's the truth, man.'

'And Charlie? Do you think he may have set you up?'

'You know what, even though he put me on to Roberto, I don't think he did.'

'They probably have something on him as well.'

'That's why Charlie was so keen to lend me a car, feels guilty, as if he owes me.'

'Why are you telling me this, Tom?'

'You'd have found out sooner or later, and because of Gianni.'

'Gianni? Your friend in Turin? What about him?'

230

'He knows Roberto. Gianni's from the Agnelli family.'

'The Fiat guys?'

'Yes.'

'Who own Juventus?'

'Yes.'

'Why did you ask for a car?'

'Look where we are. Look at what we're doing. We're on the road to bringing them down.'

'So you knew I'd be arranging this trip?' I could see Doug and Rich slowly walking back. 'Thanks for telling me, Tom. Tell me, did you know I was being set up?'

'They're using you to hide the original.'

'So the one returned to the Arts and Antiques squad wasn't the original?'

'Of course not. Even they were fooled. Look, if it's recorded as missing or stolen the value goes up, gives it more credibility. There's probably a lot that's been ordered since it went missing. These people have no morals, Steve. I spent three months in jail for them.' He sounded angry. 'Greed and excitement has consumed them,' he added.

'Does Doug or Rich know?'

'Not as far as I know. They think I stayed on here in Italy for business.'

'Wondered why I hadn't seen you. Can I tell them?'

'It might be better,' he said.

After some more of the now obligatory cheese, bread and water, it was a good time to relay the story Tom had told me. The drive to Turin then took on a new meaning. There was now an ambience of seriousness. The bond was stronger, I could feel it. A 'them against us' mentality prevailed. 'Rich, how far is Turin?' I said. He pointed to a sign above. *Torino: 55 km.* I hit the gas as *Violator* by Depeche Mode was inserted.

Doug was impressed with Tom's spell in an Italian jail. 'What's it like?' he asked.

'More freedom, not much hassle. But, you know, jail is jail. I was in the same one as Valerio Viccei.'

'The Knightsbridge robber? Wasn't he shot by the Italian police?'

'Ambushed whilst on leave. The powers that be obviously wanted him out.'

'Didn't you know him, Doug?' I asked.

'Met him in the Scrubs. Bit flash, but a good guy.' He quoted from a book Viccei had penned from his cell. 'I was as addicted to robbery as I was to cocaine. The rush from pulling off a job was better than anything in the world, including sex,' he said.

'Sounds heavy,' Tom remarked.

'Got an estimated sixty million from the Knightsbridge Security Deposit robbery in eighty-eight. Man, was that really eleven years ago?' he said, with a slight frown. '"A Little Respect", Erasure, was the tune for me.'

'"Shattered Dreams", Johnny Hates Jazz,' said Rich.

'"Tell it To My Heart", Taylor Dayne,' was for Tom.

'"Every Day is Like Sunday", Morrissey,' I added.

There was a text from Laila. '*Good news, call me.*'

'*Arriving soon. Can you research Zhou's ceramic plates please?*' I replied.

I looked up again, Torino was now fifty kilometres. The bleak Italian landscape was now set against a cloudy grey day. Tom handed me a CD. 'A new band,' he said. I pressed play. A few seconds later, the haunting intro of 'Wide Open Space' by Mansun filled the car. The melancholic guitar riff suited the drizzle as we began to catch sight of the snow-peaked Alps. They looked fresh and inviting in the distance.

The mood was changed as Vivaldi's *Four Seasons* took hold. A conversation based on anecdotes of prisons and their inhabitants followed. Doug and Tom were in charge. They had a competition to see how many jails and football grounds each had been to. Tom won, he'd attended 101 football grounds in England, Scotland and Wales. This was excluding the numerous grounds on the Continent. Doug had done time in over thirty prisons. He was still impressed with Tom's incarceration here. To enhance the theme, he recited some poetry by Jean Genet called 'Our Lady of the Flowers'.

'My good, my gentle friend, my cell.'
'My sweet retreat, mine alone, I love you so!'
'If I had to live in all freedom in another city, I would first go to prison, and acknowledge my own, these of my race.'

With these word echoing, we zoomed into Turin's city centre ahead of time. Finding another suitable hotel within budget was easy. *Finally on Italian soil*, I thought, as I unpacked. After showering we rested for a while. We were on a roll.

'Tomorrow's our day, so Rich and myself will go to the auction house tonight, see what needs to be done,' I said, a little later in the lounge area. It had begun to take on a different meaning, started to feel a little like a military operation, and, in a way, it was.

Tom made another call to Gianni. He spoke for a few minutes before making an announcement. 'Gentleman,' he said. 'This evening, we have a dinner date with the Torino Ultras.'

'What time?' Tom asked.

'Seven.'

'What's the time now?'

Rich pointed to a corner behind me. A gorgeous Italian Baroque cherub grandfather clock was standing there. It was four o'clock.

'How do you say "let's go", Tom?'

'*Andiamo.*'

I wanted to check out the Mole, Turin's iconic landmark. '*Andiamo,*' I said, as Rich and myself got ready to leave.

'Be careful of the trams,' shouted Tom.

The receptionist gave us a map. '*Chi compare billeti quasto.*'

'We're English,' I interrupted.

'Sorry, heard you speaking Italian. You can buy passes from a kiosk.'

'Now, there's a compliment,' Rich said, as we left the hotel.

Tom was right. This yellow mode of transportation had no mercy, especially concerning a couple of visitors from London. They came from all directions, zigzagging through the streets. They were a bright yellow, with thick chrome trimmings. 'Beautiful creatures,' Rich said, pausing and gazing in awe before we leapt on one.

'Unbelievable to think that London once had these,' he said. 'From the 1920s to 1952.'

'In Islington?'

'The 33 went along Holloway Road, before turning into Upper Street, then down the City Road towards Moorgate. The 35 went from Forest Hill to Archway.'

There was a sadness in his voice. Seemed at odds with the conversation about embracing change a few days ago.

'Fascinating,' I replied, looking attentively in both directions as we were about to jump off. 'Still have the Routemasters though, Rich,' I said, offering some kind of consolation. 'They ain't going nowhere.'

'Couldn't imagine the Smoke without them.'

'Only a fool would even think about getting rid of them. They glue the capital together. Bring tourists in. Known around the world, iconic,' I said.

We paused for a moment on the street as he consulted the map. 'Need to take another one. That's handy,' he said.

'What is?'

'The auction house is not too far from the Mole.'

'There it is,' I said, excitedly. The Mole is to Turin what Big Ben is to London. The skylines would be unimaginable without them.

'What's your favourite landmark?' I asked, as we walked.

'I'd have to say Chelsea Bridge.'

'Nice choice. Love those bulbs hanging along each side. It reminds me of the movies from the sixties. It's a romantic image.'

'What's yours?'

There was no hesitation on this one. 'The Old Post Office Tower,' I said. We both agreed on the second one. Alexandra Palace, we said, should be one of the seven wonders of the world.

Inside the Mole was a museum. It was dedicated to the history of Italian cinema. 'Can't believe it, they're showing my favourite film, *The Bicycle Thieves*.'

'You mean *Ladri di Biciclette*,' I said, reading a poster of the acclaimed movie on a wall.

We sat on a reclining sofa and watched a piece of Vittorio Di Sica's masterpiece that was being screened above us. 'Italian neorealism is something else,' Rich said, as we left to go to the auction house. 'I mean, what a story, all because someone gets their bicycle stolen. The consequences, incredible.'

'The actors aren't professional, either,' I said.

'And being shot on locations. Gripping stuff.'

'And realistic.' We were walking down the street. I looked at him. 'What a trip it's been so far,' I said. His face had a look as if to say that the best was yet to come.

The St Augustine Auction House was on the Corso Tassoni Alessandro. Though ornate, it looked a drab affair from the outside, especially after the splendour of the Musée des Beaux-Arts de Nice. It was open for business, wine and furniture being the commodities. Fine European wines from France, Italy and Spain were represented. The New World – South Africa, Australia, and the US – were unfortunately, and predictably, excluded. The furnishings were mainly of a French and Italian design, with some Russian and German pieces included. We got to the door, and looked at each other. 'Why not?' Rich said, after some hesitation.

So as not to arouse suspicion, we took a buyer's sheet. After entering the main hall, we found a discreet place at the back. 'Be careful on the bidding,' I said, as we sat down.

'Don't worry,' he replied. I mean, the thought of winning cases of Provence's best Burgundy or Tuscany's finest expensive Sassicaia, or an Italian throne chair from the eighteenth century, wasn't exactly what we needed at the moment. Rich took extra care with his hand-raising, bidding only in the initial stages. The purpose was not to be successful. I couldn't help but wonder how many of today's produce had the authentic '*Denominazione di origine controllata*' stamps and papers with them. On the way out an attractive dark-haired Italian lady gave Rich a brochure that had forthcoming auction dates in it.

On the way back to the hotel, I purchased a copy of the iconic pink *La Gazzetta dello Sport* from a yellow kiosk. *What is it with Turin and yellow?* I thought, as we jumped on a tram. I opened the heavy typeset paper. Andriy Shevchenko was banging them in for AC Milan. Interesting to see that Roma's Sven-Göran Eriksson was the only non-Italian manager in Serie A.

'The same items showing tomorrow will be at Christie's,' Rich said, as he browsed through the brochure.

'So the show will be rolling into London. Can't wait,' I said, as we entered the foyer of the hotel.

Tom and Doug had returned not long before. Tom waxed lyrical about his first ever visit to the Fiat factory. 'Have been here several times, never been, couldn't believe being there. Was moving,' he said, shaking his head, as in shock from the occasion. 'The race scene from my favourite film was filmed on a roof at the Fiat factory here, in Turin, and I've just been there.' He continued, still in disbelief.

'My favourite film is *Carnal Knowledge*,' uttered Doug.

'After today, *Ladri di Biciclette*,' said Rich, complete with correct pronunciation.

'Impressed,' remarked Tom.

'*Midnight Cowboy* for me,' I said.

'Do you know what Turin is famous for?' Doug asked.

'Juventus,' said Tom.

'Fiat,' replied Rich

'No idea,' I said.

'I went to the most famous place in the city for the hot chocolate. Wooden panelling, with authentic Lincrusta Italian Renaissance wallpaper, and no damn tourists!'

'Didn't know that the House of Savoy introduced the drink to Italy,' he said.

'Probably how Piccadilly or Great Portland Street would have looked during the Regency period,' I said.

I knew he had an obsession with this era. Both he – and his then best friend, David Martin – were forever playing the West End dandies. They were the real deal, parading up west in the seventies with their bespoke jackets, detailed shoes and cravats.

David Martin was one of a kind. An exquisite armed robber, safe breaker and escapist, all carried out with panache and aplomb. A Londoner, Martin gained notoriety as he pillaged his way across the capital in the seventies and early eighties, during which he was classed as Britain's most wanted man. In 1982 the police mistakenly shot at a yellow Mini in the Earls Court Road thinking Martin was a passenger. He wasn't. Stephen Waldorf became a household name as a result of the mistaken identity.

Martin was then arrested after shooting a police officer in Marylebone, central London. During a court appearance at Great Marlborough Street Court, he escaped by running along the rooftops and somehow entering the empty London Palladium. He'd escaped from custody four times before, boasting that no prison could hold him. Seemed like it became a reality.

The escapade finally came to a halt after his apartment in the Edgware Road came under surveillance, but even that didn't go to plan. Not much attention was paid to the smartly dressed blond lady coming and going from the block. Took a while for the police to realise this was actually Martin.

The beginning of the end for this flamboyant character was when he was confronted by police in Hampstead. They were again given the slip. This time he opted to run into Hampstead underground, down the stairs, then onto the track. He fled southwards towards Belsize Park where he was met by the waiting police, who took no chances. He was to end his life whilst in Parkhurst Prison on 13 March 1984.

'Took me a long time to get over that one,' Doug said. As with Martin and Vicci, he also found that giving up crime was a little more difficult than anticipated. 'You know, I'm having a great time here,' he said.

'Time to give up the smack,' Tom said, in a straightforward, but truthful, way.

'I'm gonna give it a go,' Doug replied.

We all agreed on one thing: that so far, Turin was one cool city. 'Not everyone shares the same opinion,' he said, 'especially the Italians. They think it's a cold, industrial city that's had its day. Hasn't got the best reputation,' he added.

'That's a good thing, if you ask me,' Doug replied. 'Who wants trendies and tourists anyway. What purpose do they serve, except to destroy a community? I'm fortunate to live in Whitechapel. No tourists to be seen there.'

'At the moment,' Rich said.

'What, derelict warehouses, rundown clothing retailers. Who wants that?'

'Cutting-edge artists?'

'And as for the fume-filled, desolate Commercial Road, I mean, forget it. Anyway, Gilbert and George are good people. They were there when others didn't dare. They were there when no one else would.'

'I have a feeling that in a few years' time, it will become very hip,' I added.

As we were debating the future of the capital, Tom received a phone call. 'Luigi's waiting downstairs. *Andiamo*,' he said.

Doug was confused. 'What?'

'Gianni's sent Luigi, his driver, to pick us up. He's waiting downstairs.'

It was getting a little chilly, so we each took a coat.

A shiny looking black Fiat was parked next to the Triumph. Luigi was admiring the sleek machine. As we walked, Tom came up beside me. 'Steve, listen, to these guys we are like rock stars yeah, they look up to us. Just make the most of it, enjoy.'

'Nice car,' said Luigi, peering inside the window. After a brief introduction, we got in the car. After lighting up a spliff, and cranking some Cult, we were whisked away towards the Alps.

The Ultras, of any club, were a serious outfit and carried weight. For any incoming transfer, the owners had to go through them. They were prominent not only within football, but also, it seemed, with organised crime. Some were now even entering the political arena. This was another difference – I couldn't imagine the ICF, the Zulus, or even the Bushwackers sending a car to collect guests, let alone forming a political party.

We were driven to the northern outskirts of the city, passing the dreary, industrial climes Tom had spoken about earlier along the way. The drizzle didn't help the cause, though, and definitely highlighted its desolate and barren landscape. Luigi didn't speak much English. His way of communicating was to play music. After sharing the doobie with Doug he changed the tunes. 'You guys have the best music,' he mustered, in his best broken English. A new band were on the scene, called Coldplay. 'Yellow' added to the bleakness.

After thirty minutes we turned into a side road. This really was off the beaten track, I thought. 'We're here,' announced Luigi, as we approached what looked like a bungalow. Outside someone waiting for us, 'Don't mention Juventus,' Tom said, as we got out of the car.

'Gianni, Doug, Steve and Richard. Doug, Steve, Richard, Gianni.' We were then individually greeted with a warm smile and hospitable hug. Twenty or more ciaos followed before Gianni took us inside. Outside, it looked shabby and unkempt. Inside, though, was a different story. He introduced us to the five associates dotted around the room. Two were on the sofa, two playing pool, and one on a stool at the bar.

The lounge was spacious with large polished marble tiles. On one wall were two framed flags. One of FC Torino, the other a regional banner of the province. The latter looked beautiful, a resplendent piece of tapestry. It held my attention for a few seconds, especially the detailed badges within the coat of arms. Similar in style to the map Roberto had in his apartment, only this was way larger. 'Should never have given up our status to Roma,' stated Gianni, noticing my intrigue.

'I'll fill you in on the history of Italy later,' said Tom, quietly. They seemed to be fascinated by us. Looking at our mannerisms, what we were wearing, and how were conducting ourselves. As if we were the real deal. 'You see,' Tom whispered.

'Like royalty,' I said, to which he nodded. Taking centre stage on the other wall was a huge framed photo of a football team. They were lined up in a fetching maroon and white kit. 'Who are they?' I asked Tom.

'The *Grande Torino*. Multiple champions of Italy, 1948 to '49,' he answered, again quietly. Around the picture were various signed photos of players both past and present.

'*Vengo*,' Gianni said, as he gesticulated for us to follow.

'Means "I'm coming",' said Tom, as we followed him and Luigi.

We were given a tour of what was a clubhouse of sorts. It was a large one-floor apartment with several rooms, discreetly located in the hills of the Piedmont. *Very similar to what the Hell's Angels have*, I thought, as we glided from room to room.

We ended up in a room that had a wooden tiled floor with a stucco balcony. We sat down outside looking into the blue darkness. 'We are on top of a lake,' Luigi explained. 'I like The Cult, man. When they come to Turin, we go and see them. Electric rocks, man,' he added.

'Good live band,' I agreed.

It was getting a little windy, so we went back into the room. It was a study, with a desk, a chair and a leather sofa. On a shelf was a statue of Mussolini, and various nude male pieces were aligning the room, creating a somewhat homoerotic ambience. It had everything, apart from a female presence. As we left I noticed a book on the shelf: *Ultras Torino Granata Orgoglio* by Gianni Agnelli. 'Who wrote this?' I asked Luigi.

'Him,' he replied, pointing to Gianni.

Other rooms included a small gym space in the basement, and a small cinema to watch DVDs and listen to music. There was even a press room. Gianni ' being the senior Ultra ' would conduct press conferences there. 'Who too?' I asked Tom

'The executives and directors of the club, and the media.'

Gianni's English was sporadic, but understandable. I got the feeling he wasn't interested in other languages, including other Italian dialects. Only the local dialect was to be. 'We speak the real Italian language,' he said, making a gesticulation I'd witnessed countless times on Channel 4's *Football Italia*.

'Love *Football Italia*,' I said.

'James Richardson, what a job he has,' Tom remarked.

'And the theme tune,' said Rich, as Tom hummed a little, just to remind ourselves.

'*Vengo*,' announced Gianni, as we followed him back to the lounge.

Three of us didn't drink alcohol, much to the surprise – and bemusement – of our hosts. So it was left to Doug to fly the flag. We then sat down and relaxed, speaking about football and music, before it came around to what our favourite English and Italian teams were.

'Oxford United and Verona,' I said, starting off the proceedings.

'Hellas Verona? Why?'

'They play in yellow and blue,' I replied, with logic and reason.

'Arsenal and Lazio,' said Tom.

Doug had joined us from the bar area, where the smell of moist hashish was prevalent. 'Spurs and Roma,' he said.

'Arsenal and Fiorentina,' added Rich.

'Torino and Millwall,' Gianni responded.

'Why Millwall?' I asked.

'I like the name of the stadium, Cold Blow Lane,' he said.

Fair enough, I thought.

'Torino and Chelsea,' said Luigi.

'*Vengo*,' Gianni announced, as we followed him and the others to the cinema, to watch his prized collection of DVDs, all of the Torino Ultras in action.

He led the narrative throughout, becoming a little animated on more than one occasion. '*Distruggi! Distruggi!*' he shouted, as the Torino fans led the offensive in the centre of Naples against Napoli. '*Non correre da loro! Non correre da loro!*' he exclaimed, as they went on the defensive a few seconds later.

I soon noticed that there wasn't actually that much violence. It was more posturing, and theatrical. Like Italian football itself, it had a sense of drama, as if rehearsed. The accompaniment of smoke – and its different colours – did look good though, as the participants did lots of shouting, and lots of running to and fro.

After some more spectacular footage of fans running amok in ancient Italian city centres, we made our way back to the lounge area. The drink was again being generously poured, and spliffs continued being constructed. The Cure's *Live in Orange* was the choice of music. 'Shake Dog Shake' sounded awesome.

'Why Oxford United?' I was asked as we sat down.

'First game I went to, against Manchester United. We won with a Derek Clarke header,' I said, as they looked a little bewildered.

Tom explained that Manchester United were once in the second tier of English football. 'The equivalent of Serie B here,' he said, holding up two fingers. To say they found it difficult to comprehend that the team who had just been crowned the Champions League winners a few months ago – with a win over Bayern Munich – were in such a state was an understatement.

'Tax?' asked Gianni.

'Money laundering?' inquired Luigi.

'No, it was neither. Just weren't good enough,' Tom said. He tried to explain – much to their continuing disbelief – that no financial irregularities were involved.

'The beauty of English football,' I said.

'True. Would you ever find Real Madrid or Barcelona in La Ligua two? Don't think so,' said Rich.

Gianni showed me the crest of FC Torino, a bull, to which I lifted the right side of my T-shirt. On the side of my upper arm was the Oxford United badge. I slapped it for emphasis. *Still very much proud of this masterpiece*, I thought.

'Similar. But ox stronger than bull,' I said.

'Ox get castrated,' said Luigi.

'Because we are more selective,' I replied. I then quoted a Chinese saying: 'Before taking action, an ox will have a definite plan, with detailed steps.'

'The bull is revered in India,' said Gianni. 'Represents masculinity, virility, strength, aggression and fighting power.'

'Oxen exhibit a strong sense of loyalty,' I said.

With the drink and weed kicking in, Gianni announced it was a good idea to drive to The Superga. '*Andiamo!*' he bellowed.

'Where?' Doug asked, surprised, and not too happy about leaving.

'The Superga. It's a church on a hill, not too far. The entire Torino Grande squad – the one you saw in the photo – all died there after the plane they were on crashed into the side of the hill. It's like a pilgrimage.'

'Like the Busby Babes?'

'Exactly.'

Doug went over to a cabinet in the hallway. 'Nice piece,' he said, commenting on a blue vase on top

'What is the symbol? Can't see it from here,' asked Tom.

'Looks like a serpent,' Doug answered.

'We say snake,' said Luigi, who ushered Doug away.

I looked at Rich, who looked at me. We both looked at the familiar looking vase not saying anything to anybody.

The five others stayed at the house as we crammed inside the Fiat. 'The players come here to pray and pay respect before a game,' said Gianni, as we drove back towards the centre of Turin.

Similar to Jim Morrison's grave in Paris, I thought, as we sat opposite the wall the plane had actually hit fifty years ago. Both were adorned with sentimental graffiti, and both attracted people who just sat around. Morrison's tombstone was in the Père Lachaise Cemetery. I'd visited it in eighty-six. A lot of people just sat there, speechless, as if searching for answers. The searching continued until the security moved them on when the cemetery closed.

'He's in good company anyway,' said Doug.

'Because Oscar Wilde is there?'

'And Edith Piaf,' said Tom.

'Also Frederic Chopin,' added Gianni.

There was no closing time here, so no security asked us to leave, but it was getting late so we went to the nearby Sassi–Superga tramway station. From there a train ran down the side of the hill, taking you back to the city centre. Gianni and Luigi walked with us. I spoke with Gianni. I liked him. He was warm, engaging and had a sense of humour.

We embraced by the platform. '*Ci vediamo un altro giorno,*' he said, as the train arrived. '*Ciao, ciao, ciao,*' we all exclaimed. On the train, Tom said that the Savoys were also buried at the Superga.

When we reached the bottom, he said that he had to go. 'Location in the arcade,' he shouted, as he walked ahead. Doug also excused himself. 'See you back at the hotel soon,' he said, racing towards the station.

Rich and myself strolled back to the hotel along the River Po. 'Liked what you said about oxen showing loyalty,' he said. 'I've always wondered why some people are tribal regarding their football teams, areas and countries, and some are not. I'm the former, and I could never figure it out. Thought there was something wrong with me. I explained it to Master, said I felt ashamed about my behaviour around football. His response surprised me. He said it was an honourable trait, and that all the educated philosophers in feudal China were not only good teachers and spiritual beings, but also warriors and fighters.' He stopped, you could just about hear the water in the background. 'It was an answer I'd been searching for.'

'Master seems to have a lot of insight, Rich. Appears to understand many things. Seems to not only know the past and present—' I paused '—but also the future.'

'We're talking a lineage of nearly three thousand years, that hasn't been broken.'

I wanted to ask him about the fifth painting, but it wasn't the right time. Besides, I wanted to go with the flow. Sometimes I enjoy being on the edge.

We went to the bank and looked out to the river. The Po wasn't that inspiring. It was devoid of any life. Just a few branches hanging low, sweeping across the shallow piece of water. Totally the opposite of Zhang's scenic sketches. The bite of winter became noticeable.

'*Vengo*,' I said, after a few minutes. We then began to walk a little faster. 'They must be hitting it, I mean, how many copies of the same picture or ceramics can you sell?' I added.

'There'll be different buyers at each venue.'

'Busy people,' I concluded, as the rest of the walk was conducted in silence.

Tom was back at the hotel when we returned. We sat in the lobby for a while. Immense pride was taken in showing us pictures where the Minis were driven in the shopping arcade. 'This was inside, and this was—' he was in such a rush he had difficulty in finding the intended polaroid '—outside. You see this La Stampa neon? It's still there.'

There was still no sign of Doug, as we went to bed at one in the morning.

'What a useless place Turin is,' he snapped, in the morning. This was in direct contrast to yesterday, when the hot chocolate and surroundings were awesome. The inevitable comparisons then began. 'Not as good as Nice or Marseilles, nothing here, bland.'

We knew the answer to the apathy and cynicism, it was simple: he hadn't been able to score. The worry was that he'd soon be entering the withdrawal stage – not the best preparation for the auction house. He didn't even drink his coffee, only picking up the brochure from the auction house. 'See you later,' he said, as he slammed the door behind him. He'd be back soon, such was the determination. He returned less than an hour later. The success was evident.

'Tom, what did Roberto ask you to bring?'

'Huh?'

'When Roberto asked you to carry some antiques to the UK, what were they?'

'It was only one, a figurine.'

'A man with his head in his hands?'

'Yes.'

'The woman looking at him? Both sitting on a chair?'

Tom looked up. 'How do you know?'

'Lot fifty-five. An ancient porcelain piece from Mu Ling Zhu, master craftsman of the ancient Zhou dynasty,' Doug said, reading from the brochure. He held up the page. Tom got up to take a closer look, confirming the exact item he'd sacrificed four months of his life for.

'Who owns it?' I asked.

'Good question. Doesn't say.'

'Probably a private seller.'

'That's how it's done,' Rich said. 'The buyers and sellers will all be anonymous.'

'And all by telephone. Makes it more difficult to trace.'

'Going to be hard to track them to the top. If we can't actually give solid evidence of what's being sold – and by whom – it's pointless,' I added.

'Wouldn't stand up in court,' Doug said.

'Wouldn't it be great if we could bid on something and win? Then we could get the item checked, proving it's fake, showing these auction houses and galleries are not dealing in legitimate goods,' Tom added.

'Don't have that sort of money,' I lamented.

'They must know some of this stuff ain't real?' Doug said.

'The buzz of the bidding is part of it,' Rich said. 'Then, after a couple of years, the items go back into the mix for another spin of excitement.'

'Must be a wicked buzz, though,' said Tom, showing some empathy.

'Murky world,' I added.

'Very,' Rich acknowledged.

'Part of it,' Tom replied, as his phone rang. 'Gianni!' he said, excitedly. *'Come stai?'*

After a few minutes he turned to us. 'He really enjoyed our company yesterday,' he said.

'So he should,' remarked Doug, as he got up to make some coffee.

'You said his family own Fiat cars?' I asked.

'And Juventus. They carry a lot of weight in this city and region.'

'More than the Savoys?'

'Different. The Savoys are like royalty. They have history – since 1003 – and prestige. They ruled the kingdom of Italy from 1861 until 1946. They're more traditional. The Agnellis are, however, more contemporary, more businesslike. They also own Ferrari, Alfa Romeo, and of course, Juventus FC.

'New money, you mean?'

'One thing puzzles me,' asked Doug, as he placed a fresh pot of coffee on the table and began to pour it into four cups. 'Why does Gianni support Torino? Juve's rivals?'

'The Agnellis are Turin, so I guess it doesn't really matter. It's not like it's Milan, Roma, or a team from another region.'

'Does he know about Roberto, what he's up to?'

'Hasn't said anything.'

'Have you said anything?'

'Nothing,' he said, as he took a sip of coffee.

I used Rich's laptop to email Laila, and sent her some pictures of the auction house and brochures. I told her about meeting Gianni, the Agnelli family, and the figurine. *About to step the game up to another level*, I wrote.

Rich said he had something to say. 'Steve, what you said about not having the money.'

'And?'

'Made me think. If only we knew someone who did.'

'You mean someone local, from a wealthy family?' There was a pause before we all looked at Tom.

'No way,' came the abrupt answer, as he got up.

'Ask him. The thought of nailing Roberto may appeal,' I said.

'Too risky.'

Tom then told us he had met Gianni in prison, not at a football match, as he been saying.

'Football related?'

'No.'

'Fraud?'

'You could say that.' He went to his bag before placing four tickets on the table. Internazionale v. Napoli, tomorrow at the San Siro. 'Gift, from Gianni,' he said. We now knew where he was getting his new supply of tickets for the Italian games from.

'We have to go to the auction house tomorrow,' I said, looking at the tickets in more detail.

'I do like the look and feel of tickets,' said Doug, taking them from me.

'Kick-off is in the evening,' said Tom.

'Yes!' I exclaimed, as we hugged. The feeling of being elated and joyous was shared. 'Let's get ready,' I said, as I saw a pattern emerging. The picture was now becoming more focused. The Savoy family – with the Agnellis – were Turin. The old and the new. Both formidable and prestigious outfits. Both lay claim to the province since the formation of a republic and the disposal of the Italian monarchy. The Agnellis were in front, slightly edging it – replacing the Savoys by proxy, if you like.

They both liked art, and both wanted a piece of the action with both brokering for dominance of the art market. They each had a loose cannon. Roberto for the Savoys, Gianni for the Agnellis. Both seem to want a bit of excitement that conventional wealth couldn't provide. Both were liabilities, and both were convicted fraudsters. Because of this, the four visitors from Londra had the upper hand.

Chapter Seventeen

Monday, 18 October 1999

Rich wired his speakers to the laptop. We were treated to *Violator* by Depeche Mode as we prepared. As one showered, the other ate, and so on. This was the system.

'Thought China was Communist,' said Doug, preparing his blue silk cravat in the mirror.

'It was Buddhist before,' Rich stated.

'Now they've gone the other way, capitalist,' Tom added, pulling on his dark blue Armani sweater.

'Confusing,' I said, sipping the hot espresso.

Rich was the last to join us. Having been showered, clothed and fed, we were ready for action.

The early afternoon air was cold. A chilled wind was whipping up through the Alps and filtering through into the city. Doug and Rich were the willing participants to go inside the auction house. Myself and Tommy walked a little with them, before parting on the Corso Svizzera.

'Let's walk around the block,' I suggested, as the cold began to take hold.

'Look.' Tom showed me a photograph of Denis Law and Joe Baker, both transferred to Italy to play for Torino from England. 'Original press photo, 1962,' he added.

They were grappling with each other, being playful and smiling, as though they hadn't a care in the world. Baker had come from Arsenal, Law from Manchester United. Both were popular players before being transferred to the then promised land of Serie 'A'.

He pulled out his Polaroid from his bag. 'Are you serious?' I asked.

'Won't take long.'

'This one will be impossible,' I said, noticing that there were only a few trees in the background to go on.

'Gianni said that it could be one of two parks. Both not far from here.'

First was the Parco Dora, which was under construction for a future science museum. 'Too flat and small,' I said, as we made our way to the second, the Parco della Pellerina.

As we walked along the Corso Svizzera, I said it seemed like we'd been there ages.

'Happens sometimes. You mean you feel at ease in some places? With the people and surroundings? As if you belong?'

'Not only here, but in Nice and Marseilles. Strange to think that it's only been three days.'

At the turning with the Corso Regina Margherita, Tom stopped to look at the photo. 'Look at those clothes,' he said. 'The shirts, the jumpers. Proper wool. The shirt would have been bespoke, made to measure, wonder where? Here or England?'

'Here we go,' I said, as we entered the Parco della Pellerina.

'Did you tell Gianni about why we're here?'

'No, thinks we're here for the football. My oh my!' he said, holding the photograph up against a backdrop of some overgrown shrubs and trees. A childlike sprint then followed, as he ran to an area where some benches were. *If he's like this now, what's going to happen when we approach the scene to the opening of* The Italian Job *tomorrow*, I thought, as a pursued him.

'Only one tree has gone, the rest have grown a lot in the thirty-seven years,' he said, as he handed me the Polaroid camera.

I took some shots, trying to best capture the mood years on. The chill had gone, so we just hung around for the next hour. He was pleased with the photo, constantly comparing them to each other. After an amazing espresso in a cafe, I called Rich. 'Just left,' he said.

'*Vengo*,' I announced, as we went to meet them on the corner of the Coso Potenza and Corso Regina Margherita.

'How did it go?' I asked.

'Not that many people. Previews are like that. Was more like a showcase.'

'Everything was in cabinets. I saw that piece you was accused of, Tom,' said Doug. 'And the three porcelain plates, there were also there.'

'Guess what else he saw?' said Rich. 'You'll never believe it.'

'Roberto? Zhang? Peter?' Tom asked.

'You know I told you about some lady on the train to Menton?' said Doug.

'No,' Tom and I said, in unison.

'Anyway, we'll come to that later,' said Rich wisely, before continuing. 'There were more items there than advertised in the brochure, many claimed to be found after being lost during the Opium Wars.'

'They don't want to advertise them, Rich, in case of publicity. Want to save them for the punters with the money.'

'The first and third painting were also exhibited, though not for sale until tomorrow.'

'Shame we won't be here,' I said.

'There were three sales today, all by the same person.'

'She was so beautiful,' Doug said.

'Who?'

'The lady from the train. She sat at the front, bidding.'

'She bought the three pieces? What were they anyway?'

'The porcelain piece from Mu Ling Zhu. A plate, and a painting.'

'Who is she?' I asked, in vain.

'No idea,' said Rich. 'Anyway, let's go to the place Doug went for a hot chocolate yesterday before going to Milan.' Oddly enough, Doug declined. 'See you back at the hotel,' he said, before heading in the direction of the train station.

'Don't forget the match,' I shouted.

The three of us had a spring in our step as we boarded a yellow tram. The thought of a football match and more evidence being the obvious reason. Rich showed me photos of the lady, the items she'd bought, and copies of Zhang's work. 'Don't forget to email me them,' I said, as we jumped off the tram.

Doug was right. What a place. Salmon pink wallpaper, with polished dark wooden trimmings. Superb. Tom passed around the new set of Polaroids. Everyone agreed they were up there with his best. 'Can't wait until tomorrow,' he said.

Back at the hotel, Doug was bang on form. 'No tourists whatsoever,' he said, waxing lyrical about a visit to a local fruit and veg market. A huge pile of strawberries on the table was the proof. 'Turin's not that bad a place after all, even though I nearly got dipped there,' he added, with a newly found vigour.

Rich tuned in to a local radio station. 'Love Song' by The Cure was playing.

'Brilliant,' I remarked.

'Sounds different here,' said Tom. Which was true. It did.

After a shower and change of clothes, we had a feast of fresh vegetables, cheese, bread and the strawberries. Tom stood up. '*Andiamo!*' he bellowed.

'*San Siro, arriviamo!*' we replied.

As the train was heading out of Turin towards Milan, I turned to Rich, as something occurred to me. 'Wonder where Roberto is sourcing the ceramics from?'

'Maybe here, then exporting them to London,' he said.

'I'm not so sure, too much hassle.'

'You mean somewhere closer to home?'

'I think so,' I said, as we were leaving the city centre. 'Not impressed with Turin's bland, steely grey suburbia though. What's Milan like, Tom?' I asked.

'Same, I'm afraid. Overrated. Only the San Siro for me, and maybe a few shops.'

'What about all the designer gear. Isn't that what Milan's about?'

'You can get it all in London.'

'Who you gonna support, Steve?'

'Inter,' I said. The truth was, I could only support Oxford. I mean, I liked Tottenham as well – as all the other London teams – and for some reason Blackpool was in the mix – must be the unique tangerine colour – but I could only get into Oxford. I kicked every ball when I watched them, something I found difficult watching other teams. International football just didn't do it for me either, don't know why, it just didn't.

'You have to watch Napoli,' Tom warned, 'rough lot, will be North v. South.'

There was a large police presence in and around Milano Centrale. We were clocked straight away – both by fans and by the police, with their snarling dogs.

'Beautiful interiors,' said Doug, as we made our way through the imposing hall to take a bus to the San Siro.

The station was indeed stunning. A juxtaposition of art nouveau and art deco, it stood out, despite the edgy ambience.

'Opened in 1931,' stated Tom.

Outside the station we were bundled onto a bus with other Inter fans. It was notable how the Italian firms looked – and dressed – different. Bomber jackets, hoods and skinny jeans were the favoured attire. It was a more political look, with some clubs historically left wing, and some right wing. We were more into the look, fashion, style and music. The so-called 'English disease' had spread like a virus onto the Continent, only with different ways, styles and connotations.

The San Siro was smaller than it looked on the TV, but the atmosphere was intense, electric and awesome, with each set of fans really baiting each other. I found it fascinating, the way the Ultras surged to the front when a goal was scored. I could watch that all day, very unique. 'Bob Marley played a concert here in 1980,' Tom said.

Throughout the game Inter fans were coming up and shaking our hands. They knew we were English. '*Mi piace* Chelsea! Gianfranco Zola!' was said more than a few times. They seemed to like Chelsea. 'Gianluca Vialli!' they screamed. The only two English players to wear the black and blue stripes of their beloved Internazionale Milano were Paul Ince – who played for two seasons in the mid-nineties – and Gerry Hitchens in the early sixties. Both were spoken of fondly, as if they were childhood friends.

It finished one–one, and the Inter fans weren't happy with the result. In England, they kept the away supporters in for a short while. Here, it was more like an hour. Outside the stadium was a tense affair. Lots of police were trying their best to restrain their rabid, howling dogs, who were straining to be unleashed.

We stayed a while at the station to see if there was any action similar to the DVDs Gianni had shown us. It didn't happen, the Napoli fans were surrounded by hundreds of police who had escorted them to the station whilst we were still in the stadium. The Cathedral didn't disappoint, though, it was all lit up against the dark blue Milanese evening sky.

'Boring,' said Tom, as we waited for the train back to Turin. He wanted to visit Lake Como. 'Jimmy Greaves lived there whilst playing for Inter's rivals AC in 1962,' he said. 'Lived in one of these chateau-type things on the lake,' he added.

'Another time. We have to travel tomorrow,' I said.

On the train Tom recited most – if not all – the British players who had played for Italian clubs:

Gerry Hitchens – Inter, Torino, Atalanta, Cagliari. 1961–69.

Anthony Marchi – Vicenza, Torino. 1957–59.

Luther Blissett – Milan. 1983–84.

Ray Wilkins – Milan. 1984–87.

Jimmy Greaves – Milan. 1961–62.

Mark Hateley – Milan. 1984–87.

Charles Adcock – Padova, Triestina. 1948–50.

Joe Baker – Torino. 1961–62.

Franz Carr – Reggiana. 1996–97.

Gordon Cowans – Bari. 1985–86.

Danny Dichio – Lecce. 1997–98.

Paul Elliott – Pisa. 1987–89.

Trevor Francis – Sampdoria, Atalanta. 1982–87.

Paul Gascoigne – Lazio. 1992–95.
William Jordan – Juventus. 1948–49.
David Platt – Bari, Juventus, Sampdoria. 1991–95.
Paul Rideout – Bari. 1985–86.
Lee Sharpe – Sampdoria. 1998–99.
Des Walker – Sampdoria. 1992–93.
Dennis Law – Torino. 1961–62.

'Impressive,' I said, as his phone rang. It was Gianni.

'Wants a ride in the Triumph,' he said, after the short conversation.

After the hospitality shown last night it was difficult to refuse. 'No problem,' I said, as we went back to the hotel, dropped off our souvenirs, and drove to the clubhouse.

Gianni and his friends were there to greet us. 'Nice car,' he commented, as I parked up. '*Vai dentro, saremo mezz'ora,*' he shouted, as he Doug, Rich and Tom got out and went inside the clubhouse with the others. '*Andiamo!*' Gianni said, and within ten minutes we were skimming the side of the Alps.

'I don't want to go too far in. Want to save it for tomorrow,' I said, so as not to ruin the thrill of *The Italian Job*.

The roof was still down, and the wind was beginning to hit us hard, as we were sped into the night.

'I understand!' he shouted. 'Tell me, do you like to watch the football on television, I mean, without knowing the score?'

'What makes you say that?'

'You said you want to save seeing the Alps until tomorrow.'

'Yes, I do.'

'So do you keep away from people and the news so you don't hear the score?'

'Yes, not always possible though.'

'Me too!' he laughed. 'What's the name of that football programme you have in England?'

'*Match of the Day*?'

'Match of the day,' he repeated. 'That's it, funny name,' he added.

I increased the pressure of my foot on the accelerator even more. 'Enjoy the Silence' by Depeche Mode sounded on another level.

'Rubbish programme now,' I said. It was nothing against the current presenter, housewives' favourite Des Lynam. I was just a little angry that this once sacred Saturday evening slot for many, had somehow – over the years – deteriorated into a middle-class fumble of trendy media. 'The presenters,' I shouted. 'All university educated, not real fans.'

We stopped at a small village and – even though it was late – took an espresso. 'For the road,' Gianni said.

'Indeed,' I replied. Sensing he was comfortable in my company, the time was right for some questions. 'The Savoys. Quite prestigious in this region?'

'My friend. Fiat and Juventus are the region. The Savoys are different. They are Italy, and are as one. Nobody touches them. They are – as you say in English – above the law. You understand?'

'I understand,' I replied, not really understanding. 'By the way, thank you for the tickets, much appreciated,' I said, as we walked back to the car.

'Did you enjoy?'

'Immensely.'

'Can I drive?'

'Of course.' The theme on the way back consisted mainly of hooligan-related questions. 'What is the Billy Wizz Fan Club?'

'Bolton Wanderers' firm.'

'Their rivals?'

'There's a few. Burnley, Preston, Oldham, Blackburn, Rochdale. And to some extent I guess the Manchester clubs.'

'Accrington?'

'Definitely, though at the moment they're non-league. Accrington Stanley were replaced in the league by Oxford United. 1961.'

'What is the name of the Oxford United firm?'

'The South Midland Hit Squad.'

'The South Midland Hit Squad,' he repeated. 'The South Midland Hit Squad, I like that.'

The roof was still down, and it was getting colder. The hairpin bends were irrelevant, as he took his chances. The fact that Italy has more road deaths than any other European country counted for nothing as we raced through the sparse villages and countryside, leaving the sound of British craftsmanship at its best in their wake. Remembering how it made me feel the other day, I played 'Wide Open Space' by Mansun as a soundtrack.

On arrival, I mentioned something not that many Italians want to hear. 'Do you like Notts County?'

He switched off the engine, looked at me and smiled. '*Andiamo*,' he said, not wanting to answer the question. I got the feeling that somehow he already knew the history. Notts County FC are 137 years old. Juventus took the black and white striped shirts from them. It can be a sore point for some Italians.

The clubhouse was warm and welcoming as we entered. The predictable smell of hashish was in the air, and more people had arrived, including a very attractive lady. 'Stephen, this is Sophia,' said Gianni.

'Nice to meet you, Sophia.'

'*Piacere di conoscerti.*'

'*Grazie*,' I replied, as I noticed Tom trying to attract my attention in the background.

'*Un momento. Fammi prendere un po d'acqua,*' I said.

'Have you seen this one?' Tom said, grabbing my arm and leading me to the wall where the photos were.

'What's wrong?' I asked.

'That was the woman you're with.'

'Yes?'

'She was the one bidding at the auction today?'

'You serious? The one Doug met on the train to Menton?'

'Yes.'

I looked around. Sophia had gone over to the main group, where Doug had an audience in tow. He was on form, and the London anecdotes were flowing. The charismatic pied piper had temporarily forsaken the alleyways and pavements of east London for the Piedmont chic. They were treated to an agile performance of the Englishman in Turin, and they loved it.

I sat back to observe, comfortable in the surroundings of football and music, and now women. I felt at ease with the attention of affluent Italians, happily taking photos with Doug, Rich, Tom and myself. *There's something else about Sophia*, I thought. *I mean, she bears an uncanny resemblance to the description of one of the witnesses from the gallery in Cork Street.*

There came a time to say our farewells. It was moving into the early hours, and we had a long drive tomorrow. I invited Gianni to London. 'We'll buy a one day travelcard and visit all the football grounds of the capital in one day,' I promised.

'How many teams in London?'

'Eleven,' I replied.

'Twelve including Wembley,' added Tom.

'Promise?'

'Promise,' I confirmed. This was the cue for many hugs and handshakes between us. Sophia's hug was the best: warm, and feminine, with a subtle hint of eau de toilette.

'Why do Italians love London?' I asked Tom, as we walked to the car.

'They just do, can you blame them?'

For the first time, I thought about home. 'No, I can't,' I replied.

After reversing, we turned around, and drove back past them. I tooted the horn to the tune of 'England', as in *The Italian Job*.

'Filmed in Wormwood Scrubs,' Tom said.

'Been there,' added Doug.

The roof was still down as Doug stood up. '*Forza Torino!*' he shouted, with a clench of the fist. I pressed hard on the gas pedal, turning the gravel into a smokescreen, before taking to the autostrada for our final evening in Turin.

I lowered the roof. 'Hope nobody mentioned today,' I said, cautiously.

Back at the hotel we all lay on our beds. I sent Laila a text. '*Sorry it's late. Been a good day, got a lot done. Send details in later in morning.*'

'*Paris tomorrow, two p.m.?*' was the reply
'*Where?*'
'*Louvre – Rivoli Metro.*'
'*Of course*,' I replied. I now had something extra to look forward later.

Chapter Eighteen

Tuesday, 19 October 1999

'Farewell Turin,' lamented Doug, as he waved behind him. It was seven in the morning, and we were approaching the foothills of the Alps. I stopped at the side of the road and put my orange driving glasses on. The mountains were looming, looking immense – and different – in real life. Lyon, France, was the next destination. '*Andiamo!*' I shouted, as we roared away.

'Anyone read Kerouac's *On the Road*?' asked Doug, inspired by the early morning surroundings and scenery. 'Read it in Pentonville,' he added.

'Brixton, I think,' said Tom.

'Read it in the Scrubs, years ago,' said Rich. 'Kerouac mentions the Tao in there. He was a Buddhist,' he added.

'Same as Herbie Hancock,' Tom said.

'Kerouac said he believed in all religions. He explored many traditions and philosophies.'

Tom requested some jazz.

'Davis or Coltrane?'

'Coltrane.'

'Done,' I said, as I inserted *A Love Supreme*. I took a deep breath., it sounded superb. Right here, right now, in this precise moment, everything was as near perfect as could be. The more we ascended, the more biting the cold became, but I'd somehow manage to hit happiness.

'John Coltrane died on 17 July 1967,' Tom said.

'Twenty-three days before Joe Orton,' I replied.

The four days had been eventful and productive. We had done what we had to do. I was more than pleased with that. The portfolio to incriminate Roberto & co. was growing. Everything that could be used to secure my innocence was going to the capable hands of Laila, then passed over to Alexios in due course. That was the business side taken care of.

The social side was still ambiguous. The trust with Doug, Tom and Rich was just as inconsistent as ever. We all had different reasons for this visit, but it was all holding well. One by one I looked around.

Doug was moving from side to side. The mind, body and soul were agitated, and disturbed. Withdrawal from the junk was kicking in. A far cry from last night's performance. Guess he had to wait the few hours or so until he was safely dispatched in the environs of Whitechapel.

Tom was excited, impatiently waiting for the Col du Petit St Bernard, where the opening scene from *The Italian Job* was filmed.

Rich sat back, eyes closed, but still alert. *I love these guys*, I thought. Tom pointed to the sky. 'Look,' he said. Sure enough, there it was, a magnificent eagle soaring above, very similar to one in the fifth painting.

'Do you think Master will know the translation of the characters in the paintings?' I asked Rich.

'I think he will. Mandarin writing is complex, it can confuse the Chinese themselves. The old classical style is different. Can I drive a while?' he asked.

I pulled over, and we exchanged seats. *Headhunters* by Herbie Hancock was the choice as he took the wheel.

'Don't forget the Col du Petit St Bernard,' Tom said.

'Watermelon Man' played as he skimmed the Parc National de la Vanoise with speed and precision.

'We will soon be in the presence of one of the greatest films ever made,' Rich said, reminding Tom, upon arrival at the infamous stretch of road.

'Wow,' said Tom, looking out, after he exchanged seats with Rich.

There was a respectful silence as he indulged and savoured the moment. It took but five minutes in total. There were pauses such as stopping on the bridge, and in the tunnel. A few minutes were also reserved at the top of the ravine where the red Ferrari met its fate.

'Sure you don't want to roll a wreath down while you're at it?' shouted Doug, who had stayed in the car. He was becoming agitated, so we ignored the comment.

'We'll stop in Paris for a few hours, guys,' I announced, returning to the driver's seat.

'Give me a shout, when we're there,' Doug asked, as we excitedly headed towards the A43.

Lyon was low and open. It looked pleasant enough against the blue sky. From the autoroute we caught a fleeting glimpse of the Stade Gerland, home of Olympique Lyonnais football club.

'Had 48,552 there in 1980,' Tom informed us.

'1980? "Another Brick in the Wall", Pink Floyd,' Doug said.

'"The Second Time Around", Shalamar,' I remembered.

'"Rock With You", Michael Jackson,' was for Tom.

'"Ride Like The Wind", Christopher Cross,' said Rich.

'Brilliant song,' I agreed.

As with Marseilles, Turin and Milan, the Parisian suburbia wasn't that pretty. The sun had gone, replaced with blue-grey clouds. A decision to brighten up the grim landscape was made, as I inserted *Paris* by Stoke Newington's finest, Malcolm Mclaren.

'Can I see the cover?' asked Tom. 'Stylish shot,' he said, looking at Malcolm, standing with the Eiffel Tower in the background.

'Video's good as well, he's with Catherine Deneuve. A kinda montage in black and white,' I said, realising a purpose for him in this romantic city.

I parked near the Temple metro station. 'It's now one, can we meet back here at four?' I asked, which was agreed. We went our separate ways. Tom ran off, CD cover in one hand, Polaroid in the other. Rich was going to visit the Paris Diamond Way Buddhist Centre on the Rue Traversière. Doug began to walk solemnly towards the centre, as if he was going to do something that he didn't really want to. I quickly disappeared in the subterranean underworld of the Parisian metro.

Laila was waiting beside the Louvre-Rivoli metro. 'Looking good,' I said, as she brushed her cheek against mine.

'Thank you.'

She began to walk down the stairs leading to the subway immediately. 'Where are we going?' I asked.

'Come,' she beckoned. 'We don't have much time. I want to show you to my old house, and meet some family, it's not far.'

Within twenty minutes I was introduced to her father's brother, Cheb. Her aunt – also Laila – and her nephews and nieces: Cheb, Blaoui, Cheba and Nadine. Cheb was great. He'd visited London a few times, and – like his brother – loved it. 'Arsenal!' he kept saying. Thierry Henry and Dennis Bergkamp were his favourite players.

Football is a universal language, a great mediator. It has the ability to start a conversation, to break the ice.

'My friend Tom is a fanatical Arsenal supporter,' I said. 'And since visiting the Stade Vélodrome a few days ago, has also become a fan of Olympic Marseille,' I added.

'We are all supporters of Olympic Marseille,' he said.

He took me to another room. It was a little recording studio, with a mixing desk. He put on a track that was a mixture of Arab beats and Algerian singing. 'You like?'

'Very good,' I answered truthfully. It was. In fact, it was very good.

'This is me,' he said proudly. 'This is Rai music.'

'Never heard of it,' I said.

Laila opened the door. 'Food is ready.'

'We'll talk later,' he said.

Over dinner, Cheb's son asked what I was doing in France.

'Went to Italy for a few days. Thought we'd drive back through Paris.'

'Why Italy?' he persisted.

'Football. Milan v. Napoli, last night,' I replied, showing him the ticket.

'Was one–one,' said Blaoui, passing some chickpea cakes.

The next hour was mainly me and Cheb talking about football and music in his studio. He told me the history of Rai, and how it had evolved into a commercial business. As we were leaving, he gave me a CD.

'Thank you,' I said, shaking his hand. 'I'll keep this forever,' I added. It was true. Whenever I'm given something, it doesn't matter what it is, I'll always keep it.

'Last week Manor House, now Paris,' I said, as we walked to the metro.

'Life can be good,' came the reply. The relationship with Laila had evolved. Uncertainty had been replaced with belief, a belief that someone cared, not about who I used to be, but who I was now, and where I was going.

'Have you made any plans?' she asked, as we arrived.

'About the future?'

'Yes.'

'I want to go to university, it's always been a dream.'

'Which subject?'

'English architecture, especially castles and abbeys.'

She brushed her cheek against me. 'You can do it,' she said. 'It's getting late, you better go. Text me when you get home,' she said. She was to stay another day.

'Bye,' I said, as I walked slowly down the steps and into the subway.

Rich was waiting by the car. 'Been a few smash and grabs in the West End,' he informed me, referring to the news on his laptop. 'New Bond Street, Asprey and Garrard, and Louis Vuitton being the main ones. Seventy thousand grand worth of gear,' he added, with a whistle.

'Have the press given them a name yet?'

'The Gucci Boys.'

'Surprised it took so long. They'll enjoy that one. Make it worse.'

'Which is the point.'

'The Gucci Boys doing the Louis Vuitton store, couldn't make it up.'

'Think about it, Rich. If caught, they'll get five and serve two. Seventy grand each time. Do that five times, and it's three hundred and fifty grand. If there's three of them, that's nearly a hundred and twenty grand each.

Two years of your life for a hundred and twenty grand, that's sixty grand a year.'

'Not a bad salary,' he said.

Gucci Boys, Rolex Boys, you name them. Most hailed from Islington. Still going for the glamour, the glory and, of course, the cash. A raid on a Cartier shop could be lucrative. An hour's work could net you thousands. The estate gangs in the borough were different.

Doug looked a little better. 'Goodbye Paris,' he said, as we drove out of France's capital.

'I'm in the same place as Malcolm there,' he was saying, as he passed the Polaroids around.

Rich had the atlas on his lap again. 'How far to Calais?' I asked.

'Takes about three hours,' he replied.

'*Andiamo*,' I hollered, with Rai music in the background.

The drive to the French port was uneventful, as was the ferry journey itself. Arriving back on English soil was a little surreal. It had only been a few days, but somehow seemed a lot longer.

The capital was also a little strange at first. I dropped Doug at Aldgate. He seemed a little disoriented. It was his first time abroad, so it was understandable. 'Call you later,' I said. I gave him a hug. I had a feeling that his days of junk were coming to an end. He'd experienced a little of what life had to offer, and it seemed he wanted more.

At Finsbury Park, Rich took the Piccadilly line to Southgate. 'I'll print the photos tomorrow,' he promised, looking and behaving exactly the same as last week.

Tom had to go to Stoke Newington. He waved as he boarded the 106 bus. With the Head bag slung over the shoulder, the experience was evident.

It was nice to be home. But, like Doug – and probably Rich and Tom – I wanted to stay on the Continent a little longer. I texted Laila to say I was home, before unpacking.

I carefully placed the brochures and leaflets in one pile on the table, ready to give Laila. I lined the four paintings up. They still looked amazing. I sat back and looked more in detail. I noticed a slight representation of what had happened since I was arrested. Was my fate an analogy hidden in these thousand-year-old pieces of art? Was the outcome of the court already decided? *I have to get the fifth one from Rich*, I thought, *the one Doug gave me, all I can remember are the bright colours.* As I fell asleep, the oranges, reds, greens and blues were vivid.

Chapter Nineteen

Wednesday, 19 October 1999
London, England

I looked from the window. It was raining. The previous five days had almost vanished. France and Italy were forgotten. *Funny how travel can deceive you. In that moment in Marseilles, Nice, Turin and Paris, nothing else mattered. Same in St Tropez, the same in everything*, I thought, as I made a cup of tea. I felt connected with Doug, Tommy and Rich, which was priceless. I hoped there wasn't any deception there, who knew? They were there for me, and that was what mattered. I wouldn't forget that. I sent them all a text. '*Many thanks,*' it said.

'It's Wednesday, not Thursday,' said Alexios, as I entered his office.

'Just back from Oxford. Wanted to see if there's any news?'

He was looking solemn, as the question was ignored. 'This will be your last visit to this office. Twenty-five years. End of an era,' he lamented, as he walked towards the window looking out onto Lincoln's Inn fields. 'Moving everything over the weekend. Business as usual on Monday.'

The walls were bare. Stacks of boxes were the only furnishings. 'They say a change is as good as a rest,' I said in commiseration. 'That reminds me, when you travel to Italy, where do you go?'

'Naples, Portino, sometimes Rome.'

'Ever been to the north?'

'Never. Why?'

'One of the witnesses is an Italian lady. Have you checked her out?'

'Not yet,' he replied, in a passionless way.

'Alexios, the hearing is in less than a week.' He looked at me. 'Be honest, there's nothing you can do, is there?'

'Never will I look out onto that freshly mown lawn again,' he said, avoiding the question.

I sat there, looking at him. For once, Alexios Dimitrio looked immortal. For once, the mighty colossus, the master of the universe, was lost, facing humiliation. His old foe Smith-Cresswell would have one over on him. He would never live this one down, and he knew it. No loopholes were to be found on this one. He'd been stumped by the statements – they were watertight, he knew that, and so did I.

I got up and joined him by the window. 'You know when the robbery happened? I'd been to visit James a few hours earlier. Him – and Doug – they both knew what I was wearing. James has had his sentence reduced. Coincidence, don't you think?' I walked to the door, and had to be careful how I worded the next question. 'If it could be proven that Smith-Cresswell is involved in illegal activities, such as fraud, could you make a case?'

'If only,' he said, in a wishful way.

I got up to leave. 'Well, you never know what life can throw up,' I said, as I put my hand on his shoulder. 'I won't come tomorrow. I guess I'll see you on Monday.'

'I'm sorry Steve,' he uttered, without looking at me.

It was still raining as I left. Rich rang to say he'd printed the photos. 'Fifteen minutes,' I said, as I walked down Shaftesbury Avenue to the office.

'Zhang's probably under orders from Roberto,' I said.

Rich was busy organising an event. 'May have something on her,' he replied, as he gave me the photos. 'Give her a call, she'll accept any chance to find some information.'

'Time is now of the essence. Four more days,' I said, as I left him to it.

'Tomorrow, midday, the British Institute of Architects, Portland Place. Bring the chess,' I said, as I stopped outside the Wyndhams Theatre.

'No problem.'

'I'll be with a friend. Invite someone, we can play in pairs.'

'No problem,' Zhang repeated.

Before I went into the underground, I looked to see what was on at the Wyndhams. The play was *Loot* by Joe Orton.

'"What makes the desert beautiful," said the little prince, "is that somewhere it hides a well…"' – Antoine de Saint-Exupéry

Thursday, 20 October 1999

Doug and I spent a few minutes observing the Falun Gong demonstrators opposite the Chinese Embassy in Portland Place. We'd arrived early, so had a little time to spare. A practitioner approached us. He was from the Czech Republic. The persecution only started this year, he explained, before telling us a little about the teachings. Truthfulness, compassion and forbearance, being some of the principles that need to be practised along with meditation. 'To achieve a higher level of enlightenment,' he said.

'Why do these people always look so damn healthy?' I said, as I noticed Zhang. She was across the road with a friend, both obviously reluctant to come over. I waved, as we said goodbye and joined Zhang.

'Li, my friend Doug.'

'Steve, Doug, this is my friend Icy,' she replied.

Icy was looking at RIBA on the corner of Portland Place and Weymouth Place. 'Beautiful architecture,' she said.

'Opened in 1934, by King George V and Queen Mary,' said Doug. There was a carved figure above the doors. '*The Architectural Aspiration*, by Edward Bainbridge Copnall. Beautiful isn't it?' he continued, as we entered.

We went to the first-floor cafe. Doug and I ordered hot chocolate, Zhang and Icy opted for the same. The chess was fun. Zhang and myself – who won the game – against Doug against Icy. Before the pieces were put away, I took a picture. 'For prosperity,' I said.

The bookstore downstairs was an impressive array of design and architectural titles from around the world. Icy couldn't believe it, as she browsed through the unique selection. 'The bathrooms are the best,' Doug said, on his return. He should know, having frequented Park Lane and Knightsbridge five-star establishments.

The protesters were still there. Again, Zhang and Icy avoided them. Taking leaflets outside their embassy would be perceived as anti-government, and dangerous, I thought.

As we passed All Souls Church I looked at the steps. It was here that all the pioneering Radio One DJs had lined up to have an iconic picture taken. 1969 was the year. I thought of Tom. Did he know this location?

Both Doug and Zhang had to go home. Icy wanted to stay. 'I'm going to Photographers Gallery,' she said.

'In Leicester Square? Do you mind if I join you?' I asked.

Zhang seemed a little concerned, as Icy asked if I liked photography. 'Best you go home,' she said.

'Won't be long,' she replied, as we said our farewells. 'Speak later, Doug. Bye Li,' I said, as they both headed towards the Piccadilly northbound line. Icy and I took the exit leading onto the south side of Regent Street.

On the way down, I glimpsed over to the West End Central Police Station. Was it really two months ago? 'What do you do, Icy?' I asked, as I pointed out some Nash buildings lining the street.

'Wonderful,' she said. 'Coming to the end of my placement,' she added.

I saw Austin Reed, it was too much to refuse. 'Come,' I said, as we crossed the road. 'Where is your placement?' I asked, as we took the lift to the basement.

'The Victoria and Albert Museum,' she replied.

'Joe Orton came here,' I said, as I marvelled at the art deco ceiling in the barbershop. The original chrome settings were there, still intact. *Amazing*, I thought, as we returned to the ground floor.

'The V&A, nice. Austin Reed has been here since 1911,' I stated proudly, as we walked towards Piccadilly Circus. The Criterion Theatre looked the same. Orton's *Loot* was staged there, winning the *Evening Standard*'s play of the year award in 1966. 'Any particular section of the V&A?' I added.

'Ceramics and textiles.'

The Photographers Gallery on Great Newport Street was as unpopular – and brilliant – as ever. The exhibition was by a London-based German photographer. It was simple and uncomplicated. Icy was studying each piece intently. 'You really like photography,' I said.

'I take photographs.'

'Black and white, colour?'

'Always black and white,' she said, as I ordered a pot of peppermint tea. 'I go to a lot of galleries, you're more than welcome to join me,' I said, as we exchanged numbers. 'Nice and refreshing,' I added, regarding the hot tea.

'I love tea. When I drink tea, I am conscious of peace. The cool breath of heaven rises in my sleeves and blows my cares away,' she quoted poetically.

'What did you study here?'

'Ceramics. Chelsea School of Art.'

'And after your placement. Any plans?'

'Returning to China, next month.'

'Beijing?'

'Anyang.'

'Shanxi province?'

'Henan province.'

Same as Mei the artist, I thought. 'Is Li Xing from Anyang?'

'Taiyuan, Shanxi province,' she replied, continuing to savour the tea.

'The V&A had an exhibition at the Guildhall a couple of weeks ago,' I said.

She quickly drank her tea. 'I need to go, I'm late, was nice to meet you,' she said, as she left to go to Leicester Square station.

'Works at the V&A. Guess where?'

'Chinese art section?'

'The ceramics department. When I mentioned the show at the Guildhall, she got agitated, had to leave. Got her number, though.'

'See what happens when you keep going, Steve? Things happen that may appear strange and coincidental at first, then fall into place. Try and meet her tomorrow, she might have something.'

Laila called. 'Just got back. Can we meet tonight, start to sort the portfolio out?'

'Come here at seven,' I said. I looked at the brochures, photos and printouts collected thus far. They were spread out on the table. The four paintings were standing in the background. It did look impressive. *This will be enough I'm sure*, I thought, but at this stage, no chances were to be taken. I called Icy. An arrangement to meet tomorrow for a day out to Cliveden House was agreed.

'Ready for some history?' Laila asked.

'Most definitely,' I replied, sitting back on the couch.

'Okay, here we go… When Chairman Mao seized power in 1947, previous teachings – such as Taoism and Buddhism – were not considered Communist. Books, art and philosophy deemed as such were forbidden, and ordered to be destroyed.'

As she spoke I thought of Zhang and Icy yesterday, not wanting to be associated with the Falun Gong demonstration.

'Many works of art – books and paintings – were quickly moved from village to village, and, eventually, taken out of the country. Taiwan was the most popular destination, taken by the Chinese who had fled the mainland. Mei's artwork was always revered, and his set of the "Five Paths of Buddhism" paintings ended up in Taipei. Up to now, only three have been recorded, the second, third and the fourth.'

I took a deep breath. 'But the first had been on public display, and I've seen a copy of the fifth, so they do exist,' I said.

'Or do they?'

'Where are they recorded?'

'I haven't got that far.'

'We only have a few days, Laila,' I said. 'So they went to Taiwan?'

'Taiwan was then the opposite of China. It was progressive, pro-western and capitalist. Clever businesspeople. They would have seen them as a commodity – not as sentimental value – even then.'

Something dawned on me. 'You mean that they knew the value, and maybe didn't record all of them, knowing that the missing ones would have more value in the future?'

Laila reached to the table, picking up the third painting. 'This was bought two years ago by the chairman of Lexus.'

'The original?'

She shrugged her shoulders. 'Who knows? But it was sold on a year later to another company whom Lexus have shares with.'

'Another car company?'

She nodded her head. 'Not Fiat?' I said, to which she nodded her head again.

'What? But that's the Agnellis, rivals of the Savoys. Roberto is with the Savoys.'

'More history?'

'Of course,' I said, becoming intrigued, as well as fascinated.

'I found out why the paintings were commissioned. The Zhou dynasty – under their ruler King Wen – commissioned them. The Zhous had sought to bring about a new era after disposing of the preceding Shang dynasty. It's said that the most influential minds in the Chinese intellectual tradition then flourished under the Zhou, particularly towards the end period of the dynasty. It was a time of intellectual – and artistic – awakening. Laozi, Confucius, Mencius, Mozi and Mei lived during this period. Their ideas would begin to shape the character of Chinese civilisation. Wen commissioned Mei to exhibit this new era of writings and philosophy.'

'So the Shang and the Zhou were, basically, rivals?'

'Big time,' she replied. 'Still plays out today.'

'Like the Agnellis and the Savoys?' I said. 'There's an auction at Christie's on Sunday, will be interesting to see who – and what – shows up,' I added.

We drank some tea, whilst preparing the portfolio. It looked like a work of art in itself. 'Looking good,' I said. 'Can you find out which dynasties ruled the Henan and Shanxi provinces?' I asked, before forgetting.

I told her about Icy as I walked her to the station. 'I've always wanted to go to Cliveden,' she said. 'Heard the gardens are beautiful.'

I felt guilty. 'Listen, we can go another time, this is for business, not pleasure,' I said. 'I have membership for the ICA. Are you busy Sunday evening? Fancy chilling for a while? Last day before the court case,' I added.

'You promised me a football match.'

'I'll look at the fixtures,' I said.

She handed me a book. 'Tell me what you think.'

The 253 bus came. 'Bye Laila,' I said, as she got on and walked towards the back of the bus. I stood there as she sat down. I waved and then looked at the book. It was *The Little Prince* by Antoine de Saint-Exupéry.

Rich called later. 'The politician's name is Jerry Cribb. It's rumoured James was going to blackmail him, he also went to the same school as Charlie. Stowe, in Buckinghamshire,' he said.

'Then he's certain to know Roberto. Which then means he must know Smith-Cresswell, who – being in the higher echelons of the legal profession – will have contacts in the Crown. Hence the reduced sentence for James,' I said.

'You mean to shut him up?'

'Exactly.'

'Must have something big on him. He's also a member of the Sloane Club.' As Rich was speaking, I went to the window. The moon was full, bright and illuminated, as if trying to burn a hole into this dark October night with all its intensity.

'I'm confused, Rich,' I admitted, as I went and sat back down.

He laughed. 'One more thing. The School of Torino.'

'What's happened?'

'That robbery in Verona last week? Luigi's been arrested for it, was on the net. Said he was part of the gang. Seems the Ultras are moving from the hooligan stuff into organised crime.'

'Bit different here,' I said. 'Our infamous lot are moving into film, television and writing books.'

'Must mean Gianni's involved in those armed robberies in and around Turin.'

'Definitely.'

'So why aren't the authorities acting?'

'A couple of reasons. Firstly, the Italians do like a bit of drama. They don't want to catch them yet. They need to build a story. No excitement for it. They'll let them continue a while. The police and the media will make it dramatic, then – like a movie conclusion – take them out. And secondly, of course, there's his status.'

'Crazy stuff, Rich. Anyway, need to go to bed, meeting Icy tomorrow.'

'Cool, enjoy. I'm going to the temple.'

'Say hello to Master, and don't forget to ask him for the translation,' I said.

I sat back, feeling the need to read. I looked at *The Little Prince*, but first I had to finish *Mr Nice* by Howard Marks. I was nearly at the end. An hour later I closed the cover with the joy and satisfaction that only finishing a book can give you. It was eleven. I took a shower, then pressed a nice, clean pale blue shirt from Austin Reed for tomorrow. Some black corduroys were also set aside, ready to meet Icy in Marylebone tomorrow afternoon at three.

Friday, 21 October 1999

There was no arrangement, only impulse. 'Catch,' he shouted, lifting up the sash window then throwing the keys.

'Need another favour.'

'And?' Doug replied, preparing some tea.

'The gallery. Can you go there today? Check it out, see if the painting is on display?'

'Why not, nothing happening. Coming Tom?

'I'm up for it,' said Tom, as he helped Doug bring the tea.

'Love tea,' Doug said, as he raised his cup. 'A true warrior, like tea, shows his strength in hot water.'

'Impressive,' I said.

'When I drink tea, I am conscious of peace. The cool breath of heaven rises in my sleeves, and blows my cares away,' Tom added.

'Where did you hear that?' I asked

'Somewhere, can't remember.'

It was ten as we left the flat, and ventured onto the streets of Whitechapel. Even on a bleak Friday morning you could see that it was starting to smarten up a bit. There was still some of the old character to be admired though, as we walked to Liverpool Street station. 'Tracey Emin lives there,' Doug said pointing to a magnificent townhouse.

'She's alright,' said Tom.

'One of the better ones,' I added. *No more 'Cool Britannia' debates*, I thought, trying my best not to visualise the image of Blair, Albarn, Hirst and Gallagher at Downing Street.

Doug was on good form. 'The Huguenots built these. Came as religious refugees in 1700,' he said, as we passed rows of houses that – as expected – looked a little run down.

Liverpool Street was hustling and bustling and not giving a damn, regardless of time or day. 'Standard, Standard,' was the cry. The first of the four daily issues was ready. 'Can't imagine life without it,' Tom said, buying a copy for twenty pence.

'Part of the fabric that is London life,' Doug answered.

The idiosyncratic noise of the vendors, the bills with their garish headlines, the vans zigzagging through the streets. *Unimaginable*, I thought.

'Quick, the number 8,' Tom bellowed. We then gave chase towards the bus that was stuck at the traffic lights. The lights changed, and with the fumes spewing out thick smoke, we ran faster, and managed to jump on the back. The sun appeared as the bus started to weave into the city. Bank was next, its two exits still coping with the rush hour overflow. The City of London Magistrates' Court across the road had just opened. I retraced the walk from there to the station. I remembered the excitement, as I looked down onto the streets.

St Paul's needs no introduction, still magnificent and still deceiving to the eye. In the distance, the Old Bailey loomed. Lady Justice was still on top of the dome. In her left hand were the scales, used to measure a hearing's support and opposition. Depending on your take, the Old Bailey was either bright – justice and reward – or dark – conviction and fate. *We'll see which one of these awaits me on Monday*, I thought, as the bus continued regardless.

The Royal Courts of Justice were having a media frenzy. 'Probably a miscarriage of justice,' Doug said, cynically.

'Or some celebrity involved in libel,' was Tom's take on it.

We continued a little further, disembarking at Charing Cross. Trafalgar Square had seen the lot. Marches, demos, concerts you name it. For us, though, it was where football supporters used to congregate before – and after – the FA Cup Finals at Wembley. The strategically placed benches around the fountains were the resting place for many who had travelled from afar.

The London firms – including Chelsea, Millwall, Tottenham and West Ham – would come to pit their wits against whoever was in town. For some reason it was mostly Liverpool or Manchester United, and the cockney reds were always involved. Myself, Tom and Rich had regularly ventured here as young teenagers. 'Remember Liverpool against Manchester United, Tom?'

'Seventy-seven. Remember it very well,' he replied.

'"Wonderous Stories", Yes,' Doug said.

'"I Feel Love", Donna Summer,' added Tom.

'"Magic Fly", Space,' I said.

The touts were working the matinee performance at the Theatre Royal on the Haymarket. *The Phantom of the Opera* was the show. They recognised Tom with a nod of the head, as they continued to count the wads of cash. That – and *Mamma Mia* – were the money-spinners. They looked good in their Burberry macs and suntans, and some were leaning on their brollies, for emphasis of course. They illuminated this wide thoroughfare with their presence, as much a part of London life as anything, I thought, as Piccadilly Circus was waiting.

We parted outside Simpsons of Piccadilly. 'Look for any CCTV. If you can, take pictures of the staff,' I asked Doug.

'See you here at twelve,' he replied, as he continued towards Green Park.

'What a place,' I said, as we entered Simpsons.

'Portland stone,' Tom said, touching the wall. 'The home of Daks, opened in 1936. Three royal warrants, can't be bad,' he added.

'From the East End to the West End,' I said, as we ascended the marble staircase to the fifth-floor cafe.

On the way, I imagined how the finest tailors would assemble here, and the craftsmanship it had seen. The bespoke elite at work. 'Still in good hands, though,' I said, referring to the Waterstone's book chain who'd taken it over this year.

The Houses of Parliament and Westminster Abbey – usually in focus, and sharp – were becoming distant and faded. The brief tenure of sunshine was slowly giving way to increasing cloud.

Tom passed me a photo of the Rolling Stones. 'Green Park in 1967,' he said.

Brian looked so cool. A white fedora hat, brushed velvet jacket, with psychedelic trousers – he really did look the part.

After the short walk to Green Park, we tried to locate the exact spot where the photo was taken during a press conference. Tom stopped on a patch of grass that ran parallel to Piccadilly. 'Over there,' he said, walking towards a bench. 'That's exactly where they sat, thirty-two years ago Steve, can you believe it?'

I looked at the photo. He was right, behind the bench were the exact buildings. 'Well done,' I said.

'Right up there with the best,' he said, getting himself into the correct position for the picture.

'Which are?' I asked, after being handed the Polaroid.

'The Keskidee Centre in Gifford Street, King's Cross. Bob Marley filmed "Is This Love" there. The Rainbow in Finsbury Park. David Bowie was photographed in front of the backstage door. And the Marvin Gaye you saw. He was having an affair with the owner of the Embassy Club

– some aristocrat. Hey, it's around the corner, shall we go?'

'It's in Cork Street, where the gallery is, Tom.'

'Then what about Curzon Street? Look.' He showed me some newspaper cutting from *The Times*. Bing Crosby was walking down Curzon Street. It looked like the fifties. 'There's a cigar shop behind him, it'll be easy to find.'

'Tom, come on,' I said, feeling it was getting a little obsessive. 'We have to meet Doug,' I added.

We took a slow stroll back, stopping at 139 Piccadilly, Lord Byron's house. 'Could you imagine it then?' I said, looking at the beautiful Georgian townhouse property.

'St James for some oysters and champagne, and Piccadilly if you fancied some Landau. What a life.'

'We'd be dead,' I stated, putting the fantasy into some logical context. 'There's Doug,' I said, as he was walking on the other side of the road.

'Didn't see the painting there,' he said, adding that he was hungry.

Quaglino's is an established eatery in Bury Street, just off St James. Having recently been refurbished, Doug wanted to see whether it was an improvement or not. 'Nice place,' Tom commented, as we walked down a spiral staircase that led to the main dining area.

This meant that fellow diners had sight of who was coming and going. Inevitably, Doug led the way, enjoying and savouring the moment. 'To think this was once the preserve of both the monarchy and stars of Hollywood's golden era,' he said, looking around, as we were waiting to be seated.

'Bankers, accountants and tourists now, I'm afraid,' said Tom, with a hint of reality.

'Who was the royalty anyway?' I asked, looking at the table arrangement, trying to figure out who would sit where back in the day.

'Queen Elizabeth, the Mountbattens, you name it. Apparently a table was permanently reserved for the regular visits by Princess Margaret, the Duke and Duchess of Kent, and Princess Alexandra.'

'Wasn't Leslie Arthur Julien Hutchinson supposed to have had an affair with one of the Mountbattens?' asked Tom.

'Now, that I couldn't tell you,' replied Doug, as always maintaining loyalty to the ruling classes.

'Well he did,' continued Tom, doing his best to labour the point.

'Who was he, anyway?' I asked, naively.

'Know as "Hutch", an American singer. Was invited to come and live in London by Edwina Mountbatten who took pity on his situation in New York. Decided to stay here, living in Belsize Park for nearly forty years.'

'Man, can you imagine what this place was like then? Aristocrats, with cool jazz dudes from the States,' said Tom, before going to wash his hands.

We were taken to a table. 'Died penniless, though,' said Doug, placing some perspective around dear old 'Hutch'.

'When was this, Doug?' I asked.

'1930s,' he replied, as Tom returned, his hands still wet.

'Why don't you dry them?' Doug asked, as I followed suit. When I returned we were shown to a table. The conversation had evolved to the clubs, bars and restaurants in and around St James's and Piccadilly during the thirties and forties.

'The Regent Palace Hotel,' said Tom, as he sat down.

'Cafe de Paris, Cole Porter was a regular, still has the best interiors,' said Doug.

'The Criterion. Setting for the original stage production of *Loot* by Joe Orton, sixty-seven. Sherlock Holmes even mentions it,' I added.

'One of them Brit mob lot has bought that,' said Tom.

'Marco Pierre White. He'll sell it on once he makes a profit,' I said.

'Why do they keep taking historical themes, then marketing them to us?'

'Destroying the character of this city in the process,' lamented Doug.

'Can't the council – or local authorities – serve some sort of banning order on these people?' Tom continued.

'They're doing it to everything,' I said. 'In music they're rehashing the Stones, The Beatles and The Who.'

The subject changed, as Doug filled us in on the gallery. He showed us some photos. 'Said I was a teacher from Turin, fascinated by English art galleries.'

'Nice photography,' I said.

'I requested a picture with the staff, to show my pupils back home. A reminder of my trip to London, I said, they couldn't help themselves.'

Doug posed individually with the two members of staff. Neither matched the description of the witness who was supposed to have worked there.

The pictures were taken from afar, so you could see the exhibited pieces of work in the background. One looked familiar, but I couldn't quite figure out from where, maybe in France or Italy. Then I remembered: it was Zhang's painting at Roberto's house, the unfinished one.

'Was the painting I'm supposed to have stolen there?'
'Definitely not, I looked at everything.'
'Strange, considering it's been found and returned.'
'Maybe they don't want it taken again,' said Tom.
'Maybe,' I agreed, giving the benefit of the doubt.

It was one-thirty, and I had to meet Icy. After Doug insisted on settling the bill, we made our way back up the stairs. I noticed a framed black and white photo hanging on the wall. 'Wait,' I said, as I took a closer look.

Anna May Wong was an actress from the thirties, like Hutch. I'd never heard of her, but man, she was stunning. *James would love this*, I thought. 'When are you visiting James next?' I asked Doug.

'Funnily enough, Sunday,' he replied.

'Tell him I said hello,' I said, as we walked out the door. The sun had made a return and was glowing. Doug had to get back to Aldgate. Tom was heading home in the same direction, so we said our farewells at Piccadilly Circus.

I had an hour and half to spare. The sun felt nice, so I headed to Regent's Park, and sat in the rose garden for a while. The roses were still intact and colourful. It was two o'clock when I decided to visit the Regent's Park open air theatre.

An Ethiopian wedding was taking place. *Good choice of location*, I thought. The colours of their country were significant. Not only resplendent, but also matching the wonder of the park perfectly. Red was for the roses that were still in flower. Gold was for the tips of the wrought-iron gates and railings, highlighted by the glorious October sun. And the green could so easily represent the lush, freshly mowed lawn.

I envied them. They seemed happy. They understood themselves. There was no class barrier, they all spoke the same language, and used the same words. They appeared unaffected by the dysfunction that our media-led society so wanted and desired, a culture that I grew up in.

Myself, Doug, James, Rich and Tom grew up in this seventies and eighties environment. Our lives were shaped mainly by television and radio. Film – and books – were a little different, you had to make an effort with them, but television and music were cheap, made to attract advertising. They dictated our lives, influencing the way we lived. These people were happy, I thought, as I received a text. '*Apologies, will be half an hour late*,' it said. I decided to make a fleeting visit to the V&A. *Time is of the essence*, I thought, as I ran to Regent's Park station.

With the silvery water of the Serpentine as the background, I walked briskly towards Kensington from Hyde Park Corner. There was an exhibition at the Serpentine Gallery. Jean-Michel Basquiat was the artist. I'd heard of him, a Warhol, New York type dude. *Definitely worth a visit*, I thought, as I ventured towards the former tea pavilion.

The works were brilliant. One that caught my eye was painted in eighty-two, titled *Untitled*. *How much will it be worth in twenty years' time?* I thought. I noticed some security as I left. *What is it with art*, I wondered.

The Albert Memorial was magnificent, the gold gilt splendid on the eye, and – as with the gates at Regent's Park – it had been constructed with thought, with the future, and light, in mind, illuminating the memorial.

The V&A was busy, as expected. I made my way quickly to the ceramics section on the first floor as fluently – and discreetly – as possible. In no uncertain terms, this was a treasure trove, an Aladdin's cave of various porcelain and artefacts.

There were different sections for different countries. The largest was shared between England and China. Interestingly, both were beautifully and meticulously hand-painted, and similar in style. *So many*, I thought. I suddenly became cynical. *How many are genuine?* I began to wonder about the administrative side. *How do they keep track? How are recorded and logged? More importantly though, by whom?* I needed to find out not only what Icy's real name was, but also the name of the curator.

Though photography was prohibited, I managed to take a few discreet shots before leaving, this time running to South Kensington station.

'Besides photography, any other interests?' I asked.

'Anything to do with the sixties, especially The Beatles,' Icy replied, as we walked down Baker Street.

'The Apple boutique was near here.'

'The Apple boutique? Can we see?'

We stood on the corner of Paddington Street and Baker Street, observing the building on the corner where the boutique once stood. '1967. Only lasted a year,' I said, as I was picturing which direction George, John, Paul and Ringo would have come from, and what they were doing in the store.

'Are you okay?' she asked.

'I'm fine,' I said. 'Do you like Jimi Hendrix?' I added.

'I think I know where we are now,' she said, as we approached Montague Square.

We stopped at number 34. 'John Lennon lived here with Yoko. Sixty-eight.'

'Take photo please,' she said, passing me a new 35mm SLR Nikon, before standing in front of the stunning Georgian house.

I took a few shots. 'You have a good eye,' she said.

'The initial occupant was Ringo, then John and Yoko stayed here a while, before Hendrix moved in. Jimi once walked up and down these steps,' I said. *And this street*, I thought.

'You okay?'

'Yes, I'm fine. Let's go. Have you heard of Christine Keeler?' I asked, continuing the sixties theme.

'Who was she?'

We took a left into Wimpole Mews. 'Nearly brought down the British Government,' I said.

'When?'

'1961. Was working in Murray's – a club on Regent Street – when she met a well-connected osteopath, who introduced her to a high-ranking government minister. They started an affair.'

She seemed unimpressed. 'Problem was, she was also having an affair with a Russian spy at the same time,' I said. This time she seemed even more confused. 'Anyway, she lived here,' I added, pointing to 17 Wimpole Mews. I didn't bother with the exciting bit, that another man she was seeing came around and fired some shots at the flat in a jealous rage.

'Would this happen in China? I mean, government ministers having affairs?' I asked.

As with the Falun Gong protesters, there was no commitment, not even an answer.

'The politician resigned, the government lost the next election, the man who owned this house committed suicide, and Christine Keeler went to jail,' I added.

'Quite a story.'

'Like Orton, Keeler was just another working-class kid seduced and destroyed by the political and media elite,' I concluded.

'Huh?'

'Nothing. Tea?'

This time there was an answer. 'Yes please,' she replied.

The fittings in the Marylebone cafe were from the sixties. The upholstery, though, had seen better days, but – akin to Alpinos in Chapel Market, Alfredo's at the Angel, and the Piccadilly Cafe in Piccadilly Circus – it felt comfortable and reassuring. *Marylebone Lane wouldn't be the same without it*, I thought, as I ordered omelette and chips. Icy decided on some toast.

'Where do you know Li from?' I asked, as we sat down with the tea.

'We've known each other a long time,' she replied, not elaborating.

'From China?'

'Went to the same college in China.' She looked away, as if she wanted to tell me something but couldn't.

'You're Zhou?' I asked.

'Shang,' came the reply. 'I have to go soon.'

We ate in relative silence, until it was time to leave. 'You said you liked The Beatles?' I asked.

'So much,' came the reply, with a little more enthusiasm.

'Come,' I said, as we walked to nearby Manchester Square.

We went to the north-west corner of the Georgian square. 'The cover for *Please, Please Me*, the first Beatles LP, was taken here, 1963. The stairwell would have been there,' I said, pointing to where was the exact location would have been.

'It looks different.'

'The original EMI house was demolished five years ago,' I said, again thinking of Westminster's stupidity.

'Can I take picture of you?' she asked.

'Of course, where?'

'Here. Can you look sideways?' she asked, as I took up a stance.

'I need one over there,' I said, walking to a corner of the square. I leant on the railings as David Bowie did in 1965. Only the Manchester Square sign was missing. I mean, there was one, but not the original. *Probably worth a fortune now*, I thought.

'Can you look sideways, with a vacant look?' she asked.

I gazed into the park itself. Diana Ross and the Supremes did a photoshoot there in sixty-four. Again, I thought of James.

As we walked back towards Baker Street, she showed me the images. I looked like Tom in his recent shots, we were both looking sideways, with a distant expression.

'Write your name and email. I have something about John and Yoko to send you,' I said, as we parted inside the station.

I ran home, not even bothering to go inside. Instead I got straight into the car, heading to Stoke Newington.

'Why didn't you tell me?'

'It's a complete coincidence, man, believe me. Didn't know she knew Zhang, remember, I only met her three times,' Tom replied.

'She was the librarian from the dating site?'

'I know, unbelievable,' he said.

'You need to talk to me, Tom. Is she playing a part for Roberto, getting hold of ceramics?'

'I don't know, man.' He got up and went to the kitchen.

I followed. 'Tom, you need to tell me now.'

He went back to the lounge, and showed me an email Gianni had sent him. There was a scanned copy of a new pamphlet of items for sale at the auction house in Turin.

I recognised some of the ceramics from the earlier visit to the V&A. 'She must be,' I said. 'Send a copy to my email,' I added.

Gianni also mentioned that he was planning a visit 'very soon'.

'Where shall we take him first, Arsenal?' Tom said.

'Tottenham,' I replied.

'He'd love the Clock End, Highbury.'

'Not as much as The Shelf.'

'What about The Shed, said he liked Chelsea.'

'That was Luigi. Gianni said Millwall.'

'Then it's The Den, Cold Blow Lane.'

'Or the Chicken Run, West Ham.'

'The Cottage at Fulham.'

'With that view over the Thames, cool.'

'Brentford? Only football ground in England and Wales to have a pub on every corner.'

'Still think The Shelf though, White Hart Lane is the best.'

'Archibald Leitch design.'

'Same as Goodison Park.'

'Also designed Fratton Park, Villa Park and Ibrox.'

'And Roker Park.'

I remembered what Gianni had said about World Cup Italia '90. How the character of the old Italian stadiums had been destroyed for the competition. 'Can't see it happening here,' I said.

Even though the European Championships were staged here three years ago, there wasn't that much development. So far we were fortunate to escape the development. 'What would we do without these iconic landmarks Tom?' I added.

'Doesn't bear thinking about,' he sighed.

'Becoming very continental now, though,' I said.

'Less American, can't blame them anymore.'

'How do you think they'll getting them out of there?' I asked, as I sat down.

'The museum? Must have someone inside.'

'Someone in admin?'

'Definitely, with someone else at the top overseeing it.'

'Thanks Tom,' I said, as I opened the front door. It had started to rain again.

On the way home I listened to Unknown FM. The techno beats fired me up. *I have to meet Icy one more time*, I thought as I raced up the Kingsland Road.

'Icy. Hi, it's Steve.'

'Hi.'

'I'm going to an English stately home on Sunday, was wondering if you'd like to join me?'

'Where?'

'A place called Cliveden House. The lady whose house we went to earlier, that's where she met the government official in the sixties. It's a beautiful location, by the River Thames. Just for a few hours. I want to see the swimming pool. It's only twenty-six miles from London.'

The power and the obsession of the sixties was a little too much, as she agreed. 'Can we go in the morning?'

'Of course, just stay for some lunch and come back,' I said.

What a day, I thought, as I finally got to rest. Little did I know what the weekend had in store for me.

Chapter Twenty

Saturday, 23 October 1999

'James, how's it going man?' I said, as we embraced.
'Am okay dude.'
'Looking good.'
'Thanks man, you too.'
'Arsenal are doing well.'
'Yeah, not too bad.'
'Bergkamp's still turning it on.'
'And Wrighty.'
'That new signing from Juventus is starting to look good.'
'Thierry Henry? Early days though, let's see how he gets on.'

We talked a while – music and football being the main topics – as an officer approached the table. 'Five minutes left,' he said. I took this as a cue to change the conversation.

'I'll go and get the last coffees,' Doug said, tactfully.
'James—' I looked at him across the table '—what's going on?' He looked away. 'You have to tell me, you have to tell me why you're playing along with this. For what reason?' I came to visit you that day. You – and Doug – were the only ones who knew what I was wearing.'

'I was approached to have my sentence reduced for a favour, that's all. I've had enough, Steve, I need a new life. Doug told me about your visit to France and Italy, and all the good people out there. I want that now, not this.' He looked around.

'How is Jerry Cribb?'

'I was going to the papers to name him. He's also involved with some London gangsters, didn't fancy the publicity, so he paid me some money to keep quiet. He also offered to get my sentence reduced if I helped his friend.'

'Charlie?'

'Yeah, and some Italian.'

'Roberto?'

'That's him.'

'To set Tom up?'

'I've had enough, Steve.' He broke down. 'Really, I can't do this anymore.'

I thought of Alexios. 'Did he mention a Peter Smith-Cresswell?'

'Heard the name mentioned a few times.'

That was what I wanted to hear. 'I'm going to tell Alexios. Hopefully he'll come and see you tomorrow. Write down everything you've told me today, and tell him.'

Doug returned with the coffees, and we spoke casually for the remaining few minutes before the officer returned. 'Time's up,' he said.

'Miss you, brother,' I said, as we stood up together.

'Me too,' he added, as we embraced before leaving the room.

The rain was pounding as we left Pentonville, and despite the downpour we walked down the Caledonian Road until King's Cross. 'Thanks for the invite,' I said.

'Had to do it,' he said. 'For you, for James, and for myself.'

I sighed, feeling he needed to tell me something.

'I feel like James,' he said. 'Feels like I'm in a prison, need to stop doing this. I need a life. France and Italy opened my eyes. I'm ready to come off this stuff,' he added in a steely, determined way.

'I understand, and you can,' I said. We looked at each other. 'You can do it,' I added.

'Thanks, man.'

'No problem,' I said, as I watched him walk towards the eastbound Metropolitan line. In some bizarre way, I felt a sense of relief on the way home.

'Ready for some more history?' Laila asked, over the telephone.

'Of course,' I replied.

'The Shang dynasty ruled for twenty-nine years in the eleventh century, before being overthrown by the Zhou dynasty. Jiang Ziya was leader of the Zhou.'

'Zhang is a Zhou,' I said.

'The coincidence doesn't stop there. What's Zhang's other name?'

A photo I took of her work was on the table. 'No,' I said.

'Ziya? I traced the linage. She's a direct descendent of Jiang Ziya.'

'Di Xin was the last king of the Shang dynasty.'

'Icy is a Shang.'

'Exactly. Do you know her other name?'

'I'll find out tomorrow. So one is Shang, the other Zhou. You think something's going on between these two? Some sort of historical feud?'

'Definitely.'

'Like the Agnellis and Savoys,' I said. 'I'll get some information from her tomorrow, Alexios needs a good, solid, watertight portfolio for Monday.'

'Remember you promised to go to the ICA tomorrow.'

I went to the window. The post-autumn flocks of swallows were out, darting to and fro against the deep, dark, blue grey October sky. 'We will, promise,' I said. After saying goodbye, I sat down and started to read *The Little Prince* when the phone rang.

'Come to Doug's,' said Tom.

'It's late. Have to get up early tomorrow. Got an appointment.'

'You'll be surprised who's here,' he said, very quietly.

'On my way,' I said, as the adrenaline started to pump. The anticipation of who was at Doug's house was too much.

In the car I had no choice except to play *Messages* by Orchestral Manoeuvres in the Dark.

'The lady from the party,' I said, as she frowned.

'*Tu sei la signora della festa*,' Tom said, translating.

'Hi,' I said, looking at Tom, a little confused.

'She's known a while,' he replied.

Before I could ask why, Doug came and joined us. 'Sophia is escorting me to the auction tomorrow,' he stated rather proudly, with a smile.

I nodded in approval. They did look good together. A couple no one would dare question.

'How's Gianni?'

'*Bene*, he's good,' she replied, understanding the question.

'He'll be making bids from the telephone. As an anonymous buyer,' said Doug.

'Doug and Sophia will bid on an item Roberto is selling. Gianni will also bid, as an overseas buyer,' added Tom.

'We'll let him win,' said Doug. 'Then we'll give you the piece to take to the Arts and Antiques squad. If they can't authenticate it, and find it's counterfeit, game over,' he added.

'*Questa volta a lunedì festeggerete*,' Tom stated, to which Sophia smiled. 'I said that this time on Monday, you'll be celebrating.'

'Hope so,' I said. 'Anyway, it's getting late, have to go.' I said goodbye, and drove back home to go to bed. As I closed the curtains, I noticed the rain had stopped. *Hope it stays this way*, I thought, looking forward to tomorrow.

Sunday, 24 October 1999

Walking Wounded by Everything but the Girl – purchased from the Nags Head market a few weeks ago – did the trick as I showered. 'Back in London '92, I think I've changed a lot since then, do you,' sounded sad. *Damn this nostalgia!* I exclaimed.

The neatly folded white The Who T-shirt placed on the bed did look the part. It was folded in the same style as taught in borstal twenty years previously. The faded blue Evisu jeans followed. The trainers I'd bought in Turin – for all those lira – completed the set.

I arranged to pick Icy up from her house in Earls Court. The drive was barely disrupted, considering it was Sunday. The sun was barely visible, and the roof lowered. 'Who Are You' by The Who was cranked as I sliced through the Marylebone Road.

'On the Earls Court Road,' I said, as I turned from the Cromwell Road. 'What's the address?'

'Twenty-five Barnham Gardens.'

After I looked at the A–Z, I drove down a side road consisting mainly of bed and breakfasts, and saw her waving from under the canopy of a neat Stucco-style house. I pulled up and stretched over to open the passenger door. 'Ready?' I asked, wondering whether the Shangs were as battled-hardened as the Zhous.

'What so special about Cliveden?' she asked, as she got in.

'Christine Keeler met John Profumo there when swimming naked in an outdoor pool one evening. Was a sensationalist story at the time. Apart from that, it has lovely gardens, and I want to see the pool,' I said.

In fact, I couldn't wait to see the pool, and the infamous cottage that Stephen Ward stayed in.

The drive down the A40 was pretty uneventful. The saving grace was that it didn't rain, and conversation was – as you'd expect – kept to a minimum. After fifty minutes we were driving down a long gravel driveway to a car park. As I turned the engine off, I suggested some tea. As we reached The Orangery I searched my pockets. 'Left something in the car,' I said.

Once Icy was out of sight, I called Doug. 'Twenty five Barnham Gardens.'

'No worries, what time you back?'

'About four.'

'Cool, come after.'

'Thanks Doug,' I said, as I walked back to the glass, observatory-type cafe, where Icy was waiting.

On the way I saw something familiar. The goose bumps were in place, as I walked to one of a few small wooden doors running along the side of a wall. One by one they were all locked. I looked through a gap, catching a glimpse of some water. This was the pool, I thought, as I made my way through the house to get there. It was not as big as I'd imagined, but there it was, right in front of me. The water was motionless and still, as if caught on freeze frame, not wanting to be disturbed, or evolved, as if silent in protest until the truth was told.

I walked to the edge, standing, staring. After kneeling at the side, I imagined the girl from the home counties creating a gentle butterfly stroke in the shimmering moonlight. Where did Profumo appear from? From which gate? Which way was Christine swimming? I circled the pool, trying to picture which door Profumo would've have come from, and how many people would have been there. So many unanswered questions. The statues were still there, surrounding the pool. They looked tired, worn and weary after succumbing to the elements. If only they could talk. They were present that night, I was jealous. Time didn't stop, though, not for anyone. Not for Christine, not for myself, and not for Icy.

'You okay?' Icy asked, her words disorientating me. The feeling had abated.

'Fine,' I answered. 'John Lennon stood here,' I said, referencing a photograph of him wearing a life-saving jacket with *Cliveden* written on it.

'Really, where?'

I took out a copy. 'Next to one of these doors. Don't know which one though, they all look the same.'

We slowly walked back to The Orangery and took tea. 'The government lost the next election, 1964. The Beatles had just started,' I said, as we both sipped our Earl Grey tea.

The cottage was secluded, and a bit of a walk from the house. Again the doors were locked. Looking through the windows, trying to visualise the cooking, the drinking and the laughter, was as good as it got. Again, it all seemed so small, I was expecting something larger than life. The walk back was a little tiresome. We stood on the rear balcony of the house, looking onto the beautiful Italian-themed garden.

'Look,' she said.

'What?' I asked, to which she pointed towards the sky.

'An eagle.'

'Well, a kestrel really,' I said. It didn't matter though, watching it soar over the Buckinghamshire countryside was good enough.

'Beautiful.'

'Very,' I agreed, aware that I was still in the fourth painting.

'What happened to Christine Keeler?' she asked, as we walked back to the car.

'Got arrested, went to the Old Bailey and was imprisoned,' I replied. I looked at her above the roof. 'Quite an ordeal for a young lady,' I added.

I showed her a picture. 'Wow, so pretty,' she said.

I held it in front of me. 'Wonder what she looks like now,' I said. I settled into the driving seat.

'Going to the Old Bailey, then being sent to prison, must be an ordeal for anyone,' she said.

'Some people were trying to ruin her life. Do you understand what I mean?'

'Yes, yes I do,' she answered.

As though moving my Warrior out, the first move has been made, I thought, as we drove to Maidenhead. As I parked by the River Thames, it started to rain. 'Going to miss London?'

'Of course.'

The rain hitting the rooftop became louder. 'When you going back?'

'Wednesday.'

'The twenty-seventh. So you'll be around tomorrow?'

'What is happening tomorrow?'

'A big event, I've been told,' I replied, as I started the engine and headed down the Bath Road, towards London.

'Have you been to university?'

'Just applied. Will know in the next couple of weeks if I'm accepted.'

'To study?'

'English history, the monarchy. I like castles. Have you ever been to a castle?'

'Leeds Castle, in Kent.'

'What did you think?'

'Beautiful.'

'They have an ambience. A presence that words can't explain. Probably similar to temples.'

'Have you been to a temple?'

'Yes. I'd like to go to the Temple of Heaven in Beijing. *Tian*, heaven, *Di*, earth,' I said, pointing upwards then downwards.' Time for another move. 'How do you know Li?'

'Through my manager.'

'Your manager at the V&A?'

There was no reply. I didn't expect one. The drive from Maidenhead to London was short and scenic. I opted for the slower B roads. The rain became heavier as we listened to Miles Davis. The silence suited me.

Earls Court – and its environs – has never really appealed to me, I guess some places are like that.

'Good memory,' she remarked, as I aligned the car with her house.

'Pride myself on it,' I replied.

'Thank you for today,' she said, as she opened the door.

'Can I use your bathroom?' I asked.

'Of course. Down there, on the left.'

I walked down the beige carpeted hallway. It had the feeling of a shared house. Not much of an ambience, well furnished, but empty.

'Well, was nice to meet you, and I hope everything works out for you back home,' I said, as I went to say goodbye.

There was a large framed black and white photo on her wall. John Lennon was holding Yoko. Both were looking each other in the eyes. 'Nice,' I remarked.

'My favourite. Real love,' she replied, as she walked me to the door.

'Don't forget your mail,' I said, as I picked up some letters from the floor.

'Strange, we always place them on the table,' she said.

I didn't know what to say. 'See you, then,' I said, as I walked to the car.

'See you,' she replied.

I got in the car, started the engine, and pulled away. I looked over, but she'd already gone in.

Doug passed me a spliff. 'No thanks,' I said, declining the offer.

'Did you find anything?'

'This.' He showed me a picture on his phone. One of her flatmates was leaving the house. 'Remember the picture I had taken with the staff at the gallery? Look, the same woman.'

I compared them. It was the same person. He also took photos of some mail that was in the house.

Lin Ziya. 'Sounds familiar. Thanks Doug,' I said.

'Come and say hello to Mo and the boys.'

'Have to meet Laila at ten. I promised her.'

'Plenty of time.'

'A quick one,' I agreed.

Mo and his firm were barely visible through the cloud of smoke. The weed was tempting, smelling sweeter and sweeter. I even played some pool, potting a few reds and colours. 'Still got it,' Doug commented.

It was six-thirty. 'Thanks guys,' I said, as I finally made my way to the faded exit sign.

'Catch you later,' Doug said, before racing back to the sanctuary of the pool hall. I decided on a slight detour and headed towards The Minories and Shad Thames Street, where a subtle press on the accelerator was definitely needed. The elixir of life had captured me again. Nowhere in the world could offer me this. I felt illuminated. New York? Paris? Rome? Not a chance. This was a city unlike any other, I thought, as I raced up the Kingsland Road towards Finsbury Park.

So far, it had been a day rich in colour. English beauty, Chinese wonder and Bengali class. All interwoven into the tapestry that is contemporary London, 1999. I was thirsty – and ready – for some more.

The quick shower was cooling. The decision was absolute. Vivienne Westwood shirt and Edwin jeans were the chosen items. It was seven-thirty as I jumped back into the car, this time the Upper Clapton Road was the destination.

She looked exactly like Laila, except the hair was tinted blond.

'My mother, Jasmine.'

'Pleased to meet you,' I said.

'You too. I'll make some tea and bring some cakes,' she said, disappearing into another room. We sat down. On the wall was a photo of a handsome man smiling. He was standing next to a palm tree in front of a house, the sea was behind.

'Your father?'

'Our house in Algiers, late fifties.'

Her mother brought some tea and cake, before going to her room to read.

'Icy's flatmate,' I said, showing the photos Doug gave me. 'Her name. Lin Ziya.'

She took a deep breath. 'The manager of the ceramics department at the V&A is Lin Ziya. I went on the website.'

'I wonder if Alexios is awake,' I said, as I called him. He was. After a few minutes of talking to him, I looked at Laila. 'One of the witnesses is Lin Ziya, and he also went to see James today. He's working on the transcript now. I knew the mention of Peter Smith-Cresswell would re-energise him,' I added.

'I think you have enough now,' she said, relieved.

'The others want revenge,' I said, abruptly. 'She obviously got Icy a placement.'

'More history?'

I laughed. 'Of course.'

'Archaeologists in the north of China found a significant amount of treasure buried in the Wei Valley a few years ago. The hoard was said to be from around 256 BC.'

'The time the Zhou were expelled,' I said.

'Exactly. Seems like the Shangs took the Zhous' treasure and hid it so later generations could claim the pieces and place them in a museums in China, where they could be shipped overseas to be exhibited and sold. By loaning them to establishments such as the Victoria and Albert Museum, and to exhibitions such as the Guildhall, they could be used to make counterfeits, which are then sold at auction houses and galleries.'

'But they'd need someone prominent to do this,' I said.

'Oh, one more thing. Lin Ziya is also a director at the Palace Museum in the Forbidden City, Beijing.'

'I'd bet anything that the fifth painting is housed in Beijing,' I said.

Laila had created a portfolio to hand over to Alexios in the morning. It looked good and professional. Though similar in look to Charlie's, it had different a meaning and reason. Almost a work of art in itself, detailed and creative. 'You have an amazing daughter,' I said to Jasmine, as we were leaving.

'Thank you,' she replied.

I parked on Pall Mall, and walked to the ICA. The big boys of the hospitality and establishment game were on show. The Royal Automobile Club. The Athenaeum. The Travellers. They were all there. This gave an extra air of unconformity and edge to the ICA. *This place is ultra-cool at the moment.*

The main room was all white, with some sparse pastel colours here and there. Aided by a Brazilian DJ, an eclectic mix of Japanese, Brazilian and Italian beats played in the background. It was a delight to sit and relax with Laila, and served as a suitable environment to tell her about the rest of the trip. Her favourite being the drive through the Pied region with Gianni. We stayed until eleven.

'Never been there before,' she said, as we stepped out onto The Mall.

'Moved here from Dover Street, Piccadilly, in sixty-eight.'

'Isn't that next to Cork Street?'

'It is. Everything seems to be connected or connecting,' I said, as we began to ascend the steps leading to the Duke of York column.

I drove to Hackney as slowly as I possibly could. 'Coming tomorrow?' I asked, as we approached her house.

'Of course.'

'You don't have to, Laila.'

'When is the auction?'

'Tonight,' I said. 'Thanks for the portfolio,' I added, as I played the tape her uncle had given me on the way home.

'Got beat on a few items,' said Doug, as he relayed the evening's events at Christie's. 'Some Chinese woman, bidding by telephone, couldn't match her. All the pieces from Nice and Torino were there, though, and they all sold.'

'Don't worry,' I said. 'The evidence looks good anyway.'

I finished *The Little Prince* then went to bed, thinking – obviously – about tomorrow.

Chapter Twenty-One

Monday, 25 October 1999

As expected, sleep was difficult, and there wasn't much of it. I was already awake when the phone rang. 'Hello?'

'Stephen?'

'Speaking.'

'It's Icy. Sorry it's early, but I need to see you.'

'I have a very important appointment at ten.'

'I know. At the Old Bailey.'

'Did you know yesterday?'

'I need to see you as soon as possible. It's very important, it will help you.'

Eight-thirty at Farringdon station was agreed. The next two hours felt a little surreal as I ate, showered, made a cup of tea, and played Marvin Gaye's *What's Going On*. It had a kinda death row feel to it, slow and laboured. The rain was consistent throughout. A dark blue Hugo Boss denim shirt with black corduroys was the chosen attire, topped off with highly polished black shoes.

I placed the portfolio in a bag, chose an umbrella, and walked to the station. I got to Farringdon just before eight-thirty and Icy was waiting. We found a cafe in nearby Smithfield to have an early morning coffee.

'Here, take this,' she said, as soon as we sat down.

They were two brown paper bags. 'What are they?'

'Open and see.'

I began to remove the packaging. I caught a glimpse of the Maitreya Buddha. He was still smiling. The second was obvious because of its bright colours. I couldn't look, my destiny had to wait a few hours. 'So it was you doing the bidding last night?'

'With help from a friend in Beijing.'

'Are these the real ones?'

'Don't know. Will you find out?'

'But you're leaving Wednesday.'

'It doesn't matter when, just find out. Please?'

'I will,' I promised. 'Why are you helping me? You are putting your life in danger.'

'We're helping each other. You can be set free, and we want our cultural relics back. They were stolen from us. We want them returned, it's our history.'

'So you and your friend bid, won, and you collected them?'

'Last night,' she replied.

'Do you know about Zhang, and your flatmate?'

'She's my manager at the V&A. Yes, of course. She's telling me what to loan for exhibitions and overseeing the invoices. Basically, apart from me and her, nobody at the museum knows what's going on. Take these as well.' She gave me five pieces of paper. They were receipts of transactions from the Palace Museum in Beijing to the V&A, and from the V&A to various galleries and museums including Nice and Turin. 'I also know the storage place they are using.'

I borrowed a pen from the counter. 'Where?'

'At the gallery.'

'Cork Street?'

'Yes. There's some storage out the back.'

It was still raining as we left the cafe. 'You can walk with me to St Paul's, take the central line to Holborn and change to the Piccadilly line.'

'I'm not going back to Earls Court,' she said. 'It's not safe.'

'Good idea. Hang around, go to the Whitechapel gallery, I'll call you when I'm done,' I said, confidently.

'Good luck,' she said, as I made the short walk to the Old Bailey in the rain with six million quid's worth of artwork in my bag.

It was nine-thirty when I arrived. I looked at the noticeboard outside. There it was. Stephen Vincent, court five, ten o'clock. *Unbelievable*, I thought. Alexios had said he'd meet me just inside the entrance. As I waited there, I read an axiom on the wall. '*London shall have all its ancient rights*,' it said.

'Give them straight away to the Arts and Antiques squad,' I said, as I gave him the first painting.

'Second one I've seen in a month.'

'Dozens more probably floating around. Did you see James?'

'I did, yesterday. Made a statement.' He handed me a typed transcript, which I read aloud.

'On 25 July 1999, I knowingly facilitated a prison visit by a Mr Stephen Vincent. The sole purpose being to obtain a description – and a time – to create a fictitious theft involving a painting from a gallery in Cork Street, London W1. This was in conjunction with another inmate called Paolo – a friend of QC Peter Smith-Cresswell. In reward, Mr Smith-Cresswell would use his influence within the judiciary to help to waver a reduction on my current sentence. This was duly executed. I have had time since to reflect on my ill judgement, and the anguish it has caused to Mr Vincent. I would like to state clearly that Mr Vincent was not – in any shape or form – involved with the theft of any painting to my knowledge.'

'Paolo?' I asked.

'Was in Brixton, same time as you. Italian.'

'Is there an English equivalent for Paolo?'

'Paul.'

'He was the man opposite. In for fraud,' I said.

'Anyway, I'm going to give this to the clerk.'

'Wait.' I took the portfolio from the bag. 'Give him this as well. Everything is in here. All the evidence from the museums and auction houses in Nice and Turin.' Alexios couldn't believe it as he went through the book. I gave him a detailed breakdown of every photo, printout, handout and brochure. 'Counterfeit paintings and various artefacts are being passed around. How much do you think a single counterfeit copy can make? You've seen two already. Imagine the sales? And because the art world is a closed shop, no one says anything to anyone. The original ceramics are housed in the Victoria and Albert Museum. They are loaned out to other museums and exhibitions – such as the Guildhall – by the curator. During transit they are then taken to make the fakes.'

He sat back, held his head against the wall, and sighed. It was a sigh of relief. It seemed as though he was fixated on one issue. 'So Smith-Cresswell is involved in a mass art fraud ring?' he said, continuing to flick through the portfolio.

'Amongst others.'

'I still can't understand why James did that.'

'In return for a reduced sentence. Something happened between him and an MP. To shut him up, they struck a deal.'

'To set someone up for the robbery?'

'Exactly, that was why he asked me to visit him that day. To see what I was wearing, for the witness statements.'

'So Paolo asked him if he knew anyone?'

'Roberto probably asked him, and because of what happened in Oxford twenty years ago, it looks good. I mean, I've done it before. As Smith and Jones said, it's seductive, addictive, difficult to give up, so why wouldn't I do it again?' I held my hands up.

'How am I going to avoid mentioning that you broke your bail conditions?'

'Don't say anything,' I replied.

He smiled as he closed the portfolio. 'Smith-Cresswell, you naughty boy. Coffee?'

'Please.'

'Look after these,' he said, leaving his bag and some paperwork with me. He had a spring in his step as he left the building, the supple leather portfolio was kept tightly under his arm.

'Quick. They're hot. That's the one with one sugar,' he said, as he returned.

'You remembered.'

'Guess who I saw in Starbucks?'

'Terence Stamp?'

'David Bailey.'

'No, really? Must live around here,' I said.

He shook his head as in disbelief. 'Was sitting there.'

'I think he lives in King's Cross,' I said.

'Really?'

'So I've heard. Probably in one of those new apartment complexes behind the station. Tom will know. An interesting man. Long-time vegetarian. Also inspired the movie *Blow-up*.'

'1966. What a time.'

There was a pause before the subject matter changed. 'Know anything about this?' He held up the cover of the first edition of the *Evening Standard*. 'Got it when I went for the coffees.'

'*Scooter gang raid Christie's*' was the headline. 'Bears the hallmark of The Gucci Gang. Very similar to how a gang in Italy operate.'

'The School of Torino?'

He looked at me. 'I'll come and get you at ten forty-five.'

'The witness statements did add up,' said Jones.

'They did say the same thing,' said Smith.

'You had done something similar before,' quipped Jones.

'It was twenty years ago,' I replied.

'It didn't matter,' added Smith.

'In my experience, the art world can be a very seductive one, extremely difficult to let go,' said Jones.

'I agree,' said Smith.

'I also agree,' I added, with a smile.

The two detectives from the Art and Antiques squad were opposite me. We were sitting in one of the interview rooms we'd been allocated at the Old Bailey.

'Don't often get it wrong,' said Smith.

'Very seldom,' added Jones, with a shake of the head.

They were profusely apologetic, probably more about being professional than genuinely sorry for the mistake.

'No problem,' I said, as we shook hands.

I'd just made an appearance. It had lasted no more than ten minutes. After the formalities – which included confirming my name and address – the judge promptly dismissed the case with immediate effect and ordered the arrest of Peter Smith-Cresswell QC. The three witnesses due to give evidence were also apprehended. Without sufficient evidence for the prosecution, he had no choice but to close the case.

As I made my way back downstairs I looked to the gallery. Laila, Rich, Tom, Doug, Sophia and Gianni were there. Gianni gave the thumbs-up.

After an hour downstairs in the cells, I was free to leave. 'What happened to Icy?' I asked Alexios.

'She was in the gallery. They're interviewing her now,' he answered.

'Smith-Cresswell?'

'Over there,' he said, pointing to one of the cells.

'Roberto? Zhang?'

'In the West End Central.'

I shook his hand. 'Thanks, Alexios.'

'And thank you,' he said, smiling. 'Go home and rest. I'm staying a while.' He passed me a brown paper bag.

I held it under my arm securely. 'The real one?'

We were still laughing as Smith and Jones approached us. 'We now have the real one,' said Smith, rather proudly.

'Being returned to its rightful owner,' concluded Jones.

'Make sure it's the correct one,' I added, as I made my way to the exit.

It had stopped raining as I looked up to Lady Justice. She was still there, standing alone in the now clear sky. 'Thank you,' I said aloud.

I heard my name. 'Stephen?'

'Are you okay?' I asked.

'Fine. They asked me as few questions, that's all,' Icy replied.

Doug, Laila, Rich, Sophia and Tom came and gave me a hug.

'Icy's coming with me to a Robert Mapplethorpe exhibition in Covent Garden,' announced Tom. 'A Polaroid one,' he added.

'Good photographer. I like the one of a New York fire escape.'

'Died in seventy-nine,' said Tom.

'Don't mention seventy-nine,' I said.

'"Message in a Bottle", The Police,' said Rich.

'"Escape (The Pina Colada Song)", Rupert Holmes,' was Doug's choice.

'"Born to be Alive", Patrick Hernandez,' said Tom.

They looked at me. '"Are 'Friends' Electric",' I added, without hesitation.

'I'm going to show Sophia and Gianni Soho,' Doug said.

'Remember what you promised me?' Gianni asked.

'When you're ready,' I said.

'Wednesday? I have to leave on Thursday.'

'Eight, Wednesday morning. Finsbury Park station. We'll start at Highbury.'

'*Perfecto*,' he said excitedly, as he ran after Doug and Sophia, en route to Soho.

'I'm going to show my friend the temple,' said Rich, as another man came to join us.

I recognised him from somewhere. 'David?'

'Hey dude.'

I ran to give him a hug. 'David!' I repeated.

'Live in Ibiza man,' he said, and it showed. Bronzed. Sun-tinted blond hair. As handsome as when I last saw him in Oxford twenty-four years ago.

'Still listening to *Tubular Bells*?'

'Of course,' he answered.

'See you soon, Rich,' I said, as they headed off for the temple.

'You promised me something,' Laila said.

'There's a match next Tuesday evening. Oxford against Colchester United, at Oxford.'

'I'll take one more day off work,' she said, as we walked in the Smithfields and Clerkenwell direction. At the junction of the Old Bailey and Newgate Street, a silver Porsche pulled up.

'Congratulations, Steve,' shouted Alexios.

'Remember David?'

'He was my inspiration.'

'He's back,' I said.

'Have to go. Oh, I've moved. See you later,' he added, before heading towards Tower Hill.

Hopefully I'll never see his new office, I thought, as we crossed the road. We walked slowly to Charterhouse Square, where we sat down.

'How do you feel?'

'Strange,' I answered truthfully. 'Mixed emotions. Happiness, joy, sadness, they're all in there.'

'Sadness?'

'Seeing David, then all going our separate ways.'

'We all have our lives,' she said, putting it into context.

'Finished the book last night.'

'Like it?'

'I liked the king on his small planet. Making the boy justice minister. Funny. Also the relationship between the prince and the rose in the glass. That was sad.'

'The rose was his love. He loved her. Just couldn't show it.'

'And she loved him. Just couldn't show it,' I replied.

'The rose was based on Antoine de Saint-Exupéry's true love.'

'The power of literature,' I said.

'He got very stressed.'

'Love can cause stress,' I had tried to avoid the word, but it was conspicuous as we spoke. This may be a fundamental similarity between men and women. Both feel, though both hold back.

'You mean in the context of the book, or in real life?'

'Both,' I replied.

'So much relevance, fifty-six years later.'

'What are you going to do with the car?' she asked, as we walked through Clerkenwell and Exmouth Market towards Roseberry Avenue. I had to take the 19, Laila the 341.

'Give it back to Charlie. No need for it anymore.'

The 341 arrived first. 'Thank you for everything, Laila. Say hello to your mother,' I said, as she boarded the bus.

She brushed her cheek against mine. 'Thank you,' she replied.

As the the bus faded into the distance, the rain began. I felt empty, the two-month adventure had finished. The rekindled friendships had – like the bus – faded. It was difficult to see if this was the beginning or the end. The rain had switched to a deluge. The 19 bus arrived soon after.

Chapter Twenty-Two

Tuesday, 26 October 1999

I needed a walk. The morning was bright, sunny and inviting. Walthamstow station was only four stops away. From the station, I walked through the market. *It's been here 114 years, amazing*, I thought as I made my way towards Coppermill Lane.

The air smelt fresh as I entered Walthamstow marshes. After a while I sat down on a bench overlooking the River Lea. Everything seemed bright and colourful. The sky was clear and blue, the water was flowing, but undisturbed, and the houseboats were painted in all sorts of vivid colours. In between were the marshes themselves. Under the sun they were a light brown hue that complemented the still, green grass. I gazed towards the sky, a kestrel was soaring in mid-flight.

The houseboats were burning wood, the smell reminded me of when I walked with Laila a few weeks ago. After cutting through Springfield Park, I walked to Stamford Hill. As the morning progressed there was no contact with Laila, Rich, Tom or Doug. Only at ten o'clock was there a phone call. It was Rich. 'You busy today?'

'No,' I answered.

'Come to the temple. David's being blessed. Master would also like to see you.'

'No problem, see you at eleven,' I said. A week ago we would have arranged to meet up, had some tea, a chat, spoken about Taoism, listened to some music. *That's gone now*, I thought, as I started to read a book I'd bought in Walthamstow. It had come out two years earlier; it was called *The Power of Now*, by Eckhart Tolle.

For some reason the car didn't feel comfortable anymore. Though the sun was shining, the roof was down, and *Magical Mystery Tour* was playing, the moment had gone.

The handshake was still warm. 'Welcome back,' Master said.

'Thank you,' I said, as I made my way upstairs to say hello to Buddha. The Maitreya Buddha looked like a long-lost friend. I looked at him for a few seconds as the sun illuminated the room. 'Thank you,' I said.

The blessing ceremony was exactly the same. I guessed it had been this way for thousands of years, untouched and unabridged. It was awesome. David was a natural, as though this was something he'd been waiting all his life for. I was asked to be his 'guarantor.' It was an honour.

The food – as always – was delicious. Many people have many justifiable reasons becoming vegetarian. Some for animal ethics and against cruelty. Mine was about ego and vanity, though – I somehow had this notion that it made you look younger. This – and walking – were the key elements of longevity, I thought. Some said the same about opiates, though. I mean, look at Doug: late forties – soon approaching fifty – and looking good.

George Bernard Shaw was a role model, a vegetarian. Looking healthy, he lived until ninety-four. Master had enthused me with more justification.

The conversation was profound over the dinner table. 'Jesus was blessed with Tao. The same Tao as you've been blessed with,' said Rich. 'There are many clues in the Bible. All the saints and sages of all religions were transmitted the same heavenly Tao as what's been transmitted to you.'

Like me, David was enthralled as Master took over. 'To attain enlightenment is difficult. Tao is the path of the truth. Cultivating Tao is very difficult. This path has many obstacles. Think of Jesus and Buddha, the abuse, the ridicule they had to endure. Keep cultivating, no matter what.' He looked at me, 'Stephen.'

'Yes,' I said.

'Do you agree?'

I paused, taking stock of the past two months, the people and the obstacles. 'Yes, yes I do,' I said, smiling.

'So Master knew all along?' I asked Rich, as we were walking down the stairs.

'Yes.'

'Then why didn't he say anything, I mean, warn me?'

'He couldn't. It's your path. Your fate. Your destiny. You have to keep going. He knew it was going to be okay. Many people come to him, some offering lots of money to know the future, even wanting to know the lottery numbers, but he cannot say.'

'Then how did he know?' I asked.

'From the paintings, and from the chess with Zhang. He is a master of Chinese astrology and feng-shui.'

'So that's why you asked me to photograph the endings of each game. Through the thousands of years of the Tao being handed down, he knows what's going to happen, but can't divulge it?'

'Exactly,' he replied.

David stayed on with Rich. He had to give the three treasure lecture to a small group of academics, bankers and other professionals.

Wednesday, 27 October 1999

'Yes!' exclaimed Gianni with a clenched fist, as we stood outside White Hart Lane for the twelfth photo, with the Polaroid Tom had lent him. 'Amazing,' he said. What a day, twelve grounds visited, and ticked off with an obligatory photo.

Starting at Highbury, home of Arsenal, we went from Underhill, Barnet, to Griffin Park, Brentford. Then Loftus Road, Queens Park Rangers, and Stamford Bridge, Chelsea. Craven Cottage, Fulham, and Selhurst Park, home of Crystal Palace – and Wimbledon – were next. The Valley, Charlton Athletic, and The Den, Millwall followed. Upton Park, West Ham United, and – finally – White Hart Lane, Tottenham Hotspur ended the jaunt.

'No other city could – or can – offer you that,' I said.

'*Bellissimo. grazie, grazie, grazie*,' he replied, making gesticulations as if he'd just scored a last-gasp winner for Italy in the World Cup finals.

We took the 279 back to Finsbury Park, where I collected the car, to drive to Tom's where he was staying.

'*Guarda, guarda, guarda*,' he was stating, as he was showing Tom the pictures.

'Favourite?' Tom asked.

'Cold Blow Lane, Millwall, *certo*,' he shrugged, before we all hugged. '*Molto grazie*,' said a heartfelt Gianni.

As I was leaving, Tom gave me a present. 'From Icy,' he said. 'Took her to the airport today. She wanted to leave early.'

'Shame, but thank you,' I said.

I walked down the stairwell and got in the car. I put on 'Can't Explain' by The Who. Tom and Gianni were looking over the balcony. '*Ci vediamo un altro giorno*,' I shouted, as I pressed the accelerator, increasing the volume. '*Got a feeling inside (Can't explain) It's a certain kind (Can't explain.)*'

'*Andiamo!*' I yelled, as I roared home.

I opened the brown paper bag Tom had given me. It was a Mapplethorpe Polaroid. The shot of the white brick wall.

'Every man desires to live long, but no man wishes to be old.'
– Jonathan Swift

Tuesday, 2 November 1999

The shower and shave were both cool and refreshing. I entered the bedroom topless and stood in front of the full-length mirror. After looking over each shoulder and turning side to side, I returned to the living room. Before you knew it, 'Leave Them All Behind' by Oxford's finest was being amplified. It was then time to decide on some suitable attire. This was no ordinary day. Today was football day. Oxford United were playing Colchester United. As well as keeping my promise to Laila, a much-needed return to the seat of learning was on the cards. It had been twenty years, a lot had happened – and who knew, members of Ride might even turn up for the game.

The days were fast becoming colder. Winter was settling in, so a grey tank top from new kid on the block designer Jack Wills would serve the purpose. The blue denim shirt and black corduroys completed the look. After returning to the mirror for one final reassurance, I grabbed the cashmere coat. The Penhaligon's Blenheim bouquet suited the fresh morning.

There was now a rival to the National Express. The Oxford Tube coach stop was on Upper Grosvenor Gardens, Victoria. I am one for tradition, but the Tube's fleet of new sleek Mercedes coaches tempted me. I was early, so I sat in the gardens. This hippy hangout of the late sixties and early seventies was now the haunt of beggars, and the homeless.

The shops adjacent to the South Korean Embassy were once called 'bucket shops'. No online bookings for travel then. You had to book the tickets over the phone, or come personally to collect them. James and myself once took the so-called 'magic bus' to Amsterdam in 1982. I was looking to see where the bus actually was, and where we boarded.

'Hi, are you okay?'

'I'm fine, why?'

'You seem miles away.'

'Reminiscing,' I answered, as we made our way to the coach.

I raced to the front seat on the top deck. I noted the same landmarks. Hyde Park. Marble Arch. Bayswater Road. Lancaster Road. I pointed out Reckless Records in Notting Hill. Easing into The Westway, I looked for the floodlights of Loftus Road – home of Queens Park Rangers Football Club.

Fifty minutes later, we were on the outskirts of Oxford. Navigating the roundabout seemed to take an eternity, as I searched for the floodlights. Rumour had it that The Manor was being sold. The selling off, subsequent demolition and housing development was only hearsay at the moment. *Why do they always choose working-class pastimes for these developments?* I wondered, as the four steel pylons – adorned with giant bulbs – magically came into view.

I pointed to a fibreglass sculpture of a shark looking as though it fell halfway through a roof. 'The Headington Shark,' I said.

'Cool,' gasped Laila.

'The council wants it removed,' I said. 'Which is ironic, as it's now become a tourist attraction.'

'Like Orton, the council prosecuted and imprisoned him. Now they use the damaged books as exhibition pieces.'

'Governments, local authorities, councils, whatever, none are appreciative of the arts. Look at Francis Bacon. Thatcher said he was repugnant, can you imagine? Do you think the Spanish president would say the same about Picasso? They revere such a person.'

'An asset,' she replied.

'Exactly.' I thought about Francis Bacon. He had a known penchant for working-class men, similar to Lord Boothroyd and Ronnie Kray. I wondered about James and Cribb. Alexios didn't mention it. In fact, no one had.

The London Road alleyway was still intact, as was Rose Lane. We got off at Queens Lane. The bus stop across the road was still there. 'Can't believe I saw David again,' I said.

'Similar to Florence,' said Laila. For a first-time visitor, the rows of bicycles stacked against the walls of familiar buildings would have looked impressive.

'What about Paris? Or even London?' I asked, remembering what the coach driver had said.

'Could be, certainly has a cosmopolitan feel to it.'

'This is the Radcliffe Camera,' I said, pointing out the iconic edifice, before stepping onto the surrounding green turf.

'Seems bigger on the television,' Laila replied, as I gave her a helping hand.

We then cut through an alley – again lined with numerous bicycles – before taking a right into Broad Street. 'Wow!' she exclaimed.

'Familiar?'

We were facing the Sheldonian Theatre. 'Beautiful,' she said. She was right; it was.

'A Wren piece. His second commission. Built in 1664, took five years.'

'Similar in style to St Paul's.'

'St Paul's was ten years later. He was interested in the Italian Renaissance and baroque style.'

'Interesting,' she said, as we walked through the city centre.

I took her to a college that had the dreaming spire of all dreaming spires. 'Guess who wrote one of the most famous books of all time here?'

'Clue?'

'Main protagonist fell down a hole.'

'*Alice in Wonderland.* Lewis Carroll wrote that here?' she asked, as we entered the interior of the famous Christchurch College. A spacious water fountain was placed in the middle of squared manicured lawns, you could hear the water as we went to the study where Charles Dodson had penned the timeless classic.

'Amazing,' Laila commented, as she looked around. 'Can you take a picture please?' she asked, before standing in front of a fireplace. 'What literature can do to you,' she said, as she bought some postcards to send to France.

I started to think about the football, and suggested Maxwell's, an American-style diner, to eat before The Manor.

Opened in seventy-two, Maxwell's was a long-serving institution. There was also another one in Covent Garden, so they obviously catered for the tastes of Oxford and London. Again Laila mentioned the similarities between the two cities.

'This is where the elite come and get educated,' I said, after our pizza and Coke. 'Our Prime Minister Blair, former Prime Minister Margaret Thatcher, US President Bill Clinton, you name it, they all came here,' I added.

The other side was, of course, the dropouts from the Oxbridge system. The ones who went with good, aspiring intentions, only to lose themselves for whatever reason. Most still hung around. I looked at the clock, it was five minutes to one. 'Need to hear something,' I said, as we walked to Carfax. The bench from twenty years previous was still there, still in the same place.

I sat down and closed my eyes. Everything seemed to stop as the Quartermen appeared and struck the bell. They hit it one time, which was enough.

'Are you okay?'
'Yes,' I said. 'Why?'
'I'm talking to you.'
'Sorry, what was it?'

'*The Alchemist*. Have you read it?'

'Brilliant book,' I said. 'I like the way it's open to individual interpretation. How I interpreted the book may be different from yours.'

'And how did you interpret it?' came the inevitable question.

'That we don't have to go elsewhere to seek treasure.' I looked at her. 'It's here, right in front of us. The boy thought the treasure was buried somewhere else. When he arrived at the destination, it wasn't there. He was told it was buried somewhere else.'

'Where he started.'

'Exactly, but it didn't matter. The experience of the journey – the struggles, the people he encountered – they were invaluable in themselves. Why seek out something that's right here in front of us? Being right here, right now, talking to you in a beautiful city, about to see a football match. That's where the treasure is.'

'What a nice thing to say,' she replied.

'*Andiamo!* Let's go,' I said, as we took a bus to The Manor.

The Manor isn't the biggest ground. The four sides were in juxtaposition, and different to each other, but – as always – the billiard-green grass was mowed to perfection. The excitement of looking out onto the lush, freshly watered pitch was still there, and that alone was well worth the travel. The tannoy was playing 'Summer on the Underground' by a new band called A. 'Dalston is a wicked place' was already bringing back memories. *Football and music never fails*, I thought, as the crowd began to build.

Some players came out to stretch on the pitch. Dressed in their yellow and blue kit, they were like gladiators, preparing for the battle. I started to feel a shiver down my spine. Momentum was gathering, ten minutes to kick-off. 'Be good today boys, don't let me down,' I uttered quietly.

The game was to and fro. I was kicking every ball, much to the amusement of Laila. One each was the result. The ball being thumped home in front of the London Road was a joy. Hearing the boot connecting with the ball, followed by the sound as it hit the mesh of the netting, was pure class. The jubilation of the home support that followed was always a treat. 'Thank you, boys,' I shouted, as the players made their way to the tunnel.

'How did you find your first football match?' I asked.

'Really enjoyed it. Didn't see or hear any racism,' she replied.

'Don't listen to the media. Football is a big thing for them. It's fodder, gives them a story. They hover, waiting for something to happen, asking loaded questions, waiting for a player or manager to say something controversial, so they can take it out of context.'

'We don't watch television anyway,' she said. 'Dad used to watch Al Atlas TV on satellite for updates on any political situations in Algeria, that was it really.'

We took the bus back to the centre. The Ashmolean Museum looked a lot smaller, but was just as popular with the tourists. I opted for a slight detour. Instead of passing through Gloucester Green, we walked down Beaumont Street until Walton Street, then took a left at New Road. Oxford Prison had closed three years previously. It looked the same, both daunting and homely. I remembered how it was always warm in there. The memories came flooding back. The consequences of the Ashmolean incident. The three-month incarceration. I looked at the mound and thought of Reg. Where was he now? Was he out? Was he alive? And Aadesh? Where was he? At least my vegetarianism was our legacy, I thought, as I looked up to 'Hangman's Hill'.

'Are you okay?'

'Let's go,' I said.

'*Andiamo!*' she smiled.

Laila fell asleep on the way back. Football can do that to you. The atmosphere, the noise and the energy. The people, and fresh air, the honesty – it was too much for a first-timer. I reflected on the day as I looked out the window. The sky was grey, and the clouds were becoming darker. A silvery moon was behind, waiting to emerge.

The coach journey was not lost on me. This time it was to my home; twenty years earlier it was to Portland in Dorset. *Life can be full of twist and turns*, I thought, as I rested my head against the seat and sighed.

As in *Midnight Cowboy*, I shook Laila lightly. 'We're here,' I said, as the coach passed Notting Hill. We got off at Marble Arch and took the Central line to Oxford Circus, then the Victoria to Finsbury Park.

'No car anymore,' I said, as we exited the station. 'Charlie collected it on Saturday morning.'

We waited for the 253. On arrival we shook hands and kissed cheek to cheek. 'Thank you,' I said.

On the way home, I called Rich. 'Can I see the fifth painting?' I asked.

'Master has it, and he's returning to Taiwan tomorrow,' he replied.

It was a joy to put the key in the front door. I shut the curtains, lit some incense, and switched the radio on.

Capital Gold was the station, Caesar the Geezer was the host, 'Sweet Talkin' Guy' was the tune. I thought about James. He'd be out soon, hopefully to start a new life. Doug had been accepted into rehab. David was moving back for a while to support him. I kept the picture Alexios had given me; it was now framed, and on a wall. The Maitreya Buddha was still smiling. I picked up *On the Road* and flicked through the pages. *God works in mysterious ways*, I thought, as I closed the book. I was pleasantly surprised by how easy the act of leaving was, and how good it felt. The world suddenly became rich with possibility.

The End